PRAIS

'An epic and intoxicating blend of secrets, power play and rebellion. Thomson creates one hell of a sequel. She really is a rare talent! Freya, a soul sucking syphon, is kidnapped and taken to an entire new world where she is trapped. But, Freya doesn't feel trapped, nor alone… as she possesses the spirit of an assassin in her head. The adventure leaves you turning pages. Thompson has created a wicked and clever new world smothered with unpredictable secrets. Although we still get the X-men vibes, there is a slight pinch of gladiator vibes in the recipe this time. The characterisation in the book is magnifying and consistent. I obsessed over the new characters and how they created new twists with diverse, relatable perspectives,' *Peta Carolan @UnfoldedEdges.*

'Freya (lead character) is a fountain of sass and an increasingly interesting morally grey character who pushes at her boundaries of 'where do I draw the line'. The author has expertly built upon characterisation established in *Welcome to Blackwood*, and Freya's struggle to keep herself and her darker impulses in check is fascinating to read. Five stars,' *Nita Delgado, Reviewer.*

'Freya is so relatable as a teenager growing into a young adult — inner voices, heartaches, temptations and new dangerous, attractive characters kept me on the edge of my seat! I want more!' *Chermaine Er, Reviewer.*

'She actually did it—the second book in the series is even better than the first. I didn't think it was possible. Absolutely 5 stars!' *Cate Sawyer, Author.*

PRAISE FOR LEAVING BLACKWOOD

'After loving *Welcome to Blackwood*, I couldn't wait to dive into the sequel, *Leaving Blackwood*! Freya is desperately awaiting her 18th birthday, since her and Beau have been banned from dating until then, while dealing with her biggest secret yet – the extra soul she harbours inside her head. One who doesn't always give the best advice and she's not sure if he has her best interests at heart. *Leaving Blackwood* is just as thrilling as *Welcome to Blackwood.* Dangerous magic, unlikely allies and desperate choices made this a compelling read I didn't want to put down. If you love fast paced fantasy, shifters and unique magic systems, make sure you pick this series up!'
Jenny DuRoss @Bookbookowl (74K followers).

'Freya's ambition to become not only magically strong but physically stronger and more capable to protect herself, all while she learns to adapt to her constantly evolving powers and changing surroundings; with the added stress of a not so little voice (and memories) of a centuries old sarcastic serial killer for hire stuck in her head made me admire the heck out of her. I would give this five stars just for Freya. I absolutely loved her and some of the morally grey choices throughout. What surprised me the most was how funny the book was. I loved Freya's sarcasm, great one liners and ability to get under people's skin. I finished this the same day I picked it up due to being so enthralled throughout the whole story, there isn't one boring chapter,' Five stars!
Bianca Barber @the_books_and_cats_life.

Leaving Blackwood

KHAIAH THOMSON

HAWKEYE
PUBLISHING

2021 Hawkeye Publishing
First published in Australia.

Cover Design by Jasmin Cameron.

ISBN 9780645309904
www.hawkeyebooks.com.au
www.hawkeyepublishing.com.au

DEDICATION

Dear Hugh,

For the time I ogled you in the elevator of the InterContinental Hotel in Sydney, consider this dedication an apology. Never in a thousand years, did I expect to meet Wolverine in the flesh. Should our paths cross again, which is most unlikely, I will endeavour to string more than two words together and prove that I am a relatively intelligent person.

Yours truly,
Khaiah

1

MY lungs burned—everything burned.

'Come on! We don't have all day!'

I clung to a small, wooden ledge protruding from a high wall. It was just big enough to cling to with my fingers. With trembling arms I pulled my body up. My legs were like dead weights. I swung them over the top and straddled the structure, letting out a triumphant shout.

'Move it!'

My arms shook as I shimmied down the rope on the other side and hit the ground. I sprinted, throwing myself to the ground and commando crawled through the mud, under the netted frame. Out the other side I broke into a run and raced over the finish line. Bent over with hands on my thighs, I drew in deep breaths. Steel capped boots crunched on the gravel, stopping at my side.

'Don't slack off, you've still got one more lap,' Bishop said.

'One more lap?' I wheezed. 'I've already done three!'

Her arms were crossed as she stared at my hunched over figure. 'Don't need a puke bag, do you?' I made a rude noise and she grinned, holding out a water bottle. 'Alright, you're dismissed.'

Standing to my full height, I wiped the mud from my face, and grabbed the bottle. I took a long swig, glaring at her.

'You enjoyed this, didn't you?'

She chuckled. 'Sure did.'

The obstacle course, christened Bishop's Circuit, was a new addition to our property, one that would "motivate" me. When I was taken by the horrible, power hungry Argyle a few months ago, Bishop and her small team of soldiers had played a big part in my rescue. After the rescue they made a temporary move to Blackwood and moved into our unused barn. It was now a fully decked out mini military base. I shuffled towards the house.

'See you bright and early tomorrow,' Bishop called.

I waved a hand over my shoulder.

'*Looking sorry for yourself won't make her go easier on you.*'

'You've been quiet. I thought you'd magically disappeared,' I said.

'*I'm not going anywhere, so suck it up.*'

'Let me hobble like a normal person,' I muttered under my breath.

'*You're pathetic.*'

'And you're dead,' I argued back.

Laughter echoed in my head. '*Point to you, kid.*'

When Argyle forced me to draw James's energy to the point of death, I'd inherited his abilities and memories. Unfortunately, I'd inherited him as well. I was just a seventeen-year-old girl, and he was a three-hundred-and-seventy-six-year-old blood-thirsty mercenary. My interests include reading and watching B-rated movies. James's interests included killing people for money, and killing them for fun. We weren't the best match.

In the beginning he'd been nasty. He amused himself by telling me how useless I was, accusing me of being a murderer and bombarding my mind with horrible recollections of his past. I had to find quiet, isolated places where I could scream, yell or sob without attracting attention. After a month or so he realised he was stuck with me and his attitude had changed… a little. Unless I was alone, I tried to keep our conversations in my head. A few times I'd been caught talking to James in public and people had assumed I was talking to myself. I couldn't afford to keep making that mistake; people in Blackwood were too perceptive.

I removed my mud-covered shoes and left them on the veranda. My socks were also soaked with mud, so I peeled those off as well. A chill ran through me and I shivered. The claw-foot bath was calling my name. I entered the house, trudging toward the stairs and the bathroom above.

Mum poked her head out the kitchen door and looked me up and down. 'I hope they're not pushing you too hard.'

I waved her off. 'I'm fine, Mum. Self-healer, remember?' It was clear she'd been itching to say something for weeks. Since my experience with Argyle, her attitude towards me had shifted. She treated me like I was fragile, like somehow, I was more damaged than I was letting on. Yeah, I killed a guy, and the memory of lifeless eyes still haunted me, but in a weird way James was still kind of alive.

'I know, baby. I'm worried you've had too many responsibilities lumped on you. You're still only seventeen and you've seemed… distant lately. I feel like all of this is making you grow up too fast.'

'*Better a grown daughter than a dead one,*' James joked.

I ignored his comment and shrugged. 'I've had a lot on my mind. School work never seems to end either.'

'I know, you're right. It's just like I have a different daughter. You even get out of bed before seven in the morning,' she said.

'Not willingly though. *Definitely* not willingly.' I wanted to sleep until a normal hour, I really did, but neither my body-clock, nor Bishop, would allow it.

Even with my fast muscle recovery, my legs still wobbled as I plodded up the stairs. With a groan I sank into the bath, lowering into the bubbles all the way to my chin. The agony of the past two hours seeped out into the warm, rose-scented water. The chiming of my phone jolted me back into a sitting position. The water had started to cool so I must've fallen asleep. It was a message from Reagan asking if I wanted to stay over Friday night. I sank back into the bath and stared at my phone. It taunted me with its blank screen.

Beau hadn't texted today.

When Beau helped to rescue me from Argyle, he'd exposed to the whole community that he was a Dire Wolf Shifter—a Shifter much more powerful than the average Wolf Shifter. He, and the Northern Blackwood Wolves, had been reprimanded by the Council for keeping it a secret. They allowed Beau to remain with his pack but he couldn't be involved in any pack rivalry. Beau and I had both broken numerous community laws, and because of the animosity between packs, the Council came up with a new rule that affected both of us. We weren't allowed to date until I turned eighteen. We could still hang out, but it had to be with others, usually the Monroes.

It sucked.

I dragged myself out of the bath and dressed, shrugging on Beau's jumper and rolling the too-long sleeves to my wrists. Beau's scent still lingered in the fabric and I inhaled his earthy aroma. My stomach grumbled at the smell of dinner cooking downstairs. I opened my bedside drawer and grabbed a handful of snacks. Levi hadn't discovered my stash… yet. Self-healing after gruelling workouts made me hungry. James's voice drifted into my consciousness.

'No slacking off tomorrow. There's a lot you can learn from Bishop. Your eye rolls and groans during training are childish.'

'I am not slack,' I argued. *'If I push myself any harder, I'll rupture something.'* I rubbed my biceps for effect.

'We both know that's a lie. I know how fast your muscles recover.'

I mimicked his words. It was difficult pretending to be normal when there was someone living in my head. Nobody knew about James, not even Beau.

'You don't seem to get that there's a huge target on your back. I would've been paid a million bucks to eliminate someone like you.'

'Unfortunately for you, if I die, you'll be dragged into the afterlife with me.'

'Death would be a better fate than witnessing your slow decline into a sad, menial existence.'

I scoffed. *'Just because my life lacks violence, doesn't make it boring.'*

'You rely on too many people. You'll be lucky to live past eighteen.'

'And you would sacrifice your firstborn child if it gave you an extra century of life. I don't see how I'm less of a person than you. You're the human equivalent of a cockroach.'

'Careful with the insults, kid, or I'll sing you a little tune,' he warned.

The last time James had made good on that threat was during an exam at school. Thanks to *The Ballad from the Gold Rush of Eighteen-Seventy-Seven* I barely scraped through the exam with a pass. Mum was not impressed.

'Not again. Okay, I'm sorry. I'll try extra hard tomorrow, just for you.'

'No, you'll do it for yourself. Remember, it's all for you, Freya.'

2

'I've discovered that each thread of energy has its own pattern of movement. This makes it difficult to pull the threads apart. It's as though each of them has its own mind, its own unique form. Meditation is the key. Removal of sight makes it easier to understand the flow of energy. I've found that in learning to understand my own energy core and the threads within it, I'm better able to understand the energies of the world around me.'

Video diary no.87, Matthew Holmes

I didn't sleep anymore – not often, anyway. If I finished my homework and couldn't find anything to watch on TV, I used the night hours to practice using my gift. Dad said that meditation would help me to understand and strengthen my gift. Once I understood my own energy, the rest would fall into place.

It was cold where I sat by the open window. Sweat dripped down my neck, making it difficult to concentrate. Closing my eyes to drown out all distractions, I focused on using senses other than sight. So far, I'd worked out how to feel the different textures of energies and sense their colour without visual aid. They flowed differently; some like water, some like molten lava, and others like electricity or the wind. If an energy signature is familiar to me, I can sense the person before I see them. I still couldn't work out how to unravel energy threads or make them flow the way I wanted them to.

James was blissfully silent during meditation. I focused on the flow of power moving through my body and distinguished the different threads; my life line, the respiratory system, nervous system, the thread of my gift that glowed sapphire blue, and dozens of the other threads. No matter how hard I concentrated, I couldn't unravel the rope of energy. If I tugged at one thread, the others came with it.

I scooted off the window ledge and stretched my legs, moving to the bed. Sitting cross-legged, I changed my focus to a different exercise. A Syphon's ability is activated subconsciously, when in danger. We draw energy from our surroundings, including people, so subtly that it's unnoticeable; an in-built defence mechanism. Now that I was aware of it, I'd been working to activate that ability on a conscious level. It had been James's idea—something to access in case of an emergency.

I focused on the potted succulent sitting on my window sill. The energy line of a small plant is fragile. Its life or death would tell me whether I was drawing too much or just enough. I'd been through four dozen of these plants, and was relieved that Mum had said nothing when she saw the shrivelled carcasses of failed experiments in the compost. This little guy had survived for a week, and I was hopeful. I concentrated on expanding distance, sitting myself two metres from the windowsill. Tendrils of energy flowed from me towards the plant. They were as fine as threads of cotton. As they neared the succulent, I spliced the ends of each of those threads into three finer tendrils that wrapped themselves around the plant's energy core. I inhaled deeply, and then exhaled, tugging on that rope ever so slightly. A tiny thread of succulent energy flowed into mine and I smiled.

But I'd relaxed too soon.

The energy lost its subtle flow and flew back towards me, like an elastic band let loose. The succulent shrivelled and died in its wake. I sighed, glancing out the window where hints of orange tinged the early morning sky. I'd need to take a trip to the hardware store for my next victim.

Bishop waited for me at dawn. My stomach protested loudly by the time I'd completed three laps of the circuit. She made me do an extra lap for good measure. I was improving, beating my times each lap. When we got back to the barn, she handed me a pistol.

'What's your weapon?' she asked.

I looked at the piece in my hand. 'SIG Sauer P-three-twenty. The M-seventeen.'

'Ammo?'

I examined the gun. 'With the current barrel it would be a nine-millimetre calibre.'

'Very good,' she said. 'Your aim has improved quickly, so today will be more of a challenge. You'll be practicing with a limited line of sight and obstacles. It's barely sunrise so you also need to take into consideration lack of light.'

I aced the challenge… well, mostly. Each of my shots was well within the kill-zone of the targets, but I had shaky hands. Much to James's disgust my shots were never quite perfect. Bishop frowned as she examined each target.

'Your improvement is impressive,' she said.

I shrugged. I wasn't about to tell her that there was an assassin living in my head, giving me advice. James complained that if I took things more seriously, I could be just as good as him. And apparently if I *grew a pair*, I wouldn't get the shakes. James was an A-class jerk.

Reagan texted and asked me to pick her up from Pete's Beach on the way to school. My windscreen wipers couldn't keep up with the downpour of rain blurring my vision of the road. It slowed to a drizzle as I pulled up near the beachfront cafe. A quick scan of the carpark left me disappointed. There was no sign of Beau or his friends.

Reagan darted across the bitumen; a paper mâché tray balanced in one hand. She fell into the passenger seat, slamming her door against the outside cold. The smell of coffee wafted through the car.

'One of those had better be for me.'

She grinned; her lips tinged blue. 'Double shot for you right? I assumed you'd want breakfast too.' She lifted a brown paper bag.

'You're a goddess!' I accepted the takeaway cup, relishing the feel of it warming my hands.

She shivered and pulled a towel from her bag, using it to dry her hair.

'Your mid-winter swims are going to be the death of you, you know. If it's not pneumonia it will be frostbite.' I waved a finger in her face. 'Don't expect me to open doors for you when your thumbs fall off.'

'Ha. Thanks for the lift.'

I pulled the bagel from the brown paper bag. 'You brought me coffee and food—no thanks required.'

Her lips curved. 'Seeing as I brought you coffee *and* food, do you mind if we stop at my aunt's salon? Mum asked me to drop off her spare phone. My aunt goes through a phone every couple of months. The last one was dropped in a bowl of soup.'

I snorted. 'Yeah, okay.'

Reagan's idea of a quick stop made us late for school. I waited in the car, scrolling through my phone. Absorbed by the screen, I shrieked when something thumped on my window. Beau's laughing face stared back at me as I rolled it down. He rested both arms on the door, leaning in until our noses almost touched.

'Hey.'

My heart fluttered. Wolf Shifters had no sense of personal space. 'Hey.'

He inspected my car, eyeing the collection of empty food wrappers behind the driver's seat.

'Umm, I was planning to recycle those.'

He chuckled, his eyes moving back to mine. 'Are we still on for tomorrow?'

'Yep. Unless you're busy.'

'Nope, not busy.'

My shoulders relaxed. 'I've-um… I've missed hanging out.'

His jaw twitched. I would've missed it if I wasn't so obsessed with his face. 'Yeah, I've missed it too.'

I felt uneasy. Over the last couple of months, it had seemed like the more we got to know each other, the more distant Beau became. It had worsened the closer it got to my eighteenth birthday. Maybe I was just being paranoid.

'Freya!'

Dillon stood waving at me from the other side of the road. He crossed the street, yanking open my back door. He seemed oblivious to the back-off vibes radiating from Beau.

'Geez, Freya, your car is a dump.' He sat on the back seat, ignoring Beau's glowering stare. 'I need a lift to school, is that cool?'

I glanced at Beau then back at Dillon. 'Yeah, that's fine.'

'Your family has a fleet of cars,' Beau stated.

Dillon shrugged. 'They're all unavailable today.'

Beau's alpha energy flared and Dillon shuffled in the backseat. There was a long uncomfortable silence. When Dillon didn't budge, he turned back to me and said, 'I'll see you tomorrow.'

I watched his retreating back as he went back up the street and out of sight. 'You said you'd never be caught dead in my matchbox car,' I said, arching a brow at Dillon through the rear-view mirror.

He leaned forward, waving at Reagan as she approached the car. 'What can I say, I needed a ride and here you were.'

'Since when is one of the family cars not available?'

'Since I saw the perfect opportunity to get under Greyson's skin.' He grinned. 'I parked my car behind Mum's office.'

3

'MISS Armitage!'

The sharp tone cut through my thoughts. I swung my head to the front of the classroom and sunk low in my chair as students around me chuckled. 'Yes, Mr Orson?'

'I understand that the social complexities of a teenager's life are distracting, but unless you are an expert on the supernatural wars, then I suggest you pay attention!'

'Yes, Mr Orson.'

He looked to the ceiling. 'Please, will you stop that incessant tapping!'

I stilled my arm, placing the pen to the side of the desk. With a final glare, he turned back to the whiteboard and I moved my focus to the history subject plastered across the screen.

'I would rather watch paint dry,' Dillon grumbled beside me. He leant back in his chair and stretched, smiling and winking at a couple of girls across the room. The chair teetered on two legs and I waited patiently for him to push it back that little bit too far—I was disappointed. The siren rang and everybody rushed to the door to get out first. As I shoved my books in my bag and moved to follow the hoard, Mr Orson's shadow appeared over my desk.

'Miss Armitage, a quick word please.'

Dillon grimaced, waving as he disappeared out the classroom door. I stifled a groan. 'Is there anything wrong, sir?' I asked.

He perched himself on the edge of my desk and plucked his glasses from the bridge of his nose, cleaning them with the corner of his shirt.

'Look, Freya, I understand that being the new kid means you need a bit of time to adjust. But you've been with us since the start of the school year and it's now term two.

That's three months, so you're well past the adjustment period.'

It had been a long three months. Four months in total since moving to Blackwood. A lot had happened in that first month, and the surprises just kept coming.

I nodded. 'Yes, sir.'

His eyes narrowed. 'I'm telling you this because I'm concerned. You're regularly distracted and that doesn't bode well for your future studies.'

'But I'm passing all my subjects,' I argued.

He sighed, setting his glasses back in place, which magnified the penetrating stare. 'Yes, I know. You're an intelligent girl, but you can't go through life flying by the seat of your pants. University will be much harder. I know you had a rough start moving here, but please try. For your own sake don't just coast through life.'

I looked to the window. When I first moved to Blackwood people thought I was a Mundane. It was the only way my family and I knew how to keep me safe. As a Syphon, I could draw energy from others, taking on their abilities as my own. Syphons are hunted, exploited, and killed because others fear us, or want to use us. My abilities became known to everyone in town because nothing stays secret in Blackwood for long, and well… I lost my temper. To make matters worse my dad's old research partner, Argyle, the maniac responsible for his death, captured me and tried to use me in his twisted search for power. Beau and others from Blackwood had to come and rescue me.

'Okay, I promise to try harder'.

He smiled. 'There's a good lass. Trust me, it will pay off in the long run.' He nodded towards the door. I grabbed my things and made my escape, nearly tripping over the leg of a table in my haste.

'You really should pay more attention in class,' Dillon taunted, as I exited the classroom. He slouched against the wall.

'Shut up,' I said, hoisting my bag over my shoulder.

'Is she in trouble for daydreaming again?' Reagan asked as she approached us. Unlike Dillon and me, who were gluttons for punishment, Reagan had art and design with my mum instead of history as her final period for a Friday afternoon.

'Give me a break, guys.'

'He is right, though. You've been distracted,' Reagan said.

We moved down the hall towards the exit. 'Well, if I'm not at school, I'm training. Bishop is a freaking slave master. I have a lot going on,' I argued.

Dillon scoffed. 'Does a little bit of exercise in the morning really hurt that much?'

Before Bishop had burst into my life, I'd been a couch enthusiast who'd never witnessed a sunrise in her entire life. I threw Dillon a glare.

'You can talk. You spend all your time in front of your computer screens.' Screens, plural. Dillon was a nerd, in an I-mix my-own-dubstep-music kind of way. When we'd gotten to know each other better, Dillon had shown me the music he created in his spare time. He was pretty good. The range of equipment he owned just for making *decent tunes* must've been worth about the same as my mum's life insurance.

'I'm making music, Freya. It's an investment,' Dillon said, waving to a couple of Southerners who were waiting for him down the hall. 'Anyway, catch you losers later.'

He jogged off to meet his friends, tackling one of them to the ground. He held him in a headlock while giving him a noogie. Reagan and I rolled our eyes as we passed. Wolves—always trying to prove who's the most alpha. The twins ran past us, jumping on top of Dillon and crushing the guy stuck at the bottom. Reagan coloured and glanced away, playing with one of the rings on her finger.

'Still weird?' I asked.

She snorted. 'Yeah.' There was a pause as we approached my car. 'They're just so stupidly competitive with each other, you know?' She pressed a hand to her chest. 'I of all people know how important family is. There was no way I was getting between them.'

Reagan had been on a few dates with one of the twins, but it never went any further than that. Both of them liked

Reagan, and when she agreed to a date with one, the other got jealous. Being wolves, they fought about it constantly. Reagan didn't want to cause conflict, so that was the end of that.

We hopped into my car, and Reagan synced her phone, picking out tunes for the drive home.

'I saw Beau accosting you in the car this morning. Is he still coming to our place tomorrow?' she asked.

'He's definitely coming this time—no work call outs.'

She grimaced. 'Dorian's helping to install the car stereo, right?'

I scrunched my nose. 'Yep…'

Reagan's brother, Dorian, loved any opportunity to make a situation awkward or embarrassing. I already had a brother for that job *thank you very much*. Somehow, in the short time I'd known the Monroes, I'd been adopted by Reagan's brothers as well. Even to the point of getting sweaty armpits shoved in my face. I admired their ability to accept someone so readily.

'Only a month until I turn eighteen,' I said in a lighter tone.

A smile lit her face. 'Speaking of, we need to plan this party of yours.'

'I've told you a million times, Reags, I don't want a party.'

'Ugh, fine! But we're going out for your birthday.'

'As long as there's no party.'

She waved me off. 'Yeah, yeah, no party.'

I pulled into the Monroe's driveway, slowing down as a ball flew across the gravel drive. Two small, black-haired kids screamed at each other as they tore after the ball.

Reagan smiled. 'Nothing like family night.'

Dishes of food were placed in the centre of the table. I sat wedged between Grams and Jonah, listening to the adults argue over the next vintage of wine, waiting to be barrelled. Tom wanted to try a new technique but the others weren't convinced. Mr Monroe's voice reached me from across the table.

'So, Freya, I was speaking with Bishop yesterday. She

told me that your training is going well.'

I nodded. 'I can keep up with some of her crew now. It will be hard staying motivated once she leaves.'

'I'll be your trainer,' Dorian volunteered.

I grimaced. 'Thanks, but I think I'll manage.'

'You'll get lazy.'

I froze and shoved James's comment to the back of my mind, humming a catchy tune. He knew better than to talk to me when Jonah was around. Jonah was a powerful empath. Until recent months, I'd barely seen him. When I'd arrived in Blackwood, he'd just had a growth spurt in power and couldn't block the thoughts of those around him. He locked himself away from most of the world until he'd worked out how to tune out the thoughts. Now he had it under control and had returned to the social world, but loud surface thoughts still made it through his defences.

Jonah stared at me with a frown. I turned back to the table and joined the conversation, keeping my thoughts quiet. His attention finally pulled away from me when Tom called out to Grams and I released a breath.

'The Sprigg's are planning to begin building on that land they bought on the east side of town. They've asked if you'd provide guidance on which trees to keep and which ones can go.'

Grams waved a hand. 'Of course. Take me out there whenever it suits them.'

Tom caught my confused expression and winked before turning to Reagan's dad.

An old hand rested on mine, giving it a squeeze. 'How are you?' Grams asked.

My heart rate dropped back to normal and I gave her a warm smile. 'I'm good, Grams. Same as always. What did Tom mean by 'which trees to keep and which ones can go'?'

Her eyes twinkled as she ignored my question and sipped her wine. She leaned in close and asked, 'How is our mutual friend? You know, the tall and handsome one with golden eyes and the great smile?'

I blushed, glancing at my hands. Grams Monroe was a pro at diverting conversation. My eyes were drawn to her bare feet beneath the table. She rarely wore shoes—an eccentric habit I admired. 'He's good. I think. We haven't seen much of each other, but in a few weeks that will change. Hopefully.'

She gave my hand a sympathetic tap. 'Don't forget he's already lived a long time, so a few months for him isn't long at all.'

'Well, it is for me,' I grumbled. It was way too long. 'And, how are you?'

'To be honest, my dear, I'm old.' She looked across the table at her sons. 'I know I'm becoming more of a burden to my boys. It's hard for them when I'm not myself.'

Grams had dementia and was also a powerful telekinetic. When she had one of her 'episodes' she was like a human tornado, destroying everything in her path. The family had managed to contain it, but the episodes grew steadily worse.

'I keep telling them to use those horse tranquilizers on me, but apparently it's *inhumane.*' She huffed and took a sip of her wine. She gave my hand a final squeeze and announced to the room that she was tired. She left the table and people began to clean up. Jonah grabbed my arm and steered me towards the study.

'Dad and uncle Tom are getting some "fresh air", so let's use the study. It's quiet.'

My heart thumped. 'Did you want to talk about something?'

He turned to me and rolled his eyes. 'You forgot, didn't you? I asked if I could make a mental lock for you, remember? I've been practicing, so you don't have to worry that I'll wipe your memories or anything.'

My shoulders relaxed. 'Oh, right.'

Reagan and Dorian followed us into the study. I sat myself in Mr Monroe's office chair, and Jonah dragged another one in front of me. He sat so that our knees touched, and my head was within reach. Remembering the last time I found myself sitting across from someone like this, I shivered. It was the day I'd taken James's gift, and as he would argue, the day I stole his soul. My life changed that day. It had been shocking at the time, but James wasn't all that bad, once you got used to him.

'Right. I want you to relax your mind. I'll be skirting around your consciousness, so sing a tune or something to keep me out of your thoughts.' He must've sensed that I was nervous—or maybe Dorian silently told him so, because he added, 'Don't worry, it's not going to hurt. If anything, you might have a bit of brain fuzz afterwards.'

I was sceptical. 'So, tell me what this does again?'

'It will protect your mind from being read or manipulated by people like me. If they try to break through the lock, it will give them one hell of a headache.' He grinned.

I sung a nursery rhyme to myself as he placed the fingers of both hands on my temples and across the top of my ears. He breathed deeply and closed his eyes. A feather-like touch brushed over my consciousness. Jonah's face was creased with concentration, and after what felt like twenty or so minutes, drops of sweat beaded over his brow. Aside from the light touch, I couldn't feel a thing. He finally pulled his hands away and opened his eyes. Dorian handed him an energy drink and he took a long swig, wiping his brow with the sleeve of his jumper.

'That should do it,' he said.

'That's it?'

'Yeah. How do you feel?'

I shrugged. 'I feel fine.'

He grinned and stood, giving me a hand up.

Dorian scowled. 'When he did it to me, I had a splitting headache for two days.'

Reagan gave Jonah a side hug. 'You're getting better, little brother.'

Jonah rolled his eyes. 'You're not even a year older than me. You can't really call me little brother.'

People who didn't know the Monroes assumed Reagan and Jonah were twins. They were only eleven months apart, which meant they were in the same year at school.

She grinned. 'Of course, I can. You could've been born two minutes later and I'd still call you little brother.'

We left the study and Reagan pulled me into the kitchen.

'So, are you up for some practice?' she asked.

Reagan had volunteered herself as my practice dummy. Focusing on someone else's energy rather than my own, or that of a plant, was necessary for me to improve. Humans were different to plants, and I couldn't draw my own energy.

'Actually, yeah. I've learned something new I'd like to try.'

'Alright then.'

She grabbed a packet of chips and a tub of ice-cream out of the freezer. I grabbed a couple of spoons. Using my gift drained my energy but the self-healing helped me to recover fast. The only set-back was that it made me ravenous. Reagan had adapted to my new appetite.

I felt a pang of guilt as she led the way to her bedroom. Reagan allowed me to practice on her, but the favour didn't go both ways—I didn't allow her to use her ability on me. I'd seen her smile drop those times when I avoided letting her touch my skin.

Reagan is a Seer. She sees people's future through direct bodily contact. She can see the person themselves in visions, but all the other details are hazy. This was changing; her visions were becoming clearer and projecting further into the future. I didn't want her to discover James, and if I was honest, I was scared of what my future held. I hated the thought of her coming out of a vision and looking at me with big, disappointed eyes.

Later, while Reagan slept, I was still wide awake. James convinced me to use the time effectively and I snuck out of the house, careful not to make any noise. After running a few K's I looped back to the house and begrudgingly did push-ups and pull-ups at James's suggestion. He threatened to sing again and had me doubling my speed. I showered, then tiptoed through the house, collapsing on the fold-out mattress. My eyes closed just as the sky outside the window began to lighten.

Less than two hours after falling asleep, I stumbled into the hallway, following the smell of pancakes to the kitchen. I rounded the doorway scratching my head and came to a halt.

Beau.

Leaning against the kitchen bench talking with Mrs Monroe. My insides somersaulted at the sight of him in ripped jeans and a black t-shirt. It was raining outside but Wolf Shifters don't feel the cold like normal humans. I looked him over, committing his features to memory. He caught my eye and grinned, the lazy grin that reaches all the way to his eyes. I responded with a wobbly smile.

'Thought you might need this.' He held out a steaming coffee cup.

I grasped the cup, and our fingers touched. I met his heated gaze and was pretty sure that my expression mirrored his. He rubbed his thumb across mine.

'Having breakfast, Beau?' Mrs Monroe asked, glancing between us.

Beau snatched his hand away, running it through his golden brown hair. It had grown since we first met and now fell just below his ears. It had a slight curl, but instead of looking scruffy, he still looked like surfer-boy model material. He threw Mrs Monroe a winning smile.

'Only if you're sure there's enough to feed me?'

She chuckled and gestured towards me with her free hand. 'Freya is here. So of course, I expected to be feeding a wolf.'

Feeling the heat rise in my cheeks, I stared down at my coffee cup. I recognised the logo and gave Beau a shove. 'You went to Pete's?' I hissed, for his ears only.

He shrugged. 'The sea breeze was blowing and there wasn't a Southerner in sight.' He studied me and smiled. 'Don't worry, Scarecrow, Pete and I have an understanding, and no one would've picked up my scent with all that salt in the air. I'm always careful.'

I scowled, twisting a lock of hair between my fingers. *Scarecrow?* The realisation hit and I gasped, lifting a hand to my hair. My bed hair *did* make me look like a scarecrow. I groaned, dashing back down the hall towards Reagan's room. Beau's laughter echoed behind me.

4

'WHAT does this wire do?'

Beau looked at me across the centre console. 'Why don't you leave the technical stuff to me? You can provide emotional support.'

I rolled my eyes and dropped the green wire. 'What am I supposed to do? Just sit here and watch you?'

I actually didn't mind doing just that. The angle at which he sat, hunched over as he installed the stereo, provided me with a good profile. The black t-shirt was stretched taut over muscular arms that flexed as he twisted the screwdriver. It sure was stuffy in my small car. My gaze moved up and our eyes met. He winked at me.

'Keep looking at me like that and this isn't going to get finished any time soon.'

I blushed, angling my head towards the back of the car. Dorian was muttering curses from the boot.

'Need any help, Dorian?' I asked, ignoring Beau's smug grin.

'I don't need help,' he growled. 'I just need this to sit flush with the back seats.' The car rocked as he forced the speaker boxes into place.

A hand on my knee brought my attention back to Beau. 'Why don't you hold these?' he said, holding out a bunch of tools. 'You can hand them to me when I need them.'

I grabbed the tools, studying each one.

'Finished!' Dorian exclaimed, slamming the car boot shut. He dusted off his hands and leaned inside the passenger side door. 'Anyone for a beer?' Beau lifted a hand. I didn't like beer so it was a no from me. Dorian poked me in the shoulder. 'I might be a little while. Have to call someone. You know, I'm a wanted man.' He winked, pushing away from the car. Was Dorian being nice and giving us time alone?

Beau asked me to hand him a tool, explaining to me what it looked like and what it was used for. Each time he asked for a new tool I was given a rundown of its uses.

The conversation I'd been avoiding was going to be easier when his intense gaze wasn't on me, so I swallowed hard and said, 'Has everything been okay lately?'

He faced me. 'What do you mean?'

I gestured between him and me. 'You know… between us.'

He turned back to the stereo. 'We're fine, why?'

I shrugged. 'I haven't seen much of you. I thought—' I paused, clenching my eyes at the neediness lining my words. *I'm not needy, I just need clarity.* '—I thought you might've been avoiding me.'

'I've just been busy with work. Everything's fine, Freya.'

'Okay, if you say so.'

He straightened in his seat. 'I've been busy, and the rules make it difficult. I'm not even allowed to hug you.'

'Yeah, I know. I thought you might be having second thoughts. Like, I dunno, maybe you didn't like me as much anymore or something.'

He leaned in close, his eyes meeting mine. He rubbed his thumb along the side of my jaw, staring at the spot where his thumb met my skin. Even that small gesture was pushing the rules. His eyes moved to my lips and my stomach knotted.

'Trust me, I more than like you.' He pulled his hand away, resting his arm on the steering wheel. 'I have been a little distracted—I've had contact from my family.'

I raised my brows. 'Your family? Is everything okay?'

Beau's family, like most Dire Wolves, lived discreet lives. They kept their identities a secret, because like me, their kind are hunted. A single Wolf Shifter couldn't take down a Dire Wolf, but a whole pack might if an alpha felt his authority was challenged. Other Wolf Shifters were only one of the possible threats to their kind. Beau hadn't told me much, but I knew he and his family members didn't contact each other often. They made contact on an "as needs" basis.

'They were just checking in.' He plucked one of the

tools from my hand and continued with the stereo. 'We like to keep in touch when there's been an incident, in case rumours spread that a family member has resurfaced.'

I felt a pang of guilt. It was my fault there was any concern at all. Argyle's people had seen Beau in wolf-form, and some of them had escaped before their memories could be wiped. 'I'd like to meet them one day.'

He grinned. 'I don't know about that. My sisters are protective.'

'I'm sure I can handle them.'

He chuckled. 'Yeah, I think you could.' He sat up, and handed me the screwdriver. 'Finished.' He wiped his brow, then pressed the power button. I connected my phone and opened my playlists to find that everything had vanished.

All my music had been replaced with classical.

'Dorian!' I screeched.

The screen door to the house swung open and shut. I saw his toothy grin as he sauntered towards the car.

'What?' He feigned innocence and handed Beau a beer.

'Where is my music?' I hissed between clenched teeth.

'I have no idea what you mean,' he said brightly. Beau laughed, and we both hopped out of the car.

I shoved my phone in Dorian's face. 'Fix it!'

He smirked. 'No.'

'No?'

He nodded, eyes twinkling. 'No.'

I channelled my best death stare. 'Fine. What will your mum think when I tell her about that redhead you've been hanging out with?' His skin paled. 'And no, I'm not talking about Dillon, I'm talking about the female redhead. Her gift is gravity control, right?' I tapped on my chin. 'That's pretty cool. Can she fly? Like, you know, using anti-gravity?' Dorian glared at me, then held out his hand. With an angelic smile I handed him my phone. 'Touch my phone again, and I might accidentally let slip that her name is Leah.'

He snorted. 'You'll run out of blackmail soon, you realise that? Then what will you do?'

'As long as Leah holds your interest, I'll be safe.'

Dorian rolled his eyes. 'I underestimated how nosey you are.'

'I've been hanging around with Monroes for too long, I guess.'

He groaned and turned to Beau. 'Isn't there a rule that forbids the use of one's parents as blackmail?'

Beau chuckled and shook his head. 'You're not dragging me into this one. You know I'm going to side with Freya.'

Dorian made a rude noise and I laughed. 'And that's one of the things I love about him Dorian. He'll always side with me.'

An eerie stillness fell over us and I realised what I'd said. The 'L' word. It wasn't like I'd said that I *love* him—It wasn't *that* big a statement. *Sheesh, we weren't even dating.*

But Dorian and Beau stood like statues staring at me. My mind blanked. I couldn't think of a way to smooth it over. Dorian took a swig of his beer then waved my phone in front of us.

'I'm going to go fix this.' He looked between the two of us then slunk away.

'Sorry. I ah, didn't mean . . . well I did mean. . .' I laced my hands around the back of my neck. He wasn't saying anything, just staring blankly at the spot where Dorian had been standing. 'Look, what I meant was—'

'Don't worry about it,' he interrupted. He still wouldn't look at me.

His dismissive statement stung. 'Well, obviously I've upset you.'

He finally met my gaze. His lips were curved but it wasn't one of his usual smiles. 'You haven't upset me.' He ran a hand through his hair. 'Look, I've got to go. Mick has some jobs for me to do this weekend. There's a backlog of work for next week, so he wants us to get ahead.'

I frowned. 'I thought you were free to hang out today.'

'Plans change,' he said, breaking eye contact and looking over at his motorbike, like he couldn't reach it quick enough.

'Aren't you at least going to stay for lunch?'

'Maybe next time.'

'Come on, Beau.'

He swung himself onto the motorbike and didn't look at me as he said, 'I'll see you later okay?'

The engine started with a roar, and my shoes were splattered as the wheels of his motorbike spun in the mud. I stood there dumbfounded, staring at the taillight of his bike.

James' smug voice echoed across my brain. '*Normally I don't say I told you so . . .*'

The backs of my eyes burned. '*Not now.*'

I stood under the front veranda, talking sense into myself. *It's okay. He's busy today, that's all.* Dorian handed me my phone as I entered the house, then looked past me, his eyebrows raised in question.

'He had work,' I said.

He eyed me. 'You want to play CTR?'

Reagan was at work and I'd given up my Saturday shift at the vet to hang with Beau . . .

'Okay. No cheating though,' I warned.

'I'd never cheat you.'

A few hours of CTR couldn't pull me from my brooding mood. I went home and did a few laps of Bishop's circuit, then practiced throwing knives. There were a few new ones Bishop had added to challenge me. They weren't weighted like the others, so I had to adjust my hold and the rotation of the blade. It took a few practices to get my throw right.

There was no chance of me sleeping with all the thoughts rattling my brain. I kept picking up my phone to text Beau, then thought better of it. Meditation was a good distraction. The night was warm enough to sit in the garden. The distraction paid off, because hours of practice resulted in me being able to draw from more than one plant at a time. I was confident I could do it with humans if I had to.

I laid on my bed, waiting for the last couple of hours of darkness to pass. James decided to impart his words of wisdom.

'*You know, I liked a chick once.*'

I groaned. '*Really? We're going to go there?*'

'*Yes, we're going there. She was hot – in a Marilyn Monroe kind of way. She'd enter a room and everything just stopped. Her legs just never seemed to end . . .*'

I clenched my eyes shut, as his memories of this "Marilyn" flooded my mind. *'I think I'm going to throw up.'*

'You make me want to puke on a regular basis. As I was saying, she was smokin'. We dated. She liked "bad boys" and I was happy to fit the stereotype if it kept her interested. You know what happened?'

'I'm sure the memory is floating around in my head somewhere. No need to dig up the past.'

He ignored me. *'I'll tell you what happened. I'd been hired to assassinate the French ambassador who resided in London. After a few too many drinks I bragged to her about the clean kill. You should have seen it, kid, this guy had a tight security team and I was still able to execute my mark perfectly.'* An image flashed before my eyes of a small bearded man, with grey hair and glasses, standing next to a window. He poured himself a drink into a crystal glass. A bullet shattered the glass window and just like that his life was ended. *'As I said, perfect shot. Anyway, my little Marilyn decided to tattle didn't she. We'd been seeing each other for nearly eleven months, and she sold me out for fifty pounds.'*

'She was definitely overpaid.'

'You're hilarious. Her betrayal didn't end well.'

Nausea hit me hard as the image of the blonde woman, eyes wide with fear, assaulted my mind. I could feel the hate and bitterness pouring from James, and the satisfaction.

'You're horrible, James.'

'You've established that many times. The point of the story is, you can't rely on anyone but yourself. That boy is gonna leave you the minute things get too hard.'

I dragged a pillow over my face. Trying to talk reason with James was pointless.

5

BISHOP sensed my simmering mood and decided that I needed more of a challenge. She added a tyre flip to the circuit and increased my laps. I channelled my irritation at the lack of contact from Beau – not even a single text – into training.

The weekend came, and there was still no text, so I worked a double shift at the vet clinic and raided the hardware store for succulent plants.

The following week passed and I worried—maybe I should've just texted him first. It reached Thursday and Levi came home a day early. We watched movies together, and it was then that my phone finally lit up.

Meet me at the Steelworks tomorrow night, the message read.

I huffed. As usual, it wasn't a request. *Okay, as long as my company isn't inconvenient*, I replied.

Good, see you then.

I wanted to growl but remembered I had company. Did he purposely ignore the dig?

Levi watched me. 'Has he decided to acknowledge your existence now?'

'He's been busy with work.' I cast my eyes to the TV screen.

There was an awkward silence.

'He's not worth—'

I lifted a hand. 'We agreed not to talk about it remember.'

'Fine. Just remember that it will be your family and the Southerners who will be here to pick up the pieces when he drops you.'

'You and Mum have already told me that. Many, *many* times.'

'Dire Wolves are a dying breed, Freya. Mr Waller said

they can't afford to bond with someone outside of their bloodlines. They need to bond with other Dire Wolves to increase their numbers.'

'Why have you been talking to Mr Waller about this? And who said anything about bonding?'

He shook his head and concentrated on the movie. 'You're just angry because you know I'm right.'

'Levi, when I want your advice, I'll ask for it.'

As much as I hated to admit it, there was a small, nagging part of me that wondered if he was right.

***

I dressed up a little more than usual for the Steelworks. I wore heeled ankle boots instead of my Docs, with jeans, and a nice navy-blue sweater. I even applied a little makeup. Reagan agreed to come along, and when I arrived at the house, Jonah and Dorian jumped in the back of my car as well. We claimed a booth on the ground floor, where a few others joined us. The Steelworks was quiet. It was a full moon, so all the Wolf Shifters were absent. Beau didn't need to reinforce his bond with the pack in the way other Wolf Shifters did, and I got the impression pack dynamics within the Northerners had changed since he rescued me. I scanned the room but he wasn't there.

I slid into the booth next to Reagan. The band on stage, a group of guys from school, was doing covers of nineties grunge music. One of Jonah's friends played drums. A tray of drinks was placed on the table and I grabbed my glass of lemonade. I was designated driver. Watching the crowd, I sipped on it absently, listening to the drone of conversation around me. A large stack of pizzas was delivered to our table, courtesy of Dorian. As the pizzas were demolished down to the last box, a pair of hands rested on my shoulders. I looked up into Beau's golden eyes.

'Sorry I'm late,' he said. His breath tickled my skin and I could feel the colour rising in my face.

He scooted into the booth beside me. It was a tight fit with Reagan and Jonah on my other side, and our thighs and arms pressed together. My skin tingled. The smell of his signature scent made me want to lean in closer. I remembered the day I'd first been dazzled by that scent, when he'd cornered me in the hardware store.

He joined in the conversation around the table. The discussion became heated as Jonah and Dorian argued over football. Beau's hand rested on my knee and all thoughts fled my brain. He leaned in close so that I'd hear him over the noise.

'Play a game of pool with me.'

I somehow forgot that I'd been annoyed at him for the past two weeks. 'Sure.'

He surprised me by grabbing my hand and helping me to my feet. He was bending the 'no touch' rule in front of a crowd of people. He held onto my hand and led me towards the pool table. I felt the inquisitive stares boring into my back. A cold feeling settled in the pit of my stomach. He'd followed the rules to the letter, up until now, only two weeks from my birthday. *What was he doing?* If it wasn't for the smile he threw my way as he set up the table, I would've thought he was trying to get himself thrown out of town.

'Do you want to break?' he asked, handing me a pool cue.

'Okay.'

Single word sentences seemed to be all I could manage. Balls scattered across the table. We made it through half the game in silence. He seemed to be over-thinking something. I edged around to his side, placing my hand over his, and his troubled eyes met mine.

'Tell me what's wrong,' I said.

He scanned the room. 'Come with me.' He grabbed my cue, placing it on the table beside his, then grabbed my hand and pulled me through a door at the back of the building.

'Where are we going?'

He didn't answer as he led me down a hallway and past the storage rooms, before opening a set of double doors that led out of the building.

'I get the impression that you've snuck out of this building more than once,' I whispered.

'There've been a few occasions when things got heated

between Southerners and Northerners and I had to make a quiet escape.'

We walked around the side of the building and he scouted the carpark. He ushered me towards an old muscle car, painted cherry red. He unlocked the doors and gestured for me to get in.

'Whose car is this?' I asked, running my hand along the cream leather. He dropped into the driver's seat and slammed his door shut.

'It's mine,' he answered, pulling onto the road.

'Yours? Since when?'

He shrugged. 'About a year. I finished the restoration a month ago.'

'You never talked about it. But I guess we don't talk much.' Restoring a car seemed like something you'd talk about.

He glanced at me but said nothing. He pulled his attention back to the road and accelerated. We drove through town, passing into Southerner territory. I stared at Beau with wide eyes.

'It's fine. All main roads are neutral territory,' he explained.

He turned onto a road that followed the coast and headed south.

'Where are we going?' I asked. 'You know this is against the rules.'

'I want to show you something.'

We passed the Southerners boundary line and Beau kept driving.

'The land here is considered a reserve. The Monroes are one of the only families who can claim any kind of ownership,' Beau explained.

'Really, why?' I asked.

'Because their ancestors were the first people to walk this land. Grams was born here and never left. As the birthplace of her ancestors, the land holds some kind of spiritual connection for her kin.'

'I knew their ancestors were the first people, but I didn't know they had roots specifically in Blackwood…it makes sense.' The Monroe family tree was a mixture of different cultural heritages; Grams could trace it back generations. 'Didn't some of their family migrate here?'

'Great-great Grams migrated from Spain. She met a local and fell in love.'

We fell into awkward silence at mention of the 'L' word. The road moved with the land, weaving in and out of trees. After a few songs had played through the stereo, the road opened up. Beau pointed to a river on our left. When the river mouth met the ocean, we pulled to the right. The road hugged the coast, and beaches became clifftops as the road inclined. A light flashed in the distance, drawing my attention to a lighthouse perched on the edge of a cliff. Beau pulled up in front of the gates and cut the engine. I hugged my body as the sea breeze found its way through my shirt. Beau pulled off his jacket and placed it over my shoulders.

'A lighthouse? We're breaking the rules for a lighthouse?'

'Have you been up one before?'

'No.'

'Come on, then.' The gate was made of chain-link fencing, at least three metres high. Beau crouched beside the fence and held out his cupped hands.

I glanced up at the fence and back at Beau. 'Are you serious? I can't climb that.' Not in stiff denim.

'Sure, you can. I'll give you a boost.'

It was not my idea of a date… or whatever it was. With a long-winded breath, I placed my hands on his shoulders and a foot in his hands.

'Give me to the count of—'

He launched me without warning. I grabbed the top of the gate and with a loud grunt, pulled myself to the top. If not for Bishop's gruelling workouts, I would've dangled there like a fish. Climbing half way down the other side I let go, landing on my feet. The gravel was loose and I fell on my butt with an *oof.*

'You could've given me some warning,' I muttered.

Beau jumped, grabbing the top of the gate with his hands and launched over, landing on the other side effortlessly. He towered over me where I sat sprawled on the ground and ignored my glare, offering me a hand. *Show off…* His warm hand engulfed mine. He held onto it as we approached the lighthouse and I stared up at whitewashed walls.

'Please tell me we're not climbing that too.'

He pulled out a set of keys and jingled them. 'I've got friends in high places.'

I frowned. 'You'd think your friend would've given you a key to the gate.'

'Oh, he did. I just wanted to see if you could climb it.'

I slapped his arm as he chuckled. The old, wooden door opened with a groan and I climbed the steel staircase ahead of Beau. We reached the top and stood in front of another door. Beau squeezed in beside me to unlock it and we stood face-to-face, only a hands distance apart. My stomach did flips. He pushed open the door with a wink. I moved past him onto the viewing deck and gasped as I looked out over the water. The reflection of the full moon was cast out over the sea, creating silvery ripples in the waves. I leaned against the railing and looked down at the ground below. Beau leaned beside me, placing a hand over mine. He pointed to the left of the lighthouse and then the right.

'This is where the two oceans meet.'

'Wow, it's beautiful.' I glanced up at the light shining above us. When I looked back at Beau, he was watching me.

'I really like it, but why did you bring me here?' I asked.

'We needed to talk somewhere private.'

'A lighthouse is your idea of private? We can talk over the phone, or we could've just waited for two weeks. Two weeks, Beau,' I stressed.

'It won't take long.' His tone made it clear that I wouldn't change his mind.

'What's wrong?'

He pulled away from the railing, running both hands though his hair as he turned to face me. His expression showed that something wasn't right. I could feel it in the air—in the space between us.

'Everything and nothing. I can't make sense of anything.'

'What do you—'

He closed the space between us and I forgot my words.

'The smell of you drives me crazy,' he murmured, leaning into the crook of my neck and inhaling deeply. 'It's like spring flowers and the earth after it's rained—my two favourite scents.'

My heart raced. 'Ah, you smell pretty nice yourse—'

He pulled me against him, locking his mouth with mine. The warmth of his body always surprised me. I wound my arms around his waist. The taste of him made me forget why we'd avoided this for so long. We kissed until I pulled away to catch my breath. He ran kisses down my neck and a sharp pinch made me jump.

'Ouch! What was that?'

He grinned. 'Sorry. Couldn't help myself.'

He placed a kiss on my forehead then rested his chin on top of my head. My mind floated back to reality.

'Couldn't we have waited two more weeks for a kiss?' I asked. 'If the Council finds out, you'll be kicked out of town. We can't hide this from Mr Monroe.'

He said nothing so I pulled back to look at his face. His resigned expression made my chest tighten.

'Beau?'

'I have to leave.'

'What do you mean, you have to leave?'

He studied my face. 'I'm leaving Blackwood.'

A vice squeezed my chest. 'That was a goodbye kiss?' He nodded and I pulled away. 'Why? Is it because of what I said the other week?'

'No. My parents have asked me to come home.'

Other than the fact that Beau had two sisters, and a brother who passed away, I knew nothing about the Greyson family. Not even their names. I still knew nothing about him and yet he knew everything about me. Well almost everything… except James.

'When?'

'Tomorrow.'

'*Tomorrow?* For how long?' I asked.

He shrugged. 'I'm not sure.'

'*I told you, kid, that the minute things got complicated he'd cut you loose.*' James was smug.

Shut up!' I growled.

'I'm sorry, Freya, I have no choice,' Beau said, defending himself.

I hadn't realised I'd responded to James out loud. 'No sorry, I wasn't talking to you, I was talking to myself.' He frowned and I followed up with another question. 'You won't be here for my birthday, will you?'

His jaw tensed. 'Probably not.' He grabbed a lock of my hair and twirled it around his finger. 'I want you to have access to my house if you want it, because I could be gone a while. I'll text you the passcode, okay?'

I nodded and rested my head against his chest. 'At least we can text and call.' He was silent so I pulled away. 'We can text and call, right?'

He grimaced. 'My parents are off the grid.' I threw my hands in the air and turned away. 'I'll try to make contact when I can.'

The world was out to stop us. I leaned against the railing with my head in my hands. Grams Monroe was right, a few weeks or months was nothing for someone who'd lived more than a century. We could do this. Beau grabbed my shoulders, turning me to him.

'We can do this right?' I asked.

'We've made it this far.'

He reached under the collar of his shirt, and pulled a chain and pendant over his head. He dropped it into my hand and I studied it. It was a coat of arms with two wolves on their hind legs facing each other. A shield sat between them with a crown on top.

'I want you to have this, it's my family crest,' he said. 'Wear it until I get back.'

I liked the idea of having a part of him with me. He placed it over my head, stepping back with a grin.

'It looks good on you.' He leaned in and gave me a quick, hard kiss. 'Time to take you back.'

'Can I see you off tomorrow?' I was sleeping at Reagan's, so I didn't need my family's permission.

He nodded. 'Dorian is driving me to the airport in Belfield.'

'I'm going to miss you.'

'I'm going to miss you too.'

6

THE next morning was dreary, reflecting my mood. I stood on the front porch of the Monroe's house with Reagan, Dorian, and Jonah. I didn't get any more time alone with Beau. When he arrived, he spoke with Mr Monroe in the study. Alone.

Both emerged looking solemn. Mr Monroe glanced at me, then shook hands with Beau, holding his gaze—some kind of unspoken exchange. We were at least allowed a hug before he left.

'Be careful alright?' he said when he pulled away, still grasping my shoulders. 'Argyle's family is still out there somewhere. Don't leave Blackwood on your own, and if you do, take a Monroe or one of Bishop's people with you. I've texted you the passcode to my house if you need it.'

Apparently, my own family or the Wallers weren't good enough. 'I'll be careful. Call me when you can, alright?'

He nodded, his eyes glancing away from mine. A little piece of me ripped open as he walked back to the car. He gave me one last smile before his head ducked under the roof. Reagan hugged me from the side, as the taillights disappeared. He didn't look back.

'You want to hang out tonight?' Reagan asked.

Something was building inside me—like hot coals being heaped on a fire. Whatever it was, it felt close to erupting. 'Thanks, but I think I'll go home.'

I went for a long drive and bypassed home, ending up at Pete's Beach. I sat on the beach until the sun began to set. The roiling, uncomfortable feeling inside me grew and I recognised it for what it was—anger. I had no right to be angry. Beau's family needed him. Family was important.

'Use it, kid. Use the anger, don't wallow in it.'

'And what would you suggest I do?' I asked James.

'You're angry because he left you. Just like the Dire Wolf, people will always fail you. Become good enough that you never need to rely on anyone but yourself.'

'Good enough?'

'You have the potential to be at the top of the food chain. Be ruthless.'

'As much as I shudder to ask, what would you suggest?'

'Train harder.'

I rolled my eyes. *'I already train hard.'*

He snorted. *'You need to live and breathe it. Make you, your number one priority. No more slacking off. It's the best way to distract yourself from all that teenage angst.'*

I clenched my eyes shut. *'Okay.'*

'Okay?' He sounded surprised that what he'd been pushing at me since that first night he'd spoken in my head, was actually sinking in.

'Don't sound so shocked.'

'Well then . . .' I could almost hear his train of thought kicking into overdrive. *'Let's start with pain.'*

I threw myself back on the sand. *'And you call me dramatic!'*

He ignored me. *'Pain is a good teacher, so learn from it.'*

'You've told me this rubbish before! And how do you suppose I do that, oh wise one?'

'Learn to push yourself through it. When you want to stop at four laps of Bishop's circuit because everything hurts, you do two more. Once you push through the pain barrier, anything is possible.'

'That's it?'

'No, that's just the start.'

I wanted to wallow in self-pity. I wanted to go home and throw myself on the bed, cry and punch my pillows, pretending they were the heads of my enemies. And I wanted to eat cartons of chocolate ice cream while watching sappy movies. But I'd made a promise to myself that I wouldn't be weak anymore—I wouldn't be a liability.

'Alright.' I lurched to my feet, dusting the sand from my butt. *'Where do we start?'*

As if it were even possible, I felt him grin. *'Follow my instructions, kid, and we'll be a force to be reckoned with.'*

I got home close to dinner time. As I lifted my bag of clothes from the back seat of the car, a roar echoed through the house. The front door slammed open and Levi stalked towards me. His eyes glowed and his energy flared. He was close to shifting.

'Where is he?' he growled.

I took a step back. 'Who?'

'Greyson, who else? I'm going to kill that cocky piece of—'

I placed a hand on his chest. 'Hey, calm down. Am I missing something here?'

His nostrils flared as he eyed me from head to toe. 'I could smell you from inside the house. That jackass has marked you and I'm going to rip him to pieces!' He stormed past me, wrenching open the door of his car.

'What do you mean he's marked me? And you won't find him anywhere, he's gone.'

He stopped. 'What do you mean gone?'

I crossed my arms. 'He left Blackwood.'

'He marked you and left!' His voice was loud enough to shake the windows. 'That makes him a spineless jackass!'

'What do you mean he's marked me?'

His eyes rolled skyward. 'He's marked you, which means he's claimed you. A Dire Wolf's scent is much stronger than the average Shifter which means no other male Wolf Shifter will come near you, let alone touch you. Even the Wallers will be able to smell you from here.'

My eyes grew wide. 'Surely I'd remember him marking me? I don't remember him doing anything.' *Other than kissing me blind.*

'We're not dogs, Freya. It's not like he would've peed on you.'

'I'm not *that* stupid.' *Well… the thought did briefly cross my mind.* 'How does a Wolf Shifter mark someone?'

'A scratch or a bite would do it.' My face must have given me away because his eyes narrowed. 'Did he bite you?'

'Umm…'

'He bit you! Son of a—' He clutched the back of his head and paced in front of his car.

I knew enough about Wolf Shifters to know that a claiming was significant. 'Let's say he did bite me, does that mean we're bonded?'

He snorted. 'When a Wolf Shifter marks someone to bond and be their mate, they don't just up and leave. A bond forms by building the relationship and building trust. If a Wolf marks you and leaves, he's just being a territorial jackass who doesn't want you but wants no one else to have you either. A Dire Wolf mark could last months!'

I leaned against my car. *So much for a spark of hope.*

Levi moved beside me, his nostrils flaring. 'Look, I'm sorry but—'

'Don't, Levi. He might only be gone a little while.'

'You don't sound convinced,' he said.

'I don't want to discuss it.'

'Fine, but as you've probably already worked out Mum is going to go mental.'

'I know…'

7

MUM was furious. So furious that after screaming the house down with all the different ways she was going to kill Beau, she shifted and disappeared into the night. She didn't come back for hours. I made a late dinner and when she walked into the house, she sat at the table and ate her food in silence. It was not a good sign.

By the end of the meal, she stood and said to Levi and me, 'It's fine. If he's gone for long enough the mark will fade and it will mean nothing.'

With that she left the table and slammed the bathroom door.

James didn't give me time to think, let alone wallow in pity, from that first night onward. I didn't sleep and instead practised using my gift at greater distances. I progressed enough that I could draw energy from across my room. I breezed through drills with Bishop, volunteering to train longer hours. It helped to clear my head. I went to school and concentrated on my classes. I ignored the snarky comments whispered in the halls by the Northerner She-Wolves. There was a rumour that Beau had left town to get away from me. I seethed over it, channelling that anger into my training with Bishop. She still kicked my butt at everything, but I was getting better.

The day before my birthday, I sat in biology class, staring out the window, pondering whether Reagan had somehow planned a party that wasn't 'technically' a party. The only instructions I'd been given was 'to dress in something nice.' What kind of dress code equalled nice?

Dillon elbowed me, drawing my attention to him. Dillon sat with me in biology and history; the two classes I didn't share with Reagan or Jonah. There were half a dozen Southerners who sat in the room, so I appreciated the effort he made to sit with me. Especially considering the fact that I now *stank* of Beau. The Southerners crowded to the left side of the room, while the Northerners sat to the right with a buffer of non-shifters in the middle. *Ridiculous.*

He leaned in towards me, staring at the teacher's back. 'Hey, I need you to do me a big favour. You know, because you're a caring friend.'

I narrowed my eyes. 'What kind of favour?'

He tilted his chair back on two legs. As always, a part of me was tempted to give him a little shove. 'I'm going to tell Mum that I promised to take you to see Echo Land for your birthday and you're going to go along with it.' Echo Land was the master of electronic dubstep, and one of Dillon's idols.

'Okay, why is it such a big deal?'

He shrugged. 'It just happens to fall on the day that the Morrison family are visiting.'

I frowned. 'Who are the Morrison's?'

The teacher shushed me. I sank back in my chair and scribbled in my notebook. One of the twins sitting behind us leaned over his desk and whispered loudly, 'The Morrison's are Dillon's future in-laws.'

Dillon shoved him hard and he fell backwards. The teacher evil-eyed us into silence. When her back was turned, I stared at Dillon with raised brows. He made an effort to look interested in the diagrams on the board.

I stared until he glanced at me and growled, 'Fine.' He looked over his shoulder, giving the twins the middle finger. 'The Morrison's are the alpha pair for a large town a few hours inland from here. They're friends of my parents.' His lips twitched. 'The Morrison's have a daughter, and both of our mums are trying to play matchmaker.'

My lips curved. 'What's she like?'

He shrugged. 'She's okay.'

'She's *okay?* You may as well have called her average.' I looked him in the eye. 'Just a hint—never tell a girl she's *okay*.'

'*Okay*. She's nice. . . and pretty.' A tinge of red stained his cheeks, matching his hair.

'And the problem is?'

He quirked a brow. 'You really need to ask? How would you feel about your mum trying to control your dating life?'

I grimaced. 'Yeah, I see what you mean.'

'So, you'll come?'

'As long as my ticket is free.'

He grinned. 'Deal.'

That afternoon I pushed myself through seven laps of Bishop's circuit. Bishop and I practised hand-to-hand combat and throwing knives. She pushed me extra hard as I had the next afternoon off for my birthday.

A note was on the kitchen bench when I got home saying that Mum was at Grandma and Pa's, helping them set up a new mobile phone. I pulled out the ingredients to make mac 'n' cheese. I needed carbs and lots of it. As I slid the dish into the oven, the front door opened and Levi walked into the kitchen followed by Ben.

'Hey.'

'Hey yourself,' Levi said; kissing me on the forehead. He walked past me to the fridge, pulling out a can of soda for Ben and one for himself.

'Did you want to stay for dinner?' I asked Ben. 'It's just mac 'n' cheese.'

His lips twitched into an almost-smile. 'Mum doesn't know I'm home yet, so mac 'n' cheese sounds good.'

I pulled a bag of salad leaves from the fridge and placed it on the bench.

Ben glanced at my brother. 'You're right, she reeks of Greyson.'

The bowl I'd pulled from the cupboard clattered on the bench. 'You know what, I need a shower. Levi, you can make the salad.'

I waited for the oven timer to ding before I went back downstairs. The three of us sat at the table and I listened to Levi and Ben discuss their plans for the break. I pushed a lone salad leaf around on my empty plate.

'So… Greyson left town,' Ben said. I glanced up. Levi was preoccupied reading the label on his drink.

'Yeah,' I replied. 'He had family business.'

He sipped his drink, holding my gaze. He placed the can

on the table and said, 'Did you want to run with us tomorrow?'

I studied him; he was serious. 'I doubt I could keep up with you guys.'

His lips twitched; the Ben Waller version of a smile. 'Dillon says you're acing Bishop's circuit, I think you could keep up.'

'Dillon is a stalker.'

He pointed to my chest. 'You'd have fun. There's still a bit of wolf in you, even if you're not a Shifter.'

During the full-moon and at pack gatherings, the pack ran as a group, but at other times they ran individually or in small groups. An invite to join a run was an offer of friendship—of sorts.

'It's my birthday tomorrow, and I think Bishop is drilling me extra hard.'

He nodded. 'How about the day after?'

I smiled. 'Yeah, I'd like that.' After all my training, I might just be able to keep up.

'Don't fall for it. He knows you outrank him in power. He's getting you on his side, so he can manipulate you later.'

'Not everybody thinks like you, James,' I argued.

'Most people do, kid. Guys like him just play nice to get what they want. If you showed what you're capable of every now and again, people will think first before manipulating you.'

'Oh yeah? How?'

I wasn't prepared for the onslaught of memories that flashed across my mind. James had discovered many creative ways to take a life. The wave of nausea that washed over me made me shiver and I pushed away from the table. The guys helped me clean up and then Ben said his goodbyes.

'Happy birthday for tomorrow, Freya. I'm sure the next year will be an interesting one with you around.'

His slight smile didn't escape my notice as the front door closed behind him. A smile? For me? There had to be a catch. Unlike his brother, Dillon, Ben's thoughts weren't written all over his face. Ben Waller was an enigma.

I grabbed ice-cream and Oreos, mixing them together in a large bowl. Chris's ute pulled up in the driveway and I waved to him and Mum from the front door. I snuck upstairs before I witnessed any cringe-worthy goodbye kisses.

Levi was sprawled on my bed flicking through the channels. I kicked off my shoes, jumping onto the bed next to him. He grabbed the bowl of ice-cream from my hands and shovelled a spoonful into his mouth.

'I would've brought the whole tub if I'd known I had to share. Go and get your own.'

'And run the risk of witnessing Mum and Chris sucking face? No.' I jabbed him in the ribs and yanked the bowl from his grasp. 'Is this the thanks I get?' he whined. 'I rushed home to be here in time for your birthday.'

'I'd rather have the whole bowl of ice-cream.' I scooped the biggest amount the spoon could carry and shoved the whole thing in my mouth, gritting my teeth against the brain-freeze. 'Oh, and guess who's going to see Echo Land? Me.' I gave him my biggest grin.

'How? Those tickets were sold-out in minutes.'

'Dillon needed to get out of one of Mrs Waller's match-making attempts.'

Levi chuckled. 'That's why Dillon could never be an alpha. He's got no backbone.'

'Hey!' I jabbed him in the ribs again. 'He's brave enough to be friends with me, surely that earns him brownie points?'

He hooked his arm around my neck shoving my head against his chest. I managed to get the ice-cream bowl to safety then flailed my arms, pushing against him.

'He's lucky to be your friend,' Levi said, scruffing my hair.

'Let go, you idiot!'

I found the spot just above his collarbone and dug my fingers in until he growled and loosened his grip. He grabbed at me but I slipped free and sat back on my heels, heaving air back into my lungs.

'Ha! I know all your weaknesses, remember,' I said, combing the hair out of my face with my fingers.

He smiled, rubbing the red marks on his skin. 'You're not as easy to beat anymore. Has Bishop got you doing weights training?'

'Tyre flips.'

He shook his head and studied me.

'I can't believe this still surprises you,' I said. 'Bishop's been kicking my butt for months now.'

Levi leaned back against the headboard. 'Yeah, I know, you just seem more motivated recently.'

I shrugged. 'Well, tomorrow I'm technically an adult, so I want to be prepared for the *big bad world.*'

He laughed and grabbed the remote. 'Turning eighteen doesn't mean you're on your own, you know. We're all still here.' He eyed me. 'Mum said you've seemed off. Are you sure this new motivation doesn't have anything to do with Greyson?'

'Levi—'

'Yeah, yeah, I know.' He flicked through the channels, finally deciding on a violent sci-fi movie. 'I don't like to see anyone make you unhappy.'

'Since when do you care about my eternal happiness?' I said with a snort. 'We fight all the time.'

He shrugged. 'But we're family. The rules don't apply to family. But everyone else—they answer to me.'

8

I must've dozed, because when I woke Levi was gone. I'd had a weird dream about Beau, but the details were foggy. It was odd; I'd never had a dream before where I felt the cool air on my skin, or smelled bread baking. I yawned, scratched my head and rolled out of bed. My phone displayed the time as 3:52am. I changed into gym gear, shivering as I hopped from one leg to the other, pulling on running tights. Mum, now catering for my increased appetite, had filled the fridge with a variety of snacks. I downed a carton of fruit juice and ate a couple of bananas before heading out. I'd done three laps of Bishop's circuit when she arrived. We did another four together and headed to the barn for firearms practise.

'What's your weapon?' she asked, as she handed me a rifle.

'SA80 A2.'

'Very good. And what's your ammunition?'

'5.56mm rounds.'

She crossed her arms. 'Wrong answer.'

Puzzled, I looked at the gun. I knew this answer off by heart, even James confirmed it. I studied the gun barrel and frowned. 'It's been altered.'

She grinned and held out her hand. 'The team and I have been having a little fun.' I returned the gun to Bishop, and she switched off the safety, aiming it at one of her guys as he walked past us towards the kitchen. I flinched as she triggered the gun, and a bullet hit him in the side of the neck with a loud splat. He howled, clutching his neck as blue paint seeped through his fingers.

'You didn't have to demonstrate on me,' he growled.

Bishop laughed, turning back to me. She waved the gun in her hand. 'Paint gun.'

She gestured to the corner of the barn that had been

converted into their weapons workspace. All sorts of gear lined the shelves on the walls. The workbench had an assortment of guns on display. Bishop waved over the selection. 'Pick the weapon of your choice.' I slid my gaze across the variety of weapons, stopping at an M110 semi-automatic sniper rifle.

Bishop called, 'Open the door.'

The roller door screeched open, revealing a crowd of people smiling back at me. Reagan, Jonah and Dorian stood smirking. Levi, Chris, and even my mum were there. Tom, the Waller boys, and the twins. They wore black padded clothing, and held paint guns.

Bishop clapped me on the shoulder. 'Happy birthday, Freya.'

I grinned. 'Are you serious? This is awesome.'

We walked across the border from our property to the Waller's. The back field revealed a dozen scattered car shells, trenches and barricades built from oil drums and wooden planks.

We split into two teams, Bishop and I the team leaders. As soon as the whistle blew, pellets flew. I managed to sniper one of the twins and Mum, both with shots to the helmet. Reagan squealed, closely followed by a curse that would make her mum scowl. She was out.

As the game dragged out, I lost sight of the other team. I snuck out from behind my barricade, creeping forward to a burnt-out car and plastered myself against the frame. Edging out to the side of the car, I peered around to the front, searching for signs of the opposing team. There was a chuckle from behind and I froze.

'Well, well what do we have here.'

I turned towards the voice. Ben and Dorian towered over me; grins plastered on their faces. I'd never seen Ben smile like that before.

'Sorry, birthday girl.' Ben shot me not once but three times, in the shoulder, chest and thigh. I cried out in surprise as each pellet met its mark. Those little suckers hurt.

'And I owe you for blackmailing me,' Dorian teased as he raised his gun to shoot me as well.

SPLAT! Dorian yelled, as a splatter of paint hit his helmet. Another *SPLAT* and Ben shouted as he was hit between the shoulder blades. Dorian pulled off his helmet and spat out paint that had seeped through the grill of the helmet, splattering his mouth a shade of green.

A laugh echoed from the edge of the field and I chuckled. It was Tom. To Reagan's disgust, he'd been my first pick for the team. We walked off the field and sat with the rest of the paint splattered people. I looked at each person and smiled when I realised it was only Tom and Levi left on the field. Mum and I sat together as we waited out their game of cat and mouse. She smiled at me. 'Was it a good birthday surprise, baby?'

I hugged her from the side. 'It was the best.'

A frustrated growl sounded and my team cheered as Tom emerged waving his gun in the air, a paint splattered Levi following behind.

Everyone parted after the game ended. I walked through the front door of our house, determined to have the first shower and ran into Grandma and Pa waiting for me in the hall. I was assaulted by the smell of pancakes and frying hash browns.

'Happy birthday, Sprite,' Pa murmured.

He hugged me while Grandma gave me a beaming smile. Stray splatters of paint from my hair were now smeared on Pa's shoulder. I wiped at it with my hand as tears burned behind my eyes. I sniffed back the tears, and felt James roll his non-existent eyes.

'Typical female.'

I ignored his comment and smiled back at my grandparents. Considering they lived only five minutes away, I hadn't spent much time with them since arriving in Blackwood. There was no excuse for my neglectful behaviour. 'You made me pancakes? And hash browns?' I asked, adoration lining my words.

Grandma laughed, wiping a stray tear from my cheek. 'If I knew making pancakes and hash browns would affect you like this, I'd make them for you every day.' She patted my cheek. 'Now up the stairs with you.'

I stood in the shower, the warm water washing away the remains of paint. I smiled to myself—Beau would've loved paintballing. He would've relished cornering me, just as Ben had done, and pelting me with bullets. I could envision the sly smile on his face. My mood dimmed. I hadn't heard from him. The day had barely started, so maybe he'd message or call later.

For the first time since moving to Blackwood we had breakfast together as a family – inclusive of Chris, who was almost family anyway. I glanced at my phone numerous times. Wherever Beau was, I hoped he and his family were safe.

The school day dragged as usual, and each class that I had with Reagan, I attempted to weasel out the details of my birthday surprise. Even my sulkiness at the lack of contact from Beau didn't sway her. Final period reached its end and she glanced across the desk at me.

'Let's get your stuff,' she said, grabbing my hand, and pulling me towards the classroom door.

We entered the hall and Dillon approached us. 'We're meeting at yours right, Reagan?' he asked.

She nodded and he winked at me, disappearing into the crowd that piled out the doors to the carpark.

'What did he mean? I told you no party, Reagan,' I warned.

She smirked. 'Don't worry, I haven't broken any of your rules. Now stop asking questions and get in your car.'

'When did you become so bossy?' I grumbled, doing as I was told.

We pulled up at her house and she grabbed a bag full of my clothes out of the boot. Mum had packed me a bag. I relaxed when I saw that the clothes included jeans. It meant that wherever we were going, it wasn't a party. The Monroe's had a dress-code for parties.

I pulled on the jeans, a black knit top and heeled boots. We did our hair and makeup and I was ushered out the front of the house. Dillon waited on the front steps and held out a fan of tickets. I frowned.

'Echo Land isn't for a few weeks,' I said.

Dillon grinned. 'I know.'

I grabbed the tickets from his hand, my mouth forming an O as I realised what I held.

'You got tickets to the Black Vultures?' I squeaked.

Dillon bent into an exaggerated bow. 'Reagan asked, and I delivered.'

I turned to a grinning Reagan and squealed, wrapping my arms around her in a tight hug. As I held Dillon, he scrunched his nose and I remembered that I smelled of Beau.

'Oops, sorry.' I waved the tickets in Reagan's face. 'These were sold out months ago! How did you guys get tickets?'

Reagan looked smug. 'I asked Dillon to get them when they were released.'

'But that was just after I moved here,' I said, amazed.

'Yeah. I told you that I knew we'd be friends remember?'

I hugged her again. 'How did you get permission for me to leave town?'

She pointed to the black SUV in the driveway. Bishop and one of her crew waved from the front seats. 'Levi and Ben are gonna hang out in town as well, just in case. Plus, those guys are coming too.' She gestured behind her as Dorian and one of their cousins walked out of the house, towards the SUV.

We piled into the vehicle. Somehow, thanks to Dillon, we were able to skip the line-up and go straight into the venue. Bishop disappeared as we entered, and Reagan bought me a drink. Everyone shouted me drinks for my birthday. I'd gotten through two glasses and was surprised that I didn't feel the effects of the alcohol.

'Yeah, you're not gonna feel anything, kid.'

The support band left the stage and I was handed my third cocktail. '*What do you mean I won't feel anything?*' I asked James.

'Your healing abilities override the effects of the alcohol. Drink a bottle of spirits and you might feel a slight buzz, but that's it.'

I shrugged. I wasn't here for the drinks anyway. Grabbing Reagan's hand, I drew her to the front of the stage where the crowd was chanting for the band. The lead singer walked on stage, his signature neon blue and black electric guitar in hand, and I screamed. The crowd went wild as the first chord was struck and I fell into the trance of the music.

Three songs in, James whispered to me, *'This is the perfect opportunity for you to practise.'*

His comment cut through my trance. '*Practise?*'

'Yeah. Practise the little trick you've been working on.'

I looked at the people around me. I'd never have this kind of opportunity in Blackwood. '*What if they feel it?*'

'Most of them are drunk. And they'd have no idea what they were feeling anyway – they'd blame it on claustrophobia or social anxiety.'

I took a deep breath and exhaled, scanning the people around me. I'd practised this so often in the last weeks on my succulent plants that I could do it without full concentration.

'Okay. I can do this.'

I sent out a tendril of energy, splicing it into smaller tendrils, and attached it to the nearest person: a guy with long greasy black hair who was jumping with the music. He didn't notice as I drew from him. I smiled to myself then sent out another tendril, attaching it to the girl standing in front of me.

'Go big or go home, Freya. You can do better than that. Remember how many fragile little plants you drew from without harming them.'

I nodded. '*Don't get used to this, James.*'

'What?'

'Me listening to you.'

'You're just starting to see my value.'

I grinned and closed my eyes, feeling the energy pulsing within me, and in the crowd around me. I sent out another six tendrils, attaching them to the people nearest to me. Nearly a third of them were Supers. I inhaled sharply as their energy drew into mine. Drawing tiny amounts from so many people felt good. Like the time I'd drawn from the great-grandfather tree but better. Like the time I'd drawn from James.

Mundane energy is okay, but Supernatural energy is so much better. I threw my head back and sighed as the energy poured like ice through my veins. I tugged a little harder at the threads and groaned as euphoria washed over me. When my eyes opened, I studied the people around me. No one stopped or even flinched.

I laughed. *'This is amazing, James. If only you could feel it. It's like nothing else.'*

James chuckled. *'I'm sure it is. And look around you—they feel nothing. You can have your kicks guilt-free.'*

Someone tugged on my arm and I turned to find Reagan smiling at me. 'Come on, let's find the others.'

I looked back at the stage and saw that the band had finished and left. A part of me was disappointed I'd missed half the concert, but the other part of me thought that the euphoric experience was worth it. We found Dorian and Dillon, and Dorian laughed as we reached him.

'Had a few too many on your first night out, Freya?' he asked. He must've sensed the euphoria running through me.

I smiled. 'Something like that.'

I had a last look around the room and froze as I met with a pair of brown eyes. I blinked and they were gone. They were familiar, but I couldn't place where I'd seen them before. We followed the buzzing crowd out into the street and Bishop ushered us into the SUV. Dismissing the niggling concern, I collapsed into my seat, leaning my head back against the headrest. Reagan squeezed my hand and I turned to her.

'Best birthday ever. I don't know how I'm going to top this for your birthday.'

She grinned. 'I'm sure you'll think of something.'

9

I stood at the pathway connecting the Waller's property to mine. A canine whine brought my attention to Levi and I looked down at his furry form.

'I'm going to kick your butt, and when I do, remember that you have two extra legs than me, and I still beat you.'

I wasn't good at reading wolf body language, but I could read the equivalent of an eyeroll on a Wolf Shifter as well as any person. Another five wolves joined us, including Ben and Dillon. Of the other three, one was a girl. Someone I'd probably met. They stared at me as I stretched my calves. I guessed a non-Shifter had never run with them before. Ben sniffed and padded to the start of one of the tracks. He howled, and the sound of it hummed through my blood, making me shiver. He shot off at a lightning pace, followed by the others. I muttered a curse—they'd moved faster than I expected.

I ran, trailing behind, trying to keep sight of a furry tail in case they changed course. If I lost track of them on my first run, I'd never be invited again. I gained momentum and picked up my pace, dodging a branch that crossed the middle of the track. I passed the She-Wolf, grinning as adrenalin coursed through me. The wolf in front of me took a sharp turn and I followed, slipping in the leaves that covered the forest floor. I caught myself before I fell and chased after the small pack in front of me, passing another wolf. My muscles burned, but it felt good. I was catching up to Levi. Sibling rivalry was a great motivator.

We hit a clearing. My feet hit bitumen and I realised we were crossing a road. We entered scrub on the other side and I winced as a sharp branch lacerated the side of my thigh. It didn't slow me down. The scrub became sparse and the trees grew bigger until we reached the ancient trees that lined

Blackwood Valley. Dillon was in between Levi and me; I had to pass him first to get to my brother. I pushed myself to run faster.

The ground became sandier and it was difficult to keep my footing. We were getting close to the beach. As I reached Dillon's tail, the trees opened up into another clearing. Ben slowed to a stop and howled. I pulled to a halt, panting with my hands on my knees as I drew in oxygen. *Bummer.* I'd beat Dillon and Levi next time. I'd never outrun Ben, not without charging up on energy first—that would be cheating.

I straightened and admired the view. We'd stopped on the edge of a cliff overlooking the ocean. The sky was painted in orange and pink hues as the sun began to rise. I walked to the edge of the cliff and looked down. Waves crashed against the rocks, way down below. It was amazing. *How have I not been here before?* Ben padded up beside me, looking out over the water. His fur was covered in a sheen of sweat, turning to steam in the cold air.

'Thanks for inviting me today, for bringing me here. This has to be the best view in Blackwood,' I said.

He lowered his head in a nod. We stood there, staring out over the ocean as the sky began to turn blue. I observed the wolf beside me. He was bigger than the average Wolf Shifter, his alpha blood giving him an advantage over the others. His head was level with my chest and his paws looked as though they could do a lot of damage to a fragile human body. Still . . . he was nothing compared to Beau, who was taller than me in wolf form and had paws that could crush a bear's skull. My heart squeezed at the thought of his golden eyes and that soul-melting smile.

Ben walked back to the others and Levi yipped at me. It was time to go back. I stood by Levi's side and gave him a condescending scratch behind the ears. He nipped me on the wrist which only made me laugh. Ben howled and the pack took off, but I was ready this time. I remembered some of the twists and turns in the track, making it easier to keep up. I was once again a paws distance away from overtaking Dillon when an unexpected tree root caught my foot and I hit the forest floor, the air rushing from my lungs. A hacking growl that sounded suspiciously like a laugh came from my brother as he disappeared in the distance. I arrived at our house last and waved off the others, heading straight for the barn. *Next time.*

'I have some news,' Bishop said as I approached her at the workbench.

She wasn't in her usual training gear or yelling at me to get moving. Her team were loading bags and equipment into their SUVs.

'You're leaving?'

She nodded. 'Tom Monroe's been doing some recon for me. We think we've found Argyle's family.'

My eyes grew wide. The Blackwood Council and Bishop's team had combined their efforts to track down Argyle's family, to help prepare us for any backlash from his death. Bishop was a wealth of information but any leads she'd followed were dead ends.

'What have you found?' I asked.

Tom approached us from the make-shift kitchen at the back of the barn. He handed Bishop a mug of coffee. 'Not as much as I'd hoped but better than nothing,' he said. 'I've pinpointed a broad location; a section of Northern Europe. I did some digging in the local cities and heard whispers of a powerful family who wield influence across the continent. Argyle's name was mentioned on one occasion.'

Tom's gift was Astral Projection. He could travel to any place in an instant without a trace. His Astral form was invisible to most people. A trip to Europe was like a trip to the grocery store for Tom. He leaned against the bench and pulled out a cigarette.

'May I?' he asked Bishop, holding out the cigarette.

She arched her brows. 'Just don't set fire to my base, Monroe.'

He lit it and took a drag, blowing the smoke away from us. 'The name is Clemonte. They're old money. I'm almost sure there's French royal blood in their bloodline somewhere. They lead a community like Blackwood, but we don't know where. Wherever they're based is well protected.'

James was perplexed. *'Clemonte… it sounds familiar but I can't place it.'*

'Did you hear anything about me?' I asked.

He took another drag of his cigarette and shook his head. 'There's been no mention of a Syphon.' He smiled. 'I think you're safe for now.'

'We're going to do an in-depth search. Tom's coming with us. I'm not thrilled to be leaving you here with matters unresolved, but I'm confident you'll be well looked after,' Bishop said.

I bristled and felt James bristle too. 'I can take care of myself.'

Bishop arched her brows. 'Maybe I worded that wrong. I meant that you've got good people here to watch your back.'

When my expression didn't change, she stepped closer. 'I've got years of experience and am one of the best in my field. Do you see me running around as a one-woman show? You need a team behind you, Freya.' She narrowed her eyes. 'You're not going to run off and play the lone ranger when we leave, are you?'

'No. I don't have a death wish… I just don't need babysitting all the time.'

'Just keep an old woman happy, and let people watch out for you while I'm gone, okay?'

Bishop's hair was silver, but it had nothing to do with age. She was close in age to Mum, and Mum would argue that she wasn't old.

'Alright . . . so, you're coming back then?' I couldn't hide the hope in my voice.

The corners of her mouth curved. 'You'll be seeing plenty of me. But just so we're clear – no going solo, you got it?'

'Yeah, yeah, I got it.'

She's a killjoy. There's nothing wrong with getting a little trigger-happy.'

I rolled my eyes at James' comment and Bishop caught the gesture. She studied me.

'You might think I'm joking, but I'm not. There's

determination in you, and that's a good thing. Aside from the self-healing, it's helped you improve at a remarkable rate.' She placed a hand on my shoulder and leaned in. 'What concerns me, Freya, is I don't know what's feeding it.'

I lowered my gaze, scuffing a shoe on the concrete. 'I don't want to rely on others to come to my rescue all the time. I want to look out for myself. Surely you understand?'

'I do. But we always need people in our lives. People who'll have our backs. It's those people that keep us human, no matter how hard storms may hit us. Understand?'

I glanced up at her dark eyes. 'Yeah.'

A car door slammed and someone motioned that they were ready to go. Bishop gave me a final warning to behave and climbed into the driver's side of one of the big black SUVs with her coffee mug still in hand.

'She's right you know.'

I'd forgotten Tom was standing there. 'Right about what?'

'We all need people in our lives. Don't learn the hard way like I did.' He ground out the cigarette on the bottom of his shoe, then clapped me on the shoulder. 'Stay out of trouble.' He followed Bishop to the car and as he got in, she wound down the window.

'Keep the burner phone on you at all times, Freya.' She pointed a finger in my direction. 'Don't think I haven't noticed that it's been sitting on your bedside table more often than not. I know you think I'm babying you, but it's for your safety.'

'Sorry, I won't forget again.'

She gave me a warning stare. 'Be sure you don't.'

I waved as the window closed and they drove away.

My fourth period of the day was calculus—I hate calculus. Jonah sat with me in class. He helped me when I couldn't get my head around the formulas. I pinched the bridge of my nose as the siren sounded.

'You haven't had any side-effects from the mental lock, have you?' Jonah asked as we left the classroom.

'What kind of side-effects?'

'Nausea, seizures, migraines… that kind of thing.'

I shook my head. 'I've been fine.'

'You just always look, I dunno, angry. Just for the last week or so. It's the same face Mum gets when she's having a migraine.'

'It's just RBF, Jonah. A condition I have no control over.'

His brows creased. 'Reagan has resting bitch face. This is different.'

I exhaled and looked him in the eye. 'I'm fine, Jonah.'

He glanced away but stuck beside me as we walked to our last class. We reached a quiet section of the hallway when he said, 'You know, I understand that you're upset with Beau. But don't think the worst of him just yet.'

Jonah was a quiet guy, but he noticed everything. 'I don't think the worst, I'm just worried about him. I get that Dire Wolves are solitary beings, but what if he's in trouble and needs help?'

He glanced away from me. 'I'm sure he's fine. He has a family of Dire Wolves to watch out for him. Besides, I doubt he needs help, he probably thinks he's protecting you.'

The way he muttered his words made me suspicious. I tried to catch his eye, but he wouldn't look at me. He looked at everything but me.

'Protecting me? What is that supposed to mean?'

He scratched his head and met my eye. 'Nothing. He's a genuine guy; he wouldn't leave without a good reason.' He stalked off ahead of me, not once looking back.

One thing Jonah and I had in common—we were both terrible liars. He knew something I didn't which meant that Beau had been in contact with someone in Blackwood. Beau's parents lived off the grid, so it made sense that he'd make contact through someone with psychic or psionic abilities. If the Monroe's were in contact with Beau, then they'd intentionally kept that information from me, which meant they didn't trust me.

'Of course, they don't trust you. I've told you before, your gift puts you at the top of the food chain. Nobody trusts someone with that level of power.'

'I could be reading this wrong. I've made that mistake before.'

'What does your gut tell you?'

A cold shiver ran through my body. *'It tells me that I need to be careful.'*

'Good. You're learning. You might actually live long enough to enjoy the gift you took from me.'

I walked to my next class but stopped at the door. I'd learned from a young age how to bluff my way into getting the answers I wanted. It was the only way I ever got dirt on Levi to use as blackmail. I pulled the phone out of my pocket and dialled Reagan's number. She had a study period and had gone home to keep an eye on Grams. Either I'd be right, or she'd think I was paranoid. She answered with a cheery hello.

'We're best friends, right?' I asked.

'Of course. Are you alright?'

'I'm surprised you haven't seen this.' *I suppose she wouldn't when I didn't let her touch my skin.* I threaded a hand through my hair.

'Freya, what's going on?'

'How long has Beau been in contact with you guys?' There was silence on the other end of the phone. 'Reags, I know he's been in contact.'

Her voice was quiet. 'How did you know?'

My stomach knotted. 'That's not important. How long?'

She sighed. 'A while.'

I moved away from the classroom door and down an empty corridor. I leaned against the wall. 'How long is a while?'

'Since a couple of days after he left. He called in to let Dad know he'd arrived safely.'

My head snapped forward. 'Wait … he called?'

'Freya, I'm sorry, but I couldn't say anything. Beau asked Dad not to mention anything. I had no choice.'

Beau had lied about being 'off the grid'? My grip on the phone tightened. 'I don't get it, Reagan, why didn't he just break up with me?' I ran a hand down my face. 'Oh right, we're not technically dating, so I guess it's not a break-up. Did he think I was so fragile that I couldn't handle a rejection?' I paced the corridor as I rambled.

'You guys are great together, Frey. I'm sure he has his reasons.'

'Do you know those reasons?'

'No, I just know he calls every now and then.'

I stopped pacing and drew in a deep breath. The haze of anger simmered and my thoughts cleared. 'You know what, Reagan, I think I get it.'

'What do you mean?'

'Beau and I both have gifts that attract the wrong attention. We create a bigger risk to each other by being together. Just by coming to my rescue Beau put himself and his family in danger. We'll fail each other eventually, so by leaving Blackwood he's put a stop to whatever this is before it even begins.'

'You're overthinking this. Maybe he has a simple reason and just doesn't know how to tell you?'

'What else could it be?'

'I don't know…'

I pinched the bridge of my nose. 'I should just end it. Save us both the heartache.'

She paused. 'Are you sure that's what you want?'

I nodded to myself. 'I'm starting to see the bigger picture, so yeah, that's what I want.'

'Just do yourself a favour and cool off first, alright? Then you can do what you have to do.'

I blinked back tears. 'Yeah, okay. I'll see you later.'

I hung up the phone and stared at the screen. Chastising myself for not trying it earlier, I brought up Beau's number and pressed call. The engaged tone sounded through the speaker. *Has he blocked my number?* My hand shook as I ended the call. I wanted to be sick. I passed my classroom and headed for the parking lot. My brain kicked into overdrive on the way home. I parked in the driveway and sat in my car, staring out the windscreen and rubbing that spot on my chest that seemed to grow tighter and tighter. A few laps of the circuit would help me to get control.

10

A week passed by. I did laps of Bishop's circuit and ran every day, with or without Levi or Ben. I ran further distances and pushed myself harder through all the drills I'd memorised, to block out any thoughts of *him*. It was more than Bishop would've expected of me—more than *I* expected of me. James managed to keep the 'I told you so's' to himself.

I started to notice a subtle change in my energy. My abilities thread had grown brighter—stronger. Meditation helped me to keep control but I couldn't tell if the growth in power had altered my ability. It seemed normal. I reached a point where I'd pushed my emotions far enough away that I could think of Beau without anger or hurt. I felt nothing. That was, until Thursday. I finished third period with a lecture from Mr Orson about my inattention… again. I'd forgotten the burner phone *again* and Bishop had sent me a berating text. Reagan was sick and had taken the day off school, so I walked the school halls by myself. I reached my locker and stopped. Snickers sounded from behind me. Scrawled across my locker in dripping red paint was the word *LEECH*.

Resting a hand against the locker, I took a deep breath to calm the anger bubbling in my chest. I sensed the insta-perfect She-Wolf approach me from behind. She'd been trying to sink her claws into Beau long before I arrived in Blackwood. I didn't bother to turn around.

'What do you want, Emily?'

She sidled up beside me, admiring the graffiti. 'Oh, nothing. I just wanted to say I told you so, before your little world starts to unravel.'

I glared at her. 'What's that supposed to mean?'

She shrugged. 'I've heard that you're the reason Beau has decided to stay away from Blackwood.' She saw a change in my expression and her lips pouted in false pity. 'Oh, didn't you know? He's gone indefinitely now. I knew he'd tire of you sooner or later. It was just a matter of time.'

Dillon and the twins walked past me, continuing to their next class when they saw I was speaking with the Northern She-Wolf. It was an unsaid rule in Blackwood that guys never got involved in girl trouble. It was an irrational fear that they'd get cried on or something.

'You know he had no interest in you right? Even before I moved to town,' I bit back.

Her eyes flashed. 'You may have Shifter blood, but you're not one of us. In the end Beau will want someone like him, not a *leech* like you.'

'Don't let her speak to you like that, Freya. Top of the food chain remember?'

I didn't need encouragement from James—I'd had enough. Anger ripped through me and I shoved against her shoulder. She slammed into the lockers and flinched as I thumped my fists on either side of her head. Her pretty blue eyes grew wide and I grinned. My strength surprised her, and so it should. I'd been working hard. I'd also been pulling energy from her, but she didn't need to know that.

I leaned in close and hissed, 'Call me a leech again, and I'll make you suffer.' She didn't move; her eyes stayed locked on mine. I'd never shown aggression towards her before, regardless of the taunts. I murmured low enough for her to hear, 'I won't kill you. I'll take your ability to shift. I'll take away your sense of identity so that a part of you will always be missing. No running with the pack, no pack bond. Your precious Northerners won't want you without your claws, will they?' I couldn't separate energies yet, but I would. I'd keep that promise if she so much as turned up her nose at me.

A hand rested on my shoulder. 'Freya, I think you should back away.'

I snapped my head sideways, glaring at Jonah. 'She needs to learn a lesson.'

The She-Wolf's energy flared as she fought the need to shift. She wouldn't want to ruin her perfect clothes, plus shifting in them would be uncomfortable, especially in shoes.

'One of her friends has gone to get the Principal. Let go,' he warned.

His grip tightened on my shoulder, concern reflected in his light blue eyes. I eyed the crowd that had formed behind him. Students were peering around each other for a better view.

'Show her, Freya. Show her what you can do,' James goaded, his voice echoing through my brain.

Jonah's eyes widened and I winced. I turned back to Emily.

'Leave. Me. Alone,' I warned, dropping my arms to my side.

She nodded, peeling herself away from the lockers. The sound of the principal's shoes thudding on the linoleum made us step apart. He approached us where we stood facing each other.

'What's going on here?' he asked.

Emily flicked her hair over her shoulder and produced a shaky smile. 'Nothing at all, Sir. Just a little misunderstanding.'

He turned to me, catching sight of my locker. 'Who's responsible for this?' His voice echoed down the hall.

'It was just a joke, Sir,' I said, still holding Emily's stare.

She sniffed and turned her back on me, moving down the hall, surrounded by a protective huddle of She-Wolves. The principal clicked his tongue, wiping a finger against the dried, red paint. 'Do you know who did this?' he asked.

'Not a clue.'

Jonah's gaze bore into the side of my head. The Principal turned to me.

'You shouldn't cover for them. I'll make sure this is cleaned off by tomorrow.'

I was just glad Mum wasn't here. It was her free period which meant a coffee date with Chris.

I sat through the next two periods staring out the window, unable to concentrate. Today had felt good. I'd shown just a little of what I could do and Emily had run off with her tail between her legs. When the siren rang, I hurried to the exit. A few Southerners stopped me and slapped me on the back for challenging Emily. According to the twins, she'd submitted like a Shifter who'd only just found her claws. I threw my bag in the back of the car and opened the driver's door. Jonah stood on the passenger's side.

'Can I get a lift?'

'You have plenty of friends to give you a lift. I've really got to get home.'

He hopped in the car without giving me a chance to refuse. 'Everyone else is busy.'

I sat in the driver's seat with a sigh. Jonah stared out the window as I pulled onto the road. We'd passed through town before he decided to say what was on his mind.

'What was that, Freya?'

I tensed. 'I have no idea what you mean.'

He turned his frown on me. 'That wasn't nothing. I heard a voice—a male voice. How is that possible?'

'Maybe you just heard the thoughts of a teacher in the classroom next to us?'

'It came from your consciousness. I know your thought pattern.'

We pulled into the driveway and I braked, bringing the car to a sudden halt. I twisted in my seat, facing Jonah.

'Just leave this alone and stay out of my head.'

He flinched. It was a low blow. I knew he had no control over hearing surface thoughts. He opened the door of the car and slammed it shut, casting me a glare before trudging into the house. I pulled back onto the road and drove towards Pete's Beach.

'You owe me a day of silence for that screw up, James.'

He sniffed. *'He would've worked it out eventually.'*

'Well let's just hope he keeps this to himself.'

'Doubtful.'

I pulled up at Pete's Beach and shrugged on my coat, pulling up the hood to protect my face from the blistering wind. The café was closed. I sat myself in the damp sand and stared out over the water. I'd enjoyed putting Emily in her place, but her comment about Beau had upset me. *Is he really not coming back?* I pulled out my phone and typed the text I'd been avoiding.

You were right to blow me off like you did. A cowardly way out, but right none-the-less. I'm going to be the adult and end things now. We're both better off without each other.

Goodbye, Beau.

My thumb hovered over the screen before I finally pressed send. I sat on the beach, lost in my thoughts until the sun began to set. My phone buzzed and I let out a dry laugh—Beau.

My heartbeat staggered. Ignoring the phone I pulled off my jacket. There wasn't another warm body in sight, so I stripped off my clothes and jumped into the icy cold water in my underwear. Anything to numb those feelings and stop myself from answering that call.

11

HE called at least three times a day. The sudden phone reception was nothing short of a miracle, made possible because no one had dared to break up with him before. That was my guess anyway. Eventually he gave up and called Reagan. She tried convincing me to speak to him, but I'd already made my decision, and I was sticking with it. I ran with Levi and Ben every morning while they were on break and almost beat Levi twice. Bishop called in regularly to give an update, but they'd still not located Argyle's family.

My last period on a Wednesday was free, so I arrived home before Mum. I walked into the kitchen, surprised to find Pa sitting at the breakfast bar. He stared at a picture on the fridge, one of Levi and me when we were kids. I moved behind the kitchen bench, turning on the kettle and asked him if he wanted tea. He nodded, swiping the leftover crumbs from Levi's lunch into a pile on the bench. My brother was a slob.

'No hug for your pa?' he grumbled. 'You never used to walk past me without a hug.'

'Sorry, hunger makes me forget.' I opened the fridge, pulling out last night's left-overs. I made tea for Pa and I. He didn't look up from the bench.

'You alright, Pa?'

He leaned back and scratched his head, finally meeting my eye. 'The Council wants to meet with you, Sprite. Tonight.'

My brows creased. 'Tonight? I thought they'd give me to the end of school to decide whether I join the pack.'

He grumbled under his breath. 'The Council don't tell me everything.' He wouldn't look at me.

'You *do* know something.'

'You'll know soon enough, Sprite. They wish to speak to you directly.'

We sat at the bench, quietly sipping our tea. Aside from Mr Monroe and the pack leaders, I didn't know who made up the Council.

The drive into town was quiet. I stared out the passenger window of Pa's ute. *Why hadn't Mum told me about the Council meeting?*

'You haven't seemed yourself recently,' Pa said, breaking the silence.

What was with everyone saying that? 'I'm okay. Just busy with school.'

He gave a disbelieving sniff, pulling up at the town hall. A large gold plaque dedicated to Rowan and Christina Waller was placed near the front door of the building; for their generosity in completing the recent restoration. We entered through a set of oak doors that opened up into a large hall. Twelve people sat in a semi-circle of chairs towards the far end of the room. I recognized most faces. My steps slowed as I saw the people standing behind the Council members. My mum, Levi and Grandma were there. Ben stood beside his dad. Mrs Monroe stood alongside her husband and so did Jonah and Dorian. I moved forwards until I stood directly in front of the semi-circle. Pa moved to stand with Grandma.

Something in my mind clicked. 'This is an intervention, isn't it?'

Mum began to scold me, but Mr Monroe held up a hand for silence.

'Freya, we've called this meeting due to some concerns. Please, take a seat.' He gestured to a chair that had been placed behind me.

I dropped into the seat. 'So, what's the problem?'

He tapped on the arm of his chair, eyeing the other Council members. They bobbed their heads in succession. I turned to my family. They all held concerned expressions. The only thing that could draw me to the attention of the Council was—

Jonah.

I eyed Jonah and glared. He shrugged, plugging in his

headphones to block the rather loud, unhappy thoughts I was projecting his way. I turned back to Mr Monroe.

'Look, whatever Jonah told you, he's wrong. Even Telepaths make mistakes sometimes.'

Mr Monroe exhaled a long breath. What was I thinking? I couldn't lie to Mr Monroe – a Truth Seeker. I'd just lied to a man who had always been good to me, and it wasn't even a well thought out lie.

'Freya, you were brought to the attention of the Council long before Jonah mentioned his concerns. School staff have advised us that you've been distracted in classes. We were concerned that the ordeal earlier this year had a greater impact on you than we imagined.' He turned to my mum. 'Your family agreed to tend to the matter, however things haven't improved. Bishop and your mother have expressed concern with how hard you're pushing yourself.' He turned back to me. 'You no longer sleep, you haven't been attending any social outings, and you had an uncharacteristic outburst at school. None of these things alone would overly concern us, but when Jonah mentioned what he heard, we became alarmed.' He stood up, and approached my chair, crouching down in front of me, so we were at eye level. 'We've done our research, and there's not much of it out there in regards to Syphons, but the little information that we found made us worry. The fact that you may be harbouring someone's soul, that concerns us.'

I flinched. 'I think it's an echo of him, rather than his soul.' Mum sobbed from the side of the room and I tried to reassure her. 'He's not that bad. A bit of a jerk, but I've gotten used to him now. He's the reason I've progressed so fast with training.'

'You said he was a mercenary, Freya. That his memories were sickening,' Mum screeched. 'How can he not be that bad?' Pa placed a hand on her shoulder.

'When did he begin speaking to you?' Mr Monroe asked.

I shrugged. 'The night I was rescued.'

Mum let out a gasp. 'You should have told us!'

'And what would you have done about it? What would any of you have done about it?' I stood, gesturing around the room. 'None of you could've done a damned thing! You would've all just stared at me with the same concerned looks you are now, and wondered when poor Freya was going to lose her mind!'

The Northern alpha, Theo, leaned forward in his chair. 'This mercenary, does he have a name?'

I gritted my teeth. Theo had never liked me. 'James. His name is James.'

'We don't know the level of influence this *James* has on Freya. She's already brought trouble to our town. How much more will we tolerate?'

My hands clenched into fists. My family surrounded me and Levi growled, lunging towards Theo.

Ben held him back and Levi spat, 'This is ridiculous! He's just pissed at Freya because Greyson's secret was exposed, and now he's run off with his tail between his legs. The Northerners are weak without him.'

Theo's eyes glowed.

'Back down, both of you!' Mr Monroe warned.

I moved to defend my brother and James said, *'Sit this one out, kid.'*

'He's been a jerk from the start!'

'Now's not the time for a temper tantrum. Do something about it when you have an advantage, not a room full of people to stop you.'

'He's talking to her now.'

The whole room fell silent at Jonah's words and I caught his gaze. He pulled out his earphones. 'Sorry, Freya. But they need to know.'

'Stay out of her head, boy. Eavesdropping is impolite.'

Jonah's lips quirked. 'He just told me to stay out of her head.'

The room erupted. Everyone argued over what to do with me. It dragged out as people talked over each other. Some bright person suggested that I should be put under house arrest and another thought it would best for me to be treated at one of those hospitals for Supers. Mum nearly bit his head off. I considered storming out of the room when Mr Waller stopped and turned to Pa.

He grabbed a hold of Pa's arm. 'John, are you okay?'

I faced Pa. He looked like he'd seen a ghost. Mum yelled his name and I rushed to his side, latching on to his free hand. It was cold and clammy.

'Pa!'

He pulled his hand from mine, clutching his chest. His face paled. Mr Waller lowered him to the floor as someone called an ambulance. I heard the words 'heart attack' and my ears rang. It didn't feel real. *This was happening to someone else, not Pa.* I was moved out of the way as Mum and Grandma moved to his side. An arm rested across my shoulders and I grasped onto Levi's jumper. Pa was the anchor in our family—he couldn't leave us.

The medics arrived, bursting through the door with a stretcher. Pa needed a Healer, but there was no Healer in Blackwood or nearby strong enough to heal more than a minor laceration. My healing abilities were useless for anyone but me. He was hauled into the ambulance and Grandma held his hand. The doors slammed closed and my arms fell loose at my sides.

This is my fault…

Levi and I followed Mum to the Blackwood hospital in Pa's ute. The hospital waiting room was painted a horrible shade of light green; the kind you'd find on clearance at the hardware store. I sat with my feet pulled up against my chest and leaned against Levi. Chris turned up not long after us and held Mum as she cried. She rested against Chris with her eyes closed. We'd know the second Pa was okay, or not okay. Well, the others would know… they'd feel it through the pack bond.

I stared out the waiting room window. It was past midnight. Levi fell asleep against my shoulder and the hours passed. I stifled tears as I thought back to our conversation that afternoon. Pa had complained I didn't hug him enough anymore. He'd seemed so worried.

This is all my fault.

Pa was fighting for his life because of me. I hadn't spent time with him in recent months. I hadn't hugged him enough. I hadn't told him how much I love him.

12

THE others stirred. Mum jolted upright, staring off into the distance. She turned to me and her face relaxed into a relieved smile—Pa was going to be okay.

I hung back in the doorway as everyone piled into Pa's room. He lay asleep between the stark white sheets of the hospital bed. The Doctor told Grandma he wouldn't be able to shift until his heart was in a stable condition. Wolf Shifters were fast healers, but it slowed with age, and aside from the brain, the heart took the longest to mend. I stared at Pa, who for the first time, seemed frail. John Armitage had always been a pillar of strength.

Everyone listened to the Doctor's instructions and didn't notice as I turned and walked away. I needed air. The green exit sign glowed before me and I pushed through the doors. It was raining. I felt for the car keys that Levi had thrown in my bag and sprinted through the carpark, shielding my head from the rain. I jumped into Pa's ute and headed home.

The wheels skidded in the mud as I pulled into our driveway and slammed the brake. The rain fell harder as I jumped out of the ute, and my wet clothes clung to my body. I peeled off my jumper and kicked off my shoes, leaving them scattered on the grass. Shoes would just slip in the mud.

I ran.

Rain streamed down my face and plastered my hair in thick tendrils down my back. Branches whipped my arms. My toes dug into the earth and I picked up speed. Rocks slashed my feet but I barely noticed. I pushed myself until my body ached and my muscles burned. I didn't stop until I reached the clifftop and stood with my muddied toes hanging over the edge. Angry black waves crashed against the rocks below.

As I stared over the water, my chest heaving, my phone rang. I grabbed it from my pocket and saw Beau's name light up the screen. My heart squeezed painfully and I pulled back my arm, throwing the phone into the sea with an angry shout.

'Leave me alone!' I screamed.

My heart felt fractured. It wouldn't take much more to shatter it into a million pieces. When my breathing slowed, I sat down on the cliff edge, resting my chin on my knees. Tears mixed with the raindrops running down my face and I sniffed.

'I get that you're angry, but that was a waste of a good phone.'

'Can't you just leave me alone!' I hissed.

'Hey, you need me. You know he's going to die sooner or later, right? The longer you live, the faster the years go by. All of those people you love, will drop one by one, until there's no one left. It's easier cutting them loose now. It'll hurt less.'

The waves grew angrier, crashing against the cliff below with a loud *boom.* I clutched my head, attempting to ignore James's words. The truth of them stung too much. I stayed there on the clifftop until the rain stopped and the waves calmed.

A rustle from behind caught my attention. The wolf padded up to my side, his light brown fur brushing against my arm. He sat beside me and whined, his big, green eyes staring up at me.

'I'm fine, Levi. I just needed some air.'

He looked me over, his gaze stopping at my feet. He let out a growl and nudged my knees. I saw my feet and cringed. They were covered in blood and mud.

'It's fine, honestly. I didn't even feel it. My shoes were wet.'

He snorted and leaned into me, sharing his body warmth. I buried my hands into his fur, resting my head against his neck. We stayed that way until daybreak. I broke the silence with a shaky apology.

'I'm sorry if I worried you. I just… I feel like this is all my fault.'

He grunted and pawed his muzzle. My mouth curved—the gesture was his way of telling me we needed to talk, but he couldn't while stuck in wolf-form.

'I dunno, Levi, I kind of like you as the silent, listening type.'

He snorted and pawed the ground.

'I'm sorry I never told you about James. I didn't want you to look at me like some kind of basket case. I didn't tell anyone, not even Beau or Reagan, if that makes you feel better.'

He gestured with his head to the track behind us.

I let out a long breath. 'Yeah, okay. We can go home.'

I brushed the crusted dirt and blood from my feet and followed Levi at a light jog. We reached the main road and he stopped on the other side as two more wolves appeared before us. Silent communication passed between them and Levi looked back at me with a yip. He was needed elsewhere.

'I'll be fine. You guys go.'

They leapt into the ferns and disappeared with a rustle of leaves. I instinctively reached into my pocket and grumbled, remembering that my phone lay somewhere on the ocean floor.

At home, I sat on the kitchen bench, warm and dry after a shower, with a tub of ice-cream on my lap. Mum would have scolded me for my choice of breakfast. I stopped mid-scoop as the house phone rang. I'd forgotten it even existed. Shoving the scoop of ice-cream in my mouth, I answered the phone with a mumbled 'hello'.

'Finally! I've been texting and calling you for the last couple of hours,' Dillon huffed.

I winced. 'Yeah, I lost my phone…'

'I'm glad to hear your Pop is okay. Don't worry, the pack will all help out and make sure he sticks to the Doctors orders.'

Pa was well-loved. 'Thanks, Dillon. It's good to know.'

'Also, I thought you might like to get away from the stress for a few hours. Echo Land is tonight, if you still want to come. A guy I know found me some more last-minute tickets so there's a whole heap of us going now. It'll be a fun group outing.' In other words, I wasn't allowed to go unless I had an entourage of babysitters. 'No pressure, one of the twins will take the ticket if you don't want it.'

'No, no. I still want to come.' After everything with the Council and then Pa, a few hours of mind-numbing music sounded great.

'I figured you wouldn't be coming to school today so I'll pick you up at five.'

I drove into town to buy a new phone, only to be told that I'd have to go to Belfield if I wanted something with a touch screen. The burner phone was 'Bishop only' *and* leaving town without an escort wasn't an option, so it would have to wait. It was after lunch by the time I got to the hospital. I reached Pa's room and hesitated outside the door. Grandma caught sight of me lurking near the doorway and hustled me inside. She left us alone while she went looking for some tea.

'There's my Sprite,' Pa said.

My heart pounded as I approached his side of the bed. 'You're looking better, Pa.' I wanted to touch him, but was worried I'd hurt him somehow.

He raised a single brow. 'Still no hug for your pa?'

I leaned across the bed and he pulled me into his arms. It wasn't as tight as usual. I pulled away and bit my lip hard. 'I'm so sorry.'

Pa's brows creased. 'Sorry for what? This isn't your fault, Freya. You didn't give me a faulty heart.'

'I made you worry. You were stressed out because of me.' I hugged my arms to my body, watching the heart-rate monitor to the side of the bed beep a steady rhythm. Pa patted the side of the bed and I sat down. He grabbed my hand and held it tight.

'Yes, I was worried. I've told you before that parents and grandparents will always worry. But that didn't cause the heart attack.' He tucked a strand of hair behind my ear. 'I'm getting old, Sprite. My body is telling me that I need to slow down.'

I nodded. Everyone would get old. Eventually they'd all die—I'd be alone.

13

DILLON sat out the front of my house with the car in idle at five o'clock, as promised. Mum said I was allowed to go. The Council had postponed any decisions about my future, so I was given a small reprieve. Ben and Levi sat in the car behind Dillon. Levi eyed me from the driver's seat with one brow raised. He hadn't forgotten about our chat. I wrapped a thick scarf around my neck to keep out the winter chill. Reagan rushed to me from the passenger's side of Dillon's car and hugged me tight.

'Sorry to hear about your pa.' She pulled away. 'I get that you're upset, but I had to find out what was going on with you from my baby brother, of all people,' she scolded, glancing at the car. Jonah sat in the back seat.

'Sorry, Reags.'

'I understand why you didn't tell me about the guy in your head, but I still wish you had.' She held out an arm. I zipped up my jacket with a grin, looping my arm through hers as we walked to the car.

'I'm surprised Jonah is coming to such a crowded event,' I said, pinning him with a glare.

'He's doing it for you, Frey. He's worried about you.'

I snorted. 'James can't force me to massacre a crowd of innocents or anything. He's more like an annoying buzz in my ear.'

'Either way, Jonah cares. So be nice.'

'I'm always nice.'

'Then stop giving him the stink-eye.'

Echo Land played at the only club in the backstreets of Belfield. I walked straight for the bar and ordered a lemonade. I sipped my drink, scanning the crowd for Reagan and Dillon. Levi and Ben had stationed themselves on the loft as lookouts and Jonah would've found himself a quiet corner. I spotted Dillon and pushed through the crowd. Echo Land walked onto the stage just as I reached my friends.

'Their concerts are meant to be epic!' Dillon yelled into my ear.

I glanced up on stage and smirked as the lead singer greeted the crowd with a, 'Hello, Belfield!'

'It's probably something to do with his gift!' I shouted up at Dillon.

'What?'

'His gift is projected through his voice. He's throwing energy out over the crowd like a blanket. I'm pretty sure what he's doing is illegal.'

Dillon shrugged. 'Doesn't matter. They're awesome anyway.' He pushed through the crowd towards the stage and Reagan grabbed his hand, following behind. She attempted to pull me along with them.

'I'm going to stay here,' I said, taking a step back as a group of squealing girls pushed into the open space in front of me.

I sent out tendrils of energy into the crowd. Most were Mundane but there were a few gifted people. I gave into the urge to draw from the people around me, sighing as energy flooded my body. A woman in front of me danced in a trance-like state; her abilities thread glowing bright. I closed my eyes and reached out, mentally tugging on the thread a little harder than the others. Her power flowed through my body and when I opened my eyes I gasped.

The music was visible—each note and instrument producing a different colour. I laughed, basking in the kaleidoscope of colour. My body relaxed as I continued to draw energy from the people around me. A hand grasped my shoulder and I was pulled back to reality. Reagan screamed in my ear that she was going to check on Jonah. I stopped the flow and forced myself to focus, edging my way out of the crowd and back to the bar. The room had grown stuffy so I pulled the scarf from my neck, placing it on the counter in front of me. The musical colours had faded by the time I was passed my second drink. I finished it in one mouthful and placed the glass on the counter, turning to look up at the loft.

Levi and Ben stood near the front, expressions sober as they scanned the crowd. I met Ben's gaze and he nodded, his attention quickly drawn away by a fight breaking out in the mosh pit.

'This drink is on me,' a voice said from beside me.

I cringed and turned back to the bar. 'Thanks, but I have a b—'

I froze, staring at the man standing on my right. It was the Teleporter. The same one who'd worked with Argyle. I hadn't even sensed his energy signature; he was just there. I'd seen those eyes recently… at the Black Vultures concert. He slid a glass of amber liquid my way.

'A bit of hard liquor for a barely-there adult, so take it easy.' He lifted a finger and his lips curved. 'Oh, that's right, you're a self-healer now. It won't do much, will it?'

My voice shook. 'What do you want?'

He clicked his tongue. 'Such a broad question. I want what everyone wants; the means to support my lifestyle. I'm not a greedy man; a little house on a private beach somewhere will do me just fine.' He leaned in, careful not to touch me. 'Now, if you're asking what *I* want with you, well that's the wrong question. What you should be asking, is *who* wants you.'

The blood drained from my face. He finished his drink, then picked up my untouched glass and finished that too. He placed a twenty on the counter, turned back to me and winked.

'I'll be seeing you around, you can count on it.' In a blink he was gone.

I turned from the bar, scanning the people around me. Reagan and Dillon were nowhere to be seen. I pushed my way to the staircase leading up to the loft and searched for my brother. A group of people formed a barricade in front of the stairs. I looked around for my friends—*we need to get out of here, now!* I manoeuvred my way around the group and searched for the others. Jonah's icy blue eyes caught my attention and I stopped.

It wasn't Jonah.

He looked around my age; lean, with black hair and pale

skin. He wore black jeans, and a black shirt with the sleeves rolled up. Aside from his face, his skin was covered in tattoos. He smirked and my heart jumped. I sent out a thread of energy and flinched. Something wasn't right. His abilities thread wasn't there… but I could feel it. It was like a deep well, and at the bottom of the well something powerful roiled. His gaze didn't waver from me, and I knew…

He was here for me.

'Get out now!' James roared.

Shoving people aside, I rushed to the exit. I needed to get this guy away from my brother and friends. The door loomed in front of me. I pushed past the security guard but stopped as the door disappeared. Only a black gaping hole remained. I staggered back as the security guard also vanished.

One by one people dissolved into darkness. The buzz of noise dimmed into silence –deafening silence. I couldn't hear myself breathe. An overwhelming sense of aloneness hit me and my knees buckled. Tears streamed down my cheeks. It was like my soul had been ripped from my chest. The non-existent ground was hard against my knees as I hunched over and a heavy cloud of darkness surrounded me. Even James was gone. I never thought I'd miss his irritating voice.

I sat curled into myself until the silence was broken by the sound of footsteps. A pair of black boots appeared in my line of sight. I lifted my head to the figure looming above me. My eyes were drawn to the tattoo wrapped around his neck; it glowed blue. I lashed out with all the power I possessed and fell backwards as my energy hit an invisible barrier.

Cold, blue eyes sparked with amusement as he crouched in front me. The darkness swirled around his body like a living shadow. I lashed out again, pushing through the exhaustion. My energy hit the barrier and it shimmered. The shimmer rippled and I saw that it surrounded him like a shield.

'Go ahead and wear yourself out. We have all night.' His voice was low and smooth. He'd have seemed bored if it wasn't for the curious glint in his eye.

'Who are you?' I asked.

'I'm the person entrusted with your safe delivery.'

'What have you done to me?' I asked between clenched teeth.

He tilted his head. 'I've made everything disappear—sight, sound, purpose… I can take everything from you. If you play nice and do as I ask, I'll give it all back.'

'What's the point? Just do it,' I hissed.

'Do what?'

'Kill me!'

He chuckled. 'It hurts that you've stereotyped me already. The tattoos and clothes don't make me a bad guy, you know. For all you know I could be all squishy on the inside.'

'The Teleporter led you here which means you're with the Clemontes.'

He leaned in. 'How do you know that name?'

I attempted to calm my breathing. 'I have my sources.'

His lip quirked. 'It doesn't matter. You'll know the family soon enough. Now, can you promise to play nice?' He stood and extended a hand. The air rushed from my lungs as the feeling of hollowness lifted. I eyed the hand but didn't reach for it. He continued, 'You have two choices. Either you come without a fuss and your friends keep their lives, or we do this the hard way and you still leave with us, but your friends die. This place is crawling with my people… It's your choice.'

I clenched my eyes shut. There was no alternative. It was the only choice. I opened my eyes, thrusting out my hand and he pulled me to my feet. The darkness withdrew and the buzz of noise once again filled my ears. People reappeared in an instant and everyone continued on like nothing had happened. I spun around, looking for a face I recognised.

'If you don't want trouble, don't draw the attention of your friends.' He gestured for me to walk ahead.

I noticed a brunette standing to his side. She sneered at me, a sheen of sweat covering her brow and upper lip. From her energy, I saw that she'd created the barrier surrounding her companion. I moved towards the exit, and Jonah walked into my line of sight. He strode towards me and I opened my thoughts.

'Stay away, Jonah. They'll kill all of you.'

His footsteps faltered. I felt as he entered my mind. *'What's going on?'*

'It's them—Argyle's family. We can't win, I have to go with them.'

'No, there's enough of us here.'

James butted in. *'Think of your sister, boy. You're outnumbered and they have an Aegis, which means you'll be useless too. Go home, gather your numbers and develop a plan—no one needs to die today.'*

Jonah's nostrils flared and I shook my head. He hesitated.

'Please,' I begged.

His mouth thinned. He gave a slight nod and stepped back into the crowd. I lowered my head, walking past him to the exit. A tattooed hand latched onto my elbow, steering me out the door towards an SUV with blacked out windows. There were another two cars lined up behind, with people standing near the doors. They all watched me.

Mr Tattoos opened the car door and gestured for me to get inside. It was like a limousine, with seats facing each other. Climbing into the forward-facing seat, I scooted to the far side. I patted my pockets and cursed. The burner phone was sitting on my bed at home where I'd left it, as a reminder to take it with me. My other phone still laid somewhere on the ocean floor. *He* sat in the seat opposite me. This guy could compete with an alpha with his unwavering gaze. I was used to challenging stares, so I lifted my chin and held it.

'Don't show any weaknesses. Tom said the Clemontes were old money. Old money means old school—it's all about power, hierarchy and control. Give away nothing.'

James's observation calmed me and helped me to focus. The brunette sat next to my captor, followed by a hulking mass of a man who sat next to me. He slammed the door shut and rested an arm across the black leather window-ledge. My heart squeezed as the car pulled onto the road.

'So, this is the Soul Sucker who dragged us across the world,' the hulk said.

I gave him a tight smile. 'That's Miss Soul Sucker to you. And what do they call you? Fridge?'

He barked a laugh and turned to the guy with tattoos. 'And you thought this would be boring, Kilian. She's feisty. I wonder what our king will make of her.'

'Shut up, Tank,' the brunette hissed. 'The less she knows the better.' She turned her scowl on me and I scowled back. I could handle this woman—I'd dealt with her kind of nasty before.

Kilian's hand shot out, silencing his companions. 'Relax, guys. She's not the type to risk her friends... or her family. The blonde was her brother.' The slight smirk seemed to be stamped permanently to his face. He turned to the brunette. 'Security has them in sight?'

She nodded. 'I blocked the Telepath from reaching her, so they won't trace us. They've called in back-up but it will take them time to travel from Blackwood. The Wolves from the club have shifted and are being led on a wild goose chase through the city. One of the boys has her scarf, courtesy of the Teleporter.' I clutched at my bare neck.

Kilian leaned back, stretching his arms over the back of the seat. 'We'll be gone by the time the rest of them reach this pitiful town.'

He continued to watch me. If he hoped for a reaction, he'd be disappointed. Every muscle in my body was tense when the car pulled to a stop. These people either wanted me dead, or I'd become a lab rat in their quest for the all-powerful Super. I didn't like either option, but if death was on the cards, I'd rather get it over and done with.

'When you have someone who's a risk and you want them dead, it's better to be quick and efficient. Mind you, this is about revenge—who knows what they want to do with you.'

'Thanks, James. You really have a way with words. I'm surprised someone didn't sink you to the bottom of the ocean with a ball and chain centuries ago.'

'There were many who tried.'

The door on my side of the car swung open, and I

stepped out onto smooth bitumen. Coloured lights flickered around us. I turned at the sound of whirring turbines and saw that we stood on a runway.

Tank prodded me towards the staircase and into the plane. The stewardess was a Mundane. She patted me down, removing from my back pocket the thin wallet containing my bank cards. She handed it to one of Kilian's men and led me to a seat. She offered me a drink which I declined. I doubted they made the effort to kidnap me, just to poison me, but I couldn't be certain.

Kilian spoke to the pilot. The Aegis followed behind him, sticking to him like glue. Her shield of energy surrounded the both of them like a glittering sphere. I probed it a couple of times but there was no sign of a flaw or a way to break through.

My stomach growled as the plane moved forward. I'd spent a lot of energy trying to smash through that shimmering barrier. Kilian and the Aegis sat across from me, speaking in hushed tones as the plane took off. I watched them, confused. Aside from now being ignored, I was being treated like a guest, not a prisoner. It didn't make sense. I was relieved that Kilian's attention had moved on from me. His demeanour changed once the plane was in the air. He seemed to draw into himself, silently staring out the window. The stewardess placed by his seat a glass and a bottle of vodka which he consumed like water. His energy confused me. His gift was cloaked somehow, but I could see tiny threads of energy attached to it. They came from the tattoos that covered his body and anchored to his strange gift—almost like they were holding it in place.

When the plane levelled out food was served and I gave into the urge to eat. The Aegis sneered as I accepted a second plate of food. I grinned, buttering my second roll and bit it in half. Kilian's food remained untouched.

'Wouldn't it have been easier for the Teleporter to teleport us to wherever we're going?' I asked.

Kilian pulled his attention from the window and looked down his nose at me. 'Easier, yes. But risky.' I waited for him to continue and his jaw clenched. 'The Teleporter is slippery.

He can only teleport one person at a time. He'd more than likely disappear with you and auction you off to the highest bidder. I promised your safe delivery, so that's what I'll do.'

'And I'm being delivered to someone you call a king?'

His eyes glittered. 'Enough questions. You'll know everything soon enough.' He left his chair, moving to the front of the plane. He spoke to the hulking mass of muscle, Tank. Tank glanced my way and winked.

I turned back to my food and felt the eyes of the Aegis boring into me. I glanced up. 'What?'

She sniffed. 'You're less than I expected.'

'Remember, Freya, It's all a power play. Think of it as pack hierarchy; she's challenging you. Show her how sharp your fangs are.'

I grinned, leaning forward in my seat. 'Good. Then you'll be surprised when I rip the life from your body. I'll find the chink in your armour, and when I do, it's game over.' Her sneer faltered as I eyed her from head to toe. 'Your gift would be a good one to add to my collection.'

She turned away as Kilian returned to his seat. He stretched out, placing his feet on the seat beside me. His legs brushed mine and I struggled not to pull away. He seemed amused. Another woman approached us as Kilian reclined his seat and closed his eyes. She touched his temples, releasing a cool, pale-yellow energy into his mind and body. When his shoulders dropped and his breathing slowed, she moved back to her own seat at the back of the plane. The Aegis plugged in her earphones and reclined her chair, ignoring my stare.

I faced the small, oval window, watching as the twinkling lights disappeared, replaced by the vast black ocean. A cold, uncomfortable feeling settled inside me as my eyes grew heavy—I was on my own now.

14

I was in the Monroe's house. The smell of Mrs Monroe's cooking filled my nostrils. I was drawn to the backyard by the sound of yelling. Mr Monroe, Dorian and my brother stood on the back lawn facing an enraged Beau. The muscles in his arms and neck were tense and his expression was stone-cold. I'd only seen that expression once; in the video I'd been sent of Beau bargaining with Argyle's people for me. It had been one big set-up and not one of my proudest moments.

'What do you mean they took her? She never should've left Blackwood in the first place.' Beau's voice was strangely calm, but somehow it felt worse than if he'd yelled.

His eyes glowed and the beginning of fangs protruded from his mouth as he stalked back and forth. Levi shifted into wolf-form, leaning back on his hind legs. He growled a warning. Dorian's energy flared and the tension reduced a little. Beau's fangs retracted into his mouth.

'She's not a prisoner here, Beau,' Mr Monroe said. 'We ensured she was well protected, but they had power we've not fought against before. Aegises are rare.'

'I never should've left. I thought she meant more to you. I thought she meant more to her family,' Beau growled at my brother.

Levi moved back into human-form and I got an eyeful of man-butt as he shoved Beau in the chest. They stood nose to nose.

'You're the one who marked her then left. I should kill you for that,' Levi spat.

Beau sneered. 'Please, try. I'd rip you in half, but I don't think Freya would appreciate it.'

'Enough!' Reagan's mum stalked out of the house and walked up to Beau waving a tea towel in his face. 'That is enough from you, Beau Greyson. All this finger pointing doesn't help Freya.'

Mrs Monroe and Dorian's combined empathic power was effective. Beau stepped back, stretching his neck from side to side. The glow in his eyes dimmed. He turned to the driveway and walked away. Dorian grabbed his arm.

'We don't even know where she is, Beau. Wait until we know.'

I stepped towards them, careful to not look at my brother's naked form. Yuck, yuck, yuck. 'Ummm hello,' I said, waving my hands in their faces. 'I'm right here.'

Beau's nostrils flared and he turned, looking straight at me.

***

I blinked awake. The pilot announced over the speaker that the plane was beginning its descent. I rubbed my eyes. It was just a dream. Beau wasn't in Blackwood and I was somewhere far away. The people around me stirred. As the wheels of the plane touched the ground, a sense foreboding settled in my chest. Tank opened the door of the plane and I was hit with a rush of cold air. The stewardess ushered me to the door and I stopped at the top step. Wherever we were, it was late afternoon. The landing strip was small, nestled into the side of a mountaintop. What stopped me was the wall of sand coloured stone. A gate, leading inside the wall revealed a ginormous castle: a real-life fairy-tale castle, complete with turrets, courtyards, and sculpted gardens.

'I have memories of this place.' James seemed confused. *'Seeing it has triggered things I'd forgotten. They have a Telepath like that friend of yours. She must've wiped my memory when I left.'*

A finger prodded me in the back. They were brave enough to touch me with the Aegis keeping them safe. I moved down the stairs towards a line of waiting cars. These guys were rich enough that they didn't have to walk anywhere. The cars drove in a procession up a winding driveway, stopping at the castle entrance. I stepped out of the car and was surrounded by a dozen Supers; all of them powerful. Their energy cores shone like beacons. I was wary of the Water Elemental. Water was the most lethal of all the elements. A lot of things are made up primarily of water—including humans. He caught me staring and grinned.

A woman sauntered down the front steps, her bronze-coloured hair glittering in the sun. It was cut short, framing an angular face. She approached us, eyeing me with a predatory glare. I stepped back. Something about the flow of her energy made me cautious. Kilian moved to my side, placing an arm in front of me.

'She's not here for your entertainment, Tarryn,' he cautioned. The slightest hint of darkness brushed my consciousness. Feet shuffled around me, so I guessed everyone else must've felt it too. Either he couldn't target his power, or he didn't care. My guess was the latter.

The woman stopped in front of me, so that we almost touched noses—well, her nose nearly touched my chin. Her mouth broke into a grin.

'Kilian, you do like to spoil my fun. Fear and pain run deep in her veins. If I coaxed it to the surface, I could live off it for weeks.' She leaned in, inhaling my scent. Her eyes looked like they were about to roll back in her head. 'I won't kill her, I promise. Just a couple of broken bones, maybe. A few minor abrasions.'

'She belongs to the king,' Kilian said.

She leaned towards him, running a sharp pointed fingernail across his jaw. 'What Lucien doesn't know. . .'

'Top of the food chain, Freya,' James reminded me.

I was in a gothic castle on top of a mountain, surrounded by powerful – and some seriously disturbed – Supers. I might not have had a choice in coming here, but I wasn't about to become someone's plaything. I lifted a hand, and the people around me shifted into alert mode.

'Hey, first of all, I don't belong to anyone. Second of all, touch me and I'll. . . I'll break your face.'

'Nice.'

Before I could flinch, a clawed hand grabbed at my throat. Kilian gripped her wrist and twisted it behind her back, wrenching it until she hissed. She didn't seem to be in pain, just irritated that she couldn't tear my face to shreds. He rolled his eyes and bent towards her ear.

'Don't. . . touch her.'

She stumbled as he pushed her away. She sneered at me and stalked back up the stairs, disappearing through a set of doors.

Tank moved beside me, whispering, 'She's one of the king's guardians and she's Pain Empowered. She gets a kick out of other people's pain—thrives off it, actually. She'd kill you without a second thought.'

'I wouldn't die, I—'

Kilian's irritated glare turned to me. 'Some advice – don't piss off people you can't handle.'

With that piece of wisdom, he stormed up the stairs, and we followed. I gaped as we entered a large reception area. Painted ceilings with chandeliers towered above us. Tank prodded me in the shoulder and I moved down a hall on our left. By the time we stood in front of a set of carved wooden doors, there was only the original four of us left. Kilian, Tank, the Aegis, and me.

Kilian didn't bother to turn to me as he spoke. 'You're about to meet Lucien Clemonte, our master and king. I suggest you leave the attitude behind. If you can't be civil, then shut up.'

He pushed through the doors, revealing a large ballroom. Elegantly dressed people milled around the room, the buzz of their voices filling the air. Everyone stopped as we entered.

'Hold your head up, kid. They'll be watching your every move.'

I ignored my growing nerves, lifted my chin and followed Kilian. The crowd parted for us, people whispering amongst themselves as I passed. I glanced up at the ceiling. Glass panels lined the roof, providing a view of the sky above. Grey clouds tinged with green blanketed the sky. I lowered my gaze. At the far end of the room was an actual throne. A line of people stood to the back of the throne and all of them wielded potent gifts. The Pain Empowered woman stood with them, smirking at me. The Aegis moved to the side of the throne and her shield engulfed everyone in the throne's inner circle.

I observed the man sitting in the middle of it all. He leaned back in the throne, his hands clasped over the ends of the ornate arms. His hair was dark with streaks of grey and his black eyes were impassive. This was the guy who decided whether I lived or died.

I studied his abilities thread which was a dark brownish-black. It's texture and the way it swirled through his body was like thick, dark oil. Kilian approached him and bowed.

Without a word he nodded and Kilian moved to his side. Tension filled the silent room.

'So… you're the child who killed Argyle.' His glittering eyes bore into mine.

'No fear, Freya.'

I swallowed the lump in my throat. 'Um… to be fair, he kidnapped me first.'

His face could've been carved from stone. Not a single muscle in it twitched. 'Do you think I care *why* you killed him?'

'Well, technically I didn't kill—'

He was fast. He appeared in front of me, his cold, black eyes making my heart thump. 'What matters, is that he's dead and *you* are responsible. I will know the truth.'

He nodded to a woman and she approached me. She held her nose in the air, her sharp features giving her the appearance of a witch—the kind that ate children. She was the Telepath who'd wiped James's memories. In his memories she was younger; younger than me. She stopped in front of me and tipped my chin with a pointed fingernail. I met her eyes and felt her consciousness like talons brushing against my mind.

Her voice echoed in my head. *'Let me in, child. Or it will only hurt you more.'*

I had no idea what she meant. The prodding became more forceful and she frowned.

'There is something preventing me from entering her thoughts,' she said.

'You're meant to be the best. Try harder,' Lucien commanded.

Her brows furrowed in concentration. She placed her hands on my temples and closed her eyes. There was a forceful shove against my consciousness and then nothing. The woman pulled back, clutching her head with her hands. She stumbled and people rushed to steady her. When she opened her eyes, she glared at me.

'There's a lock on her mind. It's sophisticated. I can't get in.'

Lucien narrowed his eyes. 'Then I have no use for you,

do I?' He gestured to the door.

Her mouth dropped open. 'Lucien?'

His face showed nothing. 'Go.'

Her lips thinned and she turned away. The doors banged behind her as she stormed out of the room.

Lucien turned to me. 'I'm tempted to kill you and be done with it.'

I clenched my shaking hands into fists at my side. James triggered some of his darker memories so they flashed across my consciousness. They made this situation feel like a regular Tuesday.

'We can do this. Don't show weakness.'

He was right. I could handle this. As long as my family and friends stayed safe it didn't matter.

I held Lucien's gaze. 'If you're hoping I'll beg for my life, it's not gonna happen.'

The crowd around me stirred.

Lucien's mouth curved. 'Do you think it would be that easy?' He walked in a slow circle around me. 'The Teleporter tells us you can self-heal. Do you know what we do to Self-Healers?' A shiver ran through my body as he stopped in front of me. 'We place them in a tank of water. They drown—over and over again. We left one traitor in the tank for three months.'

I had flashes of memories. Lungs burning as they choked on water, over and over again. James had been the one they tortured. *No wonder he chose to leave with Argyle over staying here.* The associated fear and anger ran through my body. I felt his rage and it became my own.

Lucien leaned in and whispered, 'Can you imagine what that would feel like?'

He had no idea.

He grabbed my forearm and his energy flared. 'I do have other methods, like my personal favourite.'

His power wrapped around my arm like tentacles. I stifled a scream. My skin aged before my eyes. It turned to the colour of ash as it dissolved, revealing the pink flesh beneath. I couldn't stop the groan that escaped my lips. The flesh rotted away until ligaments and bone showed through. I resisted the urge to vomit, forcing my gaze back to Lucien. His eyes narrowed, ever-so-slightly. He released me and I hissed out a breath as coolness swept through my arm. His cold eyes scrutinised me. My hands shook and my stomach still clenched with the need to puke. He held my gaze for a moment longer, then his lips curled and he laughed. It was the first emotion I'd seen on his face: amusement. The crowd of people joined in. The only people not laughing were the Aegis and Kilian. Kilian's expression was blank.

The rage inside me exploded.

I threw my energy towards Lucien with all the power I had, slamming into the shield with force. The Aegis fell backwards. I slammed into the barrier again and again, determined to kill him. It would be the last thing I did, considering the power contained in the room. Even a Self-Healer couldn't outlast these guys. There was a sharp sting against my throat. I ignored it and continued slamming into the shield. My energy burned fast, but the wall between me and Lucien's lifeline was weakening.

'*STOP!*' James's shout echoed in my head.

I hesitated and my knees slammed into the stone floor. I blinked once, then twice. I looked up and the room stood still. The people around me were deathly silent. The Aegis sat crumpled on the floor; a palm pressed against her head.

'How is that possible?' she hissed, her eyes following Lucien as he crouched in front of me.

It was then I felt the razor-sharp blade pressed against my throat.

'Well, well, what a curious creature,' Lucien said. He tilted his head to the side. 'You might yet prove to be valuable. We'll keep you for now.'

The Aegis whipped her head towards me, her mouth hanging open. Lucien returned to his throne and a man with a briefcase moved to his side.

'But you said an eye for an eye,' I argued, struggling against the arm looped around my neck.

Tank held me in a stranglehold. I recognised the meaty arms. He lifted me to my feet but his arm remained tight around my neck.

'Stay still and you might live through today,' he hissed in my ear.

Lucien opened the briefcase, revealing a large syringe filled with silver liquid. I tensed and considered the people around me. If I could take out Lucien, I might have a chance of escape.

Lucien faced me. 'You will take Argyle's place.'

I stopped my struggle against the steel forearm holding me in place. 'What?'

'An eye for an eye. Argyle was a contributing member of our community, so you will take his place.'

'I think I'll take option two.' *Was that an eye twitch?*

'Either you stay and pay your debt, or I kill you and seek retribution from another source. That little town of yours seems a good place to start. Perhaps your mother's body will decay from the inside out. I'll leave her heart and mind until last so that she feels everything. Or do I save that treatment for your new friends?'

I loathed this guy. 'What's the catch if I stay?' I asked. He grabbed the syringe and I stepped back, slamming into the human wall behind me.

'You will do what I ask, when I ask. You will be a cog in the machine that is my city. Step out of line and I erase Blackwood from its pathetic existence. Understood?'

I clenched my jaw and gave a tight nod. As far as blackmail went, one person's service to save a whole town was a pretty good deal.

He shoved the needle into his arm. His body turned rigid as the silver liquid poured into his veins. His body began to change. First the grey in his hair turned black. The age lines in his face smoothed, and his skin firmed. Within seconds he'd turned from a middle-aged man to a guy in his early thirties.

'There are benefits to joining us, Miss Armitage. Or is it Miss Holmes?'

How could he possibly know that name? Holmes was my dad's original surname, before he'd changed it multiple times. Lucien stood, adjusting his suit jacket and tie. He nodded behind me then turned and left the room followed by his guardians, the Aegis and Kilian.

The arm around my neck loosened. A Mundane woman approached me with a stapler-like object. I yelped as it was pressed into my forearm.

'This is the only form of identity you require here,' she advised, as I rubbed the small bump. She handed me a warm cloth and gestured to my neck. I wiped away the blood that had started to dry against my skin. Tank led me away from the ballroom and I breathed a sigh of relief as the doors closed behind us.

'What is this place?' I asked, staring at the towering stone ceilings.

'We call this the citadel.'

'Does the citadel have a name?'

He raised a brow. 'Clemonte Citadel.'

'Right...'

He smirked. 'The Clemonte family claimed the citadel and the city surrounding it over two hundred years ago. The city's original name and the name of this castle was struck from the record and replaced.' He gestured to a window and the city visible below. 'Welcome to Aurore.'

'Aurore?'

'Aurore is the French word for dawn. This city was a new start for the Clemonte family empire.'

'I'll bet the people who used to live here weren't happy about it.'

'They conformed or died.'

He glanced at me and I looked away. *Yeah... I got the hint.* We climbed two flights of stairs to the third floor. The passing windows revealed snow covered trees and more stone walls.

'There are three things you need to know,' he said. He began counting off fingers. 'First, you can go anywhere you want within Aurore, but you are not to leave the city without permission. That won't happen until Lucien believes he has your loyalty. Second, as a guest you can access any amenities you need, just ask the staff. And third, outside the usual courteous behaviour, everyone is for themselves here. Aurore functions under a classist system. You are either born at the top, or you are powerful enough to work your way to the top.'

He stopped at the end of the hall and opened a door. My jaw dropped. It opened up into a suite of rooms fit for a queen. He stopped me as I walked past. 'You're considered one of the Favoured. Someone like you could do well here.'

'The Favoured?'

'Those favoured by King Lucien. They make up the top classes of society. People considered 'favoured' can access anything and everything in the city. They receive the star treatment. You could say they are considered Supernatural royalty. Don't waste it.'

He closed the door, leaving me alone in the small palace. I explored each of the rooms. There was a lounge and dining area, a bathroom and a bedroom. The bed was the biggest I'd ever seen. I pushed through a set of French doors at the far end of the bedroom. They led onto a balcony overlooking the city below. The air was icy and the balcony railing cold beneath my hands.

The citadel sat on the top of a mountain. I had prime views of the city. Ancient buildings were mixed with newer architecture, designed to merge with the old. One building stood higher than the rest, and as night fell, lights flashed in vibrant colours from the windows and balconies. A club—Aurore had a club. As the last rays of sunlight peaked through the thick cloud cover, I caught a glimpse of a shimmering light in the distance. My eyes narrowed, attempting to focus on it, but it disappeared with the sunlight.

I felt the sting of cold against my skin. White fluff covered my clothes. I gazed up at the sky and watched the snowflakes fall. It was the first time I'd seen snow. Tears burned at the back of my eyes as I thought of my family and friends back home. They were safe. Beau was safe wherever he was. I clasped my hands together to stop them from shaking.

'It's better this way, kid. No ties mean no vulnerabilities.'

I was better off alone here. 'You shouldn't have stopped me earlier. I would've broken through that shield.' I spoke aloud. Even if someone heard, I didn't care. They could think

I was crazy here, what did it matter?

'Think, Freya. You would've had your head severed the second that barrier dropped—if it dropped. This isn't the time for rash decisions. Think of it as a game of chess. Every action has a consequence, every move needs to be planned. Play the right moves and you can win.'

'Chess… really?'

'I know these people. You'd have a place in Lucien's inner circle if you wanted it. You're already Favoured. You put aside your fear today and it impressed him.'

'That was you, not me. Your rage rubbed off on me.'

'I gave you a push, but that was all you, Freya.'

I tightened my grip on the railing. 'It didn't feel like me.'

He clicked his non-existent tongue. *'It's the part of you that you keep chained with me in the back of your mind. The part of you that's blood-thirsty. You set it free today and it was glorious.'*

I showered, trying to scrub away James's words. The soft mattress of the colossal bed engulfed me and I stared up at the painted ceiling. It depicted a battle scene: white-clad angels fighting shadowy demons. It was like a reflection of what was going on inside my head.

I couldn't tell who was winning.

15

I stood in Beau's loungeroom, light streaming through the windows. I'd never been here during the day.

Glass crunched beneath my feet and I stood still, surveying my surroundings – splintered furniture and torn books were scattered across the floor. Windows were broken and even the door to Beau's room had been torn off its hinges. My eyes caught on the figure by the fireplace. Beau sat on the floor, his back against an armchair with his eyes closed. I moved to his side, clasping my hands together to stop myself from reaching out.

'Why is it that the one person I'm trying to forget, is the one I dream about?' I whispered.

Wide, golden eyes pinned me where I stood. He shot to his feet, towering above me. 'Freya?'

I smelled his signature scent and shook my head. 'I'm even dreaming about how good you smell.' I stepped back as his eyes drilled into mine. 'You can actually see me in this dream?'

He grabbed my shoulders, eyeing me from head to toe. 'You've seen me in your dreams before?'

I nodded. It felt real. It shouldn't have felt this real. He pulled me into his arms.

'I thought I was seeing things yesterday at the Monroe's. I kept thinking you were dead. But I'd feel it if you were gone.' He ran a hand through my hair. 'You chose to come here, to my home, in your dreams. I'm glad that you feel safe here.'

I pushed away. 'Alright this is enough. I'd like to wake up now.'

Emotions I'd pushed far, far away were crowding back in. I didn't want them. He grabbed my face, turning it so I'd meet his eyes. They glowed and I was hit with the force of his persuasion.

'Tell me where you are, Freya.'

It didn't work on me. 'Wow, you're just as demanding in dream form.'

'Where are you? Have they hurt you?'

I pushed away, wrapping my arms around my middle. 'You're such a jerk.' I turned to the window and took a deep breath. 'You ran off like a coward. You didn't even call on my birthday. Worst of all, you lied to me!' I turned to the fireplace. 'This isn't even real. The real Beau will find himself some beautiful pureblood Dire She-Wolf and breed dozens of kids in an effort to re-populate the planet. He won't even remember me in a few years.' I faced him. 'And you know what, dream-Beau? It's better that way. I'm never getting out of this nest of vipers anyway.'

His grip was firm as he grabbed my shoulders. The muscles in his jaw tensed as he said through clenched teeth, 'Freya, this is real. I don't want anyone else—I want you. I'll explain it all when I come for you. Tell me where you are.'

I shrugged out of his grip. 'It's time for me to wake up.'

His wolf was close to the surface. I could see it in the erratic pulse of energy. 'Not yet. Tell me where you are.'

Pain could pull me out of a dream, right? I ignored dream-Beau's pleas and reached out to the fire. Pain shot up my arm as flames engulfed my hand…

***

I sat up in bed, cradling my hand. The burning felt so real. I lifted my arm, turning it back and forth. The burning sensation had tapered down to a light tingle across my skin, but it was still there. *How was that even possible? It was a dream.*

A knock on the door made me scramble to my feet. A woman came into the room, advising me that Tank had sent food. She pointed out a bar fridge in the loungeroom filled with drinks and snacks and told me to call if there was anything specific I wanted. She entered the bedroom and showed me a chest of drawers and walk-in robe filled with clothes in my exact size.

Why was I being treated so well? It wasn't like I was about to leave and put my family and friends in danger. Lucien knew that. Everyone else earned their way to the top, but I was already considered one of the Favoured. What would it cost me?

The woman told me that I'd be summoned when King Lucien required my presence. It could be days, or even months. She left and I glanced at the clock. I'd only slept for fifteen minutes. I ate the food that was left for me and went back out to the balcony. It was dark and the lights of the city twinkled. I sat on the cold stone surface and closed my eyes, fumbling with the pendant hanging from my neck. When I'd cleared my mind and my emotions were sufficiently numbed, I focused on the energy running through my body. I needed to be stronger and smarter if I was going to survive here.

I'd worked up a sweat and consumed all the snacks in the fridge by dawn. I was beginning to see something new in the energy threads. It was like my eyes could focus where they hadn't before. Not only could I see the texture and flow of each thread, I was beginning to notice patterns. Like the time that Grandma had tried to teach me to knit; there were different weaves. *Maybe this was part of the growth spurt?* James's spirit thread was intertwined with mine, but it was a loose weave. If I could find some way to unravel it, I'd be free of him.

But, James had been useful since arriving in Aurore. He understood the place and kept me focused. I didn't need to be free of him just yet.

I opened the door to my rooms and peeked into the hall. People passed me; serving staff and other residents of the castle. There were no guards waiting to jump me. The few guards I passed gave me a curt nod. I stopped one and asked her where I could find Tank. I was surprised when she told me that Tank wasn't a guardian or part of the security team, so she wasn't sure where he was.

I had better luck with one of the serving staff; he told me I'd find Tank in the gymnasium. After a few dead ends I found the place. It wasn't your average gym; it had everything. There was the usual weights section, exercise equipment and a pool. Then there was a basketball court, a tennis court, a fencing court, a shooting range, and what looked a series of gift-proof rooms for Supernaturals. A Fire Elemental was making fire tornadoes and scorching one of the rooms.

It must've been the jacked-up-muscle-head hour. I walked through the mirrored weights section, ignoring the stares. Tank sat on a weights bench doing presses. I stood over him and waited for him to acknowledge me.

'What do you want?' he asked between grunts.

'I don't know what I'm meant to do.'

'Whatever you want. Lucien will summon you when he needs you. It won't be often.'

'Whatever I want?'

The weight bar slammed into its holder. He sat up and ran a hand over his sweaty brow. 'Look, I'm not your babysitter. Go sightseeing or something. Don't girls like shopping?'

I scowled. 'Shopping… That's the best you could think of?'

I ignored his grumbling and followed him to an area where the floor was covered in blue mats. People were sparring or wrestling.

'I guess I could go for a run or something. I could jog into town.'

He gave an exaggerated grunt. 'You want people to think you're gutter-class? Take a car.'

'A car. And where do I get one of those?'

He glanced at the ceiling and sighed. 'Look, I can give you all the time you want once I've finished here. Otherwise find someone else to bother.'

'You're just standing here.'

'I'm waiting for a boxing partner.'

I eyed the other people on the mats. 'I could be your partner.'

He raised his brows. 'You sure you want to do that?'

One of Tank's biceps was the size of my thigh. 'Nope, not really.'

He laughed, the loud rumble catching the attention of the other meat-heads. He threw me a pair of boxing pads. 'At least you're honest.'

He moved onto the mat, thumping his gloves together and dancing back and forth on the balls of his feet. He was nimble for a big guy. I stood in the defensive stance Bishop had taught me. He did a few small practise jabs then hit the right pad with force. The strength of his punch made me stumble. I moved the pads close to my chest and braced myself for the next move. He jabbed the right pad again and followed up with a left hook.

'So, you're not one of Lucien's guardians?' I asked between punches. I'd figured out that his gift had something to do with strength, but it was more than that.

'No.'

'Why not? It seems like the perfect job for someone like you.'

He gestured to himself. 'You think this is all I have to offer?'

I coloured and he chuckled. He did a series of uppercuts and I struggled to hold the pads still, yet I could tell he was going easy on me.

'Your gift is something like super-human strength, right?'

He met my eyes. I relaxed my guard and he took advantage, throwing a punch and slamming my right hand and the boxing pad into my chest. It winded me and I stumbled backwards gasping for air. He peeled off the gloves, indicating that we were finished and I dropped the pads, bending over to catch my breath.

'I'm called Tank, not just because of my size. I'm invincible.'

I raised a doubtful brow. 'Invincible?'

'Yeah.' He stretched his arms and continued, 'My gift gives me an unbreakable body. You could nuke me and I'd come out unscathed.'

'So, you can self-heal?'

'No, if I get sick, I suffer like everyone else. I guess I'm semi-invincible.' He held out the boxing gloves and I just stared at them.

'Me?'

'That's how this works, *partner*. It's your turn.'

I slipped on the gloves, scrunching my nose as my hands met with sweaty leather. *Ewww*. I'd done a few boxing sessions with Bishop and her crew. I moved into the basic boxing stance and began with a jab and cross combo. Tank rolled his eyes.

'Make this worth my time, kid.'

I bristled. *Kid?* James called me kid and I hated it. I threw quicker and harder punches and still he seemed underwhelmed.

'Let me in and I'll help you,' James said.

'Let you in? You're already in.'

'No, you keep me in a box in the back of your mind. You pick and choose the advice I give you, then shut the rest out. Accept me into your mind fully instead of fighting against me and I can help.'

I punched the pads hard, jolting my arms. *'How do I let you in?'*

'Visualise it.'

In his video diaries, Dad had said that visualising energy as a common object such as a rope, lasso, or net, would help to control it. I pictured my mind as a house. James was confined to a small room and all the doors and windows were closed. I unlocked the door to the small room.

'That's it, let me help you.'

I gave a mental shrug and wrenched open the door.

'That's better…'

Memories flashed through my mind like a movie reel, but it was more than just visual. James was an expert in hand-to-hand combat. Living for centuries gave him the time to be an expert at many things.

'Hey, you alright?' Tank asked. I opened my eyes and saw him staring at me through furrowed brows. 'You looked like you were having a seizure or something.'

I blinked and rubbed my forehead. 'Just a headache. I'm fine.'

He grunted and lifted the pads again. The whole scene in front of me looked different somehow. The moves came to me without thought. It was as though my muscles remembered the movements. I did a variety of different combos and saw the surprise on Tank's face. I pushed myself harder, until my clothes were drenched with sweat. It dripped from my hair into my eyes. I pictured the pads as Lucien's face and hit them with all my strength. Tank called a time-out and I laid on the mat, exhausted.

He stood over me, his frown so intense it gave him a mono-brow. 'You train?'

'Yeah.'

He reached out a hand and pulled me to my feet. 'What else can you do?'

I shrugged. 'Why do you want to know?'

'These people respect anything that makes you a threat.'

'These people? Aren't you one of them?'

He ignored my question, moving away from the mats. We walked past the shooting range and he picked up a gun, shooting the cardboard target between the eyes three times in succession. He handed me the gun and I re-loaded, hitting the target twice in the heart and once in the head. As usual my shots weren't quite perfect. I looked down at my shaking hands. Even with James taking a new and improved front-row seat in my mind, it didn't get rid of the shakes.

'Who taught you?' Tank asked, studying me with renewed curiosity.

'That's none of your business.'

He grabbed a couple of towels on our way out and handed me one. 'You should shower; you stink. I'll be out the front of your room in ten minutes. I'll show you where to get a car but you can work out the rest yourself. Some of us have to work.'

Tank knocked on my door exactly ten minutes later. I'd picked an outfit from the range of clothes left for me, and I was thankful they'd included jeans. The tops were all too flashy. It felt like I was going out to a party, not driving into town. Tank led me to an elevator. It blended with the wall panelling. I would've missed it if he'd not been there. He pressed the button for the basement floor and the doors opened up to an underground garage. There were at least a hundred different cars.

'You can pick any car that has a fob key in it,' he said.

'Any car?'

'Yeah. That's what I said.'

I rolled my eyes. Levi would like Tank. They'd swap sarcastic comments and grunt at each other all day long.

'How do the Clemontes make their money?'

His expression turned serious. 'Chems development is a part of it.'

'Did Argyle's death cause a dip in profits?'

'Not as much as you'd think. His obsession with Syphons made him unproductive. His focus on achieving the impossible was a drain on the family's resources.'

I rubbed my sternum. 'Will Lucien want to continue Argyle's research?'

'No. The family understand that with current technology, manipulating DNA to wield more abilities is unachievable. Argyle wasn't practising under Lucien's direction when it came to you. At this stage Lucien considers himself *influential* enough without added abilities.'

'So, Lucien doesn't want to harness Syphon abilities?' I asked, just to be sure.

'Technology like that would be hard to control. If someone else got hold of it, it would create more competition for the Clemontes. Together, they are powerful enough—for now.' He stepped back into the elevator and the doors began to close. He propped it open with a hand. 'Oh, and there are no speed limits here. Just try not to kill anyone.' The doors closed on his amused face, leaving me in the garage alone.

I walked down the aisles, finally stopping at a bright yellow sports car. The key was in the centre console. With the push of a button the engine roared to life. Reagan would've been so jealous. Even Beau would've been jealous. My chest tightened. I ignored the sensation and pulled out of the garage, following a tunnel that opened up to a road outside of the castle walls. Guards stood on top of the walls, but no one paid attention to me. The road was steep and winding, surrounded by snow covered trees. I planted my foot on the accelerator and adrenalin coursed through my body. It was fast. The car hugged the road as it curved in and out of the mountainside. I reached the residential part of town and skirted around the city centre. The houses thinned out into small farms and forest and I floored it, exhilarated by the speed and power of the car. Up ahead I saw the shimmering light I'd noticed the night before. Curiosity had me driving towards it. As I neared it, I saw that a large arched gate framed the road. Guard towers with gun turrets sat on either side. A figure stood in front of the gate, forcing me to stop. The guard approached my open window.

'You've reached the outer boundary, Ma'am. Unless you have a permit, I'll need to ask you to turn around.

'Sorry, my mistake.'

I did a u-turn, glancing at the shimmering wall before closing the driver's window. It curved into the sky, creating a dome—It was a forcefield. The arched gateway was the only place free of the shimmer, the only way in or out. I frowned. The shimmer was made of human energy. That amount of energy was impossible for a human to control on their own. Multiple people would have to control and contain it, but I couldn't pinpoint a source. It was as though it was powered by the earth.

I drove back to the city, and found my way to its centre, parking on one of the main streets. I could feel the eyes of people assessing me as I got out of the car. Or maybe it was the bright yellow car that caught their attention. Aurore was more like a large town than a city. I located a clothing store that seemed more to my taste than the clothes I'd been given. The assistant smiled when I admitted that I had no idea how to pay for clothing and told me that the Favoured paid for nothing. By the end of the day, I'd wandered through countless shops and cafes.

Even though every fibre of my body was telling me to drive in the opposite direction, I drove back to the citadel. I parked the car and got lost in the maze of vehicles before finding the elevator. The doors opened just as I reached for the button and I locked eyes with Kilian. He stepped out of the elevator and walked straight past me, not even saying hello. The elevator doors closed, blocking his back from my view and I sniffed.

Jackass.

16

A whole week passed and still I hadn't been summoned. The gymnasium was empty at midnight so I used the space to train. Accepting James into my mind instead of fighting his presence helped me improve. His memories didn't just flash across my mind, I absorbed them and they translated into new skills and instincts.

My time was spent exploring the city during the day, then I'd train and meditate at night. I became irritated with waiting—it put me on edge. A fresh cover of snow fell over the citadel. We were in the opposite hemisphere to Blackwood, so this was summer snow; one of the *benefits* of being close to a glacier. Aurore was located somewhere in Europe, that much I knew. No one would tell me more than that.

The colourful lights of the club flashed in the distance. There was no reason I had to stay in at night; I was eighteen, not eighty. I dressed for a night out, complete with ripped jeans and boots. I hopped into the yellow sports car, following the road in the general direction of the towering building and pulled up in front of it. The line to get into the place went all the way down the street.

The door of my car opened. A guy in a dark green uniform welcomed me to The Tower and offered to park the car. I was hesitant to give him the key but handed it over. Up close, I saw that the line to get into the place not only stretched all the way down the street but around the corner. The girls all wore sparkly sequin dresses that barely covered their butts and the guys were in tailored suits. I glanced down at my jeans, shirt and leather jacket and gave a mental shrug. *Oh well*… The line was barely moving but it wasn't like I had anything better to do. I moved towards the end of the street and was stopped by one of the security guards. He held a scanner to the chip in my arm then gestured to the doors.

'You've got priority access. You can access anything up to level twelve.'

I stared at him, confused, and he gave me a light push towards the doors. I followed a couple to the elevators and watched as they held their arms to the scanner on the control panel. The buttons for the first four floors lit up. I copied their action and another eight buttons lit up, all the way to level twelve. Their eyes grew wide as they eyed me from head to toe. Twelve floors must've been a good thing.

James graced me with his presence. *'This place is new. The levels must represent your rank. The people on the twelfth floor will be considered in your class.'*

I snorted. 'That's insane.'

The couple in the elevator backed away from me and I realised I'd spoken out loud. I waved them goodbye as they got off at the fourth floor and continued all the way to level twelve. The doors opened and I halted. It was like I'd stepped into Hollywood. I stepped back into the elevator and tried the floor below. It must have been the pool party floor; I didn't like that one either. I continued back down floor by floor. They all had a different theme, becoming less glamourous as the elevator descended. The doors opened to the third floor and I exhaled. There was a stage and a dance floor, a normal bar and pool tables. It reminded of the Steelworks—it reminded me of home.

'The whole point of this place is to build your level of influence with people in your class. That's how you move up the food chain.' James didn't keep the disdain from his voice.

'You're the one who told me not to rely on anyone. Well, this is me relying on myself and not some toxic classist bull-crap. I like this floor.'

He sniffed. *'You could catch hepatitis from those carpet stains.'*

'I like them. They add to the atmosphere.' I chuckled at James's disgust.

The bartender appeared in front of me as I reached the corner of the bar. She was taller than me by at least a full head, with a short bleached-blonde pixie cut, and a sleeve tattoo. She caught my chuckle and raised a pierced brow. When I didn't explain myself, she moved down the bar to someone else. I sat back on the stool, watching the crowd around me.

'You could at least move out of your dark corner and be seen. People need to know you exist.'

'Hey, I can pick up a lot by sitting and watching,' I said.

'While you sit and watch, how about I make you something?' The bartender had reappeared. Her brows were raised as she waited for my answer.

I cringed; I'd spoken out loud again. 'Lime and soda?'

She shook her head and mixed a pink concoction. 'So, you're the new Favoured everyone's talking about.'

'I guess.'

'I heard you messed up Lucien's Aegis pretty good. It's about time someone put her in her place.'

'I didn't mess her up.'

'From what I've heard, she got knocked on her backside. They say you were savage—that you were out for blood.'

I flinched at her choice of words. 'Why do you care?'

She held my stare without wavering. 'I don't.'

'It sure sounds like you care.'

She placed the drink in front of me and leaned across the bar. 'All I see is a reckless girl with no sense of self-preservation. But others will care… not everyone appreciates change in the order of things.'

The cocktail tasted like fairy floss and strawberries. It was liquid happiness.

'I've heard of the exploits of one of your kind, you're dangerous,' she said.

Aside from my dad, I'd not heard of other Syphons. I watched her energy flare golden brown, its texture like steel. She was a Dire Wolf. 'Funny… I would've said the same about your kind. Except I'd have to add cowardly liar and bad boyfriend material into that description as well.'

She sniffed. 'Who's claimed you?'

'Excuse me?'

'A Dire Wolf has marked you. Who are you dating?'

I waved her off. 'We never dated. It was over before it began. And as if I'd tell one of Lucien's minions.'

Her expression turned to stone. 'I would never betray one of my own.'

'But you'd betray me, right?'

She turned away, moving down the counter. I didn't even get the chance to ask for a second drink.

By two in the morning the crowd had thinned. I'd found a different bartender who made me more pink cocktails and brought me food. I thought about making my exit when the elevator doors opened. A rowdy group entered from the upper floors. I watched the reflection in the splashback of the bar as two guys approached me. I took a deep breath; all I wanted to do was wallow alone in self-pity.

'*Do you think they're carrying?*' James said.

'I'm pretty sure everyone here carries some kind of weapon.'

'The pretty one is the leader. It looks like he spends more time in the bathroom than you. I say he carries on his left. Let's make a deal, if I'm right, you head back up to the twelfth floor and follow my lead, alright?'

'Fine. But If I'm right, you shut-up for a whole twenty-four hours.' I studied the reflection of the leader. *'The guy's a peacock. I say he's carrying two guns.'*

The guys approached my side and ordered drinks from the bar. The pretty one's arm brushed against mine. The Dire Wolf looked between them and me and I sensed her heckles rise. Either these guys were bad news or she thought I was bad news.

I refused to look at them. I could feel them staring, trying to get my attention. From the reflection in the splashback, I had to admit that the one James called pretty was good-looking. He smelled amazing. So amazing, that I was tempted to lean in and take a deep sniff.

'So… you're the new girl everyone's talking about.'

I sculled the rest of my drink. 'Yep.'

'You don't look that crazy.'

I turned to him and arched a brow. 'What does crazy look like? Did you expect a tin foil hat?'

He grinned, showing his pearly teeth. It was stunning. 'You're a funny one. My friend and I were just thinking that maybe you'd like to join us on level ten.'

I studied his purple energy. It wafted towards me like perfume. The desire to go with him hit me like a wrecking ball.

He was a Siren.

My fingers clenched around the pretty cocktail glass. I reached out with small threads of energy, weaving a lasso around his energy line and gave it a tug, just enough that his dazzling voice and scent didn't affect me so much anymore.

'No thanks, I'm happy right here.'

I waved my empty glass at the bartender. The Siren and his friend looked between each other. The purple haze wafted closer as he leaned in front of me. '*No?* No one says no to us.'

'I just did. Go find someone else to dazzle.'

He grabbed my wrist, his energy flaring around me like a suffocating cloud. 'But we want *your* company.'

Anyone else would've followed him like a love-sick idiot. How many people had he Siren-called? How many people had he left when he became bored, their hearts torn to shreds? How many of them had walked off the nearest cliff, heart-broken?

'*Now would be an appropriate time to release all that pent-up anger,*' James suggested.

I yanked my wrist from his grip and grabbed the back of his head, slamming it into the bar. There was a satisfying crunch. I booted him in the knees and he fell to the floor like a sack of potatoes. Straddling his body, I pulled both guns from his jacket, aiming one at his chest and the other at his friend. Pretty-boy reached for his broken nose and I pressed the gun into his chest. Adrenalin thrummed through my body along with the satisfaction that Bishop's training was paying off.

'Uh-uh, don't move. My finger might just slip on the trigger.' His friend moved in my peripheral and I flicked off the safety of the gun in my right hand. 'Stay where you are.'

The room was silent except for pretty-boy's whining.

'You crazy bi—'

'Finish that sentence and I will shoot you. When a girl says no, she means no, Moron.' I looked at the guns in my hands. 'I'll accept these lovely pieces as a gift of apology, what do you say? They're too pretty for you anyway.' He nodded, wincing with the movement. 'You really need to be careful around hard surfaces. You might slip and break that pretty face.' He nodded again, his eyes wide and full of loathing. 'Try to use that Siren voice on me, or any other person here again, and I will finish you.'

Standing over him, I shoved the guns in the back of my jeans. I stepped over him, shot his friend a warning glare and sat back at the bar. His friend helped him to his feet, followed by one of the security guards who gave him a less than friendly shove into the elevator. I watched the reflection in the bar's splashback as the doors closed on his bloodied face. My body twitched as the adrenalin wore off and my hands shook.

'Nice job, kid. Your taste for the dramatics worked a charm.'

I managed a wobbly grin. 'Yeah, I thought so too. Now, I won the bet, so zip it.' I sat back with my eyes closed and enjoyed the silence.

17

'YOU do know you can't keep those, right?'

I didn't bother to open my eyes. 'Someone should put a bell on you. I can't sense that dark energy of yours.'

'You wouldn't want to.'

I turned sideways. Kilian sat on the stool next to me, dressed completely in black. Diamonds glittered from the cuffs of his jacket. He lifted two fingers, nodding to one of the bartenders. He returned with a whiskey and another of those delightful pink cocktails. The blonde Dire Wolf was gone.

Kilian scrunched his nose at the sight of my drink. 'What is that?'

'I don't know, but it tastes like fairy floss.'

'You do realise it's just sugar and food dye?'

I shrugged. 'Shouldn't you be on one of the top floors?'

'I can be on any floor I want.'

I snorted and sipped the cocktail, exhaling a happy sigh. 'What do you want?'

'Very little. Anything I want, I take.'

I took another sip, tapping a finger against the glass, watching him in my peripheral. 'What are you, exactly?' I asked. His lips curved and I realised that I'd just asked a socially inappropriate question. I didn't care.

'My *gift* doesn't have a name.'

'Okay then, what does your gift do?'

He drank his whiskey in one gulp, placing the glass on the counter. 'It's emptiness. It can rip everything away from a person. Sight, sound, taste… feeling. I can destroy a person's life without lifting a finger.'

'Mmm, very useful. Your mother must be so proud.'

His mouth hinted at a smile. 'About as proud as yours?'

'Yeah, probably.' My body tensed as I thought of Mum.

'What did you do to disappoint Mummy dearest?' he asked.

'I didn't tell her about the guy living in my head.' He stared at me. 'That expression is the exact reason I never told her. People think I'm enough of a freak as it is.'

He studied me. His icy blue stare made me twitch. 'I get it.'

I raised a brow. 'Get what?'

'Dealing with the voice in your head.'

'Hey, I have a legitimate reason, okay? It's a side effect of syphoning someone's life force. If you're hearing voices, you need help.'

His lips curved. It wasn't a lazy smile like Beau's—it was something controlled. The expression didn't reach his eyes but it made him look nice-*ish*.

'I don't hear voices. But my ability also comes with side effects. If I don't keep control of my gift, the emptiness consumes me. Each time gets worse. I've been told it'll eventually drive me insane.'

I pointed to the tattoos on his neck. 'And what do they do?' His expression shuttered and I lifted my hands. 'I can't help what I see. That big one on your neck glowed when you dragged me into your happy pit of nothingness.'

He tapped his fingers on the bar in a rhythmic pattern. I frowned as I realised it was the only sound I heard. I looked around the room. The entire floor was empty except for the two of us. It unsettled me that I didn't know if it was real or not. His voice pulled my attention back to him.

'They stop me from getting dragged too far into the emptiness. They pull me back to reality.'

'Are you sure that's what they do?'

'What do you mean?'

I gestured to the big tattoo on his neck. 'That one acts like an anchor for your consciousness; it probably helps to keep you sane, but some of the others look like they do the opposite.'

His eyes narrowed. 'Explain.'

I shrugged. 'It's hard for me to know without physical contact.'

'If you're lying, there will be consequences.'

'You're the king's errand boy. Why would I risk lying to you?'

He pulled off his jacket and threw it on the bar, then rolled up a sleeve, his intense gaze burning into mine. 'Do it.'

'Do what?'

He held out his arm. 'I want to know what they do. Do whatever you need to do to find out. I'll owe you.'

I'd already figured out that money held little value in Aurore. Instead, people dealt in favours. 'Fine, just hold still and keep quiet.'

I grabbed his hand. It was surprisingly warm. It wasn't that I thought he was a cold, bloodless vampire, but with the vibes he gave off, he sure came close. I relaxed and closed my eyes, letting my energy flow into his and his into mine. Following the path of energy flowing towards the central core, I skirted around the dark void. I felt its pull as it tried to drag me in. Examining Kilian's lifeline left me confused. He studied my face as I opened my eyes.

'Who gave you these tattoos?'

He ignored my question. 'Tell me what they do?'

I turned his arm and pointed to a tattoo that ran along the inside of his forearm. 'This tattoo, along with one on your back and one on your abdomen, are tethering you to the emptiness. Each time you use your gift it pulls you further in.'

His eyes narrowed. 'How?'

'I see different forms of energies as threads. Picture a piece of thread sewing two pieces of material together. The threads coming from those tattoos have stitched your abilities thread to your psyche. Usually an abilities thread is free-flowing. It's a part of our lifeline but it flows in and around it, without connecting to other threads. It gives us the ability to use our gift without negative impact on ourselves, aside from energy loss.'

'English, please,' he said through clenched teeth.

I exhaled a frustrated breath. 'Your gift has been attached to your lifeline—the energy force that keeps you alive. Whenever you use the emptiness, it affects you just as much as the person you're using it against.' I sipped my cocktail and turned back to Kilian just as he pulled his shirt off over his head. My stool screeched on the wooden floor as I scooted back.

'What are you doing?'

'I want you to point out the exact tattoos.'

I admired the art covering his torso. He wasn't Shifter-fit, but he clearly worked out. Definitely *not* a vampire. Tattoos covered almost every visible inch of skin and most of them glowed with some form of power. He started to undo the buckle of his pants. I launched to my feet and the barstool crashed to the floor.

I waved my hands. 'Woah, woah, keep your pants on. All the offending tattoos are above the—ah—hips.' My face was on fire as I looked at everything but Kilian. He smirked as he redid the buckle and held out his arms.

'Well?'

I cringed and stepped close, looking over his torso. One tattoo ran down his side, from beneath his ribcage to the top of his hip. The other ran across his shoulder blades. They were written in a language I didn't recognise. I pointed out the offending tattoos to Kilian and he began to shrug his shirt back on.

I placed my hand on his shoulder. 'Wait. I think I see one more.'

I yanked my hand away—I was touching his bare skin. As if it was even possible, my face heated further. I heard his small chuckle as I concentrated on his energy. There was a tiny thread, as small as a piece of hair, running from a small tattoo at the top of his spine, right along the hairline. There were hundreds of tiny threads. They were small, but threaded through his lifeline in an intricate weave.

'There is a tiny tattoo right here.'

It was a single symbol surrounded by an intricate pattern. It was beautiful.

Kilian's hand brushed the back of his neck and hovered over the tattoo. He turned to me. Hurt flashed in his eyes, but by the time he fully faced me his features had smoothed.

'Let's go for a drive.' He walked to the elevator, shrugging on his jacket, and turned to me as the doors opened. 'Are you coming?'

I glanced around the empty room, wondering again if it was truly empty and stepped towards him. 'Where are we going?'

'You'll see.'

At the entrance to the building, a man in green stood beside a flashy black car. My little yellow sports car was a kitten in comparison to this beast.

'I never saw this car in the garage,' I said in wonder, sitting in the leather passenger seat.

'That's because it's mine.'

The engine roared and he tore onto the road. The lights of the city whizzed by, growing dimmer as the sun rose over snow-capped mountains in the distance. We slowed at the dingier part of town, stopping at the entrance to an alleyway. Kilian parked in the middle of the road showing no consideration for other drivers. Down the alleyway was a fluorescent sign that flashed the word 'tattoo'. He led me to the door beneath the sign and threw it open. It banged against the wall as he stalked into the small studio. One person sat reclined in the chair, an intricate scrawl of words being inked across her collarbone.

'Out!' Kilian snarled.

The girl scrambled to her feet and fled from the parlour, the door banging in her wake. The tattooist sat on a stool by the chair, staring wide-eyed at Kilian. He stood and edged backwards but Kilian moved fast, pinning him against the wall with a hand around his neck. His knuckles whitened as he squeezed the guy's throat. He struggled, clawing at Kilian's hands and his face turned purple, the veins near his temples bulging.

'You,' Kilian hissed. He rolled back the sleeve of his shirt, revealing one of the offending tattoos. 'You knew about these tattoos and never thought to mention they were the cause of my misery.'

He slammed the guy's head against the wall with a loud crack. The man groaned, renewing his efforts to loosen the fingers cutting off his air supply.

'Let the guy go, Kilian,' I said. He turned to me with a

murderous glare and I shut my mouth.

'I didn't give you the tattoos. What was I s-supposed to do? I can't undo what's been d-done,' the tattooist choked. His head slammed against the wall again.

'Not good enough. You can over-ride it.'

He shook his head, gasping for air. 'Prime words c-can't be undone.'

Kilian's grip tightened and the guy sputtered. I placed a hand on his shoulder. 'Let him go. He can't help you if he's dead.'

My words seemed to bounce off him. The guy turned grey and my body grew clammy. His eyes rolled back in his head. Kilian shrugged my hand from his shoulder and reached into his jacket, pulling out a gun. It was one of the fancy plastic ones. He held it to the man's temple.

'Well then, if you can't fix it, it's only fair that you pay for your predecessor's mistake.'

He meant it. There was no conflict in his eyes. He was going to make an innocent guy pay for someone else's sins. I pulled one of the Siren's guns from the back of my jeans and held it to Kilian's head.

'Let the guy go.'

He turned, his icy glare now directed at me. You could've heard a pin drop.

'You'd hold a gun to *my* head?'

This version of Kilian could've passed for a vamp. The guy against the wall looked at me, his eyes popping. I'd done something very stupid.

'You were about to kill an innocent guy, so yes, I *would* hold a gun to your head.' I flicked the safety off on the gun.

The world around me dissolved. The gun was gone, the tattoo parlour was gone. I choked on a breath as my soul was ripped from my chest taking with it the air in my lungs. I fell to my knees, tears streaming down my face. Kilian sauntered over to me, a smirk on his lips. His steps echoed in the darkness. He'd made two big mistakes. First, he'd allowed his energy to flow through mine, and mine through his. I knew his energy signature now, even with the void of emptiness masking it. Second, his pet Aegis was nowhere to be found.

Two could play at this game.

I threw out threads of energy, weaving a lasso around his lifeline. I tugged hard enough that his steps faltered. His eyes narrowed on me. The energy filtered through my veins and I closed my eyes, sighing as the euphoria hit. The emptiness wasn't so consuming anymore. I opened my eyes and pushed off my knees, moving towards Kilian until we were a hands distance apart.

'You think you can take me on?' he mocked. 'You have no idea who you're dealing with. I can take whatever I want, his life or yours. I can take your happiness and treasured memories so you're left with nothing but fear and sorrow.'

The emptiness caved in on me, tearing at my mind. He didn't understand how a Syphon's gift worked. I'd drawn enough of his gift that I wouldn't drown in the void.

A little switch flicked in my brain. People like him trampled on those weaker than him, and I don't tolerate bullies.

I drew his energy forcefully, watching as his eyes widened and his lips thinned. He crumpled to his knees, not once taking his eyes from mine as I pulled harder. The cords of muscle in his neck tightened. The world around us reappeared and we were once more in the dingy little tattoo parlour. The tattooist cowered in the corner of the room. My gun was gone. I felt the back of my jeans—the other one was gone too. Kilian's gift wasn't an illusion of emptiness—it was real. I stood over him.

'I helped you, and this is the thanks I get.' James's lips were zipped, but I could still sense his satisfaction as I loomed over Kilian. 'How does it feel? I've heard it feels like dying. Our *gifts* must be related.'

His lifeline flickered and I cut off the flow of energy. He gasped for air. I sensed James's disappointment. Kilian looked up at me through blood-shot eyes as he heaved in breaths. The frostiness in his expression could've frozen me solid. If I had to kill him I would. I wouldn't like him in my head, but it was better than the alternative. The thought of taking another life made me shudder. I tensed as the iciness in his gaze melted. The corners of his eyes crinkled and he chuckled.

He thought this was funny?

I leaned down and hissed, 'Try something like that again, and I'll kill you. That stupid smirk will be forever wiped from your irritating face!'

He stopped laughing, but the grin remained. I stormed from the building, the door slamming behind me and rattling the windows. At the end of the alleyway, I stopped at Kilian's car, glancing back at the tattoo parlour.

'What the hell is wrong with you people?' I screeched, holding back the urge to scream. Reaching through the driver's window, I pulled the lever for the bonnet. I ripped out the battery cables, throwing them in a nearby bin.

'Figure that out, jackass!' I yelled down the empty alley.

I headed in the general direction of the citadel. It was a long trek uphill, but that suited me. I needed to blow off steam. These people thought they could just take a life with no consequence, but they were going to work out that they couldn't take me down without a fight. Passing the walls of the citadel, I headed straight for the gym. I found a punching bag and pictured Kilian's smiling face as I pounded it with my fists. Hours later, when my fingers and knuckles were numb, I returned to my rooms, collapsing on the bed in an exhausted sleep.

18

DARK clouds rolled over the sand dunes, threatening to drench me with rain. Gulls nested in the spinifex, sheltering from the wind. I rubbed my arms; the breeze was chilly. Water rushed across my feet and I watched them sink into the sand. It was familiar sand.

I was at Pete's Beach.

Someone called my name over the sound of the howling wind. I turned to the voice. Beau walked towards me, stopping a small distance away.

'Don't pull yourself from the dream,' he said.

I turned from his intense gaze and focused on the changing water. This is the place I came to quiet my thoughts. Even when the water was wild and stormy, it anchored me. It was interesting that I came here even in my sleep.

'Why do all my dreams involve you? I barely sleep anyway, and you turn up in every single dream,' I said.

He grabbed my face, turning it towards him. 'Because I've been waiting here… for you. I'm sorry I left; it was a mistake. If I hadn't left, you'd be safe.' He stepped closer, inhaling my scent. His eyes glowed.

'Who is he?' He pretty much growled the question.

'Who's who?'

'The guy whose scent is all over you.'

I rolled my eyes. 'I can't believe you're this possessive even in my dreams.'

His eyes glowed bright gold. 'I tried to tell you last time, this isn't a dream. The interaction between you and me is as real as it would be if we were really standing at Pete's. It's called a dreamscape. Who is he?'

I stepped back. 'I've never heard of a dreamscape. How is that even possible?'

'It's possible because I marked you.'

My fingers brushed the side of my neck. The 'bite' had long since faded. 'You'll need to explain yourself better than that.'

He faced the dunes, running his hands through his hair. He sighed and turned back to me. 'I marked you before I left as a way to keep you safe. Shifter Wolves do it all the time. It tells other Shifter Wolves that you're spoken for and to back-off.'

I crossed my arms to protect myself from the cold… and him. 'I know that. I'm related to Shifter Wolves, remember? You marked me and left. I'm not stupid, Beau. You didn't want me, but you're a territorial jerk, so you didn't want anyone else to have me either.'

He closed the space between us. 'I did it for your protection. Dire Wolves have a code, a sense of duty that runs deep within our kind. When I marked you, it meant that other Dire Wolves are obligated to help you. If something happened to me while I was away, I knew you'd be okay.' He shrugged. 'And, if it just so happened to piss off the likes of Ben Waller and any other Shifters who came sniffing around, then it's a bonus.' The muscles in his jaw were rock-hard and his energy flared like he was resisting the urge to shift.

'There's more to it, isn't there?'

He grabbed a lock of my hair, tucking it behind my ear. It was pointless, the wind had turned my hair into a wild mess anyway.

His voice lowered. 'Marking is the start of a bonding process. A bond can be strengthened by developing trust and… love. Or it can be left to dissolve…'

I gave a disbelieving laugh. 'That's why you ran away isn't it? You're scared of being bonded to me.'

'I stayed away longer than necessary to see if the bond would weaken, but it hasn't. I was always coming back, Freya.' He grabbed the pendant around my neck, rubbing a thumb cross it, then tucked it back into my shirt. He lifted his burning gaze to mine. 'You've spent your life caged by what you are. I of all people understand that… I didn't want to reinforce the bars that were already there by tying you to me. Not yet.'

I hugged my arms around my waist. 'You didn't think I could make that decision myself? You know what I think? I think you were scared. I said the 'L' word and you totally freaked out.'

A host of emotions crossed his face. 'Yes, I freaked out. Because the moment you said it, I realised that you're the first person I might have those kinds of feelings for.'

I froze. My lungs refused to inhale oxygen. Was he saying what I thought he was saying? The warmth spreading through my chest was doused by the realisation that if Beau really had feelings for me, then *he'd stop at nothing to find me. He was the most stubborn person I'd ever met. He couldn't come to Aurore. Levi, Reagan and the others couldn't come here either. I couldn't be responsible for their deaths.*

'No,' I whispered.

'No?'

'I never actually said I loved you.' I stared at my feet, twisting a lock of hair between my fingers.

A drop of rain splashed against my cheek and he wiped it away with his thumb, leaning in to whisper in my ear. 'You're a terrible liar. Your face hides nothing and I can hear your erratic pulse.'

I pulled myself away. 'My pulse is erratic because I'm angry! I don't love you. I don't want to see you again. Not here and not in the real world.' I moved to the water's edge but he grabbed my arm and spun me back to him.

'Why won't you admit it? If you felt nothing for me, we wouldn't be able to meet in the dreamscape, let alone physically touch. I wouldn't be able to do this—' he brushed a hand down my arm, 'or this—'.

He pulled me towards him, tipping my head back. His mouth met mine in a desperate kiss. One of his hands threaded through my hair and the other grasped my hip, holding me in place, as though he feared I'd run. I couldn't have run even if I wanted to. I was glued where I stood as waves of un-wanted emotion bubbled to the surface. I gave in to the urge to kiss him back. A growl rumbled in his chest as I grabbed his T-shirt, pulling him closer. If I let go, he'd disappear and this would all be an actual dream. I wanted Beau to be with me in the real world.

But Beau couldn't be with me in the real world. He couldn't be anywhere near Aurore. I pushed against his chest and he let me go. I wiped tears from my cheeks.

'I can't do this.'

'Why not?'

'Because I'll never leave Aurore. Even if I wanted to leave, which I don't, Lucien would come for Blackwood. He would destroy everyone.'

'Who is Lucien?' he growled.

'Argyle's brother. And he's much worse. You have no idea the kind of power he has.'

'I'll find you, Freya. Lucien will regret the moment he decided to take you.'

My chest squeezed. 'Just leave me alone. I have a place here… I don't need you.'

'You have a place with your family and friends. You have a place with me.' His hands were clenched into fists at his side.

'Don't you get it? I need more.' I bit my lip, knowing the next words would be acid on my tongue. 'You'll never be enough.'

His body tensed. He didn't move a single muscle, just stared at me. I watched his chest rise and fall as he processed my words. His wolf was so close to the surface, but as always, he held it under tight control. He didn't try to stop me as I ran into the icy-cold water and not once did I look back as I sunk into its murky depths.

***

I woke with tear-stained cheeks and heaved in the cold air—my skin was still chilled from the sea. The balcony doors had blown wide open. I crossed the room and closed the doors, leaning my forehead against the cool glass.

I wouldn't let myself sleep anymore; I couldn't see Beau again. All he'd have to do is say my name in that mesmerising voice and I'd be putty in his hand. This so-called *bond* would fade over time and he'd forget about me. He had to.

I rested my head in my palms and let out a short sob. Pulling myself together I exhaled a shuddering breath and sat on the lounge, switching on the TV to distract me. Time passed and there was a quiet knock on the door. I opened it to find one of the serving staff standing in the doorway. It was the same woman who gave me the tour of my rooms.

'Mr Clemonte is expecting you, ma'am.'

I glanced at the loungeroom clock. It was just after noon. 'As in expecting me for lunch, or expecting me for an interrogation?'

'I'm not sure, ma'am. I just know that Mr Clemonte likes his guests to be punctual. He's in the ballroom.'

I thanked her and closed the door, careful not to slam it. I changed out of my clothes from the night before and dressed in fresh jeans and a T-shirt. I opened the door to find Tank waiting for me.

'Oh… it's you.'

He grinned. 'I hear you made a bold impression last night.'

'If you're referring to the Siren, he got what he deserved.'

I followed him down the hall. The ballroom looked the same as the first night I'd arrived. Now that I had the opportunity to observe the room, I noticed the select group of people close to the throne, aside from Lucien's guardians. They were different from the others. They carried themselves in a way that made them seem untouchable. And they were the only ones protected by the Aegis's shield.

'Royals,' Tank whispered in my ear. 'Lucien's siblings and their children. The odd-looking old man in the corner is a great uncle. He annoyed Lucien a few years ago, so now he's only allowed enough of the healing serum to keep him alive.'

The old guy in question wore clothing that looked as though it had been pulled from an eighteenth-century wardrobe. The room quieted as I approached the throne. Tank fell to a knee but I remained standing. Kilian appeared beside Lucien, his lips hinting at a smirk. It faded into an expression of boredom as he pulled out his phone and scrolled through the screen.

'It's been brought to my attention that you have assaulted a member of my court.' Lucien's black eyes bore into mine.

I glanced at Kilian, my heart pounding. *I'm dead. Very, very dead.*

I looked back at Lucien. 'Um, I'm sorry?'

One of his eyes twitched. 'Is there a problem with your short-term memory? Having trouble remembering last night's events?'

There was movement on my left. The Siren was here. My body relaxed. 'Are you talking about him?'

He leaned forward in his chair. 'Who else would I be referring to?'

'No one, sorry.'

Looking at the floor, I gathered my thoughts. When I lifted my gaze, the Siren stood to my side. His face was mottled black and blue, his pretty nose now a swollen lump bandaged to his face.

'Well, what do have to say for yourself? Or do I need to

force the answers from you?' Lucien's tone was clipped.

I swallowed the lump in my throat. 'The Siren started it. I was just defending myself,' I said.

'She attacked me,' the Siren spat. 'I only asked her to join us on the tenth floor. I thought I was making a generous offer to one of the lower-class.'

My body tensed. *What a load of bull!*

'And what do you say to this allegation?' Lucien asked me, an eyebrow arched.

'He tried to Siren-speak me into joining them on the tenth floor. I said no, and he didn't like it.' I shrugged. 'He threatened and grabbed me so I gave him a new nose.'

One of the guardians behind Lucien snickered. The Siren whined and Lucien silenced him, holding up a hand. 'And you thought to take justice into your own hands by teaching him a lesson?'

I shuffled on my feet and the Siren edged back. 'Like I said, he grabbed me and my instincts took over. What did you expect me to do, cry for help?'

Lucien's focus stayed on me. 'Kilian, you saw the event unfold. What's your opinion?'

Kilian glanced up from his phone. His eyes met mine, his brows slightly raised as though saying to me, *yes, that's right. Your life is in my hands now.* My hands grew clammy. I glanced at the doors behind me. There was no way I'd make an escape through the sea of Supernatural power between me and the doors.

'He knew she was Favoured. He deserved what he got.'

I blinked, turning back to Kilian. He winked, returning his attention to his phone. The Siren shook, his forehead beading with sweat. Lucien stood and addressed the larger crowd, his voice echoing through the room.

'In centuries past, nations have crumbled to dust because people thought themselves above the law and above social order. Aurore is not the stronghold it is today because of leniency. We will never crumble.' Lucien stepped towards the Siren, grabbing him by the throat. 'Our enemies will become the dust under our feet.'

The Siren screamed. His skin turned a strange reddish-grey.

A guttural groan filled the room. The Pain Empowered guardian edged forward, a satisfied grin on her face. She threw her head back and laughed, dancing in a small circle. She was basking in the Siren's fear and pain—she was a psycho. I turned back to the Siren. His skin was blistering.

'Don't turn away. It will be seen as weakness,' Tank whispered in my ear.

I watched as the flesh rotted from his bones. And then, he wasn't screaming anymore. What was left of him fell to a heap on the floor. I shook as his bones crumbled like dried mud. The room was still. All sets of eyes in the room stared at the remaining pile of dust. Lucien returned to his throne, making a dismissive gesture with his hand. Everyone returned to their conversations like nothing had happened. He crooked his finger, signalling for me to move closer and I willed my feet to move, focusing on one shaky step at a time. In my head I was screaming, but on the surface, I forced myself to remain calm. I stopped in front of Lucien and met his eyes. They betrayed no emotion at all.

'I expected less of you. It pleases me to see my instincts were right,' he said. He waved a hand around the room. 'All of these people have earned the right to be here. Only the strongest Supers are considered Favoured. The Siren thought he could use you to climb the social ladder. You not only humiliated him, but proved him valueless to me.' He leaned forward, hands laced together. 'When you first arrived, I thought you were a lamb among the wolves, but now I'm not so sure. Maybe you're a wolf in sheep's clothing.' His expression grew thoughtful and he lifted a finger. 'Or maybe you're a different predator all together.'

19

I was dismissed from the ballroom without an escort and forced myself to walk a steady pace back to my rooms. I slammed the door and ran to the bathroom, vomiting into the sink as images of the Siren flashed across my mind. The smell of his rotting flesh still lingered in my nostrils. When the vomiting and dry-retching ended I sunk to the tiled floor and thought of home. Pa would've been home from hospital by now. Mum would probably be curled up in Chris's arms. Levi would be… he'd be angry at himself.

I missed them.

I missed my friends. I even missed Christina Waller's sour face. Blackwood represented all that was good. Safety for my family meant staying here—staying here no doubt meant getting my hands dirty. Dirty hands didn't belong in Blackwood. I stared at the grey tiles. Images of rotting flesh flashed through my mind; I couldn't think. I needed somewhere to clear my head.

The room I searched for was located on the opposite end of the castle. I had to stop twice to ask for directions. The hallways were a maze. The music room wasn't in high demand at Clemonte Citadel. The antique piano sat by one of the large windows and I tested the keys, finding it in tune. I played through a few songs that I knew by heart, avoiding the ones that reminded me of home. The melody I'd written in remembrance of Dad flowed from my fingers and I wondered what he'd do in my place. He would've had a plan. He'd tell me I had to seize the day—but he was a braver person than I was. How could I keep my family safe, while finding some kind of freedom for myself?

I yanked my fingers from the keys when I realised I'd started playing a tune that reminded me of Beau. I chose a different song and was only a few keys in when my finger paused on G major. I wasn't leaving Aurore. My presence here didn't guarantee my family's safety as Lucien could change his mind at any time. But, the more influence and power I had in this place, the safer my family and friends would stay. I pushed back the piano stool.

'How is it, that on the rare occasion you win a bet and force my silence, something big happens.'

James had timed his twenty-four-hour silence to the second. 'Actually, I could've done with your advice.'

'You didn't need me. You did well, kid. They're all taking notice of you now, which means you need to be careful. You need to be one move ahead of them at all times.'

'Yeah, I know.'

The yellow sports car sat waiting in the garage. I drove into the city centre, passing the flashier streets. I had an idea of where I was going. Following a rough mental map I remembered from the day before, I pulled up in front of the dingey alleyway. The doorbell tinkled as I entered the tattoo parlour. A tall man leaned over the chair, a tattoo of a two-headed beast visible across his shoulder blades. The tattooist saw me and finished covering the tattoo with plastic wrap before gesturing to the customer to leave.

As the doorbell jingled behind him, I said, 'Your tattoos manipulate energy. I want to know how.'

He eyed me. 'I transfer power into symbols… that includes ink.'

'How does it work?'

His lips thinned. 'It's like an enchantment or glamour. I can ink tattoos that tweak your DNA to change minor physiology – hair, eye colour, skin colour – that kind of thing. It can also enhance characteristics such as hearing and eyesight. I can give you the ability to see in the dark if you want it.'

'How about steadiness of hand.' I spread my hands to show the slight shake. 'It affects my aim.'

'I can fix that.'

The buzzing of the needle gun sent a thrill down my spine. Mum would've killed me if she knew I was getting a tattoo. He grabbed my hand, turning it to expose my inner wrist. The tattoo was a delicate symbol. It started with a spiral at one end that flowed into a series of infinity-like symbols. It ended with three little dots pointing to the top of my wrist. With the last dot, a warm tingle ran up my arm. He grabbed my other hand and did the same. When he finished, the tattoos glowed a soft yellow. I held out my hands and admired the subtle change in my energy; flecks of yellow ran through it now. I could've done open-heart surgery on a goldfish. The Tattooist moved to the sink at the back of the studio.

'What about the tattoos on Kilian? They're something more, aren't they?' I asked.

His body tensed. 'Yes.'

'What are they?'

He clutched the sink and heaved a sigh. 'I owe you for saving my life. If I tell you, you must promise to keep it to yourself.'

'Okay, I promise.'

He turned, leaning his back against the sink. 'They're words of power. Prime words.'

I frowned.

He sat back on his stool and leaned his elbows on his knees. 'It looks like I have to tell you the whole story.' He ran a hand across his tattooed, shaved head. 'You know the story of creation, right? In the beginning God spoke the universe into being. He created Adam and Eve who became the caretakers of the earth and all its creatures. Well, when the earth was young, people didn't have Supernatural gifts; they spoke power into existence using the language of power – prime language. As earth's caretaker, Man had the ability to do anything except create life. Adam and Eve began to see themselves as God's equal and became greedy for knowledge. They were cast from the garden of Eden.'

He picked up my wrists and raised a brow at the almost completely healed skin. 'History repeated itself again and again, generation after generation, and then at Babel, God became angry. Man was no longer worthy of the language of power. Most of the words were lost that day—struck from the minds of man. But the few that God allowed to remain have been passed down through certain bloodlines and cultivated in different ways, from generation to generation. My family was one of those bloodlines. Our gift allows us to transfer power into symbols. In Kilian's case the power has been transferred into tattooed symbols, making them last as long as the body that holds them.'

'What kind of things can these words do?'

'Among many things, they can enhance and manipulate gifts. As you saw with Kilian, it is not always used for good.'

I studied the tattoos on my wrists. They'd completely healed. 'Could you enhance my gift with these words?'

His nostrils flared. 'I owe you my life, but I can't give you what you ask. Prime words come at a cost—a very personal cost. I'm here to pay a family debt to the Clemontes. I can't afford to use the words as I'd like to use them.'

I nodded. 'Sorry, I shouldn't have asked.'

He gave a small smile. 'You're not a typical Favoured. What are you doing in Aurore?'

I rubbed my wrists. 'The same as you. I'm here to pay a debt.'

I found a café on one of the busy streets in the city centre and sat up the back in my own booth. When my double strength flat white, lunch and a delicious looking pastry sat in front of me, I closed my eyes. I focused on sending out threads of energy, dozens and dozens of tiny threads. There were seventeen people in the café. I reached eleven of them. Pushing my reach further, I managed to reach two more without losing control of the pull. A familiar energy signature entered my range. I opened my eyes, taking a bite of my sandwich.

Kilian slid into the seat on the other side of the booth. 'There are more appropriate places to take a nap,' he said, eyeing the smorgasbord of food in front of me.

'Don't touch the pastry,' I warned.

He smirked. 'What happens if I do? A re-match?'

I snorted. 'You'll just lose again. How did you know I was here?'

'I know everything that happens in this city.'

I concentrated on eating my sandwich, keeping a close

eye on the chips. Why did everyone, my brother especially, assume that chips were there to share? Kilian relaxed back into his seat. Apparently, he'd invited himself to stay.

'You could do with some friends here,' he said.

I lifted my eyes. 'And you're offering?'

'I think we could help each other.'

'If you're willing to kill someone for a crime they didn't commit, why should I believe you won't do the same to me?' I dipped a chip in sauce, popping it in my mouth.

'Because when it comes to supernatural power, you and I are equals. You won't let me kill you.'

I laughed and he didn't. He was serious. I leaned forward, lowering my voice. 'I nearly killed *you* yesterday, remember? Not exactly the way to start a friendship.'

'Yes, you *nearly* killed me, but that's not quite the same as actually killing me, is it? You hesitated—you can't afford to be soft in a place like this.'

I reached for a chip and stopped, raising a brow. 'You're saying that I should've killed you?'

He nodded and I fell back in my seat. I couldn't work him out. 'Why didn't you tell Lucien?'

He gestured to the waitress. She approached the table, her eyes darting between Kilian and the exit. He gave his order and she hurried away. He leaned across the table and grabbed a handful of chips from my plate. He shoved one in his mouth and grinned. My glare didn't seem to bother him one bit.

'Because you and I, we're the same. I saw it the moment you wanted to kill me. The excitement in your eyes, the thrill of having power over life and death.'

'*We* are nothing alike,' I hissed.

'Haven't you ever wondered what it would be like to fear nothing? To have everyone fear you?'

I kept my mouth shut and he smirked. A black coffee that smelled suspiciously of liquor slid in front of him. He whispered something to the waitress who nodded and scurried behind the counter. He finished the coffee in two sips.

'The power structure in Aurore doesn't just depend on

supernatural ability. Old-fashioned politics underlies everything. You can fight your way up the social ladder, or make the right *friends* and take the elevator.' He reached across the table and took a bite of my pastry. My whole face kind of spasmed. He stood, checking his watch. 'I'll give you five days to think about it. When you realise this is the best offer you'll get, meet me at The Tower after midnight. Only gutter-class get there before midnight.' He turned away, then stopped. He reached back across the table and grabbed the rest of my pastry. 'Consider this payment for touching my car.' He consumed it in one bite, swiping at the corners of his mouth with his thumb.

He gave a dismissive wave and I glared at the back of his head as he left the cafe. I caught the smirk on his face as he passed the window. The roar of a car engine had everyone in the cafe turning in their seats. I hadn't inconvenienced him as much as I'd hoped.

I grabbed my things and approached the counter, glancing at the pastry display cabinet. I blinked.

It was empty.

The waitress gave me a sympathetic smile. 'Sorry, Miss. Mr Clemonte told me to throw out the rest of the pastries. He didn't say why, but nobody questions a Clemonte.'

'Mr Clemonte?'

She looked at me like I had an IQ of two. 'You're new here, aren't you? The man you were sitting with is Kilian Clemonte; Lucien's nephew and heir.' She glanced around the café. 'You should be honoured. Kilian rarely approaches anyone outside of his family. Not even the Favoured.'

Kilian was a Clemonte? *Oh, hell…*

'You've got that right. Somehow, you managed to catch his eye. You've scored the golden ticket,' James said.

Golden ticket my butt. *'It's called charm, James. You should try it.'*

20

I dressed up for my rendezvous at The Tower. I still wore jeans, but they were nice ones, and traded shoes for leather boots with a pointed heel. A stiletto heel to the temple would kill someone in seconds; a handy little tip from James. I chose a figure-hugging top and left my hair down. I'd managed to tame it enough that it looked stylishly messy. The days leading up to this meeting I'd spent holed up in my rooms. I meditated, exercising the reach of my gift, ate to replenish my energy, then meditated again. I could now reach a five-metre radius.

A couple of hours before midnight I arrived at The Tower. The security guard waved me ahead of the line and I reached the lift just before it closed. The Favoured might not have arrived, but the place was still packed. Sixteen floors lit up as I waved my arm over the sensor. People in the lift gasped. There was only meant to be fifteen floors. On the third floor I found a table in the corner where I could see everyone coming and going.

'You're back. I'm surprised you've lasted this long.'

I glanced up at the blonde Dire Wolf. 'Disappointed?'

Her lips pursed.'No. The last thing I want is to be held responsible for your death. The Sinclair family would have my throat.'

'You're not making sense.'

She placed one of the fairy-floss cocktails in front of me. 'You're bonded to Beau Sinclair, aren't you? It took me a while to place the scent, but I know he's the one who marked you.'

Of course, Greyson wasn't his last name. He was in hiding, so it made sense to change his name, but it still hurt that I hadn't known. That he didn't trust me enough to know.

My eyes narrowed. 'Yes, he marked me, but it's fading

now. We broke up.' I scolded myself. 'We didn't break up, because we never actually dated.'

She let out a snort. 'It doesn't work that way. Do you dream about him? Vivid dreams?' I nodded and she sighed. 'At the start of a normal bonding process you can't meet in the dreamscape. That connection is something that comes later when the bond is strong. But Beau is a Dire Wolf and from your scent I can tell that you're powerful.'

'What does that mean?'

She glanced over her shoulder then back at me. 'For alphas and Dire Wolves, the ability to sense power is a survival instinct. We can sense when someone would strengthen our pack or ourselves.'

'I know this…'

She lifted a hand and continued, 'There's something in our DNA that lies dormant until we mark someone. No one really knows how a bond works, but when a Wolf Shifter marks someone, a connection forms, a way of ensuring that the power or strength, in the form of a mate, remains tied to us. The stronger the power, the tighter the hold; we can't control it. When a Dire Wolf marks someone powerful—well, good luck breaking that bond.'

'Would Beau know this?'

'I don't know. For a Dire Wolf, Beau is still young. We don't typically bond till later, if we bond at all. And it's usually with our own kind. Bonds can be… complicated. He probably didn't realise how strong the connection would be until he'd marked you and it was too late. Trust me, as far as he's concerned, you're together. He'll be coming for you.'

'He can't come here, Lucien will kill him,' I argued.

Her eyes glittered. 'Then maybe you should leave. That family will never survive if they lose another male.'

'Why?'

'Because he is the only surviving male heir.' She glanced around us and lowered her voice. 'It's bad enough that he's chosen a Non-Shifter as a mate. The likelihood of your children being Dire Wolves is low, and even if you do produce them, their blood will be diluted. You are the last thing our species needs.'

'This isn't my fault,' I exclaimed. 'He can find himself some pretty Dire She-Wolf and have all the Dire Wolf babies he wants.' My teeth gritted towards the end of that sentence. A part of me raged at the idea of him with someone else, but I'd get over it.

She pointed where the pendant lay hidden beneath my top. 'Then why do you still wear his family crest around your neck?'

I scowled, grasping the pendent. I hesitated, just for a moment, before pulling it over my head. 'Here, take it.'

'No way. He'd kill me. I'm not about to start a family feud.'

I placed it back over my head, tucking it into my shirt. 'It's obvious you despise me, so why keep talking to me and bringing me drinks?'

Her lips thinned. 'Dire Wolves follow a code. We look out for each other and our mates, or in your case, prospective mate. I might not like you, but I'm obligated to watch out for you.'

Beau had been honest. 'So... if I ask, you have to help me?'

She picked up my empty glass and leaned over the table. 'Don't push your luck. My name is Blake; don't forget it. You'll ask for me when you find yourself in trouble.' With that she turned away and left me in my corner.

I ignored the fact that she'd ended our conversation with a command—typical Dire Wolf. In her lecture, Blake had never actually said that the bond couldn't be broken. It sounded as though breaking it would be best for Beau too. I rubbed my chest, then shook my head, focusing on what I'd come here early to do. Closing my eyes, I sent out threads of energy through the crowd. Instead of just reaching out to the people around me, I sent threads through the floor above, and the floor below. I reached people on three floors of the building, including the one where I was seated. I connected with more than thirty people and attached threads to each of them. No matter how my meeting with Kilian turned out, I could pull plenty of energy to defend myself. One of my threads brushed across a familiar type of energy.

My breath caught. *It was really familiar.* It disappeared as soon as I made contact with it. Whoever it was, they'd been somewhere on this floor. I searched for it, finally brushing against it again on the level above. I gulped my drink and pushed through the crowd towards the elevator. A hand grabbed my arm, pulling me to a stop.

'I thought you'd get here early,' Kilian said, surveying the room. He seemed oblivious to the wide-eyed stares and whispers. 'I gave you access to all floors and you still chose this one. It's a hovel.'

I scowled. '*Hovels* suit people like myself just fine.'

He grinned and I couldn't help but blush. The way his attention never wavered from me, even in a crowded room, gave me butterflies. He leaned in next to my ear, so close that his breath tickled my neck.

'People like you? Under that self-righteous mask, you know we're more alike than you want to admit.'

He placed a hand on the middle of my back, leading me to the elevator. The doors closed, leaving the two of us in the small space alone. He pushed the button for the sixteenth floor.

'I'm not self-righteous,' I stated.

He chuckled as the elevator chimed. The doors opened into a large, open-plan apartment. There were leather couches, a wall-sized TV, a floor to ceiling bookcase complete with ladder, a modern kitchen, and a balcony overlooking the city and Clemonte Citadel.

'What is this place?'

He shrugged off his jacket, throwing it on one of the couches. 'My apartment.'

I stepped back from the entryway. 'Your apartment? Here?'

He crossed to the kitchen and pulled out two glasses. 'I own The Tower. Living here is private and convenient.' I watched as he poured whiskey into both glasses.

'Right... I think I'll head back down to level three.' I turned to the elevator, and Kilian's hand appeared in front of the control panel.

His voice lowered. 'This is the only place we can speak freely. Stay until you've heard what I have to say.'

'I'm not staying anywhere alone with a *Clemonte*,' I said, hugging my arms to my body.

He arched a black brow. 'So, you've finally worked it out.'

He stepped closer and I focused on keeping my gift under control. I sent out a single thread of energy and wrapped it around his lifeline—just in case. He stopped when his toes nearly touched mine and held my gaze.

'Does knowing my name change anything? No. I could've ended you after you *nearly* killed me—I don't appreciate threats to my life—but I didn't. So, what makes you think I'm going to do it here?' He stepped back and smirked. 'Believe it or not, if I'm going to kill someone, I like to make sure they are very aware. It's more… satisfying.'

He stared at my lips on that last word and I swallowed the lump in my throat. He undid the top button on his shirt, loosening the collar, and turned away.

'So, you can stay, enjoy a two-hundred-year-old bottle of whiskey with me and discuss the terms of our friendship, or you can go back to your dingey little third floor and contemplate the rest of your life living on the end of my uncle's leash.'

He had a point. I brushed past him, grabbing the glass of whiskey off the kitchen bench and sculled it. I gasped for air. The glass clattered on the bench. Someone had poured gasoline down my throat and set it on fire.

Kilian's smirk curved into a grin. 'A bit different to that pink syrup you like to drink, isn't it?'

'You could've warned me,' I coughed.

'But I didn't—and it was amusing.'

He poured me another glass and motioned to the balcony doors. I passed through them, suppressing a cough as I took in the views of the city and the citadel. The evening fog made the citadel look haunted. It loomed over the city like an overbearing parent; a reminder to the city's citizens of who was in charge. I leaned against the glass railing and took a cautionary sip of the whiskey this time.

'You don't seem like the type of person who needs many *friends*. What do you want from me?' I asked.

Kilian leaned on the railing, brushing an arm against mine. 'People considered Favoured make up the majority of Uncle's court; the people you see milling around the ballroom. Like any good monarchy, where you fall within the ranks of the court depends on not just supernatural power, but social influence. The Favoured form partnerships with one another to increase social influence. With powerful people standing behind you, you become less expendable. I want you to ally yourself with me, because with me, you'll be untouchable.'

'But why do you need me? You're already the heir.'

He looked up at the citadel. 'I'm heir to the throne in name only. Now that my family has access to the healing serum, Lucien will never give up power. To quash any threat to his rule, he'll try to get rid of me.'

'Okay, but you haven't said why you want me?'

'I'm difficult to overpower. There are few people here who are a real challenge for me, but then along came you…' He sipped his whiskey, closing his eyes as he savoured it. He gestured to my glass and I took a sip. 'I could've told my uncle about our confrontation, but I'd prefer we be friends.'

His offer seemed too easy. 'And the catch?'

'I want you to help me find a way to undo the effects of these tattoos.'

The request made me uneasy. 'I can't fix you.'

'I know, but you might be able to find out who can. The fact that you can see the… what did you call it? Threads? It gives you an advantage over anyone else.'

'Who gave you those tattoos?'

'The current Tattooist's Aunt inked them… as directed by Uncle Lucien. It makes sense now. But this one—' He pointed to the small delicate design on his neck. 'That was my first one. My mother took me to get that tattoo.' He said it without any hint of emotion, but I'd seen the hurt when I'd first pointed it out.

'I'm sorry.'

He arched his brows. 'Don't be.'

I tapped my glass. 'Let's say I agreed to this partnership, how do I know you won't kill me?'

'You won't know. That's the beauty of the game.'

'And if I decide to kill you first?'

He chuckled, leaning in close enough that I could smell the whiskey on his breath. 'That's what makes the game fun.' He grabbed one of my wrists, turning it to reveal the tattoo. He rubbed a thumb across the symbol and my pulse leapt. 'Are these the only tattoos he gave you?'

I swatted his hand away. 'Yes,' I hissed. 'If I decide to do this, there will be rules. First rule; don't touch me. Second rule; you don't get to kill people just because you feel like it.'

His eyes shifted between mine. 'I agree to your first rule, mostly, but I'd like to make an amendment to the second. I vote that the 'n-apostrophe-t' be removed from the second word.'

It took me a moment to work it out in my head. 'Vote denied.'

He let out an exaggerated breath—he was enjoying this. 'How am I meant to show people how little I care for their pitiful existence?' My eyes narrowed and he laughed. It was a deep, raspy sound. 'I've never been treated like this before. Well, once when I was seven… but that kid died.'

I stared at him in disbelief. 'Well, you'll have to get used to it. You want my help, remember? I don't need your *friendship*.'

He smirked. 'Oh, you need me. You don't even know the true reason you're here.'

'I'm here to pay a debt.'

He shook his head. 'Argyle was the bastard son of some gutter-class woman my grandfather slept with. My family do not marry for love—they marry to breed power. Not only was he illegitimate, he was weak, a blot on the family tree. He wasn't allowed to use the Clemonte family name. Argyle's death was insignificant; you really did Uncle a favour.'

'So why am I really here?'

He held out his hand. 'My lips are sealed until you agree to be allies.'

I eyed his outstretched hand. His fingernails were cleaner than mine. 'Alright.' I gripped his hand and he lifted it to his face, placing a kiss on the inside of my wrist.

'Rule one, remember?' I pulled the hand from his grasp.

He grinned. 'Three generations ago there were two Clemonte siblings. This was in France, before the revolution. The youngest Clemonte, Fleur, wanted to escape her tyrant of a father and fled the continent. Her father and brother searched for her for decades but never found a trace of her. Clemonte blood is potent with supernatural power – as I said, we've been bred that way. He knew that a strong power signature would show up eventually and he would find his long-lost daughter or one of her descendants. That is exactly what happened three years ago.'

I was confused. I sipped my whiskey and waited for him to continue.

'My mother is a powerful Telepath. Her ability has been enhanced to reach minds across the world. Three years ago, she came across a telepathic mind more powerful than her own. He'd just come into his power and was unable to shield his mind. With a bit of digging, she discovered that this boy was the great-great-grandson of Fleur Clemonte. Do you see where I'm heading?'

I gripped the glass in my hand. 'Jonah.'

He nodded. 'Your beloved Monroe's are a long-lost branch of the Clemonte family.'

'But the Monroe's didn't say anything when they discovered Argyle was a Clemonte.'

'Fleur changed her identity when she fled, using her mother's Spanish family name. Fleur Clemonte became Rosa Gonzales. Your friends probably don't know their true heritage.'

'What does Lucien want from them?'

'Fleur married into a family that can access an ancient type of power, something Uncle calls 'old power'. Uncle Lucien doesn't like loose ties and he doesn't like competition.'

I pushed away from the balcony railing, running a hand through my hair. 'He knows they'll come after me. I'm the bait. What does he plan to do?'

'They accept their place within the family, with Lucien as leader, or they die.'

No. No, no, no. 'How do we stop this?'

He arched that infuriating brow. 'We? Why should I care?'

I moved in front of him, well within his personal space. 'Your uncle underestimates their power. If he sends you out to the frontlines, you'll discover I'm not the only one who's a match for you. And the Monroe's have all of Blackwood behind them.'

'That's why he'll use you to lure them here, where we have the advantage. Do you really think the whole of Blackwood will follow?'

'My family will.'

'They're just Wolf Shifters. Give me your loyalty and I'll give you mine. Your family doesn't have to die.'

'How will you save them?'

His eyes glittered. 'I plan to rule Aurore, and I want you to help me take the throne.'

21

MY fingertips were numb from the cold. I went inside and paced the floor, rubbing my arms.

'You need help,' I said, midstride.

A warm blanket draped over my shoulders. Kilian dropped onto one of the couches, an arm spread across the back of the seat as he watched me pace.

I stopped. 'You really think you and I could take your uncle on? His guardians have enough power between them to wipe out a small country.'

'We won't be alone. I have other people on my side.'

'Who?'

'I can introduce you. Tonight.' He looked me up and down. 'You're dressed well enough. No work boots today?' I scowled as he finished his umpteenth whiskey. He placed the empty tumbler on the side table and grabbed his jacket. I dropped the blanket and followed him to the elevator. He pushed the button for level fifteen.

'So… you own The Tower?' I asked. He arched a brow. 'The level access thing is a bit much. Isn't it just mirroring Lucien's classist system?'

'It motivates people to better themselves. Seeing an extra floor light up on the control panel is their reward for working hard to please me and my family. Why should I change a method that works?'

I crossed my arms, turning away. What the hell was I doing?

James decided to provide his invaluable opinion. *'Don't back out. Remember, this is your golden ticket.'*

'I'm not backing out. I'm re-evaluating what I want.'

'You want what everyone wants—power.'

'I want freedom.' I glanced at Kilian. *'No more cages. No more fear.'*

'That's one of the definitions of power, kid.'

The elevator stopped at the fifteenth floor. A floor had been removed to give it elevated ceilings much like the Clemonte Citadel. Hundreds of icicle lights hung from the ceiling, casting a warm light. The whole room was decorated in different shades of red with large medieval paintings lining the walls. There was no dance floor here, just tables, lounges and a bar. Elegantly dressed people sat in the lounges or stood in groups. Eyes magnetised to us as we entered the room.

Kilian leaned in and murmured, 'Don't let them intimidate you. Right now, you're indispensable to my uncle. None of these people are.'

I shoved my hands in my pockets and lifted my chin, meeting the stares. Thankfully I'd worn a high-necked top. It covered the red, blotchy evidence of my nerves and the low-light hid the rest. People seemed to hover around Kilian but weren't brave enough to approach him. One group wasn't intimidated and they stood out from the crowd. Like Lucien's guardians, they glowed with supernatural power. One of the guys held out his hand and introduced himself. Reluctantly I pulled my hand from my pocket and accepted his handshake. I'd seen him once, the day I arrived. He was an Elemental of Water.

Kilian introduced me to each person. One woman could enhance the gifts of others, another created energy blasts from her hands, one guy absorbed any and all information, and a young-looking girl with yellow-framed glasses could generate and neutralise poisons of any form. Bishop would've loved the last guy. His nickname was Blacksmith and he could make a weapon from pretty much anything. One of the girls told me not to be offended by his stand-offish manner. He rarely spoke and or looked anyone in the eye.

A corner of the room was reserved for Kilian and his friends. I sat on a small lounge. There were plenty of seats but Kilian chose to sit next to me. He laid an arm across the back of the lounge and I leaned away, resting against the armrest. The group discussed an upcoming marriage between two powerful families. Kilian shook his head and told me it was a risk for the groom's side of the family, as the bride's family had thrown a few 'duds' in recent generations; Mundanes with no power.

A pink cocktail was placed in my hand and I looked up to find the Dire Wolf, Blake, glancing between Kilian and I. Her nostrils flared and she shot me a glare. She looked at the spot on my chest where Beau's pendant lay hidden, then looked back at me. I held her gaze until she lowered her eyes and left the table. She said that I was *the last thing* her species needed and yet here she was reminding me that I belonged to Beau. I resisted the urge to grab the pendant. I didn't belong to anyone, and no one belonged to me.

'I'm taking Freya to see the sights tomorrow. If you guys want to meet us at Sergio's peak, we'll be there at noon,' Kilian said when the table had grown quiet. The group gave murmurs of agreement and the Water Elemental smiled.

'I hope she's ready for The Drop.'

Kilian smirked. 'She'll be ready. Shall we place bets?'

Low chuckles and whistles sounded as everyone placed favour IOU's on the table.

I had a bad feeling about this. 'What's *The Drop?*' I asked.

The Water Elemental looked at his watch. 'By this time tomorrow, you'll know The Drop… intimately.'

22

HE told me to dress warm. It turned out that my idea of warm clothing was something you wore on a hot day in Aurore. It might have been early summer on this side of the world, but near the glacier, temperatures were still in the minus.

Sergio's Peak was a snow-covered mountain close to the nearby glacier. It was the centre for winter sports in Aurore. I'd arrived in the city just in time, while the snow was still useable. *Yay...* I picked snow gear from the store and opted for a snowboard instead of skis. I'd skateboarded before when I was trying to impress the boys in eighth grade. It seemed pretty much the same.

It wasn't the same.

'What do you mean there's no snow?' Kilian asked.

'We don't get snow. It doesn't get cold enough. Arriving in Aurore was the first time I'd ever seen it.'

He frowned. 'This should be easy if you've skateboarded before.'

I yanked on his arm, pulling myself to my feet for the tenth time. 'Look, I've almost got it. Why don't you leave me alone and I'll figure the rest out myself?'

He smirked, closing the visor of his black and red helmet. 'Fine. I've bet on you, so don't disappoint me.' He did a little backwards turn and disappeared down the slope.

I grumbled at the board strapped to my feet.

'Come on, kid. It's not that different to skateboarding. Stance, balance and carving are the same. The key difference is fixed footing and the size of the board.'

James had snowboarded before. It was an efficient way to reach a target who'd been holidaying at her mountainside chalet. He enjoyed the sport and had perfected his skill over the centuries.

'Let me in, Freya. You've been shutting me out again. Let me help you.'

I hesitated. It felt unnatural, like I was handing over part ownership of my body.

'I've helped you get this far, don't doubt me now. If you fail this menial test, then you've lost their respect.'

'Ugh, fine.'

I opened my mind to him like I had before. As I let go, I sensed his spirit weaving itself tighter through mine. Memories washed over me; visual memories, muscle memories and reflexes. A snowboarder rushed past me and I opened my eyes, looking down the slope. All of the pieces fell into place. I pulled down the visor and kicked off, setting the board into motion. The movements became instinct. Muscles I didn't often use were aching as I practised again and again. I practised a few times on a gradual slope before moving onto the steeper slopes. Snowboarding had its perks. The adrenalin rush made my body hum with excitement. Noon arrived and I'd grown confident that I could keep up with Kilian. He found me at the top of the hill just as his friends arrived. There were a dozen people; some of them I'd met the night before.

'You ready, newbie?' one of the girls sneered.

I pointed to the steep slope I'd finally conquered. 'I managed that mountain.'

Everybody laughed and Kilian grabbed my shoulder, gesturing behind me. I turned in the direction he pointed, to the mountain that loomed above us. It was covered in dense trees and rocky outcrops. Snowmobiles sat waiting for us near a barely visible track. *Oh… that mountain.*

After a brief argument, I hopped on the back of Kilian's snowmobile and held on as he weaved through the trees, climbing the mountainside. The hike up the hill became a competition. Kilian cut across the path of anyone who tried to overtake his leading position. The engines struggled as we neared the top. We reached the peak and I hopped off the back, trudging through snow to the edge of the peak. It dropped off into a sharp slope. *Surely not…*

Kilian stood beside me. 'Welcome to The Drop.'

My stomach lurched as I stared down the slope. I pictured all the ways in which I could die. All of them were bloody and painful.

'You can't die, remember? Harness that fear.'

'It will still feel like a thousand deaths.'

I rubbed my hands together to stop them from shaking. It could've been from the cold or nerves, I wasn't sure. Everyone moved to the edge, strapping on their boards and skis.

This was happening whether I liked it or not. The worst thing that could happen was excruciating pain. It would end—eventually. I swallowed the fear and strapped my feet to the board. Kilian already stood at the edge. He turned to me and grinned.

'See you at the bottom.'

He pushed off the side and disappeared. The next guy hollered and followed him down the slope. Each of them disappeared one by one with a shout.

James yelled at me to go. I pushed myself off the edge and screamed. The trees rushed by. Blurs of white and green streaked past in my peripheral. All I heard was ringing in my ears. I focused on dodging trees, logs and anything else in my way. When I wasn't impaled or crushed in those first few minutes, I concentrated on finding a steady balance, fixating on the bright orange jacket of the girl in front of me. The board was longer than a skateboard, making the turns trickier. I focused on the orange jacket and narrowed my gaze. It belonged to the girl who'd sneered at me. Increasing the weight on my front foot, I leaned forward picking up speed. I passed her and the person in front. The key was to make as few turns as possible, only making shallow carves in the snow to get around obstacles. I passed another three guys—this was better than a pack run.

The people in front of me started to slow down and I shot past them, ignoring the Water Elemental's shout. I passed over the top of a small hill and saw why the others had slowed. There were no trees here, but the terrain was rough, with rocks jutting out of the snow. My stomach dropped.

'The other big difference between skateboarding and snowboarding is slowing down. It's really hard to slow down…' James was laughing at me. I could feel it.

I weaved in and out of the rocky patches on shaky legs. My arms flailed as I tried to keep my balance. A sharp rock ripped through my jacket, grazing my arm. When I reached the end of the rocky terrain, I shouted in triumph. It started to snow, making it difficult to see the people in front. Kilian's red and black helmet was just visible. I leaned forward, following the blur of colour. They made a sharp turn up ahead and I did the same. We entered a thicket of trees and when I came out the other side, I'd lost sight of them. I followed the tracks in the snow until I caught sight of a dark, moving blur and I sped up. I didn't want to get lost, and a part of me really wanted to win. The guy in front was only a few feet away when they made another turn. I turned the corner, and saw that Kilian and the other guys had stopped up ahead near the edge of a cliff. They were waving their arms at me to stop.

I turned the board to the side and dug in my heals, but I wasn't slowing down enough. The edge of the cliff drew closer and I panicked, throwing my body to the ground. The snow was slippery and I continued to slide. Gravity, along with my board, pulled me towards the cliff-edge. I twisted, grabbing at anything that would stop my fall. My fingers grasped something solid and I held onto it with both hands, clenching my eyes shut and waiting for the inevitable fall.

My body stopped moving.

I wasn't in excruciating pain so I forced my eyes open. My hands clung to a piece of exposed rock. I looked behind me and groaned; half of my body was hanging over the edge. The weight of the board made it impossible to pull myself up.

'You still sticking to the no touch rule?'

I looked up at Kilian. 'Just help me!'

The corners of his mouth quirked as he watched me dangling over the edge. He grabbed my hands and some of the other guys joined him, grabbing my arms to pull me up. When my whole body was on solid ground, I let out a relieved sigh. I pulled my feet from the board and sat in the snow, letting my body come down from the adrenalin rush. A dozen pairs of eyes watched me.

'Did no one teach you how to do a gravity stop?' one of the guys asked.

I glared at Kilian. 'No. No they didn't.'

One of the girls removed her helmet and held out her hand. She had black hair and green eyes. Her abilities thread was a dark maroon colour. I grabbed her hand and she pulled me to my feet.

'I'm Elle, Kilian's cousin,' she said.

'Nice to meet you.'

She faced Kilian. 'I agree with you, Kili. She'd be a good addition… if we can trust her.'

Kilian turned to me with one eyebrow arched. 'Can we trust you?'

I mirrored his expression. 'That's the beauty of the game, isn't it? You'll never know if you can truly trust me.'

His lips split into a grin and he laughed. Members of the group glanced at each other. They seemed unsure what to make of his outburst.

'Anyone who disagrees on Freya joining our *club* is welcome to withdraw their association with me, but a word of this to my uncle and you're finished.'

A couple of people shuffled on their feet, but they all stayed silent. The Water Elemental gave me the thumbs up. I understood why Kilian was confident he could take the throne from Lucien. This so-called *club* was an allegiance to him. These people were passionate, devoted and lethal. They'd be his guardians.

The snowfall grew heavier and I lifted my gaze to the mountain I'd pretty much fallen down. 'How do we climb back up there?' I asked.

Elle laughed. 'You have so much to learn.'

A thumping sound filled the air, growing louder and louder. A helicopter rose above the side of the cliff and landed in the snow. I snorted—the Wallers didn't have a helicopter.

I climbed inside the cabin and sat next to Elle. She pulled out a bottle of champagne from beside the seat and offered me a glass. With a shrug I held out a hand. I stared out the window and focused on placing James back in his confined space at the back of my mind. Sharing so much of myself with him was dangerous. It was harder than I expected; he liked sharing my space.

The helicopter lifted into the air. We passed over the mountains and the citadel which looked even bigger from above. The shimmering wall that surrounded the city loomed in front of us but the helicopter passed straight through. I glanced at Kilian. His lips were quirked, as though daring me to question how we'd passed through the wall. I said nothing.

A second bottle of champagne and a basket of food were emptied by the time the helicopter landed. I stepped out, my eyes drawn to a giant Ferris Wheel. The carriages groaned as they were rocked by the wind. I spotted other rides and lines of abandoned stalls. It was an amusement park. It looked as though it had been built decades ago, but it appeared untouched, like it was waiting for its grand opening. Nothing was rusted or rotted. I puzzled over the bronze glow surrounding every construction.

Kilian spoke from beside me. 'It opened over fifty years ago. The day after opening, a kid died on the rollercoaster.' He pointed to rollercoaster tracks that wound through the park. 'His mother was a Caster.' I frowned and he explained. 'A Caster can curse objects. In this case she was a Superior Caster. She could curse both living and non-living things. She cursed the amusement park and its owner. He died of some disease and the amusement park never opened again. Every time someone tried to re-open it, something went wrong. It's remained in a time vortex, never aging or decaying.'

'Why didn't she destroy the place?'

'Some say it was the last place her son ever found joy so she let it stay frozen in time. Others say it was an accident.'

Someone turned on the power and the place lit up. The rides powered up and carnival music played over the speakers. Kilian pointed to a guy in a hoodie, who sat playing on his phone. 'He can nullify curses. As long as he's with us, nothing will go wrong.'

Someone called Kilian's name, and he left me staring at

the illuminated wonderland. The Ferris Wheel turned at a slow pace. I hopped into a carriage as it passed along the ground and was surprised when Elle joined me, sitting on the opposite bench seat. A squeal from below drew our attention to one of the rides. It looked like a spinning top. One of the girls clung to Kilian's side with her eyes clenched shut as it spun.

'He likes you,' Elle said. 'Other than me, Kilian doesn't really like anyone.'

'Aren't these people his friends?'

She pulled her hair out of its braid and ran her fingers through it. It shimmered in the colours of the carnival lights. 'Kilian was groomed from birth to be Lucien's successor. If you think that meant a childhood of love, affection and gentle discipline, then you're not as smart as you seem. He learned from a young age to trust very few people. Kilian may have a few rough edges but he is loyal and I love him for it.' She eyed me. 'I think I could like you, but just so you know, if you hurt him, you'll answer to me.'

Were we talking about the same person? 'Me? Hurt him? I think you've got this the wrong way around.'

Her energy flared and I hissed, grabbing my hand. A small cut ran along the webbing of my hand between my thumb and index finger.

'You cut yourself with a pair of scissors when you were six. It was deeper than it looked and took a long time to heal.' The skin healed over and our eyes met. She smiled and said, 'You hurt Kilian and I'll make you relive every injury you've ever had, both physical and psychological. I'm confident that experiencing all that pain at once could kill you, even as a self-healer. Understand?'

'I still think you have this the wrong way around, but yes, I understand.'

Her smile widened. 'Good. I don't have any girlfriends; all the girls here are vultures. I hope we can be friends.' Our carriage reached the ground and she hopped out, waving me goodbye. *Yeesh…*

I wandered through the park. One of the guys climbed the frame of the Ferris Wheel and was hanging from the base of one of the carriages. He swung down to the next carriage, and then the following, continuing down until he reached the ground. These guys were adrenalin junkies. Passing the hall of mirrors I caught my reflection and groaned at the fuzz monster staring back at me. How did Elle and the other girls look like they'd just stepped out of a salon while I looked like I'd just rolled out of bed? Maybe there was a tattoo to fix that. I finger-combed my hair, catching all the strands that had fallen from my braid and pulled it into a ponytail. Wandering over to the next stall, I stopped at the 'shoot a duck' game. I jumped behind the counter and increased the speed on the control panel until the little ducks moved back and forth at a frantic pace, then I picked up scattered pellets off of the ground and grabbed a gun from the bench. Moving back to the front of the counter, I stepped backwards until the little yellow ducks were just within shooting range. I lifted my arm and aimed—no shaking. Six times I pulled the trigger, hitting each duck in the bullseye and knocking them over. If only Bishop could see me now.

'You're a good shot.'

I lifted my wrists, exposing the tattoos, and waved them at Kilian. 'These help, but I had good teachers.' I stood the ducks back up and grabbed more pellets, handing the loaded gun to Kilian. 'Your turn.'

He eyed the moving ducks, cocked the gun and took six shots. He hit every single one. I crossed my arms.

'You've done this before.'

He smirked. 'Elle and I used to come here as kids. We'd drag Jesse, the Nullifier, along with us and sneak over the border. We came here to get away. Her parents are just as bad as mine.'

'So, you can just walk through the border?'

He seemed to know what I was thinking. 'Yes, but you can't get back in, except through guarded checkpoints—well-guarded checkpoints.'

He threw the gun over the counter and shoved his hands in the pockets of his jeans. He was less intimidating in casual clothes. We walked back to the centre of the park.

'Do you miss them?' he asked.

'Who?'

'Your family.'

'Yes.' So much, that it hurt to think of them.

'Tell me about them.'

I raised a brow. 'You really care?'

'No. But it'll help me to understand you.'

Okay, then… 'Grandma cooks the best food and gives the best hugs. Pa is over-protective but a big softy. Mum is beautiful; she smiles a lot and can be fun. She also has a mean temper and tries to run my life. My brother Levi is overbearing and a know-it-all. He never apologises with words but he'll buy his way back into my good books with ice-cream. They're all Wolf Shifters so they can be intense at times and a bit pushy.'

'And Blackwood?'

'It's a quiet town. Everyone looks out for each other… mostly.'

'It sounds peachy.'

I was pretty sure he visibly shuddered. 'Peachy?'

'Yeah, peachy. Like the whole white picket fence thing. I don't do white picket fences.'

'I suppose you'd prefer barbed wire and machine gun turrets?'

He stopped, facing me. 'The white picket fence is an illusion. People feel safe and get soft.' He stepped closer and leaned over me with the little extra height he had. 'Soft people don't last in the real world. Your pristine white picket fence gets blown to smithereens.'

'Alright Mr Downer, what's your point?'

'My point is, you're never going to find that here.'

'I know that.'

I pushed past him and climbed the steps to the roller coaster. He sat in the seat next to me and called out for one of the others to start the ride. The railcar pulled forward with a jerk, climbing the track.

'The thing is, I don't want the *white picket fence.* I just want to be free to live the life I want, and I want—' My mouth opened then closed again.

He arched a brow. 'And?'

We were alone, but still I lowered my voice. 'I want to make sure that your uncle can never hurt those who matter to me… ever.'

The railcar reached the summit of the track and paused. A corner of Kilian's mouth quirked.

'I'm sure we can work something out.'

23

THE helicopter landed just outside the shimmering wall. We passed through one of the guard towers and cars waited for us on the other side. I declined Elle's invitation to The Tower because I needed time to myself. I went back to my rooms and meditated, sitting on the balcony floor with my legs crossed.

'You've been quiet,' I said to the open air. James had been silent since Sergio's Peak. He didn't like being shoved back in his box at the back of my mind.

'You're all grown-up and planning to steal the throne without even a suggestion from me. I know when I'm not needed.'

'I don't want the throne; I just want Lucien gone. Are you sulking?'

He gave a dismissive snort. *'You keep doing what you're doing, and remember, whatever happens, always keep those blue eyes wide open.'*

I released a long breath and focused inward, closing my eyes and following the thread of my gift. It flowed differently than usual. Like water in a stream, it had altered from a steady flow to a rapid torrent. It felt different too; more solid. I'd sensed it growing over the past weeks, but this was a huge leap.

'A Syphon's ability is the ultimate gift of survival—isn't that what your dad said? Maybe today's near-death experience fast-tracked your growth spurt,' James said.

I nodded, keeping my eyes closed. 'It's possible. Maybe the spike in adrenalin or fear accelerated the growth.'

There was a noise to my left. My eyes flew open and I leapt to my feet. Blake stepped over the balcony rail.

'What are you doing here?' I asked.

She glanced around then pulled me inside, closing the balcony doors behind us.

'Do you have any idea what you're doing?' she hissed.

'What do you mean?' I asked.

Her eyes glowed and she gripped my arm. 'Of all the people you could befriend, it had to be the Clemonte heir himself!'

I released a thread of energy and wound it around her lifeline, giving it a tug. She paled, releasing my arm and I stepped towards her. 'I know what I'm doing.'

She sneered, walked over to the bar fridge and pulled out a beer. She cracked it open and emptied it in one go, throwing the bottle in the bin. She glanced up at the ceiling and shook her head.

'Do you have any idea the kind of guy he is?'

'I have a pretty good idea.'

She gave a dry laugh. 'I didn't think you were that naive but I forget that you're just a kid.'

Her condescending tone triggered my temper. I stalked across the room, shoving her in the chest. I may as well have tried pushing a concrete wall. *Freaking Dire Wolves!* Blake's ability thread weaved through her lifeline in a figure eight pattern. Dad said that visualising a common object could help me to manipulate my gift. I pictured a needle, shaping my energy into a sharp point. I picked and prodded the thread of Blake's gift until it loosened, then pulled it, leaving the others behind. It began to unravel and I tugged harder. Blake's eyes grew wide and the glow in them dulled. *I did it, I actually did it.*

I shoved her again and she hit the wall with a thud. Clenching my eyes shut, I cut off the flow of energy. My emotions blew sky-high with all the Dire Wolf energy. I focused on calming the rage because I didn't want to shift. That could get ugly. I breathed in through my nose and exhaled slowly.

When I'd calmed down, I glared at her. 'You need to leave.'

Her lips thinned into a stubborn line. 'No. You think you know how to play this game, but you don't. These people are cold-hearted devils. They'll eat you alive.'

'You said yourself that I was a *savage, reckless girl.* You said my kind are dangerous and unpredictable. Sounds to me like I'll fit in just fine.'

'I don't know you, but I know you're not like them. Not yet, anyway. We need to get you out of here.'

I took a step back. 'I don't want to leave. If Aurore is so bad then why are you here?'

'Because someone needs to watch what goes on in this place. Lucien is cunning. He's a risk that needs to be monitored.'

'You're a spy?'

Her eyes flashed. 'Say anything to Kilian, or anyone, and I'll rip your throat out.'

'Why are all Shifter Wolves obsessed with throat ripping? It's your business, not mine, but I'm staying here.'

She paced the room. 'You're a complication I don't need. The whole Dire Wolf population holds me responsible for you.'

'I'm responsible for myself. I told Beau we're over when I met him in the dreamscape. I… I told him he wasn't enough for me anymore. It's only a matter of time before the bond fades, so you're off the hook.'

'Yet you still wear the family crest.'

I clutched the pendant in my fist. 'I'm just keeping it safe until I can post it back to him.'

She snorted. 'Trust me, it's not over. Beau Sinclair is ten times the man Kilian Clemonte will ever be. He's—'

A knock on the door stopped her mid-sentence. Our eyes met and she gave a warning glare before darting into the bedroom. She disappeared just as the door opened. The maid stood in the doorway and subtly scanned the room.

'The master awaits you, Miss. He's asked that you dress appropriately for the evening meal. I believe his words were 'no denim'.'

I glanced at the bedroom then turned back to the maid. 'Um. What exactly is appropriate dress?'

She waved a hand inside. I stepped back and she passed me, heading straight for the bedroom. I gritted my teeth as she looked around the room. Her eyes narrowed on something and my chest tightened. If Blake was found in my room people would question why she was there. Questions would get us both into trouble. I stepped in behind the maid and my body relaxed. She was scowling at the mess of clothes on the floor. The balcony doors were left slightly ajar.

The maid rummaged through the wardrobe and picked out a dress and heels. They weren't ones that I'd purchased. The dress was dark green. It had a high neckline and when I slipped it on, it hugged all the flattering parts. The heels were too high, so I swapped them for a shorter pair that I could walk in without breaking an ankle. The maid grimaced as I finger-brushed my hair. She ushered me into the bathroom and pulled out a set of curling tongs from one of the drawers. I hadn't even known they were there. She curled my hair in soft waves, then left me to do my makeup. I kept it light; mascara, a touch of eyeshadow and lipstick. I didn't know how to do anything else. I picked up Beau's pendant sitting to the side of the sink, rubbing my thumb over the lion rampant, then placed it over my head, tucking it into the neckline of the dress.

The dining hall contained a single long table that ran down the middle of the room. Lucien sat at the head of the table. The Aegis sat by his side and scowled when she saw me. Her shield surrounded him alone in a thick impenetrable barrier. He still didn't trust me enough to drop the shield. *Pity.* Or maybe he just didn't trust anyone. One of the servants crouched near the throne, sweeping up a pile of ash. I shivered. *Just keep walking, Freya.*

Kilian sat beside the Aegis, with Elle on his other side. Elle winked at me and mouthed that she loved the dress. I felt someone else's gaze. The Telepath who'd tried to read my mind sat next to Elle and glowered at me. She pulled her gaze away from me and faced Elle.

'Elle, would you please swap seats with Kilian. I'd like to speak with my son.'

Elle wiggled her brows at me, then ushered Kilian into her seat.

'Ahhh, your new boyfriend's mother. My instincts tell me she doesn't approve of you.'

'Of course, she has to be his mother. And he's not my boyfriend.' Now that I studied her, I could see the resemblance.

'The way he's watching you says he wants to be.'

Kilian wore his usual signature smirk. *'That's just his face, James.'*

'Uh-uh. He saves that particular leer for you.'

I turned my attention to Lucien. He watched me the way a predator stalks its prey. He gestured to the seat beside him. I glanced at the space beside the chair where the ash had been swept away. My stomach turned sour.

'So, Freya, you've been making friends,' Lucien said. He turned to Kilian. 'My nephew is not normally so hospitable.' Something more than curiosity lined his words.

Kilian tapped a finger on the table, his expression giving away nothing. He played the part of a bored, spoiled royal flawlessly.

'I find her entertaining.'

Lucien turned his black eyes back on me. 'And whilst amusing my nephew, have you enjoyed my hospitality?'

'Yes, I have.' A foot brushed mine under the table. I met Elle's warning gaze. 'Ah, yes thank you... sir.'

Plates of food were placed on the table. Lucien took the first bite and then everyone reached for their cutlery.

The way the Aegis stabbed at the meat on her plate while glaring at me, made me wonder if she was imagining that piece of steak as my face. There were five courses brought to the table. By the third course, the Aegis had shifted her attention to Lucien. As she ate, I studied her shield of energy. The threads were woven together in a tight weave, making the barrier impassable. But like my confrontation with Blake, I could now see the pattern in the weave. My ability to see threads had magnified—this was a part of the change I'd sensed in my power.

I sent a thread towards the barrier. It was a complicated weave. I shaped my energy into a needle-like strand and prodded the shield. I picked at different threads and froze, my skin tingling, as one of the threads loosened. I let it go and glanced around the table.

Kilian was watching me.

He sipped his drink, his diamond cufflinks glittering in the candlelight. I caught the slight twitch of his mouth before he turned to his cousin. My shoulders relaxed and I jabbed the peas on the plate with my fork. The plates from the last course were taken away and Lucien stood. Everyone followed his example and stayed standing until he left the room followed by Kilian, the Aegis and his guardians. They entered a single door at the far end of the dining hall and when it clicked shut, everyone sat back down or moved down the table to mingle. I was left sitting alone so when I caught sight of Elle across the room I moved in her direction. Kilian's mother, the Telepath, appeared in front of me.

'Stay away from my son,' she warned. A fake smile was etched on her face as she glanced around the room. She leaned in close to my ear. 'He'll use you and when he's finished, you'll be nothing but a shell of your former self.'

I pulled back to study her face. 'Do you think I'm a threat to Kilian?'

She laughed. 'You're no threat to Kilian or anyone in this family. We'll crush you.'

I studied her energy. Her lifeline pulsed erratically; she was nervous. 'If I'm no threat then why are you warning me to stay away?'

She stepped closer. 'Because you're not the first girl with great aspirations to fall at my son's feet. I'd rather not deal with the mess he leaves trailing behind him.'

'No, that's not it. I make you nervous. Is it my gift?' Her eyes darted to the door at the end of the room, where Kilian had disappeared. I tucked a loose strand of hair behind my ear and her gaze was drawn to one of the tattoos on my wrist. Her jaw tightened and I knew. 'It's Kilian's tattoos, isn't it? Specifically, the one on his neck.'

Her face paled. She glanced at the people around us, then back at me and whispered, 'I did what I had to do to keep my son safe. If Kilian knows…' She took a shuddering breath and continued, 'If Lucien becomes aware that Kilian knows about the tattoos, it won't end well for either of you. I'll only warn you once – if you value your life, stay away from my son.' She pushed past me.

Elle found me moments after and handed me a glass of

wine. 'You faced the dragon and lived to tell the tale. Well done,' she said.

'Your family is screwed up.'

'Yep.'

A commotion drew our attention as two men were dragged through the dining hall. They seemed paralysed, their eyes vacant as they were pulled across the floor by two of Lucien's guardians. They entered the far door and it slammed shut behind them.

I turned to Elle and she shrugged, waving at a waiter for another glass of wine. I stared down at my half-empty glass and jumped as someone cleared their throat behind me. One of the Mundane serving staff stood behind me and motioned to the door.

'King Lucien has requested that you join him downstairs.'

Elle grimaced and reached for my hand, giving it a squeeze. I followed the servant to the door at the back of the room. It opened to a set of stairs that descended two floors below. This floor hadn't been renovated and the stone walls glistened with damp. My heart thumped in my chest as I was led down a dark hallway. The servant opened a heavy, wooden door and motioned for me to walk through to a room that had no windows. Lucien's guardians stood around the room. Not a single one of them moved or said a word. Kilian stood to Lucien's side. Heavy chains and medieval instruments lined the walls. There were blood stains on the floor and the stale metallic smell of blood tainted the air.

It was a torture chamber.

Lucien stood over the two men. They were on their knees with their heads bowed. One of the guardians clicked his fingers and they lifted their heads. Their eyes cleared. They glanced around the room and began to shake, begging Lucien for mercy. Lucien lifted a hand and they fell silent. He faced me.

'Ah, Freya. I thought this would be an opportunity to show you the inner workings of my city.' He walked a slow circle around the men. 'To give the people of this city the best, and to keep them safe, occasionally we must get our hands a little dirty.'

He gestured to Kilian's mother. She pulled away from her dark corner against the wall, and gave me a warning glare as she crouched in front of the first man. She turned her attention to him and her energy flared. The man groaned. His body shuddered then stilled.

'You're right, Lucien. They've been spilling secrets to her people,' Kilian's mother said. She looked at me. 'They're somewhere close by, or at least they were. The young Telepath must be shielding their minds from me.'

My heart pounded. They'd found me. They'd found Aurore.

She moved to the second man and crouched before him. His jaw was rigid and his fists clenched at his side. She gazed into his eyes and he flinched. Sweat beaded on his brow.

She tsked. 'Blocking me is only going to hurt more.'

Her energy glowed bright and he let out a blood curdling scream, falling to the floor. His body writhed and his eyes rolled into the back of his head. I mentally thanked Jonah for the mental lock he'd placed on my mind. She stood and smoothed her dress, shaking her head at the man on the floor.

'These men have met with two of her people. I'm assuming there are more. One of them, a Dire Wolf, is particularly determined. Her boyfriend I think. He *persuaded* them to answer his questions—rather forcefully.'

I glanced at Lucien. He held my gaze until one of his guardians said, 'Let me have these two, please master.' It was the guardian who drew power from other people's pain. Anticipation filled her eyes as she stared at the quivering forms on the stone floor.

'Not today,' Lucien said, causing her to pout.

He nodded to Kilian. Kilian unfolded his arms and moved in front of the men. He tilted his head to the side and the tattoo around his throat glowed. Both men screamed. The emptiness engulfed them like a dark cloud. He took something from them—permanently. Their lifelines were transparent as the dark cloud faded, as though only a shadow of their soul remained. They screamed for a quick death as they were dragged from the room. I concentrated on keeping my breathing steady as the door slammed behind them, their screams echoing down the hallway. I turned back to Kilian, my eyes wide. He seemed unaffected. Lucien chuckled.

'My heir is rather marvellous, isn't he?' he said.

My tongue was stuck to the roof of my mouth, so I nodded.

'After a day in their cells, those men will find a way to kill themselves. No one lasts long after Kilian has taken from them.'

'Why?' I asked. 'Why not just kill them?'

Lucien's brow twitched. 'Because from the dungeon their screams will echo through the citadel, reminding everyone of the fate that awaits them if they betray me. It's rather effective.' A servant handed him his jacket and he shrugged it over his shoulders. 'Your boyfriend, the Dire Wolf, is he going to be a problem?' he asked.

'No, he was never actually my boyfriend,' I stated.

'I see. Then you agree to his disposal if required?'

'He's baiting you,' James warned.

I resisted the urge to grab the pendant around my neck. My hands clenched into fists by my side. 'Do what you have to.'

The corner of his mouth curved. 'You're full of surprises. Now, you may go.'

I focused on one step at a time and reached the door, turning the handle with a clammy hand. His voice stopped me.

'Don't go too far. I may have need of you soon.'

'Yes, Sir.'

'And Freya?'

I hesitated and turned back to him. 'Yes?'

'You will refer to me as King or Master, is that clear?'

I clenched my teeth, picturing his horrified face as I drained the life from his body. 'Yes… my king.'

24

I went straight to the underground garage. Elle called out to me as I stormed through the ballroom, but I ignored her. The yellow sports car sat where I left it, and I dropped into the driver's seat, slamming the door shut and resting my head against the steering wheel. I was in way over my head.

'Lucien likes you. You'll be fine,' James said.

'He killed most of his siblings, James. I doubt that liking me actually matters. If he so much as gives Beau a papercut, I'll break him in half!'

'And the over-dramatic teenager has returned… What happened to stone-cold Freya?'

'Can you stay out of my head for five minutes!' I screeched, flailing my hands in frustration.

The engine roared to life and I planted my foot on the accelerator. The lights faded as I drove past the city centre towards the outskirts. I reached the open road and pushed the pedal to the floor until the trees became a passing blur and I could finally breathe. A sharp turn and the shimmering wall was up ahead. What or who created it? My hands clutched the steering wheel as I turned another corner. The road was slippery with melting snow. There was a flash of light in my peripheral and I glanced to my side. Tom sat in the passenger's seat.

'Tom?'

Tom pointed to the windscreen. 'WATCH OU—'

Everything happened in slow motion. I snapped my attention back to the road just as we reached a bend. The car veered over the white lines towards a grove of trees. I tried to correct the steering but I was driving too fast and the road was slippery. A fallen tree appeared in front of us and the car slammed into it.

My vision went black.

I was lying on the ground, the stone floor cold beneath me. I sat up with a groan, clenching my eyes shut. My neck had never ached like this before—my whole body had never ached like this before. I forced my eyes open, blinking repeatedly to focus as I rubbed my neck. At first glance I thought I sat in one of the halls at the citadel, but instead of stone, the walls were softened by panels of wood. Moonlight shone through large stained-glass windows. My legs shook as I pulled myself to my feet. It felt like I'd just been through a three-hour workout session with Bishop.

The sound of voices drew me from the room into a hallway. I entered a large living room. Old leather lounges surrounded a fireplace. Beau stood in front of the fireplace arguing with an older man. Neither of them noticed me. I called Beau's name and waved my hands to get his attention but it was like I wasn't there.

'You can't just run in there like a thirty-year old hot-headed pup. She's safe for now; we need to come up with a better strategy,' the older man said. He was as big as Beau. His golden-brown hair was beginning to grey. He stood in a wide stance with his arms crossed, the same way Beau stood when he was being stubborn.

Beau paced back and forth. 'I'm not leaving her there, Da. You heard Blake's report. She's being drawn into their web of games and it's going to get her killed.' He ran both hands through his hair and clutched the back of his head. 'If you won't help me, I'll go by myself.'

'No!' I cried. I reached for his arm but it fell straight through, like I was a ghost. I stared at my hands, confused. This wasn't the dreamscape, so what was it?

Jonah appeared in the doorway. I gaped as he was followed by Levi and Reagan. Reagan held one of my jumpers: Dad's jumper. Her eyes were wide with worry.

'Sorry to interrupt, but I needed to tell you...' She swallowed and clutched the jumper in her hands. 'I had a vision of Freya standing over a woman. She looked... she was a bit crazed. She drew the woman's energy and then my vision jumped forward. Someone is angry; it's this Lucien guy, I think. They're in a large crowded room and he's giving Freya some kind of ultimatum.' Reagan's face paled and a tear slid down her cheek. She took a deep breath. 'My visions give me multiple possibilities, so I know that it might not happen... but in one of the possible futures, Freya is different—altered. She kills everyone in that room and harnesses the energy for herself. After that scenario my vision went dark.' The room fell silent except for the sound of the crackling fire.

Beau stood motionless staring at Reagan. She looked at him. 'We have to get her back,' she whispered.

Beau pulled Reagan into a hug and I tensed at the contact. 'We'll get her back, Reags, even if I have to go by myself,' he said.

'We're all going after Freya. You're not going alone,' Levi said, moving to Beau's side. 'Whatever the visions mean, I'll talk sense into her. She listens to me… sometimes.'

I fell into one of the leather lounges, my heart heavy in my chest. I could kill everyone? I thought back to the book I'd read in Mr Waller's study all those months ago. One of his ancestors had questioned whether all Syphons would go insane. Maybe he was right.

'I'm a monster,' I whispered.

Beau turned me. He studied the area where I was sitting, moving forward until he stood right in front of me.

'She's here,' he said.

'What do you mean she's here?' Levi asked.

His eyes narrowed. 'Her presence is here, in this room.'

'It must be something to do with your bond,' Jonah said.

Beau moved to the lounge where I was sitting and his nostrils flared. 'Put me to sleep,' he said, sitting in the armchair next to me. Jonah nodded and Beau's eyes closed. His body relaxed.

No, no, no.

I raced to the fireplace, placing my arm in the fire. I hissed in pain as the flames licked my skin. I didn't wake this time. Something was keeping me asleep.

'Come on, Jonah, let me wake up.'

The people around me disappeared as Beau opened his eyes. They zoned in on me. It was just us in the room now. I only blinked and he was in front of me, pulling my arm from the fire.

'Don't,' he growled. He held both of my hands in one of his. I couldn't pull them from his grasp.

'You heard what Reagan said, Beau. Do you really want me?'

'It's only one possible future, Freya. Get rid of the parasite in your head and it might not even be a possibility.'

I laughed. 'You know what, I used to blame James. But I'm not so certain he's the problem anymore.'

'If you needed to kill a room of murderous people to survive, then so be it, I get it.' He released my hands, touching the back of my head. His jaw grew rigid as he pulled his hand away. It was covered in blood.

'Who did this to you?'

I touched the back of my head and thought back to the moments before I woke up in the strange castle.

The car—Tom—fast-moving trees—darkness.

'No one did this to me, it's my own fault. I crashed the car. Tom surprised me and I kind of froze.'

I patted down my body and flinched as I brushed a spot near my left hip. My hand was covered in sticky dark blood. Beau's eyes glowed bright gold as he ripped open the patch of my dress revealing the oozing wound. Sharp canines protruded from his mouth and the tips of his fingers grew into claws. I'd seen Beau do this in another one of my non-dreams. The partial shifting was new to me; the shifting process was usually instantaneous.

'Calm down, Beau, I'll heal. It's fine,' I said, trying to soothe him.

'It's not fine! I'm going to kill Tom.'

His voice was changing. It grew deeper and gravelly. He turned away from me and growled, punching the mantle above the fireplace. Pieces of stone crumbled to the floor and he punched it again.

'Beau, calm down.' He continued punching it until his knuckles bled. 'Beau!'

I gripped his arm and he stopped, heaving in deep breaths. I stepped in front of him and grabbed his face, turning it until he met my eyes. 'I'll be fine, Beau. This isn't Tom's fault. He couldn't have known I'd react to his astral form like that.'

His breathing calmed as we stared at each other. The canines retracted and his claws turned back into normal fingernails, but his eyes still glowed.

His nostrils flared. 'I can smell him on you. It's the Clemonte heir, isn't it? The one you've been hanging around with.'

I stiffened and pulled my hands away. 'I needed allies and Kilian offered, so of course I'm hanging around him.'

A deep growl rumbled in Beau's chest. 'I doubt he sees you as just an ally.'

'What does it matter! I've told you that I want to stay here. I didn't ask you to come and save me, so don't!'

He stepped forward, his eyes searching mine. He stared at my chest and reached forward, pulling the pendant from beneath my dress. It seemed smaller sitting in his palm. He closed his fingers over the family crest then looked up at me. My pulse raced at the look in his eyes. I resisted the urge to look away.

'When I stayed away, thinking the bond would weaken, I thought I was doing the right thing. I'd come back when it had faded and we could date like normal people. But then you sent that message ending things between us and I realised I didn't want the bond to fade. I wanted to tie you to me.' He leaned closer, so our noses almost touched. 'I know you're trying to protect me but it's not going to work, Freya. I need you, just as much as you need me.' He dropped the pendant and tucked a lock of hair behind my ear. His eyes raked over me. 'The dress suits you.'

The dress had been nicer when it wasn't torn and covered in blood. 'Jeans weren't formal enough, apparently.'

He grinned and my heart melted. That smile still dazzled me and he knew it. Why couldn't he just give up and leave me alone? He lifted his hands, holding my face in his palms and waited, gazing into my eyes as though asking for permission to kiss me—as if I could ever say no. Our lips met. Any determination I had left to push him away and end this thing between us faded. I leaned into him, wrapping my arms around his neck. His radiating warmth and the smell of sandalwood, forest and Beau, felt like home. There was an awkward cough from across the room and I pulled away. The backs of my knees met one of the chairs and I fell into it with a strangled squawk.

'So, I guess you guys have worked stuff out?' Jonah leaned against the doorframe.

'What are you doing here? I thought this was our dreamscape,' I said, pointing between Beau and me.

He smirked. 'It is. I'm just crashing the party. Sorry if I interrupted.'

A blush crept up my neck and into my face. 'It's fine. We were just… um… talking.' I tucked a strand of hair behind my ear and looked at Beau. He seemed pretty pleased with himself.

Jonah cringed and stared at anything but my face. 'Righto.'

'How are you here?'

'We needed a way to communicate with you as Aurore is protected by some kind of ward. I can access Beau's consciousness while asleep and therefore meet you in the dreamscape.' He looked me up and down. 'Uncle Tom said you were in an accident. He had to leave before you crashed because some injuries can transfer to his physical body, some kind of psychological thing. You look like hell.'

'Thanks. That pretty much sums up how my body feels right now.'

Beau stiffened at the mention of Tom. I grabbed his hand and shook my head. His nose twitched like he was trying not to snarl. I turned back to Jonah.

'I saw you guys before, but you couldn't see me. I've had the same kind of dream before.'

'Like the dreamscape, it's not technically a dream. Your consciousness seeks Beau's even when he's not asleep. That's why you've come here, to Beau's family home. The only reason he can't do the same with you is either because of the mental lock I've placed on you, or the ward surrounding Aurore. You can leave the ward, but he can't enter through it.'

'That ward covers the entire city. People can leave, but you can't enter, except through a gate that is heavily guarded.

Jonah nodded. 'We're working out how to get through it.'

'You can't get through it,' I ground out.

They both shrugged.

'You need to come home. Reagan's been a pain in the neck without you around,' Jonah said.

'Reagan's powers have grown, haven't they?' I asked.

'Yes. She gets visions just by touching someone's belongings.'

That's why she had Dad's jumper. I wasn't the only one whose abilities were changing. I looked around the room where we stood. 'Where is your family home? This place looks as ancient as the citadel in Aurore.'

'We're in the Scottish Highlands,' Beau said. 'This place is far away enough to stay off Lucien's radar.'

'You're already on his radar,' I warned. 'Lucien knows about you. He knows you've been looking for Aurore.' I faced Jonah. 'Lucien didn't take me as payback for Argyle's death. He's doing it to get to your family. Kilian told me that your great-great grandmother was a Clemonte.' Beau clamped a hand on my arm at the mention of Kilian's name. 'She ran away from the family a couple of centuries ago and they've been searching for her branch of the family ever since.'

Jonah frowned. 'I've never heard the name Clemonte.'

'Does Rosa Gonzales sound familiar? She changed her name when she cut ties with the family.'

Jonah's frown deepened. 'I recognise the name from our family tree.

She was my great-great-grandmother. How does Lucien know the connection?'

'Kilian's mother is a Telepath like you. She sensed you when you first came into your power. Kilian says that Lucien is threatened by you, not only because you hold Clemonte power, but because it's been mixed with something he called 'old magic'.' Jonah's eyes darkened at the mention of old magic. 'So, you see, this isn't about me, it's about you. I'm just the bait.'

He shrugged. 'It doesn't matter, we're going to sneak you out anyway.'

I ran a hand down my face. 'Don't you get it! They'll kill all of you! You underestimate these guys. It's better if you just leave me here.'

Beau stepped in front of me. 'We're not leaving you.'

'You have to! It's best for everyone.'

'Best for everyone? We're bonded, Freya? I'm not leaving you. When I get my hands on you, I'm never letting go.'

'The bond is new, it will fade,' I argued and Beau's posture stiffened. 'I've got a plan, alright? I'll be fine here.'

'If this has something to do with Kilian Clemonte, then you can forget it,' Beau said through clenched teeth.

'Yes, it does have something to do with him. I'm going to get rid of Lucien and he's going to help me.'

Jonah stepped forward. 'Are you insane? What makes Kilian any different from Lucien?'

I pointed to myself. 'I can keep Kilian in line. If I can't keep him in line, then I'll deal with him and run Aurore myself if I have to.'

They looked at me like I'd grown a second head. Jonah waved his hands in my face.

'Are you listening to yourself? It's James giving you these ideas, isn't it?'

'No, actually. It was my idea. When will you understand that I don't belong in Blackwood?'

Beau stepped forward. 'Your crazy idea is exactly why you belong in Blackwood, where we can talk sense into you.'

I shook my head. 'It doesn't matter. The minute Lucien notices I'm gone, he'll come for the whole town. He loves to make an example.'

Jonah's head snapped to the side. His brows furrowed and he turned to me. 'Uncle Tom says you need to wake up, Freya. It's urgent.'

'I've already tried.'

'Your body was in bad shape then and needed the sleep to heal. You need to wake up now.'

I moved to the fire and Beau stopped me. He searched my eyes and leaned in close. His alpha energy flared and persuasion lined his words. 'I'll see you soon.'

Flames engulfed my arm. I flinched in pain and the room disappeared.

25

THE ground beneath me was as cold as ice. I was in a sitting position. My eyes were heavy and refused to open. A few extra minutes of sleep couldn't hurt.

'Wake up, Freya! You need to wake up.'

My vision was blurry. I blinked until the fuzzy black and white picture came in to focus. There was snow, mud and dead trees. I was outside and freezing my butt off.

I attempted to move, groaning as pain radiated through my body. My bones felt like razorblades cutting into my flesh every time I moved. I blinked again, taking in my surroundings.

'You have to get up, Freya!'

I squinted up at the glowing form. 'Tom?'

He crouched so we were at eye level, looking around then back at me. 'I'm sorry I can't help in this form. You're going to need to pull yourself off.'

'Pull myself off what?'

He grimaced, pointing to my stomach. I looked down and hissed. A branch protruded from my abdomen, just above my left hip. I panted, clenching my eyes shut. When I managed to calm myself, I forced them open and looked to the side. My body was propped against a tree trunk. The remains of the car smoked in the distance. It looked as though I'd been thrown through the windscreen.

'I've been with you for a while. When I got here your entire body was crushed. Your skull was shattered. From what I can tell you hit the pine tree behind you, then fell on this trunk, impaling yourself.'

I tried to move forward, hissing in pain. Things weren't looking great. I sat in a pool of blood and melting snow.

'How am I going to do this?'

Tom looked around. 'There's nothing useful within

reaching distance and the branch is too thick to snap.'

I leaned my head against the tree trunk and closed my eyes, trying not to focus on the pain. 'That was you that night at The Tower, wasn't it? I sensed a familiar energy, but you moved too fast.'

'Yeah, that was me. Once I knew you were there and you were okay, I had to get out before someone else sensed me.'

The sound of an engine drew our attention. Headlights flashed and tires screeched as a car pulled to a halt. I squinted through the glare of the headlights and tried to make out the figure approaching the remains of the sportscar.

'Over here!' I yelled.

Footsteps crunched in the snow and dirt. The figure walked straight through Tom's astral form.

'Great, it's you.' I stared up at Blake.

'What the hell happened?'

'I would think it's pretty obvious.' I grimaced as my muscles tensed around the branch.

She shook her head. 'You have no sense of self-preservation.'

'I got distracted.'

She grabbed the end of the branch with one of her hands and using her Dire Wolf strength, snapped it so that there was only a small piece protruding from my stomach. I shrieked at the jerky movement. She dropped the branch and cursed, rubbing the blood from her hands against her jeans.

'Right, let's get this done.' She held out her hands. I looked at Tom and he nodded.

Releasing a shuddering breath, I held out my hands. 'Okay, can we do this at the count of three?'

She grabbed my hands. 'Three.'

I was yanked to my feet in one swift movement. The sensation of having my insides ripped out made me scream and I fell to my hands and knees in the snow. The pain was so sharp I wanted to vomit. My breathing slowed as the wound began to heal. I sat back on my knees and a jacket was placed over my shoulders.

'How did you know I was here?' I asked.

'Beau, of course. He demanded that I drop everything and come find you.'

'Well, thanks.'

She sniffed and went back to the car, grabbing her phone. When she'd finished a call, I was able to stand. Astral Tom stared at me through creased brows.

'What? Am I missing a body part or something?'

He shook his head. 'No, but now that you're okay, there's something you need to see. Ask your friend for a torch.'

I walked over to Blake and did as Tom asked. She handed me the torch from the car's emergency kit. 'What's this for?'

'I'm not sure yet.' I turned to Tom. 'Can I tell her?'

He glanced behind me. 'Can we trust her?'

'I don't like her, but yeah I think we can trust her.' I gestured to the spot where Tom stood. 'There's a guy called Tom standing there. His gift is Astral Projection. I can see and hear his Astral form because it's made from energy. He's here to help.'

Blake stared at the blank space. 'Why does he want the torch?'

Tom turned to me. 'Shine the torch in the trees around the trunk where you landed.'

I approached the patch of red snow and grimaced at the sight of the bloodied branch. I flashed the torchlight up into the trees.

'What am I looking for? All I see is a dead tree.' The tree trunk was grey with age; it had shed its last leaf decades ago.

'Look at the other trees.'

I flashed the torch from one tree to the next. They were all dead. A bad feeling settled in my stomach as I walked further into the grove. Finally, I caught a flash of green. I stopped in front of the living pine and looked back along the trail I'd walked. The headlights of Blake's car were barely visible this far into the forest.

'You drained the life from every living thing in a one-hundred-metre radius. I saw a few dead deer over by the river,' Tom said, pointing towards the sound of rushing water.

'One hundred metres?' I squeaked.

'What's one hundred metres?' Blake asked, following my gaze to the blank space where Tom stood.

'Tom said I drained the life from every living thing in a one-hundred-metre radius. My body must have pulled the energy to heal itself.' Moving in the direction of the river, I searched until I found the deer. I stumbled across the baby deer first, its lifeless eyes wide open in horror.

Tom approached my side. 'Although it's a sad waste of life, it's a good thing it happened.'

'How is this a good thing?' I hissed, pointing to the deer.

'You needed to find out that your body would respond in this way. Your gift takes over when you're unconscious. Imagine if this had happened in a place full of people.'

A cold shiver ran through my body. 'This is yet another reason why I can't go back to Blackwood.'

I stared at the innocent baby deer and imagined it being replaced by one of my friends or family. Blake nudged the carcass with her shoe.

'Stop sulking. It's not that bad. Just don't pass out next time,' she said.

Tom cleared his throat. 'Now that you're healed, I need to go. I don't trust my nephews and niece to make rational choices. Beau and Levi are even less trustworthy now that they're buddies.'

'Buddies? Beau and Levi?'

Tom vanished before I got any answers. He must've been joking. My brother and Beau just didn't mix. It was getting light when a couple of silver SUVs pulled up on the side of the road. Blake and I stood in front of the smouldering wreck of the yellow sportscar.

A car door opened and Tank appeared.

I glared at Blake. 'Why did you call *him*?'

She motioned to the carnage around us. With the sun beginning to rise, it was now visible in the morning light. 'Did you think something like this would go unnoticed? Don't worry, Tank is on our side.'

'Is Tank a spy too?'

'My role is complicated,' Tank said as he drew close, surveying the damage. 'You're like a grenade, aren't you? Little package, big boom.'

'I'm not little. Aren't you worried I'll tell Kilian the truth about you both?'

Blake smirked. 'You won't tell. We're the ones helping to get you out of here. If Beau and your friends come here, there will be a showdown, and at this point in time, it's not certain who will win. It's better for everyone if you leave town.'

'And then Lucien will come for Blackwood. How is that a good idea?' I argued.

Tank picked up a twisted piece of metal from the wreck of the car and tsked. 'Such a waste of a good engine.' He faced me. 'The fight was always going to end up in Blackwood. It's the only way Lucien can eliminate the threat that the Monroes and the rest of Blackwood now pose to him. Don't worry, you've got some smart friends who know what they're doing.'

I narrowed my eyes. 'How do you know that?'

'I have my sources.' He pulled out his phone as I gave the burnt-out car a final pat. I heard him say Kilian's name and my mouth dropped open.

'You called Kilian? Why don't we just announce my accident to the entire city.'

He shoved the phone in his jacket and motioned to the dead forest. It looked worse as the sky lightened. 'He needs to see this. He needs to know you're not easily expendable.'

'Why do you care?'

He grunted and joined Blake who waited for him by her car. They spoke in hushed voices while I inspected my dress. I hugged the loaned jacket over the ruined green fabric and watched my breath turn to steam in the morning air. My stomach grumbled.

'I know you guys are busy plotting, but do either of you have any snacks? It's kind of urgent.'

26

KILIAN'S knuckles were white as they clutched the steering wheel. After witnessing the burnt-out car, the dead forest and the rather large blood stain in the snow, he'd had a few words with Tank and ushered me into his car. He'd been silent ever since. I moved between tapping the window-ledge and eyeing his brooding form. He was tense, his brows creased in thought.

'Am I in trouble?'

His lips thinned. 'No. People write off cars all the time. There'll be a replacement within a week. We can get you a different colour if you want.'

'I don't care about the car.'

'Then what's the issue?'

I looked him up and down. 'You. You're all… quiet.'

His jaw twitched and he focused back on the road. We reached the gates of the citadel and he stopped, twisting in his seat to face me. 'For you and I to overthrow Lucien, I require full use of my abilities. You are likely the only one who can work out how to fix me, and yet you're finding creative ways to test your near-immortality. If you're that determined to die, can it wait until after I rule Aurore?'

I snorted. 'That's what you're worried about? I didn't do it on purpose.'

He turned his attention back to driving and we entered the tunnel leading to the underground garage. 'I'd prefer it if you let me drive you from now on. You need supervision.'

'Not a chance. Even when you run this place, you don't get to rule my life. If you can't comprehend that in the entitled little brain of yours, then I'm out.' Yes, I was being snappy, but it had been a rough night.

He smirked. 'Entitled little brain? That's a new one. Besides I won't rule your life, you'll rule Aurore beside me.'

'And how is that going to work? How do I know you won't turn on me once this is finished?'

He arched a brow. 'You haven't figured this out yet? I'm offering you the position of Queen, so you'll have power almost equal to mine.'

I blinked. *Queen?*

James's voice drowned out my rapid thoughts. *'This is perfect. You won't have to fight to stay in power if you marry into the Clemonte family.'*

'Marry? Shut up, James. I need to think...'

'What's there to think about? Forget about the Dire Wolf, he's probably figured out it's too hard to come for you by now.'

'He hasn't. He's coming here. They're all coming here.' I allowed the memories of the dreamscape to flash across my consciousness. I'd pushed them to a corner of my mind, determined to keep them to myself and it had worked.

'And you didn't think to share these with me earlier?'

'Nope.'

A dry laugh from Kilian drew my attention.

'If I asked any other girl in this place to be Queen, they'd be in a state of ecstasy, willing to do anything I ask.' He glanced at me. 'And here you are—silent. It's extraordinary.'

'What can I say, I'm overwhelmed.'

He caught my sarcastic tone and frowned. 'Are you considering saying no?'

I thought of Beau. 'I don't know.'

The car pulled to a stop and I leapt out, ending our conversation. Instead of the lift I took the stairs from the garage to avoid the awkward silence with Kilian. He didn't follow me.

I sped-walked to my rooms and closed the door, leaning my head against the hardwood. I couldn't be Kilian's *Queen.* I couldn't have Beau either, could I? I'd have a better chance of stopping a bullet train, than stopping Beau and the others from coming for me.

'It's him, isn't it?'

I snapped my head to the side. Kilian leaned against the lounge.

'What are you doing here? And how did you beat me?'

'I can go anywhere I want. But you're avoiding the question. He's the reason, am I right?'

'Who?'

'The Dire Wolf. He's the reason you're hesitating.' He pushed away from the lounge and walked around the room, studying random items and scrunching his nose.

'It doesn't matter,' I muttered. 'We're better off without each other.'

'That doesn't mean you *don't want* to be with him.' He must have read something in my expression because he raised his brows. 'Oh, please… don't tell me you *love* him?'

I would rip Kilian's heart out with my bare hands if he so much as laid a blue-blooded finger on Beau. Was that love? I blinked, surprised at myself. *That was a bit extreme.*

Kilian laughed. 'You do love him. How charming.'

My face was hot—so hot. 'It's none of your business.'

'Of course it's my business. You didn't think I'd be asking you to be Queen in name only, did you?'

There was so much heat my hair was about to catch fire. He wandered through to my room and I stalked after him, nearly colliding with his back as he turned to face me.

'I've never had to wait for anything in my life but I can wait for you to get over him. Just try to be quick about it, I don't want to waste a century waiting.' He smirked and lifted my chin with a finger, closing my gaping mouth.

I followed him out onto the balcony. 'Wait a minute! I haven't agreed to anything yet.'

He sighed. 'You will. Consider your options for a moment… ah yes, there are no other options. None that end with you having the kind of freedom you want.' Icy blue eyes pinned me. 'You might think you can get rid of me when this is over, but I'm already three steps ahead of you. It works best for both of us if we do this together.'

I placed my hands on my hips, looking out over the city. 'I don't understand why you want this. I've already agreed to be allies.'

'Elle is the only person in this world I trust. She is the only one who always has my back. I think you're another person I could trust, and I'd be stupid to let that go. Besides, together we'd be formidable. What do I need to do to convince *you* to trust me?'

I attempted to run a hand through my hair, wincing as my fingers snagged on a knot of matted hair and dried blood.

'Well… you could start by ordering some food while I take a shower. I'm starving.'

He grinned and a responding smile tugged at the corners of my mouth. I could learn to like this guy. When he smiled, I caught glimpses of the man he might've been if he'd been brought up by a nice middle-class family. Without the sense of entitlement and sociopathic tendencies, he was kind of nice.

A long shower was a good place to think through my options while washing away the blood and dirt. I washed my hair three times to get rid of the matted clump at the back of my head. I must've looked like a total wreck standing next to Kilian. When I opened the bathroom door to the smell of food, there were dishes covering every surface in the living room.

'I didn't know what you wanted, so I ordered everything,' Kilian said, waving a hand around the room.

I eyed the dishes and my stomach grumbled. 'Perfect, I wanted everything.'

I started with something that slightly resembled pizza. Sitting on the lounge next to Kilian I devoured the calories. When I picked up the lid from a dish, revealing a small mountain of pastries, I lifted a questioning brow and he shrugged.

'I remembered you liked them.'

'I never actually had the chance to eat one, remember?'

'Are you going to share?'

'Not a chance. I'm eating every single one.'

I sat the plate in my lap, turning my attention to the TV. I shoved a pastry in my mouth and groaned, quickly following up with a second and a third. Kilian and me ruling Aurore together was a lot to think about. Could I really trust him? So far, he'd been good to me; aside from the incident in the tattoo parlour. I was pretty sure he had some kind of conscience, even if it was questionable. When I'd demolished the plate, I glanced sideways.

'So… I think I know how to fix you.'

His gaze snapped to mine. 'You can do it? Yourself?'

'My gift has advanced while I've been here. I think I can detach the energy threads from the tattoos, so they're no longer attached to your consciousness. It can't hurt to try. '

He studied my face. 'Can you do it now, or do you need rest?'

I held up a finger. 'I've refuelled so I can do it now, on one condition.'

His eyes narrowed. 'Go on…'

'Should my family or friends find their way here, you and your people won't do them any harm.'

'Does this include the boyfriend?'

'He's never technically been my boyfriend, but yes.'

He gave a disappointed sigh. 'Fine.'

He stood, shrugging off his jacket and reached for the top button of his shirt. I lifted my hands.

'Please keep your clothes on. I only need to hold your hand.'

His eyes sparkled with amusement. 'I'm just getting comfortable. But you can hold my hand for as long as you like.'

I rolled my eyes as he sat back down and held out both hands. I grabbed hold of them and glared at his smirking face.

'You ready?'

His face sobered and he nodded. I relaxed, closing my eyes. I focused on my own energy and let it go, allowing it to flow into Kilian. It didn't take long for me to find the threads binding the emptiness to his consciousness. There was a distinct weave. Creating a needle-like strand of energy, I prodded and picked the first thread until it loosened. A deep breath and I pulled it. My heart leapt as it gave way. I held the strand of energy as it tried to absorb into my energy line. It was under my complete control.

I wonder…

With a mental flick away from myself, I let it go. It dissolved into nothing and the tattoo on Kilian's arm dimmed. A triumphant grin spread across my face.

'It's working,' I said.

'I can feel it. Keep going.'

I focused on the next tattoo and did the same. The weave in the threads became easier to see and I unravelled the third one with ease. I brushed against the energy of the fourth tattoo, the one on the back of his neck, and hesitated. It may have been the smallest, but it was the most complex. Multiple tiny threads attached themselves to his energy core. They didn't just bind his gift to his consciousness, but his lifeline as well. If he over-used his power, it would kill him. My heart squeezed at the thought of a mother who'd do that to her child. The weave was different to the others; it was difficult to unravel. I'd begun to sweat from the strain, when I found a weak point and it gave way. As I pulled the energy thread and let it go, Kilian slumped against the lounge.

His face and body were relaxed. I reached out and shook his arm. 'Hey, are you okay?'

He nodded but didn't open his eyes. 'I can't explain the feeling. I just feel… light.' He opened half-lidded eyes. 'Thank you.'

'Forget it.'

'I won't forget.' He looked at the lounge then did something I didn't expect—he yawned. I'd never seen him do something so basic. He grabbed one of the scattered cushions and placed it on the arm of the lounge, glancing at me. 'Unless you're volunteering to be a footrest, please move.' I stood, watching as he kicked off his shoes and stretched out. He rested his hands on his stomach and closed his eyes.

'Wait… what are you doing?'

'What does it look like?'

'You can't sleep here,' I spluttered.

He barely opened one eye. 'Why not?'

'It's my room.'

'I've not been able to sleep without medication, alcohol or supernatural assistance since I was a kid. I won't be moving from this lounge for at least twelve hours.' He reshuffled, finding a more comfortable position.

'Surely your own bed is more comfortable? I can drive you home.'

He didn't answer. Watching the steady rise and fall of his chest, I muttered a curse and grabbed a blanket from the bedroom, throwing it over his still form. With a final glance I entered my room and locked the door.

As I stared at my closed door, I hoped I'd done the right thing, but there was the frightening possibility that I'd released a monster.

27

HE slept like the dead. Every couple of hours I peeked out my door and still he didn't move a muscle. I meditated until my legs had pins and needles and I'd grown restless, then left Kilian asleep and went in search of Tank. I needed answers.

Tank wasn't one of Lucien's guardians, or the security team. Yet, he was sent to Belfield to get me. It didn't make sense. He seemed to have inside knowledge on Blackwood and I wanted to know how. Although Blake liked me about as much as a stain on a favourite pair of shoes, she was obligated to help me. Tank, however, had no connection to Blackwood and no connection to me. For all I knew, he could be telling Lucien everything.

A guard directed me across the main courtyard to a building. It was a later addition to the citadel. The stone was the same colour as the citadel, but it didn't show the same signs of age, and the windows were a different shape. I entered the building and the man behind the desk told me that Tank was unavailable. Nothing about the reception area gave anything away and I was advised to save any questions for Mr Schulz. Now, at least I knew his last name.

Kilian was still asleep when I returned so I found my way to the music room and played one of Dad's favourites. It was a sad, depressing tune, but it was the perfect tune to ponder your thoughts. When I'd first watched Dad's video diaries, I'd questioned how he could've worked with someone like Argyle; someone so power-hungry and malicious. Now I understood that sometimes a little compromise was necessary. I knew more about the Clemontes than Dad ever had and I'd agreed to work with one of them. It was the only way to keep myself and the people I loved safe. It was the only way to get out of the cage I'd been stuck in since birth. I'd do whatever I needed to, to reach the top and stay there.

My fingers tripped over the keys.

When had I become like a Clemonte, willing to step on people to get to the top?

I pulled away from the piano, kicking the stool. It screeched across the stone floor and hit the wall with a thump.

'It's the circle of life, Freya. Besides, you won't be stepping on people… more like stepping around them.'

I paced the room. 'If I keep blurring that line, I'll become as corrupt as you.'

'Clearly, I don't see that as a bad thing…'

'Without moral boundaries, I'll be like Lucien. I've been worried about Kilian, but I have the potential to be worse.' I rubbed the tight spot building in my chest and continued to pace, finally stopping at the window. Lifting my hands, I watched the energy swirling through them. I clenched them into fists and resisted the urge to throw the vase sitting on the table beside the window, instead turning my attention to the view outside. Tank's building was visible from where I stood. He played a role in all of this and I wanted to know what it was.

I left the music room, passing my own rooms. Kilian was gone. The blanket was left folded on the lounge with the pillow beside it. A note sat on the table:

After organising dinner, I expected you'd return the favour and at least organise breakfast. We need to discuss the rules of this relationship.

K.C.

I rolled my eyes and scrunched the piece of paper, throwing it in the bin.

I arrived at the outer building, only to be told that Tank was still unavailable. The receptionist simply blinked and turned away when I glared at him, so I stormed out the doors. A shaded garden bench sat close to the building. I sat down, gazing up at the two-storey, sandstone walls. Tall arched windows lined both floors. The far side of the building sat close to the citadel's outer wall and hedges lined the gap between. If anyone walked through it, they'd be blocked from the view of the guards patrolling the top of the wall. Approaching the side of building, I watched out for any guards patrolling the ground. I edged along the hedged wall, ducking past the reception room windows where I peeked into the next room and saw it was empty. The window didn't budge when I gave it a wiggle, it was locked tight. The next window and the one after were both locked. I manoeuvred my way through thorny hedges, muffling a shriek as I fell into one. Wincing, I pried myself from the thorns. I reached the final window, hoping my efforts hadn't been wasted. The panel slid open and my heart skipped a beat.

The room was dark. Most of the natural light was blocked out by the foliage of the thorny hedges. There was no sign of movement so I lifted the glass panel until it clicked into place, and hoisted myself onto the window-ledge, carefully lowering myself to the floor. The floorboards beneath my feet gave a loud groan and I clenched my teeth, waiting for the inevitable rush of footsteps but they never came. In the low light I could see that the room was an office. My palms grew clammy as I tiptoed towards the desk and turned on the lamp. A computer, notepad and penholder were the only items on the desk. The computer was password protected. I looked around the room for clues. Shelving ran along one of the walls. I tiptoed towards the shelving and stopped as I heard voices from the other side of the door. Glancing at the open window I considered leaping through it, risking the thorny hedge below. The voices grew louder. I hurried to the window and paused as the voices passed the door. They faded until I heard another door open and close. I sagged against the wall.

'Chicken.'

'I don't fancy drowning in a tank of water over and over again, thank-you-very-much, James.'

'As I said… Chicken.'

A few calming breaths later, I crossed the room, keeping an eye on the office door. There were shelves of medical and pharmaceutical books. Some books detailed neurological conditions, and others, specific groups of drugs. I grabbed a book from the highest shelf. It was well-used, with marked sections and many of the pages dog-eared. The title read *Linking the Supernatural and the Mundane: A study of genetic mutations*. As I flicked through the pages, a photograph fell to the floor. I picked it up and my breath caught.

On the left stood Argyle. His grin reminded me of Kilian's smirk. Next to him stood a much younger Dad with a goofy smile plastered across his face. He held a golden award in his hand. One arm was draped over Bishop's shoulders and she was laughing; I never thought she could look so happy. She was sandwiched from the other side by none other than Tank who was giving a grinning salute to the camera. Dad had said in his diaries, that he and his friends magnetised to each other with a passion for understanding and developing Super abilities. Dad, Argyle, Bishop… and Hans.

Tank was Hans?

'You didn't think Tank was my real name, did you?'

I spun on my heel, clutching the photo in my hand. Tank stood in the office doorway. He switched on the light, causing me to squint. I stepped back.

'Don't worry, you're safe with me. I'd never hurt Matthew's kid.'

I lifted the photo in my hand. 'You're Hans?'

He nodded.

I blinked, looking around the room. 'This doesn't make sense. You're what, thirty?'

His brows lifted. 'I developed the healing serum. Didn't you think I'd use it myself?'

'I didn't think…' My brows creased. 'Why are you here? Dad said you gave up your research. You didn't want to continue working with Argyle.'

'You're right, I didn't want to work with him, so I left. But I never stopped my research. Then they found me.'

'Argyle found you?'

'No, Lucien.' He shut the door and leaned against it. 'It was a year or so after your dad died. Argyle had been disowned by the family and they needed a doctor with my particular set of skills.'

'You're a doctor?'

He smirked. 'It is possible to have both brains and brawn.' He grabbed a small black book from the shelves. He pulled out another photograph and handed it to me. The photo showed two blonde kids. The older boy looked to be in his teens and the girl, who sat in his lap, only a few years old. Tank pointed to the photo. 'That's me and my sister. Soon after she was born, she was diagnosed with a disease that causes muscle deterioration. By the time she was thirteen she used a wheelchair and needed support with day-to-day living. The doctors said she wouldn't live past eighteen.' He took back the photo and studied it.

'I was determined to find a way to fix Sofie, so I studied medicine. When I met your dad and the others, I'd branched off into neurology. It took me a few years of research to realise that the quickest way to cure Sofie was through Supernatural genetic mutation. I joined Argyle and the team to fast-track my search for a cure.'

He met my gaze and raw emotion flashed in his eyes. 'Argyle manipulated all of us. He knew our weaknesses and exploited them. Your dad sought to understand himself, Bishop sought to prove her worth, and me—I wanted to save Sofie. Your dad's understanding of the human DNA structure and how to tweak it, helped me to develop the healing serum. I never considered that a healing serum would be anti-ageing.' He rubbed his thumb over the photograph. 'By the time I returned home with the serum, I was too late. Sofie was gone. I buried myself in work and continued my research from a lab in my basement. That's where Lucien found me.'

'He wanted the healing serum,' I concluded.

'Lucien wanted more than the healing serum; he wanted my knowledge and skills.'

'Why?'

He placed the photo back in the black book and slid it into place on the shelf. 'It would be better if I showed you.'

28

TANK opened the door to his office, revealing a sterile white laboratory. He motioned for me to walk ahead.

'What if the others see us?' I whispered.

'I gave everyone an early lunch break when I heard you stumbling around in my office.'

I scowled and pushed past him as he pulled out his phone. 'Hey Phil, I need you to glitch microchip number three-three-seven-two. Thirty minutes should do. And turn all security cameras to dark mode… Yes, erase all footage of the girl along the east wall… Yes, including that part. I know it's funny, but we can't risk it.'

I glared, scuffing an impatient foot. He winked, shoving the phone in his pocket as he pushed through a set of doors into a wide hallway. We reached a door with a security pad. Tank typed in the code and there were three consecutive clunks before it swung open.

This hallway was narrow and the lighting was dim. There were no doors along the grey walls. Aside from the thumping of our shoes against the linoleum, it was quiet. The glint of stainless-steel elevator doors grew closer.

Tank broke the silence. 'It goes without saying, but what you see here, you keep to yourself. If it wasn't for the mental lock around your mind, I wouldn't have risked it.'

We stopped at the elevator doors and Tank punched in another code. The doors opened with a loud screech. He stepped in but I hesitated.

'Are you sure this is safe?' I queried.

'Yes.'

As the doors screeched closed I cringed. There was only one button. Tank pressed it, and the elevator lurched downward. I grasped onto the support railing as the elevator descended floor after floor. We were heading deep underground. Tank stood with his hands in his pockets. He looked no different from the picture I found in the study, aside from a grimmer expression.

'It's Bishop isn't it?' I asked and he lifted a brow. 'Your outside source is Bishop. That's how you know so much about Blackwood.'

'Yes. Bishop is a hard person to track down. When I saw you shoot the target that day in the gym, I knew Bishop was your mentor.' He gestured to his chest and head. 'Two shots to the chest and one to the head is a typical Bishop technique. I figured that she'd be looking for you, so I left breadcrumbs.'

The elevator continued its journey downward.

'Why were you sent to Belfield to retrieve me when you're not part of Lucien's security team?'

He rocked back and forth on the balls of his feet. 'Every now and again Lucien likes to test his subject's loyalty, especially the Favoured. He knew I'd have a soft spot for Matthew's offspring and wanted to see what I'd do. Fortunately, Lucien underestimates me.'

'I guess I underestimated you too. How far below ground are we going?' I asked.

'Just over three thousand feet.'

My mouth gaped. 'Three thousand feet? That's like… two-and-a-half kilometres.'

He nodded. 'Being deep underground provides a controlled environment. This was originally built as a locked *guesthouse* for powerful Supers who Lucien's father found disagreeable.'

Our journey underground continued until the elevator finally pulled to a stop. The doors opened and my eyes grew wide. Energy threads of all colours pulsed through the hallway. They wove together like a giant tapestry, blanketing the air. The strength of it was so potent it hummed. I'd never experienced power this strong—not even the great-grandfather tree in Blackwood. I studied it but didn't touch it. The pulsing was erratic, as though it was agitated. I recognised the pattern and turned to Tank.

'This is what controls the shimmering wall surrounding Aurore, isn't it?'

'You can tell?'

'The place is exploding with energy. Its pattern is always changing, the same as the shimmering wall. That's why it's underground, right? Kilometres of rock and earth make it difficult to pinpoint the source.' I moved towards a door on the left. All the threads were created by whatever was behind that door.

Tank stepped in front of me and turned the handle. 'Just to be clear, *the source* is a she.'

The room wasn't what I expected. It was nice—homey. Powder blue walls were decorated with framed pictures. There was a small kitchen to my left with the cabinets painted yellow. Floral furniture filled the room, giving it a cosy feel. I stopped at one of the windows. It was a screen showing a grassy field outside and blue sunny skies.

'I asked for these to be installed. They reflect the outside weather and conditions,' Tank explained. He glanced around the room. 'It makes it feel like less of a prison.'

A girl sat in the loungeroom. She was the source of energy; her body glowed with it. Her dark, black hair was long and glossy, falling in a long plait over her shoulder. She sat in a padded wheelchair by one of the pretend windows.

I took a step towards her and Tank placed a hand on my arm. 'Take care not to startle her.'

I stepped closer and held out my hand. 'Hi, I'm Freya.' She didn't turn to acknowledge me. Her expression was blank, but her eyes were focused. I was pretty sure she heard me.

'Aisha has limited control over her body. Simple movements take effort. She won't respond, until she wants to,' Tank explained.

I studied Aisha's form. 'Is she the reason you're here?'

'Yes. I help to monitor and keep her alive. Her body can't fully contain the power it carries. Lucien needs me to keep her stable, so that she can maintain the forcefield surrounding this city.' He moved to her side, picking up a small monitor hooked to the side of the wheelchair. 'Her vitals are steady; no dips or jumps. This is a good sign.'

I studied the energy pulsing through and around Aisha's body. The multi-coloured strands of energy changed colour and texture sporadically. Together they created a single cord of pure power.

'How is this possible?' I whispered.

Aisha wasn't limited to a single supernatural ability. She wielded energy that could be moulded into whatever gift she wanted. If she could control it, she could do or be anything—she was Omnipotent.

I was startled when she turned her head and amber coloured eyes met mine. I had a sudden urge to close my eyes and sunk into the chair beside Aisha. My eyes grew heavy and I let them close. *Only to rest them.*

The sound of trickling water reached my ears. Leaves rustled in the wind. A bird tweeted and my eyes blinked open. I was in a country garden, sat on a stone bench, sheltered by a large weeping willow. Flowers of every colour filled the garden beds and I breathed in their beautiful scent. I was drawn to the sound of water. Small white pebbles crunched beneath my feet as I followed a winding path and rounded a looming oak tree. A tiered fountain came into view. A girl sat on the fountain's edge with her hand wading through the water. Her bright blue dress glittered in the sunlight.

'Aisha?'

She turned to me and smiled. 'It didn't take you long to find me.'

My steps slowed as I approached the fountain. The breeze rustled through the garden filling the air with flowery perfume. 'This place is beautiful.'

'Much nicer than my underground tomb, isn't it?' She stood, brushing her hands against her dress.

'Is this part of the dreamscape?'

'Not quite. The dreamscape where you meet with Beau is a connection between your subconscious minds. One of you joins the other, or together you form your own meeting place. This place is a creation of my own mind. You're a guest here.'

'I'm in your head?'

She laughed, picking a flower from a nearby rosebush. The petals changed from yellow to purple in her hand. 'Yes. It's easier for me to communicate this way. And I like it here.'

She walked along one of the paths leading away from the fountain, and I followed. The pebbled path morphed into sand, and the garden faded, replaced with knee-high spinifex. We walked over a slight hill and a turquoise blue ocean spread out below us. It was Pete's Beach.

'I hope you don't mind. But I stole this likeness from your memory,' Aisha said.

'You read my thoughts?'

'Unlike your friend, Jonah, I can't control the telepathy. It's the only reason I'm thankful to live under tonnes of dirt and rock.'

'Have… have you seen all of my thoughts?'

'Yes, and don't worry, I completely understand your infatuation with the Dire Wolf.' My face turned scarlet and she laughed. 'I'm just teasing.'

I tucked a strand of hair behind my ear and studied her side profile. Her body still pulsed with erratic energy. 'It must be exhausting, trying to control your level of power.'

'It is. My physical body has almost completely shut down so that my mind can survive. I have very limited control over the power. People think that because physically I can't do many things, that I mustn't be able to think for myself either. It can be quite frustrating.'

I rubbed the back of my neck. I'd made that very assumption. 'I'm sorry…'

'Don't be. As frustrating as it is, the assumption works well for me. Lucien doesn't know I can control the forcefield. I never let his sister access my consciousness so she's not aware I can somewhat control it for short periods of time. When the forcefield drops so that you can escape this place, it will look like an accident. Hans will convince Lucien I had a spontaneous episode. I do have them at times.'

I couldn't get my head around calling him Hans. The guy was a literal tank. 'He cares for you, doesn't he?'

She nodded. 'He sees his sister in me. He couldn't help her, but he can help me. We've both lost families, so in a way we formed our own.'

'How did you create the forcefield? I've never seen an energy pattern like it.'

She looked out over the pristine blue water. 'It happened by accident. I was fourteen and Priya, my sister, was twelve. I believe you've met her; the Aegis?'

My brows creased. 'The Aegis is your sister? Lucien's Aegis?'

She nodded. 'I grew up a Mundane; there was no indication I had any supernatural abilities. But my parents and Priya were strongly gifted. We kept it a secret because in our country, Supernatural gifts are considered evil.' She walked to the water's edge, letting it wash over her feet.

'My mother was a Healer. She'd take risks to help people in need. My parents had been at a community meeting when a group of men from the village turned up at our home. Someone had told them about my mother's ability and they'd already intercepted my parents on the road and killed them. The men assumed my sister and I were the same.

'They attacked me first; all I remember was knowing I needed to keep Priya safe. One of the men grabbed her by the hair and she screamed. Something in me snapped. A power awoke and I unleashed it on them. The men, the house… the entire village evaporated. All that was left was me, Priya and the forcefield I'd created to protect us. But my body couldn't handle the power. It went into a coma-like state to protect itself and to protect my mind.' She turned to me. 'Even you couldn't handle this level of power. It consumes my entire being.'

'You were both so young.'

She dipped her head. 'We had an uncle in a neighbouring village. Priya worked on his farm while also caring for me, in exchange for shelter and food. The forcefield prevented thieves from stealing from his farm, so my uncle was happy to pretend I didn't exist. I'd gained some control over the forcefield so that it protected the people within it, without destroying everything else. We remained on his farm until Lucien and his sister, the Telepath, found us. It's not the best situation, but we did what we had to, to survive.'

'I don't understand how your sister sits by Lucien's side while you're living in a hole in the ground.'

'Don't judge her too harshly. The hole in the ground provides a stable environment for me. My power is temperamental so this is the easiest place to control it. I was able to spread the forcefield much further from down here. Priya sacrificed a lot to ensure our survival. Now that I'm cared for, she can pursue her own wants. We were born into a life of poverty and persecution. Can you blame her for wanting more?'

'I suppose not.' I studied the woman beside me, and thought of her physical form sitting by the window.

Aisha raised a brow. 'My answer to the question you're about to ask is no.'

'What question?'

She chuckled. 'You were going to offer to take away the power so my physical body can function as yours does. You assume that I need to be fixed.'

'Don't you want to be like you were before?'

'I'm capable of far more now than I was before. Although I have little control, I can use my gift to help my family and others. And when my physical limitations become frustrating, I can come here.'

I looked out over the water. 'So, why did you bring me here if not to help you?'

'I brought you here to tell you that it's time to go home.'

'Home?' I sat in the sand and hugged my knees to my chest. 'I don't know if Blackwood is my home anymore.'

'Of course it is.' She sat beside me, mirroring my posture. 'You're scared that the people who love you will see through you and won't like what they see. You're scared that you'll see through yourself and won't like what you see.'

I swallowed the lump in my throat. 'I'm- I'm not good, Aisha.'

She gave a dismissive sniff. 'No one is truly good. You think you're the only person tempted by power? We're defined by our actions, not the things that tempt us.'

I took a deep breath. 'Either way, I can't leave Aurore. Lucien needs to be dealt with.'

'And you think you're the one to overthrow him? You underestimate your allies, as you did me. You must leave, Freya. The next battle must be fought on home soil.'

'The next battle? Will Lucien attack Blackwood?'

Her smile was grim. 'Do me a favour and tell Hans to stop layering on the blankets; I'm sweating.'

I grabbed her hand. 'Come with me. You and Tank would like Blackwood; you could have freedom there.'

She shook her head. 'I'm not leaving this bunker, not physically anyway. Out there on the surface there are too many variables. If my body considered anything a risk – a slight change in temperature, a child screeching in play or a glass being dropped – I could destroy everything around me.' She squeezed my hand. 'Can I request one promise?' she asked.

'Of course.'

'Don't harm Priya. She's the only biological family I have left.' I frowned and she dropped my hand. 'Take care, Freya.'

I blinked and was back in the powder-blue room. Tank began to lay another blanket across Aisha's lap and I lifted a hand. 'Aisha said no more blankets.'

He re-folded the blanket, placing it on a side table. 'You met her?'

'Yeah… I met her.'

His phone rang and he pulled it from his pocket. Somehow, he had reception underground. After a single 'affirmative', he hung up the phone. 'We have to go. Your chip reactivates in eleven minutes.'

I fingered the microchip in my forearm. I could feel its odd shape beneath the skin. A knock sounded on the door. Tank opened it and a woman walked in. She checked Aisha's monitor and nodded to Tank as she sat beside Aisha and pulled out a bag of knitting.

'Aisha will wipe her memory so she remembers nothing of you,' Tank said, moving towards the door.

I crouched in front of Aisha, placing a hand on her knee. She didn't turn to me this time. 'Thank you,' I whispered.

I followed Tank to the elevator, taking one last glance at the *guesthouse.* The elevator hummed as it rose to the surface.

'She's definitely something,' I said.

A smile hinted at the corner of Tank's mouth. 'Yes, she is.'

'You'll be able to keep her safe?'

'Yes.'

We reached the ground floor and Tank ushered me to a door at the back of the building. 'Cameras will go live in two minutes. Follow the wall to the garden path, then head to the citadel from there. Check for guards before entering the main pathway.'

I gave a quick nod and stepped outside.

'Oh, and Freya, the head gardener takes pride in his hedges. Try not to assault any on your way out.'

29

I made it to the garden path unseen. As I reached the front steps of the castle a servant rushed down them and stopped in front of me, his eyes wide.

'I've been searching for you for some time, Miss Armitage. I have an invitation for you.'

He handed me the wax-sealed envelope and left me standing on the steps alone. I tore open the seal. It was an invitation to the Aurore Bi-annual Gladiatorial Games and it started in four hours. Lucien really embraced the whole Overlord thing.

The green dress was ruined, so I went with a black, backless dress and heels. I gave up on the curling tongs and pulled my hair into a ponytail. When I reached the dresser in the bedroom Beau's pendant was gone.

'Looking for this?'

I jumped. Kilian was sprawled on the bed with Beau's pendant hanging from a finger. It swung back and forth like a pendulum.

I held out my hand. 'Give it to me.'

He arched a brow, his gaze wandering over me. 'And if I say no?'

I sent out a thread of energy and gave his lifeline a tug. He smirked and threw the pendant to me. I placed it over my head, carefully tucking it inside my dress and watching as he stood and smoothed out his suit.

'You have to stop doing this… it's my room,' I said.

The last thing I needed was Blake spying through the balcony doors and seeing Kilian sprawled out on the bed like he owned the place.

'I think I'll keep doing as I please.'

'What are you doing here?'

'You needed an escort to the games.'

'I'm quite capable of taking myself. What are these so-called Gladiatorial Games?'

'Just a bit of fun. It's an opportunity for gutter-class citizens to fight for a position within Uncle's court. People who aren't pulling their weight within the court fight to keep their place. It weeds out the weaklings.'

'It sounds barbaric.'

He gave a slight shrug. 'It's effective and entertaining. Win-win.'

I scrunched my nose and he grinned. He crossed the room to the chair in the corner, picked up a black bag, pulled out a flat, square box and handed it to me. 'This is for you. You need to start looking like one of the Favoured.'

I eyed him suspiciously and opened the box. A pair of sparkling red earrings, matching necklace and a bracelet glittered on the black velvet casing. I ran a hand over the glittering jewels.

Kilian picked up the bracelet and placed it on my wrist. 'These are pigeon blood rubies. Very hard to find.'

He picked up the necklace and reached to clasp it behind my neck. It was then I noticed the rubies glinting from his cufflinks.

'You colour-matched us?'

His lips quirked. 'I'm making a statement. It's a good thing you wore black. Uncle won't be happy, but it sends a clear message. It's an effective power-play.'

I studied his icy blue eyes. 'What message?'

He clasped the necklace around my neck, resting his hands on my shoulders. 'That you're mine.'

I pulled back. 'I'm not yours.'

'You will be.'

He grabbed Beau's pendant and started to lift it over my head. I grabbed his hands, resisting the urge to growl. My heart pounded in my ears.

'The pendant stays,' I said. 'You can't see it beneath the dress anyway.'

His jaw tightened, but he let it go. 'Fine.'

He held out an arm and I looped my arm through his. I expected to head to the garage but instead we took the elevator to the floor below us: the staff quarters.

It was a busy floor. People darted back and forth attending to their jobs. Not a single person on this floor was gifted. People fell out of Kilian's way as he led me to a set of stairs. The air grew damp as we descended the steps and I stopped. I'd been on this level before.

'Don't worry, as interesting as it would be, the dungeon isn't my idea of a date,' Kilian teased.

'This is not a date,' I reminded him. We reached level ground and a large tunnel loomed ahead of us, lit only by torches lining the walls.

'There are dozens of these tunnels beneath the castle. Centuries past, they were used as escape routes for women and children during castle raids. Now the servants use them,' Kilian explained. 'I discovered them as a boy and memorised them in case I ever needed to escape.'

Our footsteps echoed against the flagstone floor. We reached a point where the tunnel split three ways, and took the middle tunnel. It went on and on. My feet ached and I questioned my choice in shoes.

'We're passing underneath the courtyard,' he said. 'The Pantheon, which we now call The Arena, is on the other side of the castle wall.'

'The Pantheon? Really?'

'Grandfather considered himself a bit of a god. A demigod at least. The Arena sounds less…'

'Less pretentious? The God complex must run in the family.'

His lips quirked. 'Every person must bow to someone. But not a god—a god bows to no one.'

We reached the end of the tunnel, stopping in front of a heavy wooden door. Kilian pressed his ear to the wooden panel. He cracked it open and the sound of voices filtered in. He pulled me through the door, closing it behind us. Waitstaff rushed back and forth with trays of food and empty glasses. One man stopped to question what we were doing in the kitchen. Kilian faced him and the man froze. He stuttered an apology, promised not to say anything and disappeared. Kilian turned to me with arched brows.

'See… there are benefits to being God.'

'*A* god,' I corrected.

He grabbed my hand, placing it on his arm, and pushed through the kitchen doors. They opened up into a domed room. Tiered seating lined the walls, surrounding an octagonal pit in the centre of the room. The pit was fenced to prevent people from getting in or out. It was a fighting arena. People eyed us as we walked past. I moved towards the tiered seating but Kilian pulled on my arm.

'You don't want to sit in the red zone.'

He led me to the loft above. Tables and chairs were spread across the floor. Elle approached us, a smile hinting at the corner of her lips.

'I see you've made it official.'

'It's not—'

Kilian gave my arm a warning squeeze and scanned the floor. 'Is Uncle here yet?'

Elle glanced between us. 'Not yet. You know he likes to make a grand entrance. Have you placed your bets?' She was looking at me.

'Bets?' I had to shout the question as more people crowded the room and the buzz of voices grew louder.

Kilian leaned in close to my ear. 'Your invitation came with a list of competitors.' He gestured to a man in a navy suit. He approached us and handed me a list. I glanced over the names, stopping at one I recognised—the tattooist. He was Favoured which meant he was fighting to keep his position.

'Why is his name on here?' I asked.

Kilian arched a brow. 'You wouldn't let me kill him, so I volunteered him. He needs to be reminded that I'm his future king.' He sighed at my horrified expression. 'Don't worry, he'll win.'

I ticked random boxes, and shoved the piece of paper back on the tray. Kilian guided me to a table and left me with Elle while he spoke to his mother a few tables away. The woman's glare scorched the side of my face.

A tray of drinks was placed in front of me. I saw the pink cocktail and glanced up into Blake's unnerving grey eyes.

She glared at me then grabbed the tray, moving to the next table.

'What is that?' Elle stared at my cocktail glass with a mixture of confusion and disgust.

'I don't know exactly, but it tastes better than that,' I said, pointing to her glass of champagne.

She sniffed in amusement and studied the glittering jewels around my neck. 'You're adjusting to life here, I see?'

I ran my thumb over the stones on my wrist. 'Kilian bought them for me.'

She smirked. 'I know. Who do you think helped him?'

The room hushed. People around me stood and I followed their example. Lucien and a few of his guardians climbed the stairs, moving to the central area overlooking the arena. The Aegis smirked at me as she sat beside Lucien. I reached for Beau's pendant and stopped, grabbing the ruby necklace instead. Kilian went to his uncle and bowed, saying loud enough for the floor to hear, 'May the best competitors win, proving themselves worthy of your favour. And may the sand beneath their feet run crimson with the blood of the inadequate.' He raised a fist in the air. 'Glory to the King.' Each person in the room raised their fist and chanted his words.

Lucien's eyes seemed blacker than usual. 'Thank you, nephew. You honour me with your *fine* words.'

I pulled my hand away from the necklace. At the rate I was twisting it through my fingers, I'd break the priceless thing. Lucien stood at the balcony railing, his arms spread wide as looked over the crowd below.

'Welcome to the Gladiatorial Games; an opportunity for all citizens of Aurore to prove their worth. Let the games begin!'

The crowd roared their approval. Two sets of doors opened from opposite sides of the arena. The crowd parted as the contestants made their way to the floor. The first contestant was the Siren's friend from The Towers. His eyes darted back and forth as he shuffled towards the pit. A hand rested on the back of my neck and Kilian leaned close to my ear.

'You didn't think we'd forget about him, did you?'

I clutched my glass.

'If you can't look as though you're enjoying the spectacle, adopt a bored expression. It works for Kilian,' James suggested.

I forced a smile over the rim of my glass and took a sip. Kilian dropped into the seat next to me, his lips quirked. The crowd cheered as the next competitor entered the pit. Her stride was confident and she grinned as the gate closed behind her. She was a Shifter of some sort. Her eyes were yellow and her pupils elongated. A tongue darted from her mouth and I cringed—she was reptilian.

'What's his gift?' I asked, pointing to the Siren's friend. He wielded two short blades and gave some practise swings.

'He's a Night Stalker. He's stronger and quicker at night. The full spectrum lights in here will weaken his abilities. Unless someone decides to cut the lights, this won't last long.'

A bell rang and the woman shifted. A large snake slithered out from her pile of clothes. The guy didn't have a chance as her lithe, twenty-foot form darted across the floor. She wound up his body, binding his arms to his sides. His blades fell to the sand with a clatter. She sunk her fangs into his collarbone, and he screamed. The scream turned to a gurgle as she squeezed the air from his lungs. With a final gasp, he toppled to the ground and the crowd roared. She unwound herself from the limp body and shifted back into her human form. She gave a bow to the ecstatic crowd and strode from the arena naked, picking up her clothes on the way out.

'There's a side bet running over whether her victim would die of the bite or strangulation.' Kilian said. He turned to Elle. 'It was strangulation, so it's your turn to pay up.'

Elle shrugged. 'Don't count on it. Let's wait for the final rule.'

He grinned and gestured to a waitress for more drinks. I watched as the body was dragged from the pit.

'The next one should be good,' Elle said, for my benefit. 'A Fire Elemental versus a Metal Elemental. The Fire Elemental has been climbing the ranks ruthlessly and has quite the flare for drama.'

The new contestants entered the pit and a clear glass-like cover closed over the structure. The bell rang and the Fire Elemental exploded into flames. The Metal Elemental had pockets full of small blades and shrapnel, but every object melted before it met its target. One knife managed to pierce the Fire Elemental's shoulder and he roared in anger, ripping the blade from his skin. The fire grew hotter, turning from red to yellow. The Metal Elemental screamed as his skin blistered from the heat. The yellow flames turned blue, flashing so bright that I had to turn away. The light dimmed and when I looked back the Fire Elemental was alone in the arena. The sand beneath his feet was now a smooth glassy surface. The Metal Elemental gone.

The crowd screamed his name and the Fire Elemental turned to our side of the balcony. His eyes fell on Elle and he gave a bow. She hid a smile behind her wine glass and turned to me wiggling her brows as he walked out of the pit.

'Do I need to have a talk with this one?' Kilian asked her.

Her cheeks turned a shade of pink. 'Don't be silly, Kili. I can look after myself.'

There was a break between matches as the glass was shattered and raked away from the floor, replaced with more sand. I watched each match with growing unease. Kilian continued topping up my glass, unaware that alcohol had no effect on me. The tattooist walked into the pit and I clutched the arms of my chair. He crouched down, drawing words and images in the sand beneath his feet. They acted like hexes, each word giving him temporary power. He won the match by paralysing his opponent. He chose not to kill him and the crowd booed.

It was past midnight when the final match was called. The 'best' had been saved for last: a Berserker versus a Replicator. Spiked clubs were thrown at their feet and the crowd clapped their approval. The Replicator could make copies of herself. Dozens of duplicates filled the arena, attacking the Berserker from all sides. The Berserker grew angry and swiped at the copies that turned to smoke when struck. He grew angrier, in turn growing bigger and faster, until eventually he struck the Replicator and a blood-curdling scream filled the air. Blood splattered the arena floor as well as the spectators on the other side of the fence. *So that's why it was called the red zone…* The match ended with the Berserker holding the limp body of the Replicator above his head. I wanted to spring from my chair and leave, but I stayed, my nails digging into the armrests. I waited for Kilian who was discussing the outcomes of the matches with his friends. They fell silent as the announcer's voice echoed over the speakers.

'Ladies and Gentlemen, it seems we have a last-minute entry.' The crowd buzzed as he paused for effect. 'Place your bets now. At the king's request, the next match will be fought by our King's guardian, Tarryn.' The Pain Empowered woman entered the pit. Murmurs of excitement filled the room.

'And who is a worthy opponent do you ask? None other than the newest member of the King's court—one who is yet to prove her worth.' He turned to me. 'Freya Armitage, consider this your summons.'

30

THE blood drained from my face. Elle stared at me with wide eyes as Kilian stormed across the room. He stopped in front of his uncle, the emptiness swirling around him like a heavy, dark cloud.

'Pitching a Favoured against another Favoured is against arena rules, Uncle.' The people closest to Kilian stepped away, glancing between him and Lucien.

A slight smile crossed Lucien's face. 'You forget, Kilian, that I am King. I make the rules.' His eyes met mine. 'Freya may have proven herself worthy to you, but she is yet to prove herself worthy to *me*.'

It seemed Lucien wasn't happy with Kilian and I being friends. Kilian's energy pulsed and his blue eyes were as cold as ice. The Aegis shuffled in her seat. I had the feeling he was about to do something out of character—something impulsive.

I stood, smoothing out my dress. 'I'd be honoured, my king. It seems only fair.'

Kilian's head snapped to me. I gave him a small nod and his shoulders relaxed. He faced his uncle.

'As Freya had no notice of the fight, do I have your permission to advise her of the rules and escort her to the pit?'

Lucien waved a hand. 'Of course.'

People parted for me as I walked down the stairs. Men in navy blue suits darted through the room taking people's wagers. Bets were being called out over the noise—most weren't in my favour. Kilian held my arm in a tight grip as we approached the pit.

'Tarryn's gift is Pain Empowerment. She doesn't feel pain but draws power from the pain and fear of others.'

'I know.'

'Syphon her power and kill her. Don't take any chances,' Kilian said.

He grabbed a tumbler of whisky from a passing waiter and gulped it, throwing the empty glass on the floor. People nearby jumped as the glass shattered.

'I'll do what I can, Kilian.'

He pulled me to the side of the room, staring people down until they gave us a wide berth. He leaned in. 'Don't hesitate, not like you did with me. Tarryn's murdered hundreds, possibly thousands of people, including women and children, and she does it with a smile on her face. She tortures and kills Mundanes just for fun—don't hesitate.'

My nerves were on edge enough already without the pep-talk. I looked down at my dress and ran shaky fingers through my hair. *How the hell was I meant to fight in this?* Reaching down I ripped the seams of the black fabric at both sides. I kicked off my shoes and reached behind my neck to unclasp the rubies. Kilian's hand covered on mine.

'Leave them.'

It seemed silly to leave them on, but I pulled my hand away, breathing in through my nose and out through my mouth to calm my jittery nerves. Kilian's hand rested on the small of my back as we neared the gate.

'You've got this in the bag, kid. Top of the food chain, remember?' James said.

My nerves turned into sweat. The dress that had seemed like a great choice a few hours ago, stuck to my skin. I clutched Beau's pendant and pictured his face; the face I wanted to see again. Kilian pulled my hand away from the pendant and turned it, placing a kiss on the inside of my wrist.

'Remember, there are no rules. Do what you have to do to win.'

He gave my hand a final caress and closed the gate, leaving me trapped. Elle and a few others cheered for me from the level above, but their efforts were drowned out by the crowd chanting Tarryn's name. Tarryn paced back and forth, sneering at me from across the floor. A wooden stave was thrown on the ground in front of my feet. I'd trained with Bishop using staves—this could work.

The crowd booed at the choice of weapon. Tarryn picked up her wooden stave and spun it in her hand.

'I can taste your fear, leech. Soon I'll be drinking your pain,' she crooned.

My stomach dropped as a shield of energy covered Tarryn. On the balcony above me, the Aegis smiled. *Ohhhh hell...*

'Remember your training, kid, it prepared you for this.'

'This is completely different!'

'No, it isn't. Think of it as another training exercise.'

'A training exercise with the possibility of losing my head!'

He sighed. *'Let me help you…'*

I couldn't do this on my own… *'Fine.'*

I pictured the place where I kept James locked away in my mind. I unlocked the door, opened it wide, and let out a nervous breath.

'I need more, Freya.'

My jaw clenched. *'Fine.'*

I opened all the windows and doors and James's presence flooded every corner of my mind. I clenched my eyes closed as he invaded my thoughts, my feelings and my instincts. His soul intertwined itself through mine in an intricate weave; he was determined to stay there this time.

The bell rang, signalling the start of the match. My eyes snapped open and I clutched the stave in my hand. Tiny splinters of wood dug into my fingers. Adrenalin rushed through me along with something else. Excitement. I met Tarryn's stare, and James's sense of calm and confidence flowed through me. Holding out the stave, I fell into a defensive stance, my weight resting on the balls of my feet. I crooked a finger and her eyes narrowed.

She sprinted towards me, aiming a high blow at my head. I blocked it, gripping my stave with both hands and pushing against her weight. She was faster than me, but I was bigger. I pushed her away and she came at me again. I blocked blow after blow, but she left no windows to strike back. She was gradually backing me towards the fence and from the smirk on her face I knew she was playing with me.

Time stretched and Tarryn became impatient. She attacked and I blocked. The pattern repeated itself and I grew weary. She doubled her efforts and my muscles ached from her relentless strikes. As she pivoted on her feet, I lunged to the side, but she took me by surprise, dancing to the opposite side of me, and her stave struck my spine. I cried out and fell to my hands and knees, pain ricocheting up my back. She darted towards me and I picked up a handful of sand, throwing it in her face as I stumbled to my feet. With an angry screech she swung the wooden stave in an arc, aiming for my ribs. I ducked, swinging my stave low. It caught her ankles and she crashed to her knees. I aimed a swing at her head, but she scooted backwards, out of my reach, and rubbed the sand from her eyes.

The crowd rattled the fence, yelling at us—they wanted blood. A person in the crowd dropped a small knife through the links in the fence. It landed near Tarryn and she picked it up, chuckling as she abandoned the stave and tested the knife's sharpness with her thumb.

'I'm curious,' she said. 'If I cut out your heart, will you heal?'

I grabbed my stave and snapped it in half across my knee, giving me two jagged-edged stakes. 'You'll have to get to me first if you want to find out,' I taunted.

Her lips curled into a snarl and she came at me again. I crossed the stakes in front of my face, blocking the strike aimed at my head. The blade glanced off the stakes, but Tarryn's fist caught me off guard. Her knuckles met my side with a loud *crack!* Pain radiated through my ribs and I buckled. The sound of her laughter made my teeth clench. She danced circles around me, encouraging the crowd to chant her name.

The Aegis's shield surrounding Tarryn shimmered—I needed to unravel it. I created a needle-like thread, but lost my focus as she came at me again. I blocked her attack, but the strength of her hit made me stagger backwards and I crashed into the fence. People banged on the wire, yelling at me to move. I tried to concentrate on unravelling the energy shield, but the persistent attacks distracted me. Another blow came at my face. The blade lanced my cheek as I ducked. She kneed me in the face and blood spurted from my nose. I crumpled to floor and clenched my eyes closed as stars blurred my vision.

She leaned over me. 'Come on, leech. Is that the best you've got?' She crouched and whispered in my ear, 'You know what my reward will be for destroying you today? Lucien will give me permission to eradicate that little town of yours. *Blackwood,* isn't it? I'll start with your family, then your boyfriend, then I'm going to pick off the rest one by one starting with all those filthy Mundanes.'

My eyes focused on her sneering face. The same face that would stand over the people I loved. Instead of screaming in rage I sifted through energy threads, trying to find one I could loosen. Tarryn stood and kicked my side with her boot, rolling me onto my back. She grabbed one of the wooden stakes I'd dropped in the sand and thrust it into my shoulder. A scream forced its way from my lungs as it tore through muscle and tendons, pinning me to the floor. She straddled my chest so I couldn't move, then raised her hands in victory. The crowd roared. She basked in the praise then turned her attention back to me.

'I'm gonna make this nice and slow,' she said. Steel glinted as she turned the knife in her hand. She lowered the blade to my chest, hovering above my heart, then moved it to the base of my throat. 'Will you grow a new voice box if I remove it, or will your life end on silent screams?'

I searched the energy shield, picking and pulling at the weave, hunting for the thread I knew had to be there. The knife pressed into my throat, pricking the skin, and I hissed. A thrill ran through me as one tiny strand came loose.

'Any last words?' Tarryn asked as she twisted the knife, scraping my collarbone.

My grimace curved into a grin and her confident smirk faltered. I ripped the thread from its weave. The shield unravelled and the Aegis shrieked from the floor above. Latching onto Tarryn's energy core, I drew her energy with force and her eyes grew wide. She dropped the knife and scrambled off of me. With a snarl I pulled the stake from my shoulder and pushed off of the ground. I pressed against the gaping wound with my hand and straightened my back. As the pain ebbed I released a sigh. The noise from the crowd was deafening.

Tarryn was on her hands and knees, struggling to breathe. Her face was pale. I tugged on the cord of energy and her lifeline flickered. She glared at me through bloodshot eyes; her complexion was turning a familiar shade of grey. The crowd fell silent as I picked up the fallen blade and stood over her.

I groaned, rotating my arm. The stab wound had healed, but my shoulder was as stiff as a board. Tarryn clawed at her throat as I crouched beside her.

'Do it,' she hissed.

I thought of all the people she'd killed. *She's killed kids…* 'As you wish.'

Her energy wavered and instead of letting go I pulled harder. It left her body and I sighed as power rushed through my veins. Instead of letting the thread of her gift weave itself into mine, I flung it away from me and it dissolved into the air around us. I didn't want her gift—if it could even be called a gift. Tarryn's body fell to the ground at my feet. The crowd buzzed and I could hear voices chanting my name. It wasn't until the dust settled that the announcer tapped the microphone.

'Ladies and Gentlemen, we have an unexpected winn—'

The announcement was cut short as people gasped. Tarryn moved. A hand darted out and then another. She pushed herself off the ground, standing on shaky legs and glared at me through hate-filled eyes.

Her voice shook, 'What have you done to me, leech?'

I tilted my head. 'I've made you the one thing you hate most.' I glanced from one eye to the other as understanding dawned on her face. 'You're nothing more than a *filthy* Mundane.'

The bell rang and the crowd roared, drowning out Tarryn's howl of despair. Looking up at the balcony I saw that the Aegis was gone. Lucien stared at me. I sensed the cold fury burning behind those black eyes.

I moved to the gate. Kilian stood beside it, his arms folded across his chest, mouth curved in a half smile. The smile fell and people around me were shouting. Kilian called out a warning, but I'd sensed her energy already. I turned, throwing the knife from my hand. It was a perfect shot. Tarryn clutched her chest, dropping the wooden stake. It rolled in the sand as her body fell to the ground with a thud, her vacant eyes wide with shock. I suppressed a shudder and turned away.

I lifted my eyes to Lucien and bowed, projecting my voice for the crowd to hear. 'Glory to the king.'

The air was thick with tension as people waited for him to speak. He tapped a finger on the arm of his chair, his eyes not once leaving mine. A muffled cough from the back of the room broke the silence. I sent out threads of energy, attaching them to everyone between me and the exit. Then he stood and began a slow clap. It echoed through the arena, stopping when he reached the balcony. He lifted his arms and eyed the crowd.

'It seems the newcomer has earned her place,' he announced.

The crowd cheered and my body sagged with relief. Spectators rattled the fence of the pit. The gate screeched open and people clapped me on the shoulders as I stepped into the crowd. I glanced up at the loft but Lucien was gone. Kilian moved in front of me, eyeing me from head to toe.

'It seems I was worried for nothing.' He lifted the ruby necklace from my neck, running a thumb across the stones. He showed me his thumb covered in my blood. 'Blood rubies were the right choice for you.'

His gaze made me uncomfortable, so I focused on the crowd around us. Elle appeared at my side, handing me my shoes and a drink.

'You surprised us all, Freya. None of us knew if you had it in you.'

I looked back at Tarryn's corpse. The blade protruded from her chest slightly to the left of her breastbone, exactly where I'd aimed it. I pushed away the revulsion I felt at my own actions. 'Yeah… neither did I.'

31

ELLE followed me back to my rooms and picked an outfit for me to wear while I showered. I raised my brows when I saw jeans, a white shirt and leather jacket laid out on the bed.

'You're an icon now, Freya. People want to dress like you. Rebellion against proper dress is now in fashion, even at The Tower. You'll have everyone listening to grunge music next.'

'Ha-ha.' Grabbing the clothes, I approached the dresser, reaching behind my neck to undo the clasp of the rubies. Elle insisted I wear them again.

People in the line for The Tower waved as I entered the revolving doors. We went straight to the top floor: Kilian's apartment. He and some of his friends lounged in the living area, discussing their wins and losses. They saw us and a few of the guys pretended to chant my name. I couldn't help but smile.

'That ending was epic, Freya. A lot of people owe me favours thanks to you,' the Water Elemental said, gripping my shoulder.

My smile wavered. It was just sport to them. 'Thanks.'

'Kilian's apartment is boring. Which floor shall we choose tonight?' Elle asked me. 'We can clear any floor that you want, even that dingey third floor.' She scrunched her nose.

'I don't mind. You choose,' I said, hugging my jacket closer. Her expression brightened.

'Before we go anywhere, we need to discuss what happened tonight,' Kilian said, moving to my side. 'I invited you up here because you are the few people that I trust the most.' The Water Elemental stood a little straighter. 'Freya's victory has opened Uncle's eyes. She can disable the Aegis's shield, which makes her a problem. He'll be making a move soon, so we need to be prepared.'

'What kind of move?' one of the guys asked.

Kilian looked at me. 'Either he'll test Freya's loyalty, or he'll try to dispose of her. I need you all to be alert.' They agreed and Elle led the way to the elevator, pressing the button for the thirteenth floor. I was second last and Kilian placed an arm on my shoulder to stop me from getting in.

'Freya and I will follow in a few minutes.'

Elle smirked, waving to me as the elevator doors closed. I turned back to Kilian.

'What did you want to ta—'

He pressed me against the elevator doors and kissed me. It wasn't electrifying—it was just… a kiss. He stepped closer, pulling me against him, and alarm bells rang in my head.

'Get off me,' I hissed, shoving him away. I stepped away from the doors, rubbing my arms. It wasn't cold, but guilt added a certain chill to the air. I pinned Kilian with a glare. 'What the hell was that?'

His devilish smirk made me want to kick him. 'I've wanted to do that all night. It seemed like the right time.'

'The *right* time? I haven't agreed to anything between us yet!'

'You will.'

I gave a frustrated huff and marched to the elevator door, jabbing the button until the doors opened. The button for the thirteenth floor lit up and Kilian stepped in just as the doors closed. The smirk was still plastered to his face. We waited in silence as the elevator descended. It was the slowest elevator ride in history.

Up until I turned seventeen, I'd been kissed a total of two times. Somehow in the past year, I'd been kissed by four different guys. Every single one had brought trouble. Fourteen-year-old me wouldn't have believed it.

'Just to be clear, that kiss meant nothing,' I said.

Kilian grinned as the doors pinged open. He stepped out and I attempted to grab his arm. We were not finished. I was stopped by the bright lights of a casino. People crowded around me, congratulating me on my victory. Elle was right; a few of the girls wore clothes similar to mine, instead of the usual formal dress. I sent threads of energy through the room. Kilian was out on the balcony. He was with the Water Elemental and his usual friends. I moved to the bar, ignoring the people trying to catch my eye. Surprisingly, Blake wasn't there. She usually managed to turn up wherever I was. The bartender approached me and I asked for a pink cocktail. He had no idea what I meant so I went with a lemonade instead. A whiskey was poured and placed on the bar next to me.

'We really need to stop meeting like this.' I turned to the familiar voice. The Teleporter grabbed his glass and sipped it. He sighed. 'Kilian always has the good stuff.'

My jaw clenched. 'What do you want?'

He pretended to be offended. 'A guy can't just drop in for a chat these days. You females all assume we have ulterior motives.'

'And you don't?'

'Well in this case, yes.'

I rolled my eyes and turned away.

'I came to warn you.'

'And why would you want to do that?'

He glanced around the room. 'Like anyone here, I'm happy to exchange a favour for a favour.'

I didn't trust him, but my senses tingled. He'd been involved twice at turning points in my life. 'Go on.'

He raised his glass. 'Here's to you.' He sculled the amber liquid, and asked the bartender for another glass. 'There's a woman who's going to arrive in Aurore in about forty-eight hours' time. She is very keen to meet you. Lucien didn't want her to know about you yet, but someone squealed.'

I grabbed Beau's pendant, running my fingers along the chain. 'Who is she?'

'*She* is what you'd get if Lucien and the Devil spawned a child. Her name is Csilla and she's a scheming and intelligent woman, with a soul as black as soot. Lucien would consider her the perfect wife if he didn't think she'd murder him in his sleep.'

'Why does she want to meet me?' I asked.

'Because you have the potential to be her ultimate nemesis. After what I saw tonight, I'd say that you're more of a threat than she knows. She's never met one of her kind with power to match hers. She won't be pleased.' My blood turned to ice at his words.

He chuckled. 'Yes, you heard me right. Csilla is a Syphon. You and your father weren't so unique after all.'

'Why are you telling me this?'

'I may have upset Csilla—' he pinched his thumb and forefinger together, '—just a little. And that woman has been known to hold a grudge for centuries. You're my only shot at freedom.'

'What do you expect me to do?'

'I'm not sure, but I have a feeling it will all play out by itself. I'd suggest getting away from this place though. I'd offer to take you somewhere but I can't teleport through the forcefield, only inside, or outside of it.

'What if I take my chances and stay?' I sipped my lemonade.

He made a noncommittal sound. 'It's your funeral. There's a long-standing agreement between Csilla and Lucien, one with many, many clauses. He's broken it by keeping you without telling her. Given the chance, he'll turn you over to her to save their shaky alliance. Whatever happens, remember that I did you a favour, okay? Oh, and the next time you see your Dire Wolf lover, ask him about Csilla.'

He disappeared in a blink. Panic had me on my feet and searching for Kilian. On the balcony, an infinity pool jutted out over the side of the building. The base was glass, giving an unnerving view of the ground below. Girls played in the water, trying to get the attention of Kilian and his friends. The Water Elemental flicked his wrist and a fountain of water rose out of the pool, cascading back down in the shape of a mermaid. The girls squealed and clapped their hands. I rolled my eyes. A guy was thrown into the pool, splashing me with water. The night just kept getting better. I reached Kilian and rested a hand on his arm.

'Can we talk?'

He gestured for the others to leave. Even the girls were ushered out of the pool.

I scowled. 'You didn't have to make everyone else leave.

We could've found a quiet corner or something.'

He smirked. 'If that's what you wanted, we could've gone back to my apartment.'

I wanted to sink into the pool and never surface. 'That's not what I meant.'

He sniffed in amusement. 'What's bothering you?'

'Who's Csilla?'

His brows creased. 'I have no idea.'

'Don't play me, Kilian.'

'I'm not playing you. I don't know a Csilla.'

He was lying—he had to be. How could he not know about the woman the Teleporter called Devil's Spawn? She sounded like a memorable person.

I looked up at the starless sky. 'I have to leave.'

His eyes narrowed. 'Why?'

'I can't stay here.'

'I'll make you.'

I crossed my arms. 'Remember how you owed me a favour? Well, I'm calling it in now.'

His lip twitched. 'It's *him*, isn't it?'

I could tell by the tone he was referring to Beau. 'No. But either way I can't stop him from coming for me, so it's better if I'm far away when he smells your scent on me.'

'I can handle him.'

'Not if he works out you kissed me. He'll tear you apart limb by limb. He's a Dire Wolf, so he can probably smell it somehow.' I waved a hand. 'And there's the bond thing. I think that makes it worse.'

He arched a brow. 'You're bonded to the Dire Wolf?'

'Only just. He bit me and left and then I was brought here.'

He eyed me. 'What would you do if I killed him first? In self-defence of course.'

I stepped closer, till our noses nearly touched. 'Touch him and I'll choke the life from you.' Blinking in surprise I pulled away. I had to get a grip on the random outbursts.

He sighed. 'So protective; you really are bonded.'

The bond was the reason for my violent protectiveness of Beau? Well, that made sense.

'How could you know that?'

'I make it my business to know everything about my enemies.'

'Enemies?'

'Your boyfriend.'

'Lay a finger on him and—'

He waved me off. 'I know, I know. There's still hope he'll die at someone else's hands. If, like you say, it's only the start of the bonding process, then I'll be waiting for you when it fades. Or when he dies.'

My mouth opened and closed but I had no words.

'You realise I can't help you escape? It puts my own plans at risk,' he said.

'I wouldn't expect you to.'

'Good. Until you leave, we'll pretend we're together. Uncle will be less likely to suspect your escape plans and I can pretend to be broken-hearted and depressed when you're gone.'

I turned to leave and he stopped me with a hand on my arm. He kissed the inside of my wrist, glancing up at me with a devilish smile. 'If you change your mind, you know where to find me.'

'I won't change my mind.'

'We'll see.'

I made my way to the elevator and, finding myself alone in the mirrored box, heaved a sigh.

'What are you doing, kid? You could've had it all.'

'That's where you're wrong, James. I could've had everything, except what I really want.'

32

'I haven't come across another of our kind. Neither has Bishop in all of her travels. Either persecution sends Syphons deep into hiding, or as the books suggest, there just aren't many of us. I sometimes wonder if Freya and I are the only ones left. Perhaps it's better that way. A world full of Syphons would be chaos. Not everyone listens to their conscience.'

Video no.32, Matthew Holmes

I paced my rooms, trying to come up with a plan. I'd hoped that Tom would appear but he hadn't. Laying on the bed I willed sleep to come. The figures painted on the ceiling taunted me with their anguished faces. There was a shuffle on the balcony. I sensed her wolfish energy before she appeared in front of the glass door. Blake.

'Where have you been? Aren't you meant to be my protector?' I accused, as she carefully closed the door behind her.

'Unlike a Replicator, I can't be in many places at once. I was busy planning how to haul your butt out of here.'

'Well, I nearly had my butt hauled to the afterlife, thank-you-very-much.'

She snorted. 'Hardly. From the sounds of it, you were fine. More than fine.'

I supressed a shiver at the vision of Tarryn. 'Have you heard of a woman named Csilla?'

Her body went rigid. 'How do you know Csilla?'

'I don't, but it's obvious you do. Apparently, she's coming here. For me.'

'How do you know?'

'An acquaintance told me. He has his own agenda, but I believe him. He thinks someone told her without Lucien's permission.'

She nodded. 'My guess would be Kilian's mother—she's

hated you from the start. We're getting you out of here tomorrow; it rushes our plans, but we can do it. Csilla won't waste time.' Her nostrils flared as she eyed me from head to toe. 'You stink of Kilian. Shower before Beau smells you.' She opened the door to leave then pinned me with a glare. 'Stay here until we come for you. Don't get into trouble.'

The door clicked and I fell back on the bed, rubbing my shoulder and thinking over the night's events. I was going home. Heaviness swept over me and I closed my eyes, relaxing into the feathery mattress. The image of Tarryn laying lifeless in the sand was imprinted on the inside of my eyelids. I pushed the image aside and thought of home, finally giving in to sleep.

I was in a forest. It was close to dawn; somehow, I could feel it. The tall pines towered above me, rustling in the breeze. Whispered words echoed in the wind. I turned in a circle, trying to follow the strange voice, but it was everywhere. My search brought me to the edge of a lake. The bright, full moon reflected on its still surface. I'd forgotten it was a full moon. A large wolf laid at the water's edge, his golden fur gleaming in the moonlight.

'Beau?'

His head lifted and he leapt to his feet, bounding over to me in a few strides. He sniffed me from head to toe and whined.

'Hey, I'm okay.' I patted his head.

His voice whispered across my mind. 'Blake told me about the fight. They stopped me from coming for you.' He let out a low rumbling growl.

'I'm fine, Beau.'

He pushed his big furry head into my chest and nudged me. When I didn't react, he nudged me again. I chuckled, running my hands through his fur. Seeing him eased the tightness in my chest. I pressed my forehead against his and released a sigh.

'Tell me what's wrong.' His voice held concern and a hint of persuasion.

I gripped his fur, swallowing the lump in my throat. 'I killed someone tonight. I didn't hesitate, not even a little.'

He placed his big paws on my feet. 'You did what you had to do.'

'I know, but it was too easy. I… I understand Reagan's *vision now.'*

He nudged my chest and gestured to the ground with his nose. I sat at the lake's edge and he rested his head in my lap.

'Why are you in wolf-form?' I asked.

'I haven't been able to shift back into human-form since Blake contacted me. The full moon makes it harder. Now that I know you're safe, I'll be able to de-escalate.' A low rumbling vibrated through his chest and across my legs. 'The smell of Clemonte isn't helping.'

'Don't worry about him. I don't like him like that... It's just you, Beau.'

He sniffed, laying heavier against my legs. The trees moved and the whispering voice reached my ears once more.

'Where are we?' I asked.

'Blue Lake Forest; close to Aurore. It's enchanted by a woman who lives here. Locals call her The Witch. Her wards protect us from any Psychics or Psionics who may be looking for us. It won't be long now until we find you and bring you home.'

Home... I really missed home. I missed Mum, Pa and Grandma. I even missed school. 'How's Pa?'

'The Doc gave him the all clear. Levi had to convince him and your mum to stay home. She was ready to bite heads off when Waller told her she was emotionally compromised and had to stay in Blackwood. He told Levi to stay too, but your brother is nearly as stubborn as me. Levi convinced Waller to let him go, along with Dillon and a couple of Southerners.'

'Wow.' I shook my head. 'I underestimate my brother. Do you think the Council will let me stay in Blackwood?'

He shuffled in my lap. 'They'll let you stay.'

I frowned, realising that Beau had been speaking to me telepathically. I'd gotten used to James's voice in my head. 'How are we speaking like this?'

'It's the dreamscape. Technically it's our consciousnesses intertwining, so we can communicate this way.'

'How much more will we... intertwine?'

'I don't know, but the fact that the bond still exists stops me from tearing my way through Aurore and ripping the little Clemonte imp to shreds.'

I snorted. 'He's not little.'

'Compared to me, he's tiny.'

'Don't underestimate him. He's dangerous... for an imp.'

Beau growled and nipped my thigh.

'Ow! What was that for?'

'Reassurance.'

'Reassurance?' I gave him a shove. 'You marked me again, didn't you?'

'Just a small one. I had to cover that horrible scent.'

I raised a finger, ready to lecture him, when a sharp sensation radiated through my chest. I screeched in pain and Beau leapt to his feet. Blood seeped through my white shirt. Not again…

'FREYA!'

I woke with a scream and ran a hand across my chest, ripping the knife from where it was plunged between my ribs. I threw it across the room and it hit the wall, lodging itself in the plaster. The Aegis stood at the end of my bed.

'You ruined everything, Soul Stealer,' she hissed. 'I was irreplaceable. I could've been Lucien's Queen, but you came along and made me look weak. Now I'm *worthless*!'

She lunged, her hands aimed at my throat. As I leapt from the bed she fell into it with an angry shriek. I grabbed her wrists and dragged her off the mattress. She landed on the floor with a thud and I straddled her body, pinning her hands above her head.

'What are you going to do, take my soul?' she screeched. She struggled against my grip, flailing like a fish. If only Aisha hadn't made me promise to let her live.

I leaned close to her face. 'I don't want your filthy soul. I want you out of my room.' I unravelled the shield she'd erected around herself, ripping it to shreds. I drew her energy until her face grew pale and her lips trembled. 'Get out. Now.'

She scrambled out from beneath me, backing towards the door. When she stood near the exit, she said with a sneer, 'If Lucien doesn't kill you first, Csilla will be the end of you.' She turned and fled the room.

Well, I've found my snitch.

I turned the lock on the front door, twice, before crossing the room and pulling the knife from the wall. Plaster crumbled at my feet. I felt along my forearm, my fingers finding the small bump beneath my skin. Taking the compact blade, I pierced the skin, breathing a sharp intake of air as I made the incision. I dug my fingers into the flesh, pulled out the tiny microchip and threw it in the bathroom sink.

I waited out on the balcony. Blake hadn't hinted at anything about the rescue plan. For all I knew Beau and Levi would just charge in, leaving a bloody path in their wake. I grimaced. Knowing the both of them, that option was entirely possible. I focused inward, on the energy pulsing through me. The flow of Syphon energy had forged a stronger path through my energy core. It was a bright beam of light flowing in a tight, intricate weave. When I'd totalled the car, I'd drawn power from anything with a lifeforce within a hundred metre radius. With practise I'd be able to do it consciously and no one in Lucien's court would be a match for me. I shivered; I couldn't lose consciousness again.

When the sun was high in the sky, I rose from my knees and entered my room. The blood rubies sat on the top of the dresser, carefully placed back in their black velvet box. I left a note with the box, instructions for them to be sent back to Kilian. As I signed the note someone knocked on the door.

Instead of the usual serving staff, it was one of Lucien's guardians. His deadpan stare seemed to look straight through me.

'You've been summoned,' he said. 'Try anything with me and I'll shoot you.'

He cocked two fingers, pretending to shoot me between the eyes. He had Superior Instinct. Any action from me and he'd sense it before it happened. This guy would've never had a surprise birthday party or surprise present in his life. Maybe that's why he was such a prickly guy. I glanced back in my room.

This was not part of today's plan.

In the ballroom Kilian stood in his place by Lucien. People parted as I moved through the crowd to the front of the room. The Aegis no longer sat by Lucien's side, but behind the guardians. I stood close enough to notice that Lucien's hair had begun to grey and bowed low, keeping my eyes to the ground.

'My king.'

I lifted my eyes. His expression was fixed and the cords of his neck rigid.

'I have a little problem,' he said. 'You're just the person to help me solve it.'

He templed his fingers and studied me. The guardians surrounding him hummed with power. They were on the alert and it made me nervous. I sent out threads of energy, reaching more than thirty people in the crowded room and attaching threads to each one. Lucien leaned forward. 'You have access to anything you want here… absolutely anything. All I ask for is your loyalty. Do I have your loyalty, Freya?'

'Of course, my king.'

He rose from the throne and paced in front of it. 'Good. I had the distinct impression that your allegiance may lay elsewhere, which would've been inconvenient. I was advised of the wreckage from your little accident. Putting you to death without casualties would be difficult. I don't have to worry about that now, do I? I'm lacking a guardian, so you shall take Tarryn's place.'

I blinked. '…What?'

He stopped. 'You will replace Tarryn and commence her duties.'

I shuffled my feet. 'I don't have any experience…'

'It's on the job learning. You can begin your first task now.' He raised his voice, projecting his words through the room. 'My devoted subjects, it's been brought to my attention that we have a traitor among us. Someone has been spreading lies and deceit, seeking to usurp my throne.' People gasped. 'Have I not made our city prosperous? Have I not kept you safe? Have I not ensured that Mundanes remain where they belong; beneath us?' The crowd shouted in agreement.

This was definitely not good.

Lucien turned to Kilian. 'Did you think I was foolish, boy?'

Guardians surrounded Kilian and me. His tattoos glowed. One of the guardians held his hands in the air and his energy pulsed. The crowd of people scrambled backwards as a shadow emerged from the ground beneath us. It formed into the shape of a large dog, almost as large as Beau in Dire

Wolf form. Instead of fur it had scales and in place of its feet were talons. Its face was little more than bone and sinew with gaping holes where its eyes and nose should have been. Large fangs protruded from its mouth. It opened its mouth and let out a blood-curdling howl.

'What is the meaning of this, Uncle? I'm your heir, I have no reason to betray you,' Kilian said, flexing his hands as the black beast loomed over him. It didn't have a lifeline. Instead, a ball of strange almost-transparent energy pulsed in its skull.

'Did you think that I wouldn't know of your schemes? I've had you watched from the very beginning,' Lucien boasted.

He pointed to one of the girls I'd met on Sergio's peak—the one who'd sneered at me. Now she sneered at Kilian with her head raised high. The Aegis stepped forward, strengthening the shield around Lucien. It was then I noticed something different about her energy, it had a greenish hue. I'd seen it before with Argyle and his people—she was enhanced.

'For the last fifty years I've fought schemes and murderous plots to keep this throne. I'm not going to lose it to a whelp like you.' The corners of his mouth curved and he turned to me. 'Time to test your *loyalty*. You so efficiently disposed of Tarryn. You will do the same with Kilian.'

I glanced at Kilian. His jaw was clenched. He watched me, waiting. All the while the shadow beast was practically drooling on him.

Just do it. You would've had to get rid of him later anyway,' James said.

Kilian had known nothing but betrayal since he was a kid. From his friends and even his mother. I might not like him like *that,* but I wasn't going to be another person added to that list.

'No.'

The guardians moved forward, tightening the circle around us. Lucien's eye twitched.

'No?'

I glanced to my sides as two of the guardians closed in

behind us. 'You can do your own dirty work.'

His eyes glittered. 'Well, isn't that a pity.'

The shield that had been protecting Lucien disappeared. The Aegis turned to me and a new shield covered my body like a fine layer of silk. This shield was a different weave and it was airtight. Not only was her ability enhanced, but she'd been practising a new technique. The shield didn't protect me, it stopped me from using my power.

'Let's see how long you survive now.' Lucien turned to his guardians. 'Kill them both and weed out his followers.'

The black beast bared its teeth and closed in on Kilian. Its lack of lifeline allowed it to resist the emptiness. One of the guardians targeted me. He stepped forward, bringing his hands together in a clap. A large crack of thunder sounded through the room and I was thrown backwards by the force. I slammed into a large pillar, my head hitting the stone. My body slid to the floor. I opened my eyes but only saw stars. A blurry outline of a person moved towards me but stopped as the sound of rumbling filled the room. It wasn't coming from the guardian. My eyes cleared and I saw everyone staring at the glass ceiling. I looked up. The shimmering dome surrounding the city flickered, like a television with dodgy reception. The dome completely disappeared, then in a blink it was back in place. The guardian turned back to me, his lips curled in a sneer. He chuckled as I braced against the pillar and stood.

'What are you going to do, Soul Sucker? Hit me?' he jeered.

He spun around as a loud roar echoed from outside. Gunshots, shouting and screams came from the other side of the doorway. Everyone stared at the doors that lay between us and whatever was going on in the hallway on the other side.

Lucien shouted to his guardians, 'Don't just stand and gawk! Find out what's going on.'

Two men approached the doors and the sound outside stopped. Everyone seemed to be holding their breath. One of the doors creaked open. A petite older woman, with long grey hair, stepped inside. 'Well, well. Nothing changes, I see.'

33

THE people closest to the doors backed away. The woman's bright eyes scanned the room. She met my stare and smiled.

Csilla?

She continued her perusal until her gaze fell on Lucien. Her kind smile turned into something more sinister. A chuckle sounded from my side. I turned to Kilian.

'That woman is Uncle Lucien's wife. She's supposed to be dead,' he explained.

'Hello, Luce,' she said. Her voice was smooth and melodic.

Lucien stared at the woman, his lips thinned into a grim line. He was nervous. 'Hello, Gabriella. This is… unexpected.'

I relaxed. *Not Csilla.*

She laughed. 'As the girl implied, you really should do the dirty work yourself, Husband. It would prevent moments such as this.'

His nostrils flared. 'It was nothing personal. You were a risk.'

'A threat, you mean. You always were a spoilt royal, used to having the world admire you and bow at your feet. You couldn't handle the thought of someone having more power than you, could you?'

'What do you want?' he asked.

'You've grown overconfident and irrational in the last decade, Lucien. This city needs a new ruler.' She tilted her head to the side. 'I saw an opportunity to play a part in your downfall and I just couldn't say no.'

The tall arched windows lining the east wall shattered. A giant golden wolf leapt through the central window, his teeth and claws dripping with blood.

Beau.

His eyes glowed luminescent in the light. He lifted his head to the ceiling and howled. It was echoed by the howls of his fellow wolves, and the roar of something else.

Monstrous, white, ape-like creatures burst into the room. They roared and people screamed, running for the doors. Beau's eyes met mine from across the room. He bounded towards me, followed by my brother, Levi, in wolf-form. Dorian, dressed in black body armour, ran close behind. Anyone who drew close to him fell to the ground, crying in anguish. Dorian's energy brushed against me.

Fear—deep, ominous, all-consuming fear.

The doors to the room slammed open and another Dire Wolf leapt into the room followed by Wolf Shifters. Bishop's people piled in, pushing past those trying to flee. The Metal Elemental on Bishop's team went straight for the steel chandeliers, throwing them and scattering people like skittles. Her sniper knelt in front of the windows, shooting anyone who tried to attack me or their group. His gift was Perfect Aim—he never missed. Mr Monroe and Tom entered through the broken window. I'd never seen them in action before. They were fast and very, very efficient.

'Impossible!' Lucien yelled. 'No one gets into my city.' He lunged towards his wife as she uttered words under her breath. They reached my ears in a whisper; the same whisper I'd heard in the dreamscape. Her body glowed with energy. Lucien reached out to grab her but pillars of black stone burst through the floors, curving over him like a giant clawed hand. He called on his guardians. Three of them tried to attack the woman, but as they drew close, they exploded into dust. She cackled.

Her words reached all corners of the ballroom. 'You will watch as everything you value falls to pieces. I couldn't save my daughter… but I can avenge her death.'

A glint from the corner of my eye made me turn. Silver scales glinted in the light and I shouted, moving behind a pillar, as a large reptilian head lunged at me. The Snake Shifter hissed and darted around the pillar, snapping at my legs. I leapt away, but she was too fast. She encircled my body, wrapping herself around me tighter and tighter. I had nothing to defend myself. She rose up, her head level with mine, and bared her fangs with a hiss.

Beau slammed into her, sinking his teeth into her scaly flesh. He whipped his head back and forth until bones crunched and her body went limp, releasing me from her grip. He moved in front of me while Levi circled behind me, together creating a protective barrier. I concentrated on loosening the weave of the shield that was nullifying my abilities. It was complicated and my mind and body strained with the effort. The ground beneath us shook. The vibrations grew until the glass panels of the ceiling began to crack. The entire east wall exploded. Animals of all shapes and sizes burst into the room. People were trampled and thrown across the building. Yellow energy covered the animals like a haze. I traced it back to one of Lucien's guardians who grinned as a lion attacked one of Kilian's followers.

I needed a weapon. A sharp stick, anything.

'Good to see you, kiddo,' Bishop shouted. A dagger and handgun skidded across the floor, landing at my feet as she ran past me. The dagger was made of crystal. I picked them up and watched as Bishop pulled two thin swords from the sheathes on her back, jumping onto the back of an angry rhino that was charging its way through the crowd of people. She leaned over the beast, drawing the blades across its throat and severing its neck. It crashed to the ground and she jumped from its back, landing on her feet.

She has to teach me to do that.

Kilian's shout reached my ears and I searched for him in the chaos. The shadowy beast had him pinned to the ground; one of its talons piercing his shoulder. I pulled the gun and aimed it at the beast's head. It swivelled, facing away from me, and the bullet lodged in its shoulder. It didn't even flinch. I emptied a dozen rounds into its side, until finally I caught its attention. It snapped its head towards me. The Summoner tried to redirect it back to Kilian, but the creature was angry. I threw the crystal dagger and Kilian caught it by the hilt. As the beast stalked towards me, he plunged the blade into its hindquarters. It roared, thrashing its head. The crystal seemed to hurt it. It snapped at Kilian but he was too fast. It lunged in low and Kilian sidestepped it, plunging the dagger into its skull, in the middle of the strange swirling energy. He twisted the hilt and it fell to the ground lifeless, dissolving into smoke. The Summoner ran for one of the shattered windows, but Kilian got to him first. He was consumed by a cloud of emptiness and screamed in horror, ripping at his chest. He ran into the path of a stampeding elephant and the screaming stopped. Kilian turned to me and grinned. *Oh dear.* Beau growled. I gave him a reassuring pat as Kilian winked and moved on to his next victim.

'Don't worry about him. I'm going home with you, remember?' I reassured Beau.

People were taking notice of us. The people and creatures running towards us fell one by one thanks to Tom and Dorian. Those they missed were finished by Beau and Levi. I continued working to unpick the shield. One thread loosened but didn't give way.

A man with inhuman red eyes emerged from the crowd. His muscles bulged as he flexed his hands. It was the Berserker from the Gladiatorial Games. He bared his teeth in a sneer as Beau edged forward, a low growl rumbling in his chest.

'Finally, a real challenge,' the Berserker snarled. 'When I'm done with you, Wolf, I'm going to enjoy breaking every bone in your mate's body.' He gave me a predatorial smile.

The rumbling in Beau's chest grew louder as he drew back on his hind legs, ready to spring.

'NO!'

I clutched at his fur, but he'd already lunged. The Berserker grabbed him by the throat in mid-air, throwing him across the room. He landed hard and skidded into the wall. I screeched in panic, gripping the gun in my hand. *Click, click, click*—no ammo. It didn't matter; I was going to tear the Berserker into tiny, bloody pieces with my bare hands. I stepped forward but Levi moved in front of me, baring his teeth.

'Let me go, Levi.'

Another wolf stepped in beside him; his red fur streaked with dark blood.

'Dillon? Move out of my way, Beau could die!'

'This is his fight.'

I turned to Tom's astral form. His physical body was somewhere over the other side of the room. 'I have to help him,' I ground out.

'Remember the car accident and dead trees? If you get injured enough to fall unconscious, you could kill everyone in this room.'

I clamped my jaw.

'The Berserker threatened you, his mate. That's a challenge, Freya. Let him prove himself.'

Beau's ego was big enough to fill this room, but Tom was right. I'd lived with Shifter Wolves long enough to understand the importance of a challenge. Tom disappeared and I focused on breaking the shield. After prodding every loop and weave, the loose thread still refused to unravel, so I abandoned it and started again. I grew agitated and impatient with each blow that Beau suffered. He and the Berserker were evenly matched and the battle dragged out. The Berserker grew angrier. He swung at Beau with his boulder of a fist, leaving an opening on his right side. Beau dodged the blow, biting into the muscle between the Berserker's shoulder and neck, ripping away a chunk of flesh. The Berserker roared, trying to swing his now useless arm.

'Enough games,' the Berserker spat.

He drew a black sword from the sheath on his back. It was obsidian. Obsidian was rare and sharper than steel. Obsidian weapons were supposedly destroyed during the last cold war. I'd actually been listening in history class. The Berserker swung the blade in erratic arcs. Beau avoided his swings but was unable to attack him without coming close to the deadly blade.

My search for loose threads became frantic, but the shield showed no weaknesses.

Levi and Dillon yelped, falling to the ground beside me. Waves of sound energy hit their bodies. It came from the outstretched hands of a woman in heels and a mini-dress. She caught sight of me and changed the sound frequency. I fell to my knees, covering my ears as a high-pitched ringing filled my head. My eardrums burst and bled. The soundwaves were cut off and I glanced up to see her on the ground, a long shard of ice protruding from her back. Dress shoes covered in powdery ice stepped in front of me. The Water Elemental held out a hand and pulled me to my feet.

'You owe me one, Soul Sucker,' he said with a wink. I didn't get a chance to say thanks as he ran towards the Fire Elemental I'd seen in the arena.

A roar of anger filled the air and I spun on my heel. The Berserker was on the floor with Beau's jaws clamped around his neck. The guardian who'd blasted me with shockwaves stood to the side, rubbing his hands together and creating static electricity that bounced over his skin. He was like a thunderstorm in a human body. He held out his hands, palms facing Beau. Lightning bolts flew. Beau was thrown from the Berserker and laid unmoving on the floor as electricity bounced over his singed fur.

I stopped breathing.

The Berserker stood and picked up his sword, dragging the tip of the blade across the stone floor. He loomed over Beau's paralysed body.

No.

He met my eyes, grinning as he lifted the sword high and plunged it into Beau's side.

Beau let out a blood-curdling howl and I screamed. My ears rang. My lungs struggled for air. This was different from that day in the rain, when I'd watched him leave, taking a piece of me with him. This time my whole heart was being torn from my chest, leaving a dark gaping hole. Everything was a blur but somehow I pushed past Levi and Dillon, falling to my knees at Beau's side. I clutched his fur. His lifeline was still there. It was flickering like a candle with no more wick to burn, but it was still there.

'Don't you die, don't you dare die,' I stammered. 'It's your fault we're bonded and I love you, so you can't die!'

The Berserker pulled the sword from his flesh and I lifted my head, meeting his crimson eyes. He pointed the sword at me.

'Now, little Soul Sucker, time to join your mate.'

He lifted the sword. The blade was slick with blood—Beau's blood. Mine would soon join it. My body would try to save itself and everyone else would die too. I ran my hand through Beau's fur for the last time and everything around me slowed.

There it was—the elusive thread I'd been searching for.

The Aegis's shield wasn't flawless. It wasn't a loose thread that I found, but a tied-off knot where the weave ended. My heartbeat quickened as I unpicked the knot and it came loose.

The muscles in the Berserker's biceps flexed as he prepared to swing.

'Let loose, kid.'

I ripped the thread and the whole shield unravelled. I didn't hesitate. I wrenched his energy and it flowed through me like rushing water. The sword clattered on stone as he crashed to his knees. He shouted, clawing at his neck. His crazed eyes dimmed to a normal brown and his lifeline flickered.

'Don't stop now,' James said.

I didn't. Beau was dying because of him. I kept taking until the last spark of power faded from his body. He fell to the floor, lifeless. New power rushed through my veins and my head flung back. The Berserker's energy weaved itself into my energy core and euphoria washed over me. Before it could attach itself, I pulled his spirit thread and let it go. It rose above me, dissolving into the air.

Beau whined, snapping my attention back to him. My heart slammed in my chest. I ran a shaky hand over his blood-soaked flank. His lungs expanded and fresh blood oozed from the gaping wound in his side. I pressed a hand against it to stop the bleeding. His lifeline grew stronger as his body started to regenerate. The bleeding stopped and I heaved a shuddering breath.

Relief morphed into rage and it burned like fire. Flames of new energy scorched me and I shouted in pain as my body altered. I grew stronger and my senses intensified. It was like Dire Wolf energy without the shape shifting. A red haze clouded my mind. Volts of electricity struck my skin, adding to the burn. I turned to the guardian as he pulled his hands apart, static electricity bouncing along his skin as he readied to zap me again. I grabbed hold of his lifeline and pulled. The sparks of electricity protecting him disappeared and a large furry mass tackled him to the ground. The Dire Wolf looked similar to Beau. He stood over the guardian's prone body and met my stare. There was a flash of movement behind him. A man with glowing skin aimed a semi-automatic rifle at his head. I picked up the obsidian sword and hurled it through the air, skewering the man in the chest. It propelled him backwards, slamming him against the wall. He dissolved into a puddle of smoking goo on the floor. I scrunched my nose. *Gross…*

The Dire Wolf sniffed and lowered his head.

'No problem,' I said.

A coolness swept across my mind dulling the haze. I focused on calming the rage that clouded my thoughts and glanced around the room. The battle had slowed. Lucien's people had either fled or died. Some of them fought alongside my friends and rescuers, siding with Kilian instead of their king. A woman's scream drew my attention. Lucien had escaped his stone prison and held his wife by the jaw. With a smile he kissed her and she decayed, turning to ash at his feet.

Everything else faded, all I saw was his face. Something inside of me roared. I picked up the sword, hissing as the puddle of acid it laid in ate through my skin. With the sword clutched tight in my hand, I moved towards Lucien. Anyone who got in my way fell to the ground, gasping for air. I didn't kill them; the others finished them off. Lucien was my target.

Lucien was angry, turning anyone who came near him to dust, even his own people. He was desperate—he knew he was losing. I reached out, weaving a noose through his energy. As I began to draw on it, a hand rested on my shoulder.

'He's mine, Freya.'

I met Kilian's eyes and clenched the sword tighter. 'No.'

Emptiness swirled around him in a dark menacing cloud. 'Please.'

Please? Dorian stepped through the crowd and that same coolness swept through me, causing the haze to recede a little. I remembered that this wasn't just my fight and with some hesitation held out the obsidian sword. Kilian grasped it in his hand and the corners of his mouth quirked. He nodded and I stepped back. Lucien turned to us, his black eyes crazed.

'This is just precious. You think that *you* can beat me? Even your grandfather couldn't beat me, boy, and he was a greater man than you'll ever be.'

Kilian's lips curved into his signature smirk. 'We'll see.'

One of Kilian's followers, the Enhancer, stepped beside him, magnifying his ability. The emptiness moved through the room like smoke. It reached Lucien's followers and they started to scream. They fell one by one. Their bodies were empty shells; no trace of their lifelines remained.

Lucien hissed, 'You can't beat me without going mad, Kilian. I've made sure of it. Your mother made sure of it.'

He spat the final words, eyeing the sword that stood between him and any chance of beating Kilian. He couldn't use his power without physical touch. Kilian winked at me as Lucien spat and cursed his name.

When he'd finished Kilian said, 'It was you who once told me there are no certainties in life, Uncle. You should've listened to your own advice.'

The emptiness rushed towards Lucien, surrounding him in a spiral of darkness. Tendrils reached out for him, grabbing at his soul.

It froze.

I turned to Kilian who was still like a statue. The whole room stood still.

34

IT was like everyone was frozen in time. The red haze crept back in. There wasn't time to puzzle out what was going on. I pried the sword from Kilian's frozen fingers and marched towards Lucien.

'Wait!'

I stopped mid-step, recognising the voice. 'Reagan?'

I followed her voice and saw her climbing over the remaining rubble of the east wall. A wave of panic rushed through me when I saw she was unarmed. But no one attacked her. Everyone, except for my rescue team, stood frozen to the spot. She ran to me followed by a guy I'd never seen before. I glanced between her and Lucien's frozen form, clenching and unclenching the sword hilt in my hand. The creature inside me roared that I had to finish what I'd started.

'Kill him now, Freya!' James yelled.

I stepped forward and hesitated, my attention caught by Reagan's smiling face. Mr Monroe held out an arm, stopping her from slamming into me. Her smile faltered at whatever she saw on my face.

'It's me, Freya.'

'I know.'

I clenched my eyes shut, ignoring the rage inside that was trying to claw its way out. I opened them and stared at Lucien. A few more steps and this would all be over. A hand touched my arm and I flinched.

'Freya, we have to go. I've seen hundreds of possible futures. If Lucien dies today, none of those futures look good. That's why I'm here, Frey.'

I turned to Reagan. Her gentle voice cut through the haze. 'What?'

She grasped my shoulder. 'We have to go. We don't have much time.'

I turned to the guy who'd followed her in. He met my eyes and edged back.

Reagan stepped in front of him. 'He's a Binder. He can make any object or person inanimate.' She gestured to the room around us. 'At this scale he can't hold them for long.'

I reached out with my power and sensed the steady flow of Beau's energy—he was okay. The red haze dulled to a mist. Rational thoughts re-entered my mind. I looked behind Reagan at the others. A healer was moving between people, healing who she could, slapping them with bandages that looked like fish scales. Bishop's eyes met mine.

'The giant, white yetis, were they your creation?' I asked.

She winked. 'Sure were. Were they a nice touch?'

A grin tugged at my mouth.

The red mist faded. The sword became heavy in my hand and clattered on the floor. My shoulders sagged. The fire in my veins ebbed and exhaustion kicked in. I staggered back as Reagan hugged me. She pulled back and her expression sobered.

'I'd give you a lecture, followed up by how much I've missed you, but we need to go.'

The Binder, the guy who'd entered the room with Reagan, stepped forward. 'We've got ten minutes at most,' he warned.

'Okay.' She approached Kilian and he unfroze. He blinked, glancing at his empty hand then scanned the room. His gaze stopped on Lucien's frozen form then narrowed on Reagan.

'Who are you? What have you done?'

'I've saved your life, Cousin. I can call you Cousin, can't I? We're blood related after all. We don't have much time. In short: if you or anyone else kills Lucien today, we all die.'

He glanced at me.

'You can trust her,' I said.

He considered Reagan. 'He's defenceless in this state; it would be ill-mannered to kill him. But, why can't he die today?'

'One of the reasons is that Csilla's plans have changed

last minute. That is only reason I can give you without impacting the future.'

At the mention of Csilla, he glanced at me again, his brows creased. I shrugged. I didn't understand any more than he did.

He turned back to Reagan, his eyes curious. 'And you're letting me live because?'

She smiled. 'We need your help to get out of here. Besides, you helped Freya. It would be *ill-mannered* to kill you.'

He nodded. 'I suppose I have to leave too. Without your support and limited numbers, I doubt we can finish this fight. Would you be kind enough to release my friends?'

She gestured to the Binder and he released the others. They blinked in confusion, taking in the scene around them.

Mr Monroe stepped forward. 'You may seek refuge in Blackwood. We have the room.'

Kilian eyed Mr Monroe. 'Thanks, but I still plan to take over this place. If I'm going to plot an offence, I'd rather stay close to Aurore and attack while my uncle is weak.' He looked around at the rubble that was once the ballroom. 'It looks like we'll have to redecorate.'

'What the hell is going on here?' Elle screeched from across the room. Her usually-perfect hair had fallen to her shoulders in a tangled mess. I'd be lying if I said it didn't make me feel the teensiest bit better about myself.

'We're leaving,' Kilian said, before turning to me. His icy blue eyes held mine. 'My offer still stands, in case you've changed your mind.'

'She hasn't changed her mind.'

Beau stood in human-form in the same place I'd left him. Someone had found him a pair of pants but they looked a couple of sizes too small, the hems brushing just above his ankles. A red gash ran along one side of his face, stretching from his temple and half way across his cheek and a hand was clutched to his side. His gaze was fixed on Kilian. Beau's father, who I'd seen in the dreamscape, held an arm across his chest, keeping him still.

'Beau!'

Dorian and Jonah jumped as I screeched his name. Any

residual Berserker energy disappeared. I ran to him, colliding with his chest. He grunted on impact and wrapped his arms around me. He was solid, he was real. I drew back and held his face in my hands, running a finger underneath the red mark. 'You're still hurt.'

'The obsidian slows the healing.' He pulled my hands away, holding them to his chest and lowered his voice, 'I'll be fine.'

I leaned in and kissed him hard, pulling away when someone cleared their throat. I gave Levi a pointed glare.

'Save it for later, Frey. We have to go,' Levi said. He was in human-form and thankfully, decent. Someone had brought spare clothes for the Shifters.

I stepped towards Kilian, and Beau flanked my side. 'I belong in Blackwood, Kilian. But after everything you've done for me, if you ever need a favour, you know where to find me.'

Beau's body tensed beside me and I gave him a warning glare. He ran a hand through his hair.

Kilian's lips quirked. 'I was just looking out for myself. But, when you change your mind, I'll make sure you know where to find me.'

Beau tried to push past me. His dad appeared in front of us, growling words in a language I didn't understand. Beau stood down, stepping back to my side. His eyes glowed and his body flared with alpha energy. All the wolves, aside from his dad, stepped back.

Beau's voice was like the calm before a storm. 'Don't come near her again.'

Kilian's eyes sparkled. 'Does that apply if she chooses to be near me?'

He surged forward and I grabbed his arm. I didn't have a chance of stopping him, but a hand signal from Bishop worked.

'We need to move out, now. There's unknown movement on the city border, and our ride home lies outside the castle walls,' she advised.

'We'll take the tunnels. Tell your people to wait beside the large arena to the east of the citadel walls,' Kilian said.

He glanced around the room taking one last look at Lucien before leading us downstairs. We passed the servant's floor then descended another flight of stairs to the floor below where the tunnels ran underneath the castle. He led us on a familiar path. When the tunnel split three ways we stopped.

'Freya will show you the rest of the way to the Arena,' he said, pointing straight ahead. He glanced at Beau. 'She and I know the tunnels *intimately*.'

The muscles in Beau's jaw were about to snap. He grabbed my hand, pulling me down the tunnel. I looked back and smiled at Elle. She waved as she disappeared from sight. Kilian was the last to leave.

'Thanks for everything,' I said to Kilian. 'You'll be a better king than your uncle, just try not to kill people needlessly.'

He grinned. 'I make no promises.' He turned, following the others, and disappeared.

'I can't hold them for much longer,' the Binder shouted for everyone to hear.

We broke into a run. The arena was deserted. We passed the pit and the blood stains were still visible in the sand. I shuddered. Beau's grip on my hand tightened as we reached the doors leading out into the open. Four Blackhawk helicopters sat waiting for us. They were powered up and ready to fly. Bishop and Mr Monroe directed people into the cabins. The wolves shifted into human-form and I saw both Southerners and some of Beau's Northerner friends. One of his friends waved and I waved back.

'Theo allowed your friends to come along?' I questioned.

Beau tried to adjust his pants, but they were spray-painted to his thighs. He hadn't even managed to do up the top buckle. 'Theo might not agree with our relationship but he respects a bond.'

'How'd you end up with my pants, Greyson?' Dillon yelled.

He walked towards us, wearing a baggy pair of jeans—Beau's jeans. I snorted and Beau scowled. He wrapped an arm around my waist as Dillon drew closer. Dillon glanced at Beau, stopping a few feet away from me. He grinned, showing all his teeth.

'Hey you. Good to see you in one piece—again.'

I smiled and Beau's grip tightened. 'You too. Thanks for coming for me—again.'

'Any time.' He looked Beau over, his lips curling in amusement. 'Keep the pants, Greyson. They look good on you.'

He winked and moved to the second helicopter, giving me a salute as he jumped in. Beau lifted me into the first one. Reagan, Levi, Dorian and Beau's dad jumped in behind us. Bishop sat beside the pilot and called for us to take our seats. I sat by the window and Reagan dropped beside me, grabbing my hand. I squeezed it.

'You have *no idea* how good it is to have you back,' she yelled over the sound of whirring rotor blades.

Dorian leaned forward in his seat. 'Reagan's been miserable without you. The aunties have had nothing better to talk about than her love life.'

Reagan shoved him back into his seat and he laughed.

I leaned forward, looking over the people sharing our cabin. 'Where's the Binder?'

Reagan played with the rings on her fingers. 'He's in one of the other helicopters with Dad.'

'Where did he come from?'

She shrugged. 'We met up with family over here. He's friends with one of our cousins and offered to help us. I thought it was best if he stayed with me—ah—came with us, I mean.' Dorian snorted when she corrected herself.

Bishop, Levi, Beau and his dad sat nearest to the cockpit. I couldn't hear their voices over the whirring. Beau caught my eye and winked. I looked him over. The red, angry scars still marked his face and side. But he was in one piece—one perfectly *fine* piece.

As the helicopter rose from the ground, I looked out the window and watched as the body of the helicopter changed from black to invisible. I craned my neck to watch the other helicopters do the same—they were camouflaged.

'It's pretty sweet technology,' Dorian said, from his seat across from me. 'Bishop and her team modified them. They're the ultimate stealth fighter.'

We passed over Aurore, reaching the shimmering wall. I released a nervous breath when the helicopters passed straight through. Reagan moved to the adjacent seat, shoving Dorian over so she could sit across from me. Beau took her place beside me and pulled at my seatbelt, ensuring it was secure.

'Are you okay?' he asked.

I rubbed my arms and managed a small smile. 'Yeah… I'm glad to be going home.'

I glanced up at my brother, expecting him to challenge Beau or try and wedge himself between us. He arched a brow at me, grinned, then turned back to Bishop. *Okay, wow…*

I leaned into Beau's side and he rested his chin on the top of my head.

'Beau…'

He took a deep whiff of my hair. 'Mmhmm?'

'How do you know Csilla?'

His body tensed. His dad who'd been crouched by the open side of the cabin turned his attention our way and approached us, bracing himself against the closed door beside me.

His voice was deeper than Beau's and his accent was thick as he said, 'What makes you think my son would know this woman?'

I bristled at the persuasion in his voice.

'Da,' Beau warned.

'An acquaintance of Csilla told me to ask,' I explained.

His voice lowered to a burr. 'You're telling me you don't know Csilla?'

'Until yesterday I'd never heard of the woman.'

'You're a good liar, Soul Stealer.'

Beau stood, his alpha energy flaring. 'She's not lying.'

Beau's dad kept his gaze pinned to mine. 'You expect us to believe you don't know your own kind?'

'Da, leave it,' Beau growled.

He ignored the warning and his eyes glowed burnished

gold. 'Soul Stealers are far and few. Surely your father; an expert in Supernatural genetics, would've been aware of the only known Soul Stealer of our time, aside from himself.'

I leaned back. 'I wouldn't know. I can't ask a dead man, can I? Just because Csilla and I share the same gift doesn't mean we're buddies.'

His lip curled. 'You may have deceived my son, but I'm not so easily fooled. Your scent is almost the same.'

Beau launched to his feet. 'She's nothing like Csilla.'

His dad leaned in so that their noses nearly touched. 'You're blinded because of the bond. What if Csilla sent her? I'm not losing another son!'

Bishop moved between them, pushing them apart. 'You are guests on my chopper. This can wait 'til we're on solid ground.'

Beau's dad gritted his teeth and stepped back, glaring at me before moving back to the open side of the cabin. Beau dropped down beside me. He sat as still as a rock; glowering.

Dorian spoke up from across the cabin. 'Freya wouldn't have been able to keep a secret like that from my family, even if she tried. Dad can truth seek her when we get home if you'd like.'

'Who's to say she can't resist your father's truth-seeking abilities?' Beau's dad argued.

Dorian gave a tight smile. 'No one can resist Dad's skills. Even if Freya could, she couldn't resist Jonah.'

Mr Sinclair muttered in Gaelic. Dorian winked at me, earning himself a grin.

'Where's Jonah? I thought he was with you guys?' I asked.

Dorian's expression fell and he glanced at Reagan. 'He was called home. Grams isn't doing well.'

If they needed Jonah it must be bad. 'I'm sorry to hear it.'

He shrugged. 'It is what it is.'

'I'm sorry that you had to leave her to come and get me. I know how important family is to you, especially Grams.'

He turned to Reagan and they both smirked. Reagan said, 'I don't think you get it, Freya. Mum knitted you a

Christmas stocking. That makes you family now.'

Beau chuckled and some of the tension eased from his body. I faced him with a raised brow. 'Do you have a Christmas stocking?'

His lips twitched. 'Yes.'

Dorian leaned forward. 'The first time Beau was invited to our place he washed the dishes without being asked. Mum knitted Beau a stocking that night. She didn't even knit my dad a stocking that early in the relationship.'

I laughed and my own tension eased. It felt good to laugh. Really good.

We reached the coast and transferred to a plane. Bishop and her team, along with Reagan's new friend, the Binder, stayed back. Bishop needed to check in with Tank before she left. She confirmed that he and Aisha were okay. We arrived in Belfield at night. The door of the plane opened and I fought tears at the sight of my mum and grandparents waiting on the runway. Mum held me so tight I gasped for air.

'I'm never letting you out of my sight again,' she sobbed.

'It's okay, Mum. I'm okay.' I patted her on the back, inhaling the familiar scent of her shampoo. Chris smiled at me over her shoulder. 'Thanks for looking after Mum,' I said, my voice muffled as she pressed my head harder against her shoulder.

'You're suffocating her, Claire. Let the girl breathe.'

Pa smiled at me through watery eyes. I threw myself into his arms, burying my face in his jumper. Remembering the last time I'd seen him lying in that hospital bed, I pulled back.

'Sorry, Pa. Did I hurt you?'

'I'm fit and as sturdy as an ox, kiddo. My heart is even better now that you're safe.'

Grandma came next. She hugged me tight, then studied me from arm's length. She tsked and patted me on the cheek. 'You're so thin I can see your collarbones. I'm going to cook all of your favourite foods when we get home.'

My heart relocated to my throat. 'Sounds good, Grandma.'

I searched for Levi; we hadn't had the chance to talk yet. He stood next to Beau and a smile tugged at my mouth. They both had their hands in their pockets and glanced at me every few seconds as though checking to make sure I hadn't disappeared.

'What are you guys whispering about?' I asked as I reached them.

Beau grimaced. 'I have to stay behind in Belfield for a few hours. Just until Dad's flight leaves.'

'Your dad's not staying with you?'

'No. He travelled with us for added safety, but he needs to be with the family.' He looked me up and down. 'I trust Levi to make sure you don't get into trouble for the few hours I'm gone.'

My brows rose. 'You trust Levi? My brother? I thought you said all Southerners were incompetent?'

He shrugged. 'I can make an exception.'

I squinted. 'How is this'—I pointed between them—'even a thing?'

'They bonded over their willingness to break every town rule to come and get you—that's how.' Dorian stood by my side, turning to me with dimpled cheeks. 'Now that you're back, we can all get back to our obscure, abnormal lives.'

Tom approached us, clapping a hand on Dorian's shoulder. Beau gave him an icy stare.

'We need to go. It's best to keep moving until we cross Blackwood borders,' Tom said. He turned to me. 'There's a party at my brother's place tomorrow to celebrate your safe return. We'll see you there.'

Everyone moved as Tom shouted orders, until only Beau and I stood on the tarmac.

I rubbed my arms. 'So… I'll see you soon?'

He hauled me into his arms, his mouth pulling into a grin. It was *that* grin—the one that slayed me. Every. Single. Time.

I stood on my tiptoes and we kissed. Loud gagging noises from Reagan pulled us apart. I rested my head in the crook of his neck and laughed.

'Nothing will stop me coming back, I promise,' Beau whispered in my ear.

I looked into his eyes and ran a hand through his hair. It still didn't snag. 'I know. But, there's one thing I need to do before I go.' I turned and scanned the crowd of people. I spotted Mr Monroe by one of the cars. 'Let's prove your dad wrong.'

35

MY whole body sighed as we reached the red fire hydrant at the top of our driveway. I was home. The Wallers waited on the veranda. As I reached the front of the house, Mr Waller placed a hand on my shoulder and squeezed it.

'It's good to have you back, Freya. I'm sorry I couldn't come myself, but I couldn't abandon the pack, not for that length of time.'

I smiled at the warmth in his voice. 'I understand, Mr Waller. Thanks for letting Levi and Dillon come for me.'

He glanced at my brother, who was speaking to Ben. 'They always had my permission, but I wanted to ensure there was a plan so they didn't run head-first into danger. Levi provided a convincing case.' He paused and the corner of his mouth hinted at a grin. 'It's interesting how a crisis can bring people together, people such as your brother and Greyson.'

I bristled. 'Is it a problem?'

'No, your brother is loyal to the Southerners and to me. It just makes me wonder if both packs might be capable of getting along a little better.' He gestured to Dillon and Mrs Waller. 'Time to go home.'

Dillon mouthed 'you owe me' as he followed his parents down the trodden path to their property. Christina gave me a curt nod. Ben stayed behind, standing next to me as he watched his family leave.

'I'm sorry I wasn't there to help,' he said. 'We thought the Clemontes might be using you to draw us out of town. If the strongest of us were gone, it would leave the town compromised. We had to prepare a defence in case they attacked.'

'It's fine, Ben. I understand. You're the next alpha so you have to be with your pack.'

His nostrils flared. 'One should always be there for their friends.'

'Your friend's baby sister doesn't really count though, does it?' I joked, trying to lighten the mood.

He turned to me. 'I asked you to join our run. That makes us friends.'

I tugged a strand of hair behind my ear. 'Oh… thanks.'

'I understand that Greyson being back changes things, but if you'd still like to run with us, you're always welcome.' He gave a tight nod and left. *Ben Waller considers me a friend? It's not even a new moon.*

James spoke up. *'You've could've ruled a prosperous city – possibly an entire continent – and here you are right back where you started. You don't even know if they'll keep you. Not everyone on the Council likes you. You'd be better going back to Kilian.'* His tone was bitter.

'I'm right where I want to be.'

'I suppose the Dire Wolf has his uses, even if it's just brawn.' He was mocking me.

'Get out of my head.'

Grandma and Pa left with a promise from Grandma to arrive early the next morning and make me breakfast. I went upstairs and had a shower. The injuries I'd sustained had taken their toll. By the time I rolled into bed and my head hit the pillow, I fell asleep.

The sand was cool beneath my feet. I heard the sound of waves lapping against the shore. The moon was covered by a blanket of cloud and as my eyes adjusted, I saw the dark, still water and Beau's silhouette standing next to me. His skin glistened with sea water. He shook his head, splattering me with cold water drops. I screeched, lifting my hands to shield my face, and he chuckled.

'You can swim in the dreamscape?' I asked, peering out from between my fingers.

He grinned. 'Obviously. Did you want to swim with me?'

'It's black out there. Something might eat me.'

'Not with me here to protect you.'

I snorted as the image of him doggy-paddling in wolf-form popped into my head. My hands dropped from my face and I looked up at his towering figure. 'Could you put a shirt on or something, please?'

'Why?' he asked, grinning as my cheeks turned red. 'Don't like what you see?'

'We both know perfectly well that's not why,' I grumbled. I could still make out enough of his physique in the dim light.

He ran a hand through his hair, flicking water away from me this time. 'How's everything at home?'

'It's fine.'

He dropped down on the sand beside me, bumping his shoulder against mine. I sifted sand through my hands, thinking over all that had happened since I last physically sat here at Pete's Beach. Well, I wasn't technically here, but I was close by. I watched the grains of sand fall through my fingers.

'We need to talk about Csilla,' I said.

A small sigh escaped him. 'You want to do this now?'

'Is there a better time?' I gestured to the empty space around us.

'I guess you're right.' His mouth pulled into a grim line. He picked up a shell and tossed it into the water. 'I was twenty-seven when I first met Csilla—just a kid by Dire Wolf standards. My eighteen-year-old brother, Nicholas, found Csilla beaten and bleeding on the side of the road. She was young, vulnerable and had no one to care for her, so he brought her home. By her scent, it was clear to us she was gifted. She told us that when she came into her power she was disowned by her parents, so she stowed away on a boat that took her to northern Scotland. She was a talented seamstress and when she first arrived in Scotland, she quickly found work and the means to support a simple life.

'Her shop received an order for a wedding trousseau that needed to be finished within a week. She worked late nights to finish the garments and on one of those evenings she was attacked on her way home. She used her ability to protect herself, killing one of the Mundanes who'd attacked her. She was knocked unconscious and woke in a prison cell, waiting to be sentenced. Back then she would've burned at the stake. She said that she used her gift to escape.'

His jaw tightened and I squeezed his hand. 'We took her into our home, and my mother nursed her back to health. Mother took a liking to Csilla. She lived with us for a year and my family provided for her. During that time Nicholas followed her around like a love-sick pup. I always felt something wasn't right with her. She'd take stupid risks or play dangerous tricks on the servants. She treated life like a game. One morning after my run, I caught her in the stable with my brother. She was convincing him to go after the men who'd attacked her and avenge her by spilling their blood.'

He rubbed the back of his neck. 'Nicholas begged me to keep it to myself. He told me that she was just afraid and that he wouldn't have done it anyway. I did as he asked and kept it to myself for a while but Nicholas started to change. He became resentful and started spouting that as Dire Wolves we should use the power we were born with. He wanted to start by teaching a lesson to the people in the town that Csilla had escaped. Csilla had a greater influence over him than I thought.

'I told my parents about her past actions and my concerns for Nicholas. They called Csilla in for a family meeting. She became angry at the accusations and said we were mistreating her because of her gift. Her hateful words shocked my parents and they told her that she no longer had a place in our family. She just laughed when we asked her to leave.'

He clenched his jaw, looking out over the calm water. 'None of us thought to watch Nicholas when she left. He followed her and by the time Da and I caught up to him, he was lying dead in the road. His body was rigid and his skin discoloured.'

'She drew his energy,' I whispered.

'I couldn't know for sure. She was long gone.'

'I'm so sorry, Beau.'

He gave a grim smile and ran a finger along my jaw. 'That's why I was suspicious of you when we first met. Your scent was so similar to Csilla. I hadn't smelled her scent in a century but I've never forgotten it.'

He laced his fingers through mine and held my hand against his thigh. 'That day at the Monroe's, when you said you loved me, I got scared. I thought of Nicholas and his obsession with Csilla and worried I was doing the same thing. Deep down I knew you weren't the same, but I was worried that you could become like her—you were different after Argyle. I had to find out if Csilla was still alive and somehow involved with you. Most of all, I wanted to find a way to help you. I thought if I could find Csilla, it might give me some answers.'

'Did you find anything?'

'I found Csilla. I followed her for a couple of weeks and was careful to cover my tracks. Someone tipped her off that I was sniffing around. I withdrew to my parent's home where I could lay low. She wouldn't dare return to my family's home. I couldn't risk leading her back to Blackwood and to you.' He rubbed the palm of my hand with

his thumb. 'As I told you, I stayed longer than needed. I wanted to give us space to see if the bond would fade. Then you sent me that message and didn't answer my calls, and I realised I was too selfish to let you go. I got on a plane and came home to find you gone. I thought it was her; that somehow I'd led her to you.'

'You blamed yourself?'

His teeth clenched. 'It was risky following her for the length of time I did. I should've left after a few days. I stayed because I needed to know.'

'Needed to know what?'

His eyes glowed. 'I needed to know whether my brother was still there, trapped inside of her. When Jonah told me about James's spirit residing in you, I knew it had to be true. My brother has been stuck with that witch for over a century.'

I squeezed his hand. 'You don't know for sure, Beau. If she was more experienced than me, she may not have taken his soul.'

He met my gaze. 'Why didn't you tell me about James?'

'We never had any time alone, how was I meant to tell you?'

'You could have told me that night at the lighthouse.'

I snorted. 'I was scared too. Scared that you'd regret this thing between us, scared that you'd see me differently. Besides, I was kind of distracted that night, remember? I didn't even know you'd marked me.'

He ignored my indignant tone. 'I'm not sorry I marked you.'

'Even if it means we're stuck with each other?'

He leaned close, reaching for a lock of my hair and twirled it around his finger. His lips fell into a grim line. 'We can still break the bond, if it's what you want. It will be hard, but I could move back home for a while. Then we can see what we want after that.'

I swallowed the lump in my throat. 'What do you want?'

'I think I've made it clear what I want.'

'But what if I'm like Csilla? I didn't hesitate to kill that Berserker. What if this gift sends me insane?'

'You're nothing like her. You killed the Berserker defending me.' He tucked the lock of hair behind my ear. 'Csilla isn't insane—psychopathic maybe—but not insane.'

'Oh great, so I might just become psychopathic instead.'

'You won't. You'll have me to keep you accountable. You'll have your family and the Monroes.'

'For how long? Eventually they'll be gone and I'll still be here.'

My voice tapered off to a whisper.

Beau grabbed my hand and gave it a squeeze. 'I'll be here with you if it's what you want. Always.'

I relaxed a little. 'What do you think Csilla wants with me?'

His lips thinned. 'I don't know.'

If I was lucky, Csilla would never find Blackwood. If I was unlucky… well, I didn't want to think about that. I sighed, tipping back my head to stare at the sky.

'Let's just see how this thing between us goes,' I suggested.

'It will get to the point that there's no going back,' Beau warned.

'I know. I think I'm okay with that.'

The clouds parted and moonlight shone through. Beau stood and my view of the silvery moon was replaced by a pair of golden eyes. He stood over me, his lips curved as he reached out a hand and pulled me to my feet. He brushed his thumbs over my knuckles and the intensity of his gaze made the touch feel intimate.

'You've done it now. I'm never going more than a ten-kilometre distance away from you. Ever again.'

I shrugged, winding my arms around him and inhaling his intoxicating scent. 'I suppose I can deal with that.' Only then in the moonlight, did I notice the scar on his cheek. It had faded to a silvery-white colour. 'The scar didn't heal,' I said.

He shrugged. 'It's something to do with the Obsidian. Do you still want me, even with my imperfect face?'

I ran a thumb across the thin line. 'I actually think it's kind of hot.'

He gestured to his side and I hissed at the sight of the thick, jagged scar just below his ribs. I wanted to resurrect the Berserker and kill him all over again.

'And this one?' he asked, his eyes not leaving my face.

I ran my hand across his warm skin, feeling the puckered scar under my fingers. I tried to sound unaffected, but the words that came out of my mouth sounded more like a strangled cat.

'Yep, that one too.'

His lips curved into his butter-would-melt grin. He kissed me, cradling my head in his hands. I tasted the saltiness of the sea on his lips. His hands moved over my shoulders and down my sides and he grabbed my waist, gripping me tight as he edged backwards. I pulled away to catch my breath and he ran kisses down my neck and along my collarbone. I sighed. The sand beneath my feet grew damp. It wasn't until water rushed over my feet that I straightened.

'Beau?'

I could feel his lips pull into a smile against my skin as he gripped my waist tighter.

'Don't you dare,' I warned.

'I want to be kissing you while we're awake,' he teased.

He picked me up, slinging me over his shoulder like I weighed nothing. I thumped his back, screaming as he ran into the water. His rumbling laughter echoed around me as the icy cold water drenched my clothes, pulling me from my sleep.

36

I woke with a start. Mum's shallow breathing reached my ears from where she slept in the bed beside me. Easing out of the bed I grabbed the burner phone from my bedside drawer. A text showed on the screen.

'Forget this phone again and it will be my pleasure to tag you with a classy, top-of-the-range ankle monitor.'

With a smirk, I placed it in my back pocket and crept downstairs. The clock in the front hall showed it was two in the morning. I tiptoed out the front door and past the barn.

My toes dug into the cool earth at the start of the pack run. The scent of the forest and the sound of creatures in the night made me smile. I took off at a sprint, ignoring the branches whipping my arms and legs. Adrenalin kicked in and my muscles ached, waking something primitive inside me. The Berserker energy burned through my veins and the passing trees became a blur. It was like my feet barely touched the ground. A large tree trunk crossed the path ahead. I leapt over it, launching myself in the air like my legs were springs. I pushed myself to run harder, to keep going until I made it to the cliff. The cliffside loomed ahead and I stopped when my toes hung over the edge. The Berserker roared its approval. It was going to take some getting used to. Heavy clouds covered the moon, as they had in the dreamscape, so I could barely see the water below. A flash of light caused me to stagger backwards. My eyes struggled to follow the rapid movement as Tom's astral form shaped beside me.

'What are you doing here?' I asked, squinting as my eyes adjusted to the light.

'I was going to ask the same question. Can't sleep?'

'I don't sleep much these days.'

He gestured to the path behind us. 'I saw you a few K's

back near the road. It was almost a struggle to keep up.'

I heard the question in his tone. 'It's the Berserker's energy.'

'I wanted to ask; you took his energy but not the energy of the woman you fought in the arena. Why?'

Alright then, straight into the interrogation. I shook my head. 'I didn't want that kind of energy. I didn't want any part of her. The Berserker's gift helps me to defend myself and protect the people I care about.'

'And harbouring his soul doesn't bother you?'

'I didn't take his soul. I've learned how to separate different energies and let them go.'

'I see.' He reached for a non-existent packet of cigarettes in his shirt pocket and sighed.

'Were you out here looking for me?' I asked.

'Yes. I never got the chance to apologise the night you crashed. When I found you, I saw you headed straight for the city's forcefield.' He grimaced. 'To be honest, I was worried you were on some kind of suicide mission.'

'I wasn't thinking straight that night. I shouldn't have gotten in that car in the first place.' I looked him over. 'Is Beau being nice to you now?'

He shrugged. 'He hasn't spoken to me yet. He refuses to look at me, and when he does it's with a glare that would kill lesser men.'

I snorted. 'He'll get over it… eventually.'

Tom arched a brow. 'According to Jonah, you're marked. I'm lucky he didn't kill me.' I crossed my arms, staring out over the black, still water and could feel his gaze. 'You're not happy about being bonded?'

I hesitated to answer. 'It's not that. I just—I'm not the same. I'm worried he'll get to know the new me and regret our connection.'

'He won't. If you were the same as before it would mean you'd learned nothing. It's part of growing up.' He gestured to the air around us. 'This is Blackwood, Freya. Everyone has a story—everyone has shadows.'

'Yeah, well growing up sucks.'

He nodded in agreement. 'If you can separate threads of

energy, does that mean you can detach the soul clinging to yours? James, isn't it?'

I glanced away, wrapping my arms around my middle. 'Maybe.'

'You've worked out how to do it, haven't you?'

I'd figured it out the day I'd unravelled the binding of Kilian's tattoos. 'I don't know if I can remove James without adverse effects.'

'You're hesitating. Why?'

I groaned in frustration. Any time Tom asked me a question I seemed to spill my entire life story. 'Because if I let him go, I'm scared I won't like what's left. What if all those dark, horrible bits are all me, and James is just my excuse? What if I'm just one, big, ominous, life-sucking shadow?'

He looked thoughtful. 'Then you change.'

I gave a dry laugh. 'I just change?'

He stared out over the water. 'In the past I made bad decisions and did awful things. I was serving my country as a soldier, so it was seen as acceptable. I overstepped so many lines I forgot where the line was. I forgot who I was. When I returned home on leave, my mother said my spirit was sick, that my mind was at war with my heart.' He turned to me. 'She told me it was time to take a new path and start again.'

I puzzled over his words. 'How?'

He gave a small smile and pointed between my head and my chest. 'You start by aligning this and this. The rest will follow.'

'You make it sound easy.'

He arched a brow. 'It's not easy. Change hurts, sometimes a little, sometimes a lot. Only you can decide when to let go, Freya.'

Let go. Let go of James?

James's voice echoed in my head. *'Come on, kid. Where would you be without me? I've gotten you this far, you can't dump me now.'*

'I need to think about this,' I said to Tom.

'Changing your life path is always an option, no matter what choices you've made. Just remember that the longer you let James stay, the more of an anchor he is to your soul.'

I knew what he said was the truth. I felt it every time I let James in a little more and his spirit wove into mine. Tom's energy flickered and blinked out.

'You can't do it. I'm a part of you.'

I could do it. I could do it right now and be rid of James.

'Don't do it. You and I are a team, Freya. If you want to survive this world then we need to work together,' James said.

I didn't want a sick spirit. Eventually the sickness would spread to those around me.

'You can't get rid of me. You need me. You'll be a useless waste of life without me!'

'You don't belong in my head,' I said. *'I've appreciated your help, but it's time for you to face the other side.'*

'No!'

I ignored his screaming protests and sat cross-legged on the ground. Closing my eyes I searched for his spirit thread. It had weaved itself intricately through my own spirit with strands of energy knotted through my consciousness. It took me hours to loosen all the threads and knots that had embedded themselves into my lifeline. James's pleading and insults were relentless as he tried to distract me from my task. I paused on the final thread, just as a roll of thunder rumbled.

'Goodbye, James.'

I let go and the thread rose into the air, dissolving into nothing. The air rushed from my lungs and my shoulders sagged. As I took a breath, my mind felt lighter—my body felt lighter. I waited for over an hour, but the cynical voice that had become so familiar to me never spoke another word. James's memories were still there as they'd become my own, but that room at the back of my mind was empty.

Drops of water splashed against my skin. The light drizzle turned to a downpour. Rain soaked my clothes and body, washing away the sweat and dirt. I threw back my head, letting the water splash my face, and smiled.

37

AFTER breakfast, I received a call from Reagan, asking me to get to her place early. Grams wanted to see me. I reached the door to the glasshouse and Tom stood beside it.

He studied me a moment before saying, 'Mum is going to ask something of you today. We just want you to know that it's a decision we've agreed on as a family, as long as you're comfortable with it.'

'What decision?'

His smile was grim. 'That's for her to tell you.'

He walked away, leaving me standing in front of the door. The glasshouse had changed in the time I'd been away. Flowers had died off, making way for new blooms in different colours. I followed the path to the wrought iron table and chairs in the centre of the garden. The seats were empty.

'Grams?' I called.

'Over here, darling,' came the reply.

I moved to the back of the building. Grams looked up from her workbench and gave me a beaming smile. I glanced at her muddy, bare feet and smiled back. She held out her arms and pulled me into a hug, kissing me on both cheeks.

'It's good to have you back, my girl. You've been sorely missed.' She picked up a package from the workbench. It was wrapped in brown paper and white ribbon. 'A welcome home present,' she said, as I opened it.

It was an old glass picture frame. Pressed between the two pieces of glass was the electric blue flower she'd pressed for me all those months ago, when I first arrived in Blackwood. I admired it in my hand.

'I'd forgotten all about this.' I ran my fingers along the frame. 'Thank you, Grams, it's beautiful. I'll keep it by my bedside.'

'You're most welcome.' She patted my arm then leaned in close. 'There's another reason I wanted you to come over early today. There's a rare orchid that's blooming right this moment. The flowers opened a few days ago and I'd love for you to see them.'

'Have you seen them already?' I asked.

'No, I've been waiting for you.'

'Then how do you know they've bloomed?'

Her eyes twinkled. 'Care to take a drive with me?'

I smiled at her evasive question. 'I'd love that.'

Grams refused my suggestion to put on some shoes and hopped in my car. She no longer drove, so she directed me down a dirt track that ran through the heart of the forest, curving in and around the ancient trees. My small car scraped over some of the bumps in the track. We stopped at the deepest part of the valley and walked the rest of the way through dense shrub. There were no clear paths; Grams must've known the area well. We reached a small clearing and she signalled for me to halt.

'Now, watch your step. We don't want to trample anything.'

I didn't know what to look for so I followed behind her until she stopped again and pointed to her side. 'There she is.'

'Ohhhh,' I gasped.

I crouched down next to the flower. It was a beacon of colour among the surrounding shrubs. It was the same shape as the blue orchid Grams had framed for me, but instead of blue petals it had bright purple petals, with dark red spots and yellow edges. Grams sat on her heels beside me and ran a hand along the stem.

'This is the queen. Regal, isn't she?'

'Yes, she is. I haven't seen her framed on your walls.'

'No, you haven't. There are too few of them to justify picking one, even if it would look beautiful pressed between glass.' She grunted as she stood straight, pressing a hand to her back. 'She is a beauty, but there's another reason I brought you out here today.'

I straightened, dusting off my hands. 'Oh?'

She studied the forest around us, her brows creased in

thought, then nodded. 'Follow me.'

We headed back to the car and passed it, following a trail on the other side. New growth along the path showed that it wasn't used often. It opened up into the mouth of a cave. Thick, gnarly roots the size of small tree trunks ran down the outer wall of the opening, weaving in and out of the earth and rock. I followed them with my eyes, up and up to the giant tree towering over the ground above the cave. The tree I'd dubbed the great-grandfather of all trees was average compared to this one. Energy of all colours pulsed through it, reminding me of Aisha's Omnipotent power. The earth around it vibrated from the strength of it.

'No one outside my family knows of this cave,' Grams said. 'I'm about to show you something you must never speak of. Stay close to me, or you may take a tumble.' She pulled a small torch from her pocket and entered the cave.

The deeper we walked, the more eerie it became. Energy pulsed through the walls, as though the cave itself and the tree above it were the heart of the earth, pumping life through the forest around us. The air was heavy and the only sound other than our footsteps was the dripping of water. I nearly walked into Grams when she stopped. She shone the torchlight along the walls of the cave until she found what she was searching for. Five lanterns and a box of matches sat on a boulder. She lit the lanterns, placing them in a wide circle around us. Even with the light, I couldn't see the ceiling of the cave, just the sharp stalactites protruding from the darkness like sharp teeth.

My mouth gaped as I studied the walls of the large cavern. Painted images of people, animals and landscape covered the walls. There were human handprints of all shapes and sizes.

'They all tell a story. The story of my family and our ancestors,' Grams said. 'My great-great grandfather was a story-teller. He transferred magic into the stories painted on these walls.'

'Old magic,' I whispered.

'Even older than me,' she chuckled. 'Old magic, or what some call primal power, is an ancient power. It runs through our blood, passed down from generation to generation. It connects us to the earth around us. When we stand on home soil, the supply of power we can access is insurmountable.'

The tattooist had mentioned prime language; primal power must be similar.

She patted the walls. 'These caves are the primary source of that power for my family. When a member of our family dies, their souls move on, but their power transfers into these walls and the earth around us, to protect and empower future generations.'

'So, the tree above us is like nature's version of battery storage?'

She chuckled. 'Put simply, yes.'

'Incredible.' I studied the images, my eyes drawn to the picture of a person dangling their feet in a river. *The Blackwood River?* 'Thank you for showing me this.'

'I did it for a reason, Freya.' The light from the lantern cast shadows across Grams' face as she placed her hand in one of the handprints outlined on the wall. 'As you know, my *episodes* have worsened. I'm worried about the impact it's having on my family. Sooner or later, someone will be hurt.' She glanced at me. 'I want you to take it from me.'

I blinked in surprise. 'Take it from you?'

'I want you to take my gift.'

I opened my mouth and shut it again, then stammered, 'Grams, it's not that simple. I'd be taking a part of you. I don't know if I could handle—'

She lifted her hand. 'I've considered all of these things, my dear. Without you, my only option is to admit myself into one of those horrible hospitals. This is for the best. I spoke to Tom this morning and he told me you can take energy without absorbing it. You can transfer the telekinetic power back into this cave. The cave will allow the transfer of power through you. It understands my dilemma.'

'The cave is responsive?'

She nodded. 'In a sense.'

I took a deep breath. 'Are you sure you want to do this?'

She placed her hands in mine and squeezed them. 'I'm sure.'

I pushed aside the ache in my chest and closed my eyes. 'It will feel like a part of your soul has been ripped from you, Grams. Can you live with it?'

Her lifeline pulsed. 'This is my choice, Freya. It has not been ripped from me; I have given it away by choice. This part of me will never truly be gone. It will be in the earth, the trees and the creatures around me. When I need to feel it, all I need to do is seek it.'

'And you want to do it now?'

'There is no better time.'

Swallowing hard I gripped her hands, taking a shuddering breath. Our eyes met and she nodded. I closed my eyes, threading my energy through hers. The thread of her gift was a cord of glowing, white-gold power. I unpicked the thread from the weave of her energy core and loosened it. It unravelled, pulling away from Grams and leaving the rest of her energy core intact.

I opened my eyes. 'Are you ready?'

A tear slid down her cheek as she nodded. I couldn't just pull the thread and let it go, or it would disappear. It had to be transferred to the cave. Placing a hand on the wall beside us, I pulled the thread until it flowed into me, shivering as Grams's potent power flooded my veins. It was stronger than I'd imagined. I pushed it towards the line of energy running from my hand. Roots, pulsing with power, detached themselves from the cave wall, reaching towards my hand. They wrapped themselves around my arm, attaching themselves to my energy line, and I pushed Grams's energy towards them. Threads of white-gold energy dispersed through the roots, into the web of power pulsing through the cave. When the final thread left my fingertips, the roots detached from me, sinking back into the cave wall. Grams's hands shook and her lips curved into a shaky smile.

'Thank you, my dear. This means everything.'

She extinguished the lanterns and linked her arm through mine, leaning against me as we left the cave and made our way back to the car.

My heart remained lodged in my throat as we drove back to the Monroe's in silence.

38

I pulled up in the driveway and Grams gave my hand a last squeeze. 'Let me tell the family in my own time,' she said softly.

She left me sitting in the car. Out the driver's window I saw Beau's bike parked by the garage. The house was starting to buzz with activity. I gave myself a few moments to process what had just happened then entered the house, dodging the kids playing in the hallway.

'Where have you been?' Reagan demanded when she spotted me passing the kitchen. 'Next time I'll tell you to get here at lunchtime and maybe then you'll give us time to get ready.'

She grabbed my hand before I could respond and dragged me to her room. She persuaded me to wear one of her dresses. It was a metallic, rose gold dress with long sleeves to protect my arms from the cold. It wrapped around my waist, tying off to the side. She pulled my hair into a high braid, and shoved matching hoop earrings in my hand. As I placed them in my ears, she stood back with a satisfied grin.

'You look like an amazon. Beau's eyes are gonna fall out of his head.'

I rolled my eyes and grabbed her hands. 'I've missed this.'

She smiled. 'I know.'

She pulled me down the hall towards the kitchen. The place was filling with people. The wolf packs agreed that the party was neutral ground, so both Southerners and Northerners were there together for the first time in years.

I smiled as I rounded the entryway and saw Beau behind the kitchen bench wearing Mrs Monroe's floral apron. He looked up as I entered the room and grinned. My cheeks reddened. As usual he looked delicious in his semi-formal attire. *Delicious? I meant great... he looked great.*

The music started and the tealights all lit up. Mrs Monroe handed me a tray of food for the barbeque.

'You know what to do with these.'

Her eyes glistened. She gave me a lingering kiss on the cheek and ushered me to the door. The Monroe men were congregated around the barbeque. They turned when they heard my footsteps. Theo, the Northern alpha, was with them. I held his stare as I neared their group. The resentment in his gaze made the Berserker inside me stir. His expression shuttered and he gave me a curt nod, pulling his eyes from mine.

Tom rested a hand on my shoulder. 'You might want to put that down.'

I looked down. Where my hands held the tray, the metal had crushed like a can. I put it on the table beside the barbeque, pulling my hands away and uttered an apology to Mr Monroe. Theo nodded to the others and left. I watched his retreating back until it disappeared from sight.

'Your new gift is an interesting one,' Mr Monroe said, bringing my attention back to him.

I grimaced. 'It'll take some getting used to.'

'And the soul of the Self-Healer, James, is he still with you?'

This was another interrogation, a lie-proof one. I glanced at Tom. 'No. It was time to let go.'

Tom's eyes softened as he pulled out a cigarette. 'We wanted to thank you, for what you did for our mother.'

The group murmured their thanks and I wrapped my arms around my middle. 'It's no problem. You've all done so much for me.'

Mr Monroe smiled. 'Our mother can stay at home with family, thanks to you. It's the best outcome we could've hoped for.'

'I'm glad I could help.'

He looked over at the yard that was filling with people and lowered his voice, 'You have a big decision to make, now that you're home. Are you going to join the Southerners?'

'No—I'd already decided before I was taken.'

He looked between his brothers. 'In that case, I'd like to ask you to join our sub-community. You'll be the first member outside of our family.'

I glanced between each of them. 'Really?'

He nodded. 'I'm the representative for the Council, as you are aware, which means your actions will reflect on me. I will not go easy on you, do you understand?'

'Yes, sir. I'd—I really appreciate it.'

'Good. Because my mother, and of course my children, wouldn't have taken no for an answer.' He grabbed the cigarette from Tom and inhaled, puffing out a cloud of smoke as he passed it back. 'And my wife… well, she's already knitted you a Christmas stocking.'

I made my way back to the kitchen and helped finish setting up the backyard. So far, the rain had held out. I greeted my family when they arrived, then sat in my usual spot by one of the trees, underneath a string of tealights. They held a lot more heat than a small candle should have, keeping me warm. Grams wasn't waiting for me in her usual chair. She'd skipped the party. I saw the Wallers arrive and watched as they came face to face with Theo and his wife. Everyone stilled as the alphas acknowledged one another with a nod then moved on to separate areas. Just like the school classroom, the Southerners massed on one side and the Northerners congregated on the other. I sensed Beau approach my side.

'He's part Dire Wolf, isn't he?' I asked, still watching Theo.

Beau sat in Grams's chair. 'I wondered if you'd work it out.'

I nodded. 'As my gift has grown stronger, it's magnified my ability to see energy. There are tiny strands of Dire Wolf energy woven through his gift.'

'It's not common knowledge.'

'It's how you knew him, right? When you first moved here?'

He leaned towards me. 'My father and his grandfather were friends. He repaid a favour by letting me join his pack.'

I heard the tension in his words. 'I won't tell anyone, as

long as he gets off my back.'

'It wasn't personal.'

I raised my brows. 'It felt personal.'

'He knew that I'd leave the pack for you and was worried I'd swap sides.'

I sniffed. 'He clearly doesn't know you well. You'd never take orders from Mr Waller or Ben.'

'You're right, I wouldn't. Theo won't be a problem anymore, now that you're not joining the Southerners.'

'You heard that, huh?'

He pointed to an ear. 'Dire Wolf, remember? The Monroes will help you as your gift grows. You made a good choice.'

'I made the *only* choice.' I tucked a stray lock of hair behind my ear. 'My new gift makes controlling my abilities more complicated.'

'We'll work it out. I know a little about controlling the inner beast.'

I leaned into him a little more. A slow song began to play and I recognised it. He turned to me.

'I believe you owe me a dance,' he said.

It was the same song that had played at Dorian's birthday party, the first night he'd asked me to dance.

'Are you trying to salvage your pride because I made you look bad last time?'

'No one makes me look bad.'

'Pathetic then?'

His rumbling laughter sent shivers down my spine. He stepped in front of me and held out his hand, pulling me to my feet.

'We're going to dance here?' I said, as he grabbed my waist.

'Yes. I want you to myself.' He leaned in and whispered, 'I want to hear you say those words again. The words you said when you thought I was dying.'

I blushed. I didn't think he'd remember me speaking to him while he'd lain on the floor, his lifeline flickering. 'Ummm, don't you dare die?'

He pulled me close. 'I guess I'll have to make you say

them. What do you think would happen if I French kissed you in front of your mum and grandparents?'

'Don't you dare. You'll give Pa another heart attack.' I pushed against his chest, but he refused to budge. I swallowed the lump in my throat and glanced at the people around us. 'Fine… I—I love you.' It felt strange saying it out loud when I wasn't begging him not to die.

He raised a brow and waited.

'You didn't ask for an explanation,' I muttered, resting my forehead on his chest. 'I'm pretty sure I started *feeling things* for you the night you first spoke to me in Gaelic… when the Teleporter messed with my car.'

He pulled me back by the shoulders and met my eyes, running a thumb along my jaw. 'I *feel things* too. And… I'll try to give you space when you need it.' He had to force out the last words through clenched teeth.

I bit my lip to stop myself from smiling. *Who said I wanted space?* 'Can you do something for me?' I asked.

He rested his forehead against mine and murmured his agreement.

'Be nice to Tom.'

The muscles in his jaw ticked. 'I haven't hurt him.'

'If you were a Fire Elemental, he'd have burned to death with the glares you've given him.'

'Isn't a clear, non-verbal message better than crushing his bones with my bare hands?' He caught my narrow stare and sighed. 'Fine, I'll try.'

I grabbed his hand. 'Good. Come on, let's go dance with the others.'

'You go and dance. I need to talk with Theo.'

I arched my brows and he said, 'I don't like dancing, unless it's alone with you.' He kissed me on the forehead. 'Go have fun with Reagan.'

As soon as I left his side, he was surrounded by his Northerner friends. I found Reagan in the middle of the dancefloor. Dillon had taken over the music selection. I danced until my feet hurt and my cheeks were sore from laughing. Needing water, I left the floor, spotting the cooler near one of the tables by the house. I threw back a large glass of water and searched for my mum in the crowd.

'Freya?' I turned to one of Reagan's aunties and she held out the home phone in her hand. 'There's a call for you.'

I really needed to get that new mobile phone. I grabbed the phone expecting it to be an update from Bishop. The burner phone was sitting on Reagan's bed.

'Hello?'

'Hello, Freya dear. I'm so sorry to have missed you. I hope that you're enjoying your little welcome home party.'

I refilled my water glass, holding the phone between my shoulder and ear. 'I'm sorry, who is this?'

'Oh my, where are my manners. My name is Csilla—Csilla Rothenberg. I cancelled all my plans to come and meet you in Aurore. I was very disappointed to find you gone.'

I caught the phone before it dropped to the ground. All the air squeezed out of my lungs. I struggled to form a reply. 'What do you want from me?' I stammered. Beau must have sensed my distress and his eyes met mine, glowing gold in the evening light.

'Blood calls to blood, dear. It's only right that I meet my one and only great-granddaughter.'

'*Great… great-granddaughter*?'

'I'll come to you. We'll share a pot of tea and *get to know* one another. I may bring along a friend or two and we can make an event of it. We'll have such a lovely time. I'm sure you're just dying to meet me.'

THE END

ABOUT THE AUTHOR

Khaiah Thomson pens the *Blackwood Trilogy* (YA, Paranormal Fiction) series. The first book, titled *Welcome to Blackwood*, won the Hawkeye Publishing Manuscript Development Prize in 2020. The second book, *Leaving Blackwood*, was eagerly anticipated and early reviews stunningly supportive.

When Khaiah isn't in her home office writing, she can usually be found nose-deep in a book or procrastigaming. If she's not at home, she'll be at the nearest café, hovering close to the coffee machine. Khaiah lives in Western Australia with her husband and two sons.

Redeeming Blackwood is coming in 2022.

To follow Khaiah, and hear about her upcoming book releases, register for the newsletter at www.hawkeyebooks.com.au or follow her on Instagram @kthomson_author.

ACKNOWLEDGEMENTS

First of all, a prayer of thanks goes to the big guy upstairs. Without my faith in God, I never would've had the courage to put myself out there and share a piece of my soul with the world. Now look at me, here I am publishing a second book.

Thank you to the team at Hawkeye Publishing, for your support and enthusiasm. Without you this trilogy would still be a pipedream.

To my family and friends, thanks for listening to my rants, reading through rough drafts and overall putting up with the fact that I can't think of much else to talk about aside from book stuff.

To Stu, my husband, without your support, writing this book wouldn't have been possible. Keep dreaming of that vineyard in Margaret River. And don't worry, I don't hold it against you that you still haven't read the first book, let alone the second—yep, no hard feelings at all.

To my wonderful boys, Oscar and Dylan, without your constant love and attention, there's no way I could've finished this book in a year. In fact, I would've finished it in six months.

And finally, to my readers, thank you for giving the Blackwood trilogy a chance and for going on this journey with me. Without you all the wonderful characters that make Blackwood, would still be a figment of my imagination.

Khaiah Thomson

Book reviews can make or break a book. If you liked what you read today, please do consider recommending it to your friends, and posting a review on your favourite forum.

If you'd like to see Freya, Beau and Kilian and all their friends in cinemas please send us a note of support through the contact form at hawkeyebooks.com.au – we slip updated dossiers of notes from fans to producers.

The Blackwood Trilogy will be available at www.hawkeyebooks.com.au and all good bookstores and libraries.

Pre-order *Redeeming Blackwood* (due for release 2022) at www.hawkeyebooks.com.au to receive a certified first edition.

Hawkeye Publishing is an independently owned traditional publishing house in Brisbane, Australia. hawkeyepublishing.com.au

CPSIA information can be obtained
at www.ICGtesting.com
Printed in the USA
LVHW041753141221
706194LV00012B/718

9 780645 309904